"And  **this out. I d** **will."**

She nodd... ...anced away, but h... ...cing her to meet his gaze. She stared up at a smile that curved into something delicious.

That smile was her downfall. She should turn away. But his eyes were dark and tempting, like chocolate.

"We should definitely go," she whispered.

"I know, but there's one thing we need to do before we leave."

His lips touched hers in a gesture that was sweet and disarming. Then he paused and rested his forehead against hers.

"We shouldn't have gone there," Andie said.

"Andie, at least give me a chance to figure this all out before you give up on me."

"I've never given up on you. But I have to make the right decisions, now more than ever."

"And you think turning down my proposal was the right decision?"

"Yeah. It was sweet of you, but it was spur-of-the-moment and this is something that we should take time to think about."

Spur-of-the-moment was definitely a bad idea.

WITHDRAWN FROM THE RECORD OF THE MID-CONTINENT PUBLIC LIBRARY

Dear Reader,

We hope you enjoy the Western stories
The Cowboy's Sweetheart and *The Cowboy's Family,*
written by bestselling Love Inspired author
Brenda Minton.

Love Inspired books show that faith, forgiveness and
hope have the power to lift spirits and change lives—
always.

And don't miss an excerpt of Brenda Minton's
The Boss's Bride at the back of this volume. Look for
The Boss's Bride, available September 2013.

Happy reading,

The Love Inspired Editors

The Cowboy's Sweetheart
&
The Cowboy's Family

Brenda Minton

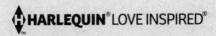

If you purchased this book without a cover you should be aware that this book is stolen property. It was reported as "unsold and destroyed" to the publisher, and neither the author nor the publisher has received any payment for this "stripped book."

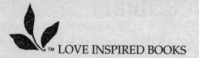 LOVE INSPIRED BOOKS

Recycling programs for this product may not exist in your area.

ISBN-13: 978-0-373-68921-7

THE COWBOY'S SWEETHEART & THE COWBOY'S FAMILY

Copyright © 2013 by Harlequin Books S.A.

The publisher acknowledges the copyright holder of the individual works as follows:

THE COWBOY'S SWEETHEART
Copyright © 2010 by Brenda Minton

THE COWBOY'S FAMILY
Copyright © 2011 by Brenda Minton

All rights reserved. Except for use in any review, the reproduction or utilization of this work in whole or in part in any form by any electronic, mechanical or other means, now known or hereafter invented, including xerography, photocopying and recording, or in any information storage or retrieval system, is forbidden without the written permission of the editorial office, Love Inspired Books, 233 Broadway, New York, NY 10279 U.S.A.

This is a work of fiction. Names, characters, places and incidents are either the product of the author's imagination or are used fictitiously, and any resemblance to actual persons, living or dead, business establishments, events or locales is entirely coincidental.

This edition published by arrangement with Love Inspired Books.

® and TM are trademarks of Love Inspired Books, used under license. Trademarks indicated with ® are registered in the United States Patent and Trademark Office, the Canadian Trade Marks Office and in other countries.

www.LoveInspiredBooks.com

Printed in U.S.A.

CONTENTS

BRENDA MINTON

started creating stories to entertain herself during hour-long rides on the school bus. In high school she wrote romance novels to entertain her friends. The dream grew and so did her aspirations to become an author. She started with notebooks, handwritten manuscripts and characters that refused to go away until their stories were told. Eventually she put away the pen and paper and got down to business with the computer. The journey took a few years, with some encouragement and rejection along the way—as well as a lot of stubbornness on her part. In 2006 her dream to write for Love Inspired Books came true. Brenda lives in the rural Ozarks with her husband, three kids and an abundance of cats and dogs. She enjoys a chaotic life that she wouldn't trade for anything—except, on occasion, a beach house in Texas. You can stop by and visit at her website, www.brendaminton.net.

THE COWBOY'S
SWEETHEART

Dedicated to the readers,
for the wonderful emails, letters and prayers.
To the editors at Love Inspired, for the opportunity
to write the books that I love and for encouragement
along the way. You're the best. To my family,
for all of the love and support you've given me.
To God, for giving me the desires of my heart.

Chapter One

You have to cowboy up, Andie. Get back on, even if it hurts.

Andie Forester swiped a finger under her eyes and took in a deep breath. She hit the control on the steering wheel to turn down the radio, because it was the fault of Brooks & Dunn and that song of theirs that she was crying. "Cowgirls Don't Cry."

Whatever.

The song made her think of her dad pulling her to her feet after a horse had thrown her. She remembered her world when he was no longer in it. And the song reminded her how it felt to have a sister so perfect the world couldn't love her enough.

Andie even loved Alyson. How could she not? Alyson had come to Dawson and back into her life, soft smiles and sunshine after a twenty-five-year separation. Andie was home just in time to help her sister prepare for her wedding to Jason Bradshaw. A beautiful wedding, with the perfect flowers, the perfect dress.

At the moment Andie wanted to throw up because she was Andie Forester and she didn't think like that. She didn't think sunshine and lace. She thought leather boots and saddles. She thought hard and tough. She was a tomboy. She knew how to hang with the crowd, with cowboys and stock contractors, and guys from Dawson, Oklahoma.

But her dad had been wrong. Brooks & Dunn were wrong. Sometimes cowgirls did cry. Sometimes, on a dusty road in Oklahoma when there wasn't anyone around to see, cowgirls sobbed like little girls in pigtails.

Sometimes, when her best friend had hurt her in a way she had never thought he could, a cowgirl cried.

But she'd get it out of her system before she got to Dawson, and she'd be fine. Ryder Johnson wasn't going to get to her, not again.

That was another thing about Foresters. They learned from their mistakes. She shouldn't have made this mistake in the first place. That's what really got to her.

She downshifted as she drove through the tiny town of Dawson, all three businesses and twenty or so houses. The trailer hooked to her truck jerked a little and she glanced in the rearview mirror, smiling because even Dusty was glad to be home. The dusty gold of his nose was sticking out of the side window, his lips curled a little as he sniffed the familiar scents in the air.

Home was where people knew her. Yeah, they knew her secrets, they knew her most embarrassing moments, but people knowing her was good. The folks in Dawson had shaken their heads, sometimes laughed at her antics, but they'd always been there for her.

The end of September was a good time to return to Oklahoma. The weather would be cooling off and in a month or so, the leaves would change colors.

She would get back to normal. Home would do that for her.

Andie took in another deep breath, and this time she

didn't feel the sting of tears. She was done crying. Her pep talk to herself had worked.

She slowed as she drove past the Mad Cow Café and pretended she wasn't looking for Ryder's truck. But she was. It was an old habit. She consoled herself with that thought. And with another one—his truck wasn't there. Hopefully he was still on the road. She didn't want to run into him, not yet.

They'd both been going in opposite directions as fast as they could, putting distance between them and their big mistake. He'd gone back to riding bulls or steer roping, whatever he was doing this year. She'd taken off for Wyoming and a rodeo event she hadn't wanted to miss. Even her trips home had been planned for the times she knew he'd be gone.

The last time Ryder had seen her, well, she'd done a lot of changing since then. She wasn't ready to talk to him about any of that.

At least Dawson hadn't changed. That was something Andie could count on. Her hometown would always be the safe place to land. Jenny Dawson, the town matriarch whose grandfather had started this little community, would always be in her front yard wearing a floral print housedress, digging in her flower gardens, a wide-brimmed hat shading her face from the Oklahoma sun. Omar Gregs would forever be in the corral outside his big barn, a shovel in hand, and that old dog of his sniffing at a rabbit trail.

And Granny Etta would always be at home, waiting.

She slowed as she drove past the Johnson ranch, past the drive that led to Ryder's house. Her best friend. Her heart clenched, the pain unfamiliar, sinking from her heart to her stomach. He'd never been the one to make her feel that way.

The truck jerked a little, evidence of a restless horse that had been in a trailer for too many hours. Andie downshifted as she approached the drive that led to the barn. It felt good to see the yellow Victorian she'd grown up in. It looked just the way it had the last time she was at home. Flowers bloomed profusely out of control. The lavender wicker furniture on the front porch was a sign that all was well in the world.

As she turned into the drive, Andie noticed a big sedan on the other side of the house, parked in the driveway that company used. Company, great.

Etta walked out the front door, waving big.

Andie's grandmother had hair that matched the furniture on the porch, kind of. It was the closest the stylist in Grove could get to lavender. And it clashed something horrible with Etta's tanned skin. A Native American woman with Irish ancestors didn't have the complexion to carry off lavender hair.

But tall and thin, she did have the ability to carry off some wild tie-dyed clothes. The clothing was her own design, her own line, and it sold nationwide.

Andie drove the truck down the drive and parked at the barn. Etta was fast-walking across the lawn, the wind swirling the yellow-and-pink tie-dyed skirt around her long legs.

Andie hopped out of the truck and ran to greet her grandmother. Andie was twenty-eight years old—almost twenty-nine—and a hug had never felt so good. When Etta wrapped strong arms around her and held her tight, it was everything.

It was a bandage on a heart that wasn't broken, more like bruised and confused. She hadn't expected it to take this long to heal.

"Sweetheart, it's been too long. And why that serious face and no smile? Didn't you call and tell me things were good?"

"Things *are* good, Gran."

"Well, now why am I not buying that?"

"I'm not sure." Andie smiled as big as she could and her granny gave her a critical stare before shaking her head.

"Okay, get Dusty Boy out of that trailer and let's go inside. I bet you're hungry."

"I am hungry." Starving. She'd been starving for the past few weeks. She was just sick of truck-stop and hotel-restaurant food. Even when she'd stopped in with friends, it hadn't been the same. Nobody cooked like Etta.

Andie moved the latch on the trailer and stepped inside, easing down the empty half of the trailer to unhook Dusty. He shook his head, glad to be free, and then backed out, snorting, his hooves clanging loud on the floor of the trailer.

"Come on, boy, time for you to have a run in the pasture."

"Where'd you stay last week?" Etta was standing outside, shading her face with her hand, blocking the glare of the setting sun.

Andie held tight to the lead rope, giving Dusty a minute to calm down. His head was up and his ears alert as he snorted and pawed the ground, eager to be back in the pasture with the other horses.

"I was at Joy and Bob's."

"You were in Kansas? Why didn't you just come on home?"

Because she didn't want to face Ryder and she'd heard he might be home. She'd planned her timing lately so that she was home when he wasn't. But how did she explain that to Etta?

She shrugged, "I was looking at a mare they have for sale."

Not a lie.

The roar of a truck coming down the road caught their attention. Dusty dipped his head to pull at a bite of clover, but he looked up, golden ears perked, twisting like radar as he tuned into the noises around him. He snorted and grabbed another mouthful of grass. Andie pulled on the lead rope and his head came up.

The truck slowed at their driveway. Etta beamed. "Well, there's that Ryder Johnson. He's been down here three times in the past week. He says he's checking on me, but I think he misses his running buddy."

"I'm sure. If he missed me that much…" He would have called. Two months, he could have called. He hadn't.

Etta shot her a look, eyes narrowing. "What's going on with you two kids?"

"Well, first of all, we're not kids. Second, he needs to grow up."

"Oh, so that's the way the wind blows."

"This might be Oklahoma, but the wind isn't blowing, Etta." Andie turned toward the barn, Dusty at her side. He rubbed his big head on her arm and she pushed him back. "Bad manners, Dusty."

"Where are you going?" Etta hurried to catch up.

"To put my horse up."

"Well, I guess I'll make tea."

Tea was Etta's cure for everything.

"Don't invite him for tea, Etta. I'll take care of this, but he doesn't need to hang out here."

"Nonsense." And Etta stormed off, like a wise grandmother who had dealt with her share of lovesick kids. Andie shook her head and unhooked the gate. She wasn't lovesick.

She was mad at herself. And mad at Ryder.

"Off you go, Dusty. Eat some green grass and I'll be back later."

She watched, smiling as her horse made a dash around the field, bucked a few times and then found a place to roll on his back. And then she couldn't put it off any longer. She turned, and there he was, walking toward her, his hat low over his eyes. She didn't need to see those eyes. Brown, long dark lashes. He had a dimple in his chin and a mouth that flashed white teeth when he smiled. He had rough hands that could hold a woman tight and a voice that sounded raspy and smooth, all at the same time.

Those were things she had just learned about him, eight weeks ago. Before that he'd had a voice that teased and hands that held hers tight when they climbed fences or arm wrestled. He had been the person she told her secrets to and shared her fears with.

More than anything she was mad that he couldn't be that person right now. Instead, he was the person she needed to talk about.

He was tall, a cowboy who wore faded jeans, ripped at the knees, and button-down shirts, plaid with pearl buttons. He was her best friend. They'd been friends for twenty-five years, since his family moved to Dawson from Tulsa. His dad had done something right with the stock market. His mom had inherited a chunk of cash. It hadn't been a perfect life though, and a little over five years ago his parents had died in a car accident.

She'd been there for him.

He'd buried his face into her shoulder and she remembered her fingers on soft, brown hair.

She remembered waking up weeks ago, knowing her life would never be the same. One night, one mistake, and her world had come unraveled.

And then God had hemmed it up again. She'd been running from God longer than she'd been running from Ryder. God had caught her first.

Ryder watched the changing expressions on Andie's face and he wondered what kind of storm he was about to face. Would it be the summer kind that passes over with little damage, or the other kind, the kind that happens when hot air meets cold?

He had a feeling that it was the hot-meets-cold kind. She had gone from something that looked like sad, to pretty close to furious, and now she was smiling. But the coldness in her eyes was still there. She had latched the gate and she was strong again.

She stood next to the barn, looking a lot like she had the last time he'd seen her. She was a country girl, born and raised in Dawson. Her idea of dressing up was changing into a new pair of jeans and boots that weren't scuffed. She was tall, slim, with short blond hair and brilliant blue eyes.

And she had every right to be angry.

He slowed a little, because maybe this wasn't a hornet's nest he wanted to walk into. It was going to get worse when she found out who was in the house waiting for her. She leaned back against the barn, the wind lifting her hair, blowing it around her face.

"Did you forget how to use a phone?" Yep, she was mad. Her voice was a little softer, a little huskier than normal.

"Nope. I just thought I'd give you a few weeks to get over being mad at me," he said.

"I wouldn't have been mad if you had left a note, called, maybe met up with me somewhere."

"I know." He cracked his knuckles and she glared. He

took that to mean she wanted more than an easy answer. "I'm not good at relationships."

Understatement. And it was an explanation she didn't need from him. His parents had spent his childhood fighting, drinking and socializing. The ranch here in Dawson had saved him. At least he'd had horses to keep him busy and out from under their feet.

Away from his parents had usually been the best, safest bet for a kid.

He'd had Andie to run with and Etta's house as a safe haven. Right at that moment Andie looked anything but safe. Standing there with her arms wrapped around herself, hugging her middle tight, she looked angry, sad, and about a dozen other female emotions he didn't want to put a name on.

"Relationship? This isn't a relationship, Ryder. This is us. We were friends."

"Oh, come on, we're still friends." He slipped an arm around her shoulder and she slid out of the embrace. "We'll go out tomorrow, maybe drive into Tulsa. It'll be like old times."

"Nope." She walked quickly toward the house. He kept up.

So, the rumors were true. "This is about church, isn't it?"

She stopped abruptly and turned. "No, it isn't about church. You think that going to church would make me mad at you? Don't be an idiot."

"Well, isn't that what people do when they feel guilty?" He winked. "They get right with God?"

"Shut up, Ryder."

She took off again, arms swinging, boots stomping on the dry grass.

"We've been friends forever."

"Right." She stopped and when she glanced up, before she could shake the look, he thought she looked hurt.

The way she'd looked hurt when he'd turned eleven and she'd been about ten, but not quite. He'd had a bunch of boys over and she hadn't been invited. He'd told her it was a guys-only party and she'd wanted to be one of the guys, because she was his best friend.

Now he realized that best friends shouldn't be easy to hold or feel soft in a guy's arms. Or at least he thought that was the case. He didn't want to lose someone who had always been there for him. He didn't want to turn her into his mom.

He sure didn't want to be his dad.

He wanted them to stay the way they were, having fun and hanging out. Not growing up, growing angry, growing apart. He didn't want to think about how selfish that sounded, keeping her in his life that way.

"Andie, I didn't plan for this to mess up our friendship."

"Neither of us planned for that. And this isn't about…" She looked away. "This is about you not calling me back."

"Because I didn't know what to say."

"Ryder, you're almost thirty and I've heard you talk to women. You always know what to say." She looked down, shuffling her feet in the dusty driveway. "But you didn't know what to say to me?"

"I'm sorry." He hadn't known what to say and he still didn't. With other women, he just said what felt right at the moment. And man, he'd had a lot of nasty messages on his answering machine over the years, because he'd said what felt right, not what mattered.

"You don't have to apologize. We're both responsible."

"I know, but we made a promise. I made a promise."

A promise to keep boundaries between them. "I don't know what else to say, except I'm sorry."

"You should have called." She had shoved her hands in her front pockets and she stared up at him, forcing his thoughts back to that. That night in Phoenix he'd found her standing behind her trailer, crying because she'd been rejected by her mother. He'd never seen her like that, hurt that way.

He shook his head, chasing off memories that were more than likely going to get him in trouble again.

"Come on, Andie, give me a break. You know me better than anyone. You know that I'm not good at this. You know that we were both there. We both…"

"Stop. I don't want to talk about what we both did. I want to talk to you about us."

Heat crawled up his neck, into his face. "Andie, you sound like a woman."

"I am a woman."

"No." He took off his hat and swiped a hand through his hair. "No, you're not. You're my best friend. You're my roping buddy. You're not like other women. You've never been like other women, getting all caught up in the dating thing and romance."

"I'm still not caught up in those things."

"No, now you're caught up in religion."

"I'm not caught up in anything. This is about faith. And to be honest, I really needed some." She looked away.

"Whatever. I'm just saying, this isn't you."

"It's me. But for a lot of years, I've been trying to be who you wanted me to be. I've done a lot of things to make you feel better about being angry." Her voice was soft and sweet, reminding him of how easy it had been to kiss her. Maybe things had changed—more than he'd realized. Being on the road he'd been able to fool himself into believing that they could go right back to being who they'd always been.

"Go to supper with me at the Mad Cow. I'll buy you a piece of pecan pie." He nudged her shoulder and she nodded. He thought she might say yes.

But then she shook her head. "I'm tired. It was a long trip."

"Yeah, I guess it was. Maybe tomorrow?"

"Tomorrow's Sunday."

"And you're going to church?"

"Yeah, Ryder, I'm going to church."

"Fine, I've got to get home and get things cleaned up before Wyatt gets here."

"Wyatt's coming?"

Ryder pulled his keys out of his pocket. This was something she would have known, before. He would have called her to talk it over with her, to get her opinion. He guessed that was a pretty good clue that he'd been avoiding her, and telling himself a whole pack of lies.

Number one being that nothing had changed.

"Yeah, he's coming home."

And Ryder didn't know how it would work, with him, Wyatt and two little girls all in one big, messy house. The girls needed to be here, though. Ryder knew that. He knew his brother was falling apart without Wendy. Wyatt was caving under the guilt of his wife's death. A year, and he was still falling apart.

"If you need anything." Andie's voice was gentle, so was her hand on his arm.

"Yeah, I know you're here." He smiled down at her, winking, because he needed to find firm footing. "Gotta run. Let me know if you change your mind about, well, about anything."

About being this new person, this woman that he just didn't get.

"Right, I'll let you know."

The back door opened. He waved at Etta and tried to escape, but she left the back stoop and headed in their direction. And then he remembered why he'd driven down here. Because mad or not, Andie was about to need a friend.

"Don't you want to come in for tea?" Etta had been filling him with tea for years. Tea for colds, tea for his aches and pains, tea to help him sleep when his parents died. He'd turned to something a little stronger for a few years, until he realized that it was doing more than helping him sleep. It had been turning him into his dad.

He glanced at Andie, and she was still clueless. "I can come in for a minute. I have to get my house clean before Wyatt shows up."

Why'd he have to feel so old all of a sudden? Last week he'd still felt young, like he had it all, except responsibility. He had liked it that way.

"When's he going to be here?" Etta stepped a little closer.

"Tomorrow or Monday. I guess I'll have to call Ruby to get my house really clean."

"You'll be fine, Ryder." Etta's eyes were soft, a little damp.

"Yeah, I'm more worried about Wyatt." Ryder didn't want to think about the house and the girls, not all in the same thought.

And then the back door opened again.

Chapter Two

Andie had forgotten about that car in the drive. She shouldn't have forgotten. It was Ryder's fault and it would have felt good to tell him that. But she didn't have time because the woman standing on the back porch was now walking down the steps. She was nearing fifty and stunningly beautiful. And she was smiling. Andie hadn't expected the smile. She wanted this woman to be cold, to live up to Andie's expectations of her.

A woman that ditched a child couldn't be warm. She couldn't be loving. Andie replayed her list of words she used to describe her mother: cold, unfeeling, hard, selfish.

The list used to be more graphic, but Andie was working hard on forgiving. She'd started with the easy "need to forgive" list. She would forgive Margie Watkins for spreading a rumor about her. She could forgive Blaine for gum in her notebook back in the fifth grade. She'd kept her mother on a list by herself, a final project. Saving the most difficult for last.

So now Andie knew that it was true—God had his own timing, reminding her that He was really the one in charge. She had really thought she'd wait a few months to contact Caroline.

"You okay?" Ryder stepped next to her. "I thought I ought to be here for you."

Cowgirls do too cry. They cry when the man they are the angriest with shows up and says something like that. They can cry when they see their mother for the first time in twenty-five years. She nodded in answer to his question and blinked away the tears, because she'd never cried this much in her life and she didn't like it.

She didn't like that her edge was gone.

Was this really the plan, really what God wanted? For her to forgive the person who had hurt her more than anyone else, even more than Ryder when he ignored her phone calls?

If so, it was going to take some time.

"Caroline wanted to see you." Etta's tone was noncommittal and Andie wondered if her mother had been invited or just showed up.

Oh, the wedding. Alyson's wedding.

"Did she?" Andie managed to stand tall. "Or is she here to see Alyson? To help plan the wedding."

It made sense that her mother would show up to help plan Alyson's wedding. She had never shown up for anything that had to do with Andie.

"I'm here to see you." Caroline was close enough to hear, to respond. And she had the nerve to smile like she meant it.

But really? Did she?

"That's good." Andie managed words that she didn't feel. Standing there in the yard, the sun sinking into the western horizon, red and glowing, the sky lavender. The sky matched Etta's hair. At least that lightened the mood.

"I know I should have come sooner." Caroline glanced away, like she, too, had noticed the setting sun. She stared toward the west. "I don't have excuses. I'm just here to say that I'm sorry."

"Really?" Apparently it was the day for apologies. Was it on the calendar—a national holiday?

"We should go in and have that tea." Etta gathered them the way a hen gathered chicks.

"Ryder, you should go." Andie squeezed his hand. "Thank you for being here."

"You're okay?"

"I'm fine. I'll see you at church tomorrow." She said it to watch the look on his face. She knew he wouldn't be there. He'd gone to church when he was a kid, until his dad's little indiscretion.

"That's one thing I can't do for you, Andie." He kissed the top of her head. "I'll see you around."

Why did it have to sound like goodbye, as if they were sixteen and breaking up?

She watched him get in his truck and drive away. And it wasn't what she wanted, not at all. She wanted her best friend there with her, the way he would have been there for her if Phoenix hadn't happened, if they hadn't spent weeks not knowing what to say to each other.

Watching his truck turn out of the driveway and head down the road, she felt shaken, and her stupid heart felt like it was about to have a seizure of some kind.

And her mother was standing in front of her, waiting for her to pull it together. Caroline, her mother. But Etta had been that person to Andie. Etta had been the one who taught her to be a woman. Etta had taught her to put on makeup, and helped her dress for the prom. Etta had held her when she cried.

Caroline had been in some city far away, being a

mother to Andie's twin, and to her half siblings. She'd left the less-than-perfect child with the less-than-perfect husband.

Issues. Andie had a lot of issues to deal with. But she wasn't the mess some people thought she should be. She'd had Etta. She'd had a dad who'd done his best. She'd been taught to be strong, to not be a victim. Now those seemed like easy words that didn't undo all of the pain.

"Come on." Etta took her by the hand and led her to the house.

"Of course, tea will make this all better," Andie whispered. As if tea could make getting steamrollered feel any better.

They walked through the back door into the kitchen decorated with needlepoint wall hangings that Andie and Etta had worked on together. They'd never had satellite, and only a few local stations until recently. Winters had been spent reading or doing needlepoint. It hadn't been a bad way to grow up.

"What's going on between you and Ryder?" Etta spooned sugar into the cup of tea she'd just poured. "If I didn't know better, I'd think that was a lovers' quarrel."

"We'd have to be in love for that to be the case." Andie leaned in close to her grandmother, loving the way she smelled like rose talcum powder, and the house smelled like vegetables from the garden and pine cleaner.

It was her grandmother's house and it always felt like the safest place in the world.

Even with her mother standing across the counter from her, fidgeting with the cup that Etta had set in front of her, it was still that safe place. Caroline looked up and Andie met her gaze.

"Well, it was just a matter of time," Etta whispered as she walked away.

"What did you say?"

"I said, I hope you don't mind sugar in this tea, and do you mind if it has thyme. It's good for you, you know."

"Right."

She sat down at the kitchen island and her granny slid the cup of tea across the counter to her. Etta sat down next to her, moving a plate of cookies between them. Peanut butter, nothing better.

Andie sipped her tea and set the cup down, not feeling at all better, not the way she usually did when she came home.

"I'm surprised to see you." Andie reached for a second cookie. "I'm the reject kid, right? The one you didn't want."

Caroline shuddered and Andie didn't feel better, not the way she'd thought she would feel the sense of satisfaction she'd expected. And now, not so much.

"You're not defective. You're beautiful, smart and talented," Etta spoke up, her voice having a loud edge.

Andie shot her grandmother a look, because they both knew better. She and her father hadn't been good enough for Caroline. He'd been Caroline's one-night stand in college, and he'd married her. A cute country boy from Oklahoma. And reality hadn't been as much fun.

One-night stands didn't work. She sipped her tea and pushed the thought from her mind. Better to focus on Caroline and her father rather than on her own mistakes.

"I'm not the prodigy. I'm the kid who struggled to read." Andie no longer felt like the kid in school who didn't understand what everyone else got with ease. She had been fortunate to have great teachers, people who were willing to help and encourage her. She'd had Etta.

"You have a challenge, not a disability." Etta covered Andie's hand with a hand that was a little crooked with arthritis, but still strong, still soft, still manicured. "She took Alyson. I got to keep you. That wasn't so bad, was it? Being here with me and your dad?"

Caroline spoke up. "It wasn't bad, was it? I mean, I know Etta loves you. Your dad loved you."

"You can't comment. You weren't here." Andie closed her eyes and tried to let go of the sparks of anger that shot from her heart, hot and cold.

"I can comment." Caroline's hand shook as she set her cup on the counter. "I can comment, because I know what I did and why I did it. I couldn't take this life. I couldn't be a cowboy's wife and the mom to two girls. I couldn't be from Dawson."

Andie shook her head, feeling a little sick with guilt, with hurt feelings. "Really, would it have been that hard?"

"I don't know."

Andie finished off the last of her cookie and drained her cup of tea, and she still didn't know what to say to Caroline Anderson—the woman who had never been her mother.

She thought about this two months ago when she'd slipped into a church service held at the rodeo arena after one of the events. She had sat there wondering how to put her life back together. The pieces were in her hands; Alyson, her mother and Ryder.

It was up to her to put it all back together. It was up to her to forgive.

Andie hopped off the stool. "I have to take care of my horse."

And she planned on spending the night in the camper of her horse trailer. It wasn't really running away. She was giving herself space and a little time to think.

Ryder woke up the next morning to the rumble of a truck in his driveway. He peeked out the window as

Wyatt jumped out of a rented moving truck and then reached in for the two little girls who resembled their mom.

As he watched them cut across the lawn—Wyatt holding both girls, looking as sad as they looked—Ryder ran a hand through his hair and shook his head. Man, this was a lot of reality to wake up to.

He glanced at the clock on the coffeemaker as he walked through the kitchen. Nearly ten on a Sunday morning. And Etta's old Caddy was going down the road, because it was time for church. And for the first time in years, Andie was in the passenger seat.

Too much reality.

Too many changes. He was nearly thirty and suddenly everything was changing. Andie was going to church and she didn't want to talk to him. Not that he really blamed her.

But he wanted her back, the way it was before. He wanted it to be like it had been before their night in Phoenix, before her trip to the altar and God. Not that he had anything against God. He knew there was one. He'd been to church. He'd heard the sermons. He'd even prayed.

But his parents had gone, too. They'd picked a church in a neighboring town, not Dawson Community Church. And that had just about done him in on religion. His parents, their lifestyle and then the day in church when someone brought his dad forward. Man, he could still remember that day, the looks people had given him, the way it had felt to hear what his dad had done.

And he remembered the clapping of a few hands when his dad was ousted from the congregation, taking his family with him.

That had been a long time ago, almost twenty years. He shrugged it off, the way he'd been trying to shrug it off since the day it happened. He walked down the hall and met his brother at the back door, coming in through the utility room. It had rained during the night and Wyatt's boots were muddy. He leaned against the dryer to kick them off.

Ryder reached for three-year-old Molly but she held tight to Wyatt. It was Kat, a year younger, who held her arms out, smiling the way little girls should smile. With one less child, Wyatt could hold the door and kick off his boots.

They would never know their mom. They wouldn't even remember her. But then, even in her life, Wendy hadn't been there for the girls. She had changed after having them. She had lost something and before any of them had figured it out, it had been too late to get her back.

"Long trip?" Ryder settled Kat on his hip and walked into the kitchen. The two-year-old smiled because his cheek brushed hers and he imagined it was rough.

"The longest." A year. That's what Ryder figured. His brother had been on a journey that had taken the last year of his life, and brought him back to Dawson.

"You girls hungry?"

"We ate an hour ago, just outside of Tulsa," Wyatt said. "I think they're probably ready to get down and play for a while. Maybe take a nap."

Ryder glanced at the little girl holding tight to his neck as he filled the coffeepot with water. "You want down, chick?"

She shook her head and giggled.

"Want cookies?" he asked. When she nodded, he glanced at Molly. "You want cookies?"

She shook her head. She had big eyes that looked like the faucet was about to get turned on. She'd be okay, though. Kids had a way of bouncing back. Or at least that's what he thought. He didn't have a lot of experience.

"They don't need cookies this early," Wyatt interjected.

Older, wiser, Wyatt. Ryder shook his head, because he'd never wanted to grow up like Wyatt. He'd never wanted to be that mature.

"Well, I don't have much else around here." Ryder looked in the fridge. "Spoiled milk and pudding. I think the lunch meat went bad two days ago. It didn't taste real good on that last sandwich."

"Did it make you sick?" Molly whispered, arms still around Wyatt's neck in what looked like a death grip. He hadn't been around a lot of kids, but she was the timid kind. That was fine, he was a little afraid of her, too.

He'd had enough experience to know that kids could be loud and destroy much if left to their own devices.

"Nah, I don't get sick." He bounced Kat a little and she laughed.

"I guess I'll have to go to the store." Wyatt sat down at the dining room table.

"No, I'll get ready and go." Anything to get out of the house, away from this. He flipped on the dining room light. "Make a list and I'll drive into Grove. When I get home, we can run down to the Mad Cow before the church crowd gets there."

"I need to have the girls back in church. They like going."

"Yeah, kids do." They liked the crafts, the stories. He got that. He had liked it, too. "I need to feed the horses and then I'll get cleaned up and run to the store."

He brushed a hand through his hair and for the first time, Wyatt smiled. "Yeah, you might want to get a haircut."

"Probably." He slid his feet into boots and finished buttoning his shirt. "I guess just help yourself to anything you can find. The coffee's ready."

A brother and two kids, living in his house. Now that just about beat all. It was really going to put a kink in his life.

But then, hadn't Andie already done that? No, not Andie, not really.

When he walked out the back door, his dog, Bear, was waiting for him.

"Bear, this is not our life." But it was. He could look around, at the ranch his dad had built. He could smell rain in the air and hear geese on a nearby pond.

It was his life. But something had shaken it all up, leaving it nearly unrecognizable. Like a snow globe, shaken by some unseen hand. He looked up, because it was Sunday and a good day for thinking about God, about faith. He didn't go to church, but that didn't mean he had forgotten faith.

So now he had questions. How did he do this? His brother was home—with two kids, no less. His best friend was now his one-night stand. He had more guilt rolling around in his stomach than a bottle of antacid could ever cure.

Did this have something to do with his crazy prayers before he got on the back of a bull a month or so earlier. Did the words *God help me* count as a prayer? Or maybe it was payback for the bad things he'd done in his life?

Whatever had happened, he had to fix it—because he didn't like having his life turned upside down. But first he had to go to town and get groceries, something to feed two little girls.

Church had ended ten minutes ago and Andie had seen Ryder's truck driving past on his way to the farm.

But they'd been stalled by people wanting to talk with her and her grandmother. Caroline had managed to smile and hang at the periphery of the crowds.

"We need to check on Ryder and Wyatt." Etta started her old Caddy, smiling with a certain pride that Andie recognized. Her granny loved that car. She'd loved it for more than twenty years, refusing to part with it for something new.

What could be more dependable, Etta always said, than a car that she'd taken care of since the day she drove it off the lot?

Dependable wasn't a word Andie really wanted to dwell on, not at that moment. Not when her grandmother was talking about Ryder.

"I think Ryder and Wyatt are able to take care of themselves." After her mother climbed into the front seat beside Etta, Andie slid into the back and buckled her seat belt. Etta eased through the church parking lot.

It hadn't been such a bad first Sunday back in church. The members of Dawson Community Church were friends, neighbors and sometimes a distant relative. They all knew her. Most of them knew that she'd gone on strike from church when Ryder stopped going. Because they'd been best friends, and a girl had to do something when her best friend cried angry tears over what his father had done, and over a moment in church that changed their lives. A girl had to take a stand when her best friend threw rocks into the creek with a fury she couldn't understand because life had never been that cruel to her.

Her strike had been more imaginary than real. Most of the time Etta managed to drag her along. But Andie had let her feelings be known. At ten she'd been pretty outspoken.

"How long have you known Ryder and Wyatt?" Caroline asked, and Andie wanted to tell her that she should know that. A mother should know the answer to that question.

"Forever." Andie leaned back in the seat and looked out the window, remembering being a kid in this very car, this very backseat. Her dad had driven and Etta had sat in the passenger side. The car had been new then. She'd been more innocent.

She'd heard them whispering about what Ryder's dad had done. She'd been too young to really get it. When she got home from church that day she'd run down the road and Ryder had met her in the field.

"Forever?" Caroline asked, glancing back over her shoulder.

"We've known each other since Ryder was five, and I was three. That's when they moved to Dawson. I guess about the time you left."

Silence hung over the car, crackling with tension and recrimination. Okay, maybe she'd gone too far. Andie sighed. "I'm sorry."

Etta cleared her throat and turned the old radio on low. "We'll stop by the Mad Cow and get takeout chicken. Knowing Ryder, he doesn't have a thing in that house for Wyatt and the girls to eat."

"What happened to Wyatt's wife?" Caroline asked.

Stop asking questions. Andie closed her eyes and leaned back into the leather seat. She wouldn't answer. She wouldn't say something that would hurt. She was working on forgiving. God had to know that wasn't easy. Shouldn't God cut her a little slack?

Etta answered Caroline's question. "She committed suicide last year. Postpartum depression."

It still hurt. Andie hadn't really known Wendy, but it

hurt, because it was about Ryder, Wyatt and two little girls.

"I'm so sorry." Caroline glanced out the window. "It isn't easy to deal with depression."

Clues to who her mother was. In a sense, Andie thought these might also be clues to who she was. She waited, wanting her mother to say more. She didn't. Etta didn't push. Instead she turned the Caddy into the parking lot of the Mad Cow. And Ryder was already there. He was getting out of his truck and a little girl with dark hair was clinging to his neck. He looked like a guy wearing new boots. Not too comfortable in the shoes he'd been forced to wear.

He saw them and he stopped. Etta parked next to his truck.

As they got out, Wyatt came around the side of the truck. The older of the two girls was in his arms. She didn't smile the way the other child smiled.

"We didn't beat the church crowd." Ryder tossed the observation to Wyatt but he smiled as he said it.

"No, you didn't, but you can eat lunch with us." Etta slipped an arm around Wyatt, even as she addressed the response at Ryder. "And you'll behave yourself, Ryder Johnson."

"I always do." He winked at the little girl in his arms and she giggled. And she wasn't even old enough to know what that wink could do to a girl, how it could make her feel like her toes were melting in her high heels.

Andie wished she didn't know what that wink could do to a girl. Or a woman. She didn't want to care that he looked cuter than ever with a two-year-old in his arms. He looked like someone who should have kids.

But he didn't want kids. He had never wanted children of his own. He said the only thing his childhood had prepared him for was being single and no one to mess up but himself.

"You look nice." He stepped closer, switching his niece to the opposite arm as he leaned close to Andie. "You smell good, too."

Andie smiled, because every answer seemed wrong. Sarcasm, anger, the words "Is this the first time you've noticed how I look?" and so on.

She didn't feel like fighting with him. She felt like going home to a cup of ginger tea and a good romance novel. She felt like hitching the trailer back to her truck and hitting the road with Dusty, because she could always count on her horse and the next rodeo to cheer her up. She could head down to Texas.

"You look a little pale." Caroline stood next to her, another problem that Andie didn't want to deal with. She felt like a tiny ant and people were shoveling stuff over the top of her, without caring that she was getting buried beneath it all.

"I'm fine."

"You really don't look so hot," Ryder added.

"You just said I look nice. Which is it, Ryder?"

"Nice, in a pale, illusive, gonna-kick-somebody-to-the-curb sort of way." He teased in the way that normally worked on her bad moods. Ryder knew how to drag her out of the pits.

But not today.

Today she wanted to be alone, to figure out the next phase of her life. And she didn't want to think about how Ryder would have to be a part of that future.

Or how he was going to feel about it.

Chapter Three

"Why aren't you eating?" Ryder had tried to ignore Andie, the same way she'd obviously been ignoring him. She had talked to Wyatt, to the girls, even to her mother.

She was ignoring him the same way she was ignoring the chicken-fried steak on her dinner plate. And her mother was right. She did look pale.

"I'm eating." She smiled and cut a bite of the gravy-covered steak. "See."

She ate the bite, swallowing in a way that looked painful.

"Are you sick?"

She looked up to the heavens and shook her head. "No, I'm not sick."

"You act sick." He grinned a little, because he just knew he had to say what was on his mind. He couldn't stop himself. "You look like something the cat yacked up."

His nieces laughed. Even Molly. At least they appreciated his humor. He sat back in his chair, his hands behind his head, smiling at Andie. Kat giggled like she knew exactly what her uncle Ryder had said. He hadn't expected to really like a two-year-old this much, but she already had him wrapped around her little finger.

He didn't think Andie was as thrilled with him. As a matter of fact she glared at him as if he was about her least favorite person on the planet. And with her mother, Caroline, sitting at the same table, he was pretty shocked that he'd be Andie's least favorite person.

"That's pleasant, Ryder. I'm sick of you asking me what's wrong. You haven't seen me in two months. Do you have something else you'd like to say to me?"

"Right here, right now?" That made his hands a little sweaty, especially when everyone at the table stared, including his nieces. Kat, who sat closest to him, looked a little worried. "No, I guess not. Well, other than wanting to know if you'd like to go the arena with me tonight. I could use a flank man."

"I'm not a man."

"Good point," Wyatt mumbled.

Ryder shot his brother a look. "Keep out of this."

Kat, two and innocent, clapped her hands and laughed.

A chair scooted on the linoleum floor. Ryder flicked his attention back to Andie. She was standing up, looking a little green and wobbly. Maybe it was the dress, or the three-inch heels. He stood, thinking he might have to catch her.

"What's wrong?" Etta started to stand up.

"I'm going outside. I need fresh air."

"I'll go with you." Ryder grabbed his hat off the back of the chair and moved fast, because she was practically running for the door.

She didn't go far, just to the edge of the building. He stood behind her as she leaned, gasping deep breaths of air.

"What's going on with you?"

"Stop." She kept her face turned, resting her forehead against the old concrete block building. "I must have caught something from Joy's kids when I stopped in Kansas. One of them was sick."

"I could take you home," he offered quietly, because he had a feeling she didn't need more questions at the moment.

"I'm fine now. I would just hate to make the girls sick. They don't need that." She turned, smiling, but perspiration beaded along her forehead and under her eyes. She was still pale.

"No," he agreed, "the girls don't need to get sick. I don't think I could handle that."

"They're just little girls."

"Yeah, and I'm not anyone's dad. That's Wyatt's job. He's always been more cut out for the husband and father gig."

And saying the words made him feel hollow on the inside, because he remembered standing next to Wyatt at his wife's funeral. He remembered what it felt like to stand next to a man whose heart was breaking.

Ryder hadn't ever experienced heartbreak and he didn't plan on it. He enjoyed his single life, without strings, attachments or complications.

"You're good with the girls," Andie insisted, his friend again, for the moment. "Just don't slip into your old ways, not while they're living with you."

"Right." He slid his hand down her back. "I'll be good. So, are you okay?"

"I'm good. I'm going back inside." She took a step past him, but he caught her hand and held her next to him.

"Andie, I don't want to lose my best friend. I'm sorry for that night. I'm sorry that I didn't walk away…before. And I'm sorry I walked away afterward."

She didn't look at him. He looked down, at the ground she was staring at—at dandelions peeking up through the gravel and a few pieces of broken glass. He touched her cheek and ran his finger down to her chin, lifting her face so she had to look at him.

"I'm sorry, too," she whispered. "I just don't know how to go back. We've always kept the line between us, Ryder. This is why."

"We don't have to stop being friends," he insisted, hoping he didn't sound like a kid.

"No, we don't. But you have to accept that things have changed."

"Okay, things have changed." More than things. She had changed. He could see it in her eyes in the way she smiled as she turned and walked away, back into the Mad Cow.

A crazy thought, that he had changed, too. He brushed it off and followed her into the diner. He hadn't changed at all. He still wanted the same things he'd always wanted. Some things weren't meant to be domesticated, like raccoons, foxes…and him.

When they got home, Andie changed into jeans and a T-shirt and headed for the barn. She was brushing Babe, her old mare, when Etta walked through the double doors at the end of the building.

"What's going on with you?" Etta, arms crossed, stood with the sun to her back, her face in shadows.

The barn cat wandered in and Etta stepped away from the feline.

"There's nothing wrong." Andie brushed the horse's rump and the bay mare twitched her dark tail and stomped a fly away from her leg. "Okay, something is wrong. Caroline is here. I don't know what she wants from me. I don't know why she expects to walk into my life and have me happy to be graced with her presence."

"She doesn't expect that."

Andie stopped brushing and turned. "So now you're on her side."

"Don't sound like a five-year-old. I'm not on her side. I'm on your side. I want you to forgive her. I want you to have her in your life. I have to forgive her, too. She broke my son's heart. She broke your heart."

Andie shook off the anger. Her heart hadn't been broken, not by Caroline or anyone else.

"I'm fine." She brushed Babe's neck and the mare leaned toward her, her eyes closing slightly.

"You're not fine. And this isn't about Caroline, it's about you and Ryder. What happened?"

"Nothing. Or at least nothing a little time won't take care of."

Etta walked closer. "I guess it's too late for the talk that we should have had fifteen years ago," she said with a sigh.

Andie swallowed and nodded. And the words freed the tears that had been hovering. "Too late."

"It's okay." Etta stepped closer, her arm going around Andie's waist.

"No, it isn't. I messed up. I really messed up. This is something I can't take back."

"So you went to church?"

"Not just because of this. I went because I had to go. As much as I've always claimed I was strong, every time I was at the end of my rope, it was God that I turned to. I've always prayed. And that Sunday morning, I wanted to be in church."

"Andie, did you use…"

Andie's face flamed and she shook her head.

"Do you think you might be…"

They were playing fill-in-the-blank. Andie wanted option C, not A. She wanted the answer to be sick with a stomach virus. They didn't want to say the hard words, or face the difficult answers. She wasn't a fifteen-year-old kid. Funny, but until now she had controlled herself. She hadn't made these choices. She hadn't gotten herself into a situation like this.

She was trying to connect it all: her mistake, her relationship with God, and her friendship with Ryder. How could she put it all together and make it okay?

"Maybe it's a virus. Joy's kids had a stomach virus."

"It could be." Etta patted her back. "It really could be."

And then a truck turned into the drive. Ryder's truck. And he was pulling a trailer. Andie closed her eyes and Etta hugged her close.

"You're going to have to tell him."

"I don't know anything, not yet. I don't know if I can face this. I'm trying so hard to get my act together and I can't pull Ryder into this."

"Soon." Etta kissed her cheek.

"When I know for sure."

Ryder was out of his truck. And he was dressed for roping, in his faded jeans, a black T-shirt and nearly worn-out roper boots.

"You going with me?" He tossed the question before he reached the barn. His grin was big, and he was acting as if there was nothing wrong between them. Andie wished she could do the same.

"I don't know."

Etta's brows went up and she shrugged. "I'm going in the house. I have a roast on and it needs potatoes."

Andie watched her grandmother walk away and then she turned her attention back to Ryder. He scratched his chin and waited. And she didn't know what he wanted to hear.

"Come on, Andie, we've always roped on Sunday evenings."

It was what they'd done, as best friends. And they hadn't minded separating from time to time. She'd go out with James or one of the other guys. She'd watch, without jealousy, when he helped Vicki Summers into his truck. No jealousy at all.

Because they'd been best friends.

But today nausea rolled in her stomach and she couldn't think about leaving with him, or him leaving with Vicki afterward. And that wasn't the way it was supposed to happen.

"I can't go, not tonight."

"I don't want to lose you." He took off his white cowboy hat and held it at his side. "I wish we could go back and…"

"Think a little more clearly? Take time to breathe deep and walk away?" She shook her head. "We can't. We made a choice and now we have the consequences of that choice."

"Consequences? What consequences? You're the one acting like we can't even talk. It's simple. Just get in the truck and go with me."

"I can't." She tossed the brush into a bucket and the clang of wood hitting metal made Babe jump to the side. Andie whispered to the mare and reached to untie the lead rope from the hook on the wall. "I can't go with you, Ryder. I'm sick. My mom is here. I'm going to go inside and spend time with Etta."

"Fine." He walked to the door. "I'm going to be pretty busy in the next few weeks. Wyatt and the girls are going to need me."

"I know." She watched him walk away, but it wasn't easy. She'd never wanted to run after a guy the way she wanted to run after him, to tell him they could forget. They could go back to being friends, to being comfortable around each other. But she couldn't go after him and they couldn't go back.

She stood at the gate and watched as he climbed into his truck and slammed the door.

Ryder jumped into his truck and shifted hard into first gear. He started to stomp on it, and then remembered his horse in the trailer. Man, it would have felt good to let gravel fly. If only he could be sixteen again, not dealing with losing his best friend to a one-night mistake.

Why couldn't she just get over it and go with him? This was what they did, they went roping together. They hunted together. They got over things together.

As he eased onto the road he let his mind drift back, to the night in Phoenix. Stupid. Stupid. Stupid. They'd both been hurting. He'd been upset by Wyatt's situation. She'd been hurting because her twin sister had arrived in town, bringing back the pain of being a kid rejected by her mother.

And then his thoughts made a big U-turn, shifting his memory back to the Mad Cow and Andie's pale face.

He was an idiot. An absolute idiot.

Consequences. He caught himself in time to keep from slamming on the brakes. He eased to the side of the road and stopped the truck. He sat there for a long minute thinking back, thinking ahead. Thinking this really couldn't be happening to him.

He leaned back in his seat and thought about it, and thought about his next move. A truck drove past and honked. He raised a hand in a half wave.

Glancing over his shoulder, he checked the road in both directions and backed the trailer up, this time heading the way he'd come from, to Etta's and to Andie.

As he turned into the driveway, she was coming out of the barn. She stopped in the doorway, light against the dark interior of the barn, her blond hair blowing a little in the wind. She sighed, he could see her shoulders rise and fall and then she walked toward him. And he wondered what she would say.

He parked and got out of the truck, waiting because he didn't know what questions to ask or how to face the consequences of that night. It would have been easier to keep running. But this would have caught up with him eventually. It wasn't as if he could run from it.

When she reached him, they stared at each other. The wind was blowing a little harder and clouds, low and heavy with rain, covered the sun. Shadows drifted across the brown, autumn grass.

"You're back a little quicker than I expected." She smiled, and for a minute he thought it might have been his imagination, her pale skin, the nausea.

He rubbed his face and tried to think of how a man asked a woman, a friend, this question.

"I came back because I have to ask you something."

"Go ahead." She slipped her hands into her front pockets.

His gaze slipped to her belly and he didn't even mean for that to happen. It was flat, perfectly flat. She cleared her throat. He glanced up and her eyebrows shot up.

"I have a question." Man, he felt like a fifteen-year-old kid. "Are you, um, are you having a baby?"

Chapter Four

The question she hadn't even wanted to ask herself. Ryder, her best friend for as long as she could remember, was peering down at her with toffee-brown eyes that had never been more serious. He wasn't a boy anymore. She wasn't a kid.

And she didn't want to answer this question, not today. She didn't want to stand in front of him, with her heart pounding and her stomach still rolling a little. She looked away, to the field across the road. It was nothing spectacular, just a field with a few too many weeds and a few cattle grazing, but it gave her something else to focus on.

"Andie, come on, we have to talk about *this*."

"Like we talked two months ago? Come on, Ryder, admit that neither one of us want to talk about this."

He took off his hat and brushed his arm across his forehead. He glanced down at her and shook his head. "No, maybe this isn't how I wanted to spend a Sunday afternoon, but this is what we've got."

"I don't want to talk about it. Not today."

"So you are…?"

"I don't know." She looked down, at dusty, hard-packed earth. At his boots and hers as they stood toe-to-toe in that moment that changed both of their lives. He was just a cowboy, the kind of guy who had said he'd never get married.

And she'd claimed his conviction as her own. Because that's what they had done for years. She had never been one of those girls dreaming of weddings, the perfect husband or babies. She didn't play the games in school with boys' names and honeymoon locations. Instead she'd thought about how to train the best barrel horse and what it would take to win world titles.

Babies. As much as she had wanted to pretend otherwise, her feminine side had caused her to go soft when she held a baby or watched children play. When she watched her friends with their husbands, she felt a little empty on the inside, because she shared her life with Etta—and with Ryder—but Ryder never shared his heart, not the way a woman wanted a man to share his heart.

"Andie, I'm sorry, this shouldn't have happened." He touched her cheek and then his hand dropped to his side and he stepped back a few steps.

"I definitely don't want you to be sorry." She looked up, trying her best to be determined. "Like I said, I don't know. It could be that I caught the stomach virus some of the kids in Kansas had. When I know for sure, I'll let you know."

"Let me know?" He brushed a hand through his hair and shoved his hat back in place, a gesture she'd seen a few too many times and she knew exactly what it meant. Frustration.

Well, she could tell him a few things about frustration. But she wasn't in the mood. She wasn't in the mood to spell out for him that this hadn't been in her plans, either. He hadn't been in her plans, not this way.

"Yeah, I'll let you know. Look, whatever happens,

whatever this is, it isn't going to change anything." She was glad she sounded firm, sounded strong. She felt anything but, with her insides quivering. "You've always been my friend and that's how it'll stay."

"What does that mean?"

"It means I'm not going to tie you down or try to drag you into this. It doesn't change things."

"I have news for you, Andie Forester, this changes things. This changes everything."

"It doesn't have to."

He shook his head. "Are you being difficult for a reason, other than to just drive me crazy? If you're pre…uh, having a baby, it changes a lot, now doesn't it?"

She wanted to smile, because even the word brought a bead of sweat across his brow and his neck turned red. But she couldn't smile, not yet.

"I'll let you know when I find out for sure."

"Fine, you let me know. And we'll pretend that this isn't important, if that's what you really want." He turned and walked away, a cowboy in faded jeans, the legs worn and a little more faded where he'd spent a lot of time in the saddle.

He waved as he climbed into his truck and started the engine. She waved back. And it already felt different. She'd been lying to herself, trying to tell herself it wouldn't matter.

She watched him drive away and then she considered her next move. Go inside and face her mother, or stay in the barn and hide from reality. She liked the hiding plan the best. Facing Ryder and her mother, both in the same day, sounded like too much.

In the dark, dusty interior of the barn she could close her eyes and pretend she was the person she'd been two months ago. But she wasn't.

A lot had happened. She turned over a bucket and sat down. She leaned against the stall door behind her and closed her eyes. Everything had changed. Most importantly, she had changed.

On a Sunday morning in a church service at the rodeo arena she had changed. It had started when she walked out of her horse trailer, a cup of coffee in hand, and she'd heard the couple who led the service singing "Amazing Grace." She'd walked to the arena and taken a seat on a row of bleachers a good distance from the crowd.

During that service, God had pulled her back to Him. She had been drawn back into a relationship that she'd ignored for years. And it hadn't been God's fault that she'd walked away. It had been about her loyalty to Ryder.

She opened her eyes and looked outside, at a sky growing darker as the sun set. The days were cool and growing shorter. She wasn't ready for winter. She definitely didn't know how to face spring, and seven months from now.

How did a person go from turning back to God, to making a giant mistake like the one she'd made with Ryder? And what about God? Was He going to reject her now?

She'd had experience with rejection.

It had started with her mother. She squeezed her eyes shut again, and refused the tears that burned, tightening in her throat because she wasn't going to let them fall.

"Forgive me," she whispered, wanting peace, something that settled the ache in her heart and took away the heaviness of misgivings.

She stood and walked into the feed room to look at the calendar tacked to the wall. It recorded dates and locations of rodeos. She thumbed back to the month of the Phoenix rodeo and tried to remember. She leaned, resting her forehead against the rough barn wood.

For two months she'd told herself there wouldn't be consequences, other than a little bit of time when they'd be uncomfortable with each other.

But she'd been wrong. There were definitely consequences, and this wasn't going away any time soon. She picked up the pencil she used to mark the calendar and she went through the next few months, marking through events she'd planned to attend, but now wouldn't.

Things had definitely changed.

Roping hadn't taken Ryder's mind off Andie and the possibility of a baby. His baby. He didn't need proof of that fact because he knew Andie. As he drove through Dawson after loading his horse and talking for a few minutes with friends, his mind kept going back, to better choices he could have made. And forward, to how his life would never be the same.

Ryder drove through Dawson. It was Sunday night and that meant there wasn't a thing going on and nothing open but the convenience store. A few trucks were parked at the side of the building and a few teenagers sat on tailgates, drinking sodas and eating corn dogs. Big night out in Dawson.

He turned left on the road that led out of town, to his family farm, and on past, to the house where Andie had grown up with Etta. He considered driving there and talking to her, trying to figure out what they were going to do. He didn't figure she'd be ready to talk.

Instead he pulled into his drive and drove back to the barn. As he got out, he noticed Wyatt in the backyard with the girls. Wyatt was sitting at the patio table, the girls were running around the yard with flashlights. They were barely more than babies.

And Wyatt didn't know what to do with them. That

thought kind of sunk into the pit of his stomach. Wyatt had always been the one who seemed to know how to do this adult thing.

Ryder stepped out of the truck and walked back to the trailer to unload his horse. The big gelding stomped restlessly, ready to be out and ready to graze in the pasture.

"Easy up there, Buddy." Ryder unlatched the back of the trailer. He stepped inside, easing down the unused half of the trailer to untie the animal and back him out.

When they landed on firm ground, Wyatt was there. Ryder smiled at his brother and got a half smile in return. The girls had stopped running and were watching. They weren't used to horses. Wyatt had taken a job as a youth minister in Florida and they had lived in town.

"Long night?" Wyatt stepped back, watching.

"Yeah, kind of." How did he tell his brother? Wyatt had always held it together. He'd held them together as best he could.

"What's up?" Wyatt followed him to the gate, opening it for Ryder to let the horse out into the pasture.

"Nothing."

"Right."

Ryder pushed the gate closed and latched it. The horse reached for a bite of grass, managing to act like he hadn't eaten in days, not hours. Horses were easy to take care of. They could be left alone. They didn't make requirements. They had to be trained, but he was pretty sure they were a lot easier to train than a child.

He ranched. He raised quarter horses and black angus cattle. He didn't raise babies.

Until now.

The girls ran up to them, tiny things, not even reaching his hip. He closed the gate and turned his attention to

Molly and Kat. And boots. They were wearing his boots. The good ones that had cost a small fortune.

He glanced up, pretty sure that God was testing him. This was a lesson on parenting, or patience. He didn't know which. Probably both.

"We like your shoes." Molly grinned, and he was happy to see her smiling. But man, she was wearing his best boots.

The look he gave Wyatt was ignored.

"Boots." Kat giggled. The pair she was wearing covered her legs completely.

"Yep, boots." He scooped up Kat and snuggled her close. She giggled and leaned back. She looked a lot like her mom. That had to be hard for Wyatt. Kat had Wendy's smile, her dimples, her laughter.

And she was a dirty mess. Mud caked her, and his boots. From the tangles in her hair, he guessed it had been a couple of days since it had seen a brush.

"You need a bath." He held her tight as they headed toward the house.

Kids needed things like baths, and their teeth brushed. They had to be tucked in and someone had to be there for them. They didn't need parents who drank themselves into a stupor and made choices that robbed a family of security.

He didn't drink. He had one thing going for him.

Anger knocked around inside him. The past had a way of doing that, and a guy shouldn't get angry thinking of parents who had died too young.

"If you need to talk…" Wyatt followed him up the steps to the back door, and then he shrugged. They'd never been touchy-feely. Sharing was for afternoon talk shows, not the Johnson brothers. They'd always solved their problems, even dealt with their anger, by roping a few calves or riding hard through the back field.

Every now and then they'd had a knock-down-drag-out in the backyard. Those fights had ended with the two of them on their backs, staring up at the sky, out of breath, but out of anger.

Talking about it didn't seem like an option.

"Yeah, I know we can talk." Ryder put his niece down on the floor and flipped on the kitchen light. Kat stomped around in his boots, leaving dirt smudges on the floor he'd mopped last night. "Did you guys eat?"

He looked around. There was an open loaf of bread on the counter and a jar of peanut butter, the lid next to it. He glanced down at Kat. She had a smear of peanut butter on her cheek. He twisted the bread closed.

"Did you feed the girls?" Ryder asked again when Wyatt hadn't answered.

"Molly made sandwiches."

"And you think that's good?" A three-year-old making sandwiches. Ryder screwed the lid on the peanut butter because he had to do something to keep from pushing his brother into a wall to knock sense into him. "Girls, are you hungry?"

Kat grinned and Molly looked at her dad. Ryder exhaled a lot of anger. He didn't have a clue what little kids ate. Wyatt should have a clue. If Wyatt couldn't do this, how in the world was Ryder going to manage?

"Tell you what, I'll make eggs and toast. Do you like eggs?" Ryder opened the fridge door.

"I can do it." Wyatt took the carton of eggs from his hands.

"You girls go play." Ryder smiled at his nieces. "I think there's a box of toys in the living room. Mostly horses and cowboys."

His and Wyatt's toys that Ryder had dug out of a back closet the night before.

When the girls were gone, he turned back to his brother. Wyatt cracked eggs into a bowl and he didn't look up. "I've taken care of them for a year."

"Yeah, I know you have."

The dog scratched at the back door. Ryder pushed it open and let the animal in, because there was one thing Bear was good at, and that was cleaning up stuff that dropped on the floor. Stuff like peanut butter sandwiches.

Bear sniffed his way into the kitchen and licked the floor clean, except he left the mud. Not that Ryder blamed him for that.

The dog was the best floor sweeper in the country.

"I'm taking care of my girls." Wyatt poured eggs into the pan. "And I don't want tips from a guy who hasn't had kids, or hasn't had a relationship in his life that lasted more than a month."

"That's about to change," Ryder muttered and he sure hadn't meant to open that can of worms. He'd meant to butter toast.

"What's that mean?" Wyatt turned the stove off.

"Remember what it was like, growing up in this house?"

"Sure, I remember." Wyatt scooped eggs onto four plates. "Always laughter, mostly the drunken kind that ended in a big fight by the end of the night. And then there were the phone calls."

Phone calls their mother received from the other women. Ryder shook his head, because memories were hard to shake. His dad's temper had been hard to hide from.

"Right. That's not the kind of life our kids should

have." Ryder let out a sigh, because he had been holding on to those memories for a long time.

"Well, as far as I know, the only kids in this house are mine, and they're not going to have that life, not in this house. If you're insinuating…"

"I'm not insinuating anything about you or how you're raising those girls." Ryder tossed a slice of buttered toast to his blue heeler. "Wyatt, there isn't a person around who blames you for having a hard time right now."

"I guess this isn't about me, is it?"

No, but it would have been nice to pretend it was. Ryder shrugged and poured himself a cup of that morning's coffee. He ignored his brother and slid the coffee into the microwave.

"No, it isn't about you." He took his cup of day old coffee out of the microwave. "I'm going outside."

Because it was still his life. For now.

"Not again." Andie rolled out of bed and ran for the bathroom. She leaned, eyes closed and taking deep breaths until the moment passed. When it was just a rolling hint of nausea, she sat back, leaning against the cool tile walls of her bathroom.

"I have gingersnaps."

She turned and Etta was standing in the doorway, already dressed for her day. Andie looked down at her own wrinkled pajamas that she honestly didn't want to change out of, not today.

"I'm not sure what good cookies and milk will do now."

Etta laughed. "Ginger for nausea. Although the milk might not be the best thing right now. Maybe ginger tea. Come downstairs and we'll see what I have."

The thought of ginger in tea made it worse. Andie

closed the bathroom door with her foot and resumed position next to the commode. Her grandmother knocked, insistent. It wasn't a good thing, Etta's insistence, not this morning.

"Give me a minute, Gran."

"It's your mother."

Oh, that didn't make it better. Mother. Andie leaned again, perspiration beaded her brow and her skin felt clammy. She stood and leaned over the sink, turning on cold water to splash her face.

"Leave me alone."

"I can't. Etta said you're sick. Can I help?"

"No, you can't help." No one could help.

But there was a clear feeling that someone could. She closed her eyes and prayed for answers, because she'd never needed answers more. She felt like she was on a traffic circle in the middle of a foreign city and she didn't know which road to take, so she kept driving around the circle, looking for the right direction, the right path.

Her own analogy and it made her dizzy. She opened her eyes and the swaying stopped.

"Andie?"

"I'm fine. I'll be out in a minute."

The door moved a little, like someone leaned against it from the other side. "I know you're angry with me."

The woman wouldn't give up.

And the term *angry with her mother* didn't begin to describe the hurt, rejection and fury, all rolled into one giant ball and lodged in her heart. Andie slid her hand over her stomach, wondering at the idea of a baby growing inside her, and wondering how a mother could leave a child behind.

People did things even they didn't understand, things they regretted. She tried not to think about Phoenix, but it wouldn't go away. Ryder's face, his smile swimming in her vision, couldn't be blinked away.

She had always cared about his rotten hide.

Hormones. All of this emotion was caused by raging hormones. She had to stop, to get her act together. She dried her face off and pulled the door open.

Her mother nearly fell on top of her.

"I forgive you." Andie walked past her mother and kept going, down the stairs, out the front door. Alyson's cat greeted her on the front porch. She scooped the kitten up and held it close. Not that she liked cats. But she had to do something.

The screen door creaked open.

"Are you pregnant?" Caroline asked as she stepped onto the porch. She looked so pinched and worried, Andie nearly smiled.

"I probably am." She glanced away from her mom. "I guess this is how you expected I'd end up."

"I never thought you'd be less than wonderful. I didn't take Alyson because I thought she'd be better." Caroline swept her hand over her face, her fingers glittering with gold and gems. "I took her because she was easier. You had so much energy. You pushed me."

"Pushed you?"

"I knew I couldn't be a good mother to you. I was worried I'd be a horrible mother. That would have been worse for you, wouldn't it?"

"You could have called."

"It seemed better this way. I can't go back, Andie. But I do want you to know that I'm here if you need me."

"I'm sure I'll be fine."

"Of course you'll be fine. If you'd like, I could go to the doctor with you before I leave in the morning."

The kitten hissed and clawed, wanting down. Andie

let him go, watched him scamper with his scrawny tail in the air and then she turned to meet her mother's cautious gaze. "I get that you want to be forgiven, but we can't undo twenty-five years of silence with a doctor's appointment and you standing outside the bathroom door offering words of support."

"I know that." Caroline hugged herself, her arms thin. "Will you call if you need anything before I come back next month to help Alyson finish the wedding plans?"

"I'll call." Andie sighed. "If it helps, I don't hate you. I wanted to, but I don't."

Caroline nodded and tears flooded her eyes. "I'm glad."

"Yeah, so am I." Andie sat down on the steps, her mother stood, leaning against the post. "I guess what you have to realize is that I'm not ready for you to play the part of my mother."

"Right. Of course." Caroline nodded and stepped away from the post. "Thank you for giving me a chance."

"You're welcome." The kitten crawled into Andie's lap, twitching its tail in her face.

Andie watched her mother walk back into the house, and then a truck was barreling down the paved road and turning into their driveway. She groaned and wondered how a day could turn this bad this fast.

Instead of sitting on the porch, waiting for him to get to her, she got up and walked inside. From the front hallway she could smell the spicy aroma of the ginger tea that Etta had promised. And now it seemed like a good idea.

Etta turned to look at her when she walked into the kitchen. Her grandmother pointed to the cup on the counter and Andie picked it up, holding it up to inhale the aroma of ginger and cinnamon.

"Sip it and see if that doesn't help settle your stomach."

Etta flipped pancakes onto a plate.

"If it does, I want a few of those pancakes." Andie sat down with the tea and watched her grandmother. It was just the two of them, the way it had been for a long time. Even when Andie's dad had been alive, it had been Etta and Andie most of the time.

"The first plate is yours." Etta glanced out the kitchen window. "You know that Ryder is here, right?"

"I know." She sipped the tea and waited, listening for the familiar sound of his steps on the porch, the song he whistled that wasn't a song and the mew of the kitten when she had someone cornered for attention.

Chapter Five

Ryder walked up the back steps to Etta's, whistling, pretending it was any other fall day in Oklahoma. It was easy to whistle. Not so easy to put out of his mind other thoughts, more complicated thoughts.

He rapped on the back door and Etta called out for him to come in, that he didn't have to knock. He'd never knocked before, but he thought that today might be a little different. Things had definitely changed.

Andie sat on a stool just inside the door. She turned to look at him, and then shifted her attention back to the cup in her hand, and the plate of pancakes in front of her. She looked a little pale, a little green. Her hair was in a short ponytail with thin wisps hanging loose to frame her face.

How many times had he seen her in the morning? They'd taken predawn rides together, worked cattle together and hauled hay together. But today she was maybe the mother of his child. Stuff shifted inside him, trying to make room for that idea. It wasn't easy to have that space when he'd never thought about his life in terms of fatherhood.

He felt nearly as sick as she must feel.

"You're up and around early." She kept her focus on the plate of pancakes.

"Yeah, well, I have a lot to do today."

"Like?"

"First of all, I want to talk to you."

"Talk away." She took another bite of pancake.

Okay, she wasn't going to make this easy. He leaned against the wall next to the door and watched her eat. He had just finished breakfast at the Mad Cow, but that didn't stop him from thinking about Etta's pancakes. No one made them like Etta.

"Want some?" Andie offered, smiling a little. Looking a little like her old self.

"Nah, I just ate. Andie, we need to talk."

"I'd rather not. I mean, really, what do you need to say? We've covered it. We made a mistake. We were both there. So we move on, we find a way to keep being friends."

"I think I should give you kids some privacy?" Etta turned off the stove and slipped the apron over her head, hanging it on the hook as she walked out the door.

"We don't need privacy." Andie stood, picking up her empty plate. She carried it to the sink and ran water over it, staring out the window.

Ryder walked up behind her, wanting to hold her. And that surprised him. She'd never been that person to him, the person he dated, the person he held. She'd been the person who helped him keep his act together, and the friend he turned to when he needed to talk something out. He'd been that person for her, too.

"We need privacy." He stepped next to her, leaning shoulder to shoulder for a second. And she leaned back, resting her head against him.

"Okay, we're alone." She glanced up, turning to face him.

Yeah, they were alone. He took a few deep breaths and told himself this was the right thing to do. Andie was staring up at him, blue eyes locking with his. His emotions tangled inside him like two barn cats were going at it, fighting to the death inside his stomach.

"I never thought I'd do this." He'd ridden two-thousand-pound bulls, fought fires with the volunteer fire department, and he'd never been this afraid of anything.

"Do what?"

He reached into his pocket and held out his hand. "Andie, I think we should get married."

And she laughed at him. He stepped back, not sure how to react to laughter. He had kind of expected her to be mad, or something. She could have cried. But he hadn't expected laughter.

"You've got to be kidding me."

"Well, no, I wasn't." But maybe he should pretend it had been a joke. They could laugh it off and move on like it hadn't happened. Maybe she'd even tell him this was a late April Fools' joke, and she wasn't going to have a baby.

"Well, you should be kidding. You know you don't want to marry me. You don't want to marry anyone, and especially not like this."

"I'd marry you. Seriously, who better to marry than your best friend?"

She didn't make a sarcastic remark or roll her eyes, and those would have been the typical Andie reactions to his comment. Instead she smiled and he couldn't believe two months of hormones could change a woman that much, that fast.

"I'm not going to marry you, Ryder. We won't even know for sure if I'm pregnant until I go to the doctor tomorrow."

"We could get a, well, one of those tests."

She turned a little pink and looked down at the floor. Her feet were bare and she wore sweats cut off at the knees and a T-shirt. She looked young.

And he felt older than dirt.

"Andie?"

"I took a test." She turned away from him, running dishwater like nothing was different, as if this was a normal day and he hadn't just had his proposal, his very first proposal, rejected. As if she hadn't just admitted to taking a pregnancy test.

He shoved his hands into his pockets and waited a few seconds before pushing further into the conversation.

"Okay, you took a test. I guess you didn't think I had a right to know?"

"Yes, I was going to let you know." She kept washing dishes without looking at him. "I took the test last night and it was positive."

So, this was how it felt to learn you were going to be a dad. Not that he hadn't already been pretty sure, but this made it official. She reached for the ring where he'd left it on the counter. It had been his grandmother's. She looked at it for a long moment and then she smiled and put it back in his hand.

"Save your ring for someone you love. I'm going to have this baby, and I'm not going to force you into its life, or my life. I'm not going to accept a proposal you probably planned while you were feeding cattle this morning."

She knew him that well.

* * *

"Now, if you don't mind, I have a lot to do today. Rob's coming over to shoe my horses and Caroline is going back to Boston tomorrow."

Andie was trying like crazy not to be hurt or mad. She'd never wanted a proposal like this, one that a guy felt as if he had to make. She hadn't spent too much of her life thinking about marriage, but she knew the one thing she wanted. She wanted love. She didn't want to start a marriage based on "have to."

That night two months ago was one she couldn't undo. She couldn't undo the consequences. She closed her eyes and her hand went to her stomach. As much as she had never thought about babies in connection with her life, she couldn't think of this baby as a punishment.

It was her baby. She opened her eyes and Ryder was watching her. It was his baby, too. Having a baby changed everything, for both of them. It changed who they were and who they were going to be. It changed their friendship.

If she had to do it over again, she would have walked away from Ryder that night in Phoenix. She would have stopped things. Because a baby's life shouldn't start like this, with parents who could barely look at one another.

A baby should be planned, shouldn't it? A baby should know that it was being born into a home with two parents prepared to love it and raise it.

So what did a person do when the perfect plan hadn't happened? Andie figured they made the best of things. They counted from this day forward and promised to do their best after this.

"When are you going to the doctor?"

"Tomorrow." She washed a plate and he took it from her to run under rinse water.

"I meant, what time?"

"I'm going to leave early, probably by nine."

"I'll take you."

Andie stopped washing and took a deep breath. "I don't need you to take me."

"Why in the world are you pushing me away?" Ryder's voice was low, calm. But she knew better. She knew him better. "If you're pregnant, I'm the father. Right?"

"Right."

"So, I'm going with you. My baby, Andie. That has to give me some rights. Maybe you don't want to marry me, but I don't think you'll stop me from being a part of this kid's life."

"I'm not trying to stop you. I'm trying to tell you that I'm not expecting this from you."

Her insides shook and she felt cold and clammy as a wave of nausea swept through her again. Ryder touched her arm, his hand warm on her bare skin.

"Do you need to sit down?"

"Yes, I need to sit down and I need for you to stop acting like this."

"How do you want me to act?"

"I don't know." She let him lead her to one of the bar stools at the kitchen counter.

"Well, that makes two of us, Andie. We're both in a place we never expected to be. We're going to be parents. That's going to take some time to adjust to. Give me a break and don't expect me to know exactly what to say or how to react."

"Fine, then you give me a break and don't expect me to suddenly think of you as my handsome prince." She blinked away tears. "You've always been my toad."

He smiled and shook his head and she thought he might hug her, but he didn't. As she was contemplating the dozens of reasons why she shouldn't want him to hug her, his cell phone rang.

Andie waited, watching as he talked, as his expression changed from aggravated with her to worried.

"I'll be right there." He slipped his cell phone into his pocket. He met her gaze and his eyes were no longer dancing with laughter.

"What's up?"

"Molly's sick. Wyatt needs to run to town and get something for her. My medicine cabinet doesn't support the needs of toddlers."

"I can go with you." Andie hopped off the bar stool and grabbed her cell phone that had been charging all night. "Let me get shoes."

"You're sick."

"I'm fine. It's over now." She tried to smile, but he was still watching her. She was suddenly breakable.

He'd have to get over that in a real hurry.

"Morning sickness, Ryder. Morning, and then it goes away."

"Right. I get it."

The back door opened. Etta walked in, glancing from one to the other, clearly looking for marks of a fight.

"Where are you two off to?" Etta kicked off her shoes and set a basket of fresh eggs on the counter.

"Molly's sick," Andie explained as she leaned to tie her shoes. "I'm going over to see if there's anything I can do."

"You're going to help?" Etta smiled a little. "With children?"

"I can do that."

"Call if you need my help."

"Will do." Andie hugged her grandmother. "Oh, if Rob gets here before I get back, tell him Dusty and Babe need shoes. Not that he won't be able to tell."

"Of course."

Ryder pushed the door open and Andie walked out, past him, his arm brushing hers. And then he walked next to her. They didn't talk. When had they ever not talked? They'd always had something to say to one another, something to tease the other about.

How did she get that back? Or did she? Maybe that was the other consequence, losing her best friend.

Ryder opened the passenger side truck door. For her. She stopped and gave him a look. "Stop." She stood in front of him.

"Stop what?"

"When have you ever opened the car for me?"

"I don't know. I'm sure I've done it before. Would you just get in?"

She shrugged and climbed in. "Sure thing."

The door closed and he walked around the front of the truck to the driver's side. Her heart clenched a little, because he was sweet and gorgeous and a cowboy. For most of her life she'd just seen him as the friend she couldn't live without. Now, watching him walk away, she wondered if she'd kept that line between them because he'd insisted on just being friends.

No, that wasn't it. She was just being overly emotional. She didn't love Ryder. He didn't love her. And maybe, just maybe, the test was wrong. She'd go to the doctor tomorrow and find out it had all been a big mistake. They'd laugh and go back to being who they had always been.

Ryder didn't talk to Andie on the short drive to his place. As he eased the truck up the driveway, he let his gaze settle on the house he'd grown up in. It was a big old ranch house that his parents had remodeled. They'd added the new windows, the brick siding and the landscaping.

It had sheltered them, but it hadn't exactly been a happy home. Wyatt and Ryder had spent their time breaking horses, roping steers and looking out for each other.

They'd been in more than their share of fights. They'd broken more than a few hearts. He knew that. He could accept that he'd always been the bad boy that most parents didn't want to see walk through the door to pick up their little girl for a date.

And now he was going to be a dad. The idea itched inside him, like something he was deathly allergic to. But when he walked through the front door and saw three-year-old Molly on the sofa, a stuffed animal in her arms and her little face red from the fever that must have come on since he left the house, he thought different things about being a dad.

He thought about a kid of his own, one that he wouldn't let down.

But what if he did? What if he messed up a kid the way his parents had messed him up? What if his kid grew up too independent for its own good, or always afraid of what was happening in the living room?

The last thing he should be thinking of was a little girl with Andie's eyes.

Wyatt held Kat. "Can you watch them while I run to Grove and get some medicine?" The little girl looked like she might be nearly asleep, but when she saw Ryder she smiled. And then she held her arms out to Andie.

And Andie's eyes widened. "Oh, okay."

She held the little girl and when she looked over Kat's shoulder at him, he felt like someone who didn't belong in this picture. Andie probably felt the same way.

"I'll be right back." Wyatt grabbed his keys, shot a look over his shoulder and walked out the front door.

Something about that look had Ryder worrying that his

brother wouldn't come back. He walked to the door and watched the truck drive away. "How about some lunch?"

He turned, smiling at Kat, and then Molly. His dog, Bear, was curled on the couch at her feet. As Ryder approached her side, Bear looked up, letting out a low growl. So, it had been that easy to steal the dog's loyalty? It just took being a little girl with big eyes.

"Bear, enough." At the warning, the dog's stub tail thumped the leather sofa.

Molly's eyes watered. Ryder sat down on the coffee table, facing her. "How about a drink of water?"

She nodded and sat up, still dressed in her nightgown with a princess on the front. His heart filled up in a way he'd never experienced. And then it ducked for cover, because this couldn't be his life.

Movement behind him. He turned and Andie was sitting in the rocking chair, Kat held against her. If Wyatt was running, he should have taken Ryder with him.

"Is her forehead hot?" Andie asked, her voice soft, comforting. He'd never heard it like that, as if she already knew how to be a mom.

Maybe women were that way? Maybe they had that natural instinct, and only men had to wonder and worry that they'd never get it right. The way he was worrying.

He touched Molly's head. "Pretty hot." He winked at the little girl as she curled back into her blanket, his dog curling into the bend of her knees.

"Maybe get a cool, wet cloth?" Andie shrugged. "I really don't have a clue, but it could be a while before Wyatt gets back and maybe cool water would bring her temperature down. We could call Etta."

"Wyatt will come back." Ryder cleared his throat. "I mean, he'll be back soon. It doesn't take that long to drive into Grove."

"Right." She was still holding Kat, her fingers stroking the little girl's brown hair. "Do you have a brush? Her hair's kind of scraggly."

He stood up. "I'll get a wet cloth for Molly and a brush for Kat."

When he walked back into the room, Molly was dozing and Kat had found a book for Andie to read. The two of them were cuddled in his big chair, Andie's bare feet on the ottoman.

His throat tightened and he looked away, because it was a lot easier to deal with Molly and not the crazy thoughts going through his mind.

Wyatt came back.

Andie breathed a sigh of relief when he walked through the door an hour later. He had a bag of medication and two stuffed animals. He avoided looking at her, and at Ryder. She wondered if he had thought about not coming back.

How did a person go on when the person they had loved the most, the one they had promised to cherish and protect, took their own life? She couldn't imagine his emotions, the loss, the guilt and the questions.

The questions about her mother leaving didn't begin to compare to what Wyatt must be asking himself every single day. She wanted to tell him he couldn't have stopped it. She wanted to tell him that people make choices, and when they're making those choices they aren't always thinking about how the ones left behind will feel. Wendy wouldn't have wanted to hurt him, or her daughters.

It wasn't her place. She and Wyatt had never been close. He'd been older, wiser and never up for any of her and Ryder's crazy antics.

She shifted and he moved, as if he had just noticed her.

Kat had fallen asleep in her arms and Molly was sleeping on the couch. Andie looked at Ryder. Without words, he took the sleeping child from her arms and placed her on the opposite end of the couch from her sister.

Bear hopped down, looking offended the way only a dog can.

"We should get you back before Rob gets there to shoe those horses." Ryder had walked to the door. His gaze settled first on the girls and then on Wyatt. "Need anything before we go?"

"No, we're fine. Thanks for watching them."

"No problem. Call if you need me."

As they walked out to the truck, Andie slowed her pace.

"Do you think he'll be okay?" She glanced back at the house. Ryder followed the direction of her gaze and shrugged.

"I guess he will. What else can he do?"

"I guess you're right. But I can't imagine..."

"Yeah, I know."

His hand reached for hers. Andie didn't say anything. She walked next to him, his fingers tightly laced through hers. When they got to the truck he squeezed lightly and then let go. His hand was on the door handle, but he didn't open it.

Andie reached to do it herself, but he stopped her.

"Andie, we're going to figure this out. I don't know how, but we will. I guess we'll do it the way we've always faced everything else—together."

She nodded, but her eyes were swimming and she just wanted him to hold her hand again. She didn't want to feel alone. His words had taken away a little of that feeling and replaced it with hope. Maybe they would survive this.

"We should go." Andie glanced away, but Ryder touched her cheek, drawing her attention back to him, forcing her to meet his gaze. She stared up at him, at lean, suntanned cheeks and a smile that curved into something delicious and tempting.

That smile was her downfall. She should turn away and not think about her life in terms of being in Ryder's life. She should definitely look away. But his eyes were dark and pulled her in.

"We should definitely go," she repeated, whispering this time.

"I know, but there's one thing we need to do before we leave."

He leaned, his hand still on her cheek. Her fingers slipped off the chrome door handle to rest on his arm.

His lips touched hers in a gesture that was sweet and disarming. His hand moved from her cheek to the back of her neck and he paused in the kiss to rest his forehead against hers.

Andie gathered her senses, because she couldn't let her heart go there, not in the direction it wanted to go.

"We shouldn't have gone there." She broke the connection and reached for the door handle. This time he opened it for her.

"Andie, at least give me a chance to figure this all out before you give up on me."

"I've never given up on you." She touched his arm. "But I can't be distracted, Ryder. I have to make the right decisions, now more than ever."

"And you think turning down my proposal was the right decision?"

"Yeah, right now it is. It was sweet of you, really it

was, but it was spur-of-the-moment and this is something that we should take time to think about."

Spur-of-the-moment was definitely a bad idea.

Chapter Six

Andie walked through the glass doors of the women's health clinic the next morning and she couldn't deny that her stomach was doing crazy flips and her palms were sweating. This time it was a good old case of nerves and not morning sickness. She rubbed her hands down the sides of her jeans and ignored the cautious look Ryder shot her as they walked across the granite-tiled lobby.

"We could skip this. I mean, the test is probably right."

Ryder laughed a little as he pushed the button on the elevator. "Right, we already know, so why bother with a doctor? I mean, who needs help delivering a kid into the world?"

Every word spiked into her heart. *Delivering. Kid. World.* This baby wasn't going to stay inside her, where it was safe, where it was a thought, something in the future. It would come kicking and screaming into her life. If Etta's calculations were correct, it would happen in May. Spring.

Andie wouldn't be riding for a world title any time soon.

But with the life growing inside of her, that couldn't be her focus. Her old plans were being replaced by new ones. Etta was looking at paint samples and fabric for baby quilts.

It was a little soon for that.

They got off the elevator at the third floor. Andie stood in the wide corridor, staring at Suite 10. Another couple stepped off the second elevator, smiling, holding hands. The other woman's belly was round and her eyes were shining with anticipation. And Andie didn't know how to reach for Ryder's hand, or how to make this about a happy future for the two of them. The three of them.

Her own belly was still flat. Her jeans still fit. Other than nausea in the morning and a positive sign on a stick, this didn't seem real. But it was.

At least Ryder was with her. Of course he was. She knew him well enough to know that he wasn't going to let her go through this alone. He just wasn't going to be the person with adoration in his eyes, holding her hand and telling her he'd always be there for her.

He'd never been that person for anyone. She knew him, knew that he'd worked hard at never letting himself get too involved. He didn't even want kids.

That was one thought she wished she would have blocked. Too late, though, because it had obviously already been swimming around in her mind.

"We're going to be late." Ryder reached for the door and glanced back at her. "Andie, you coming with me? I'm pretty sure this doctor doesn't want to examine me."

She tried to smile. "I'm coming."

They stepped into a prenatal world of soft colors, relaxing music and mothers-to-be reading magazines as they waited. The bad case of nervousness she was already experiencing went into overdrive. It was bad enough to make her reach for Ryder's hand, tugging him close.

"Relax." He walked with her to the counter. The re-

ceptionist smiled up at him. He grinned with that wicked
Ryder charm that had kept girls following him since kindergarten. "Andie Forester. We have an appointment."

"Right. Here's the paperwork for new patients, Mr.
Forester." The young woman handed over a clipboard
with a pen and a stack of papers to be filled out.

Ryder turned, handing Andie the clipboard. "There
you go, Mrs. Forester."

She smacked him with the clipboard. "You're horrible."

He winked. "Yeah, I work at it. But your color is coming back, so that's a plus."

She walked away from him and he followed. When
she sat down in a corner, as far away from other patients
as she could get, he sat down next to her. He crossed his
right leg over his left knee and leaned back in the chair
that had to be one of the most uncomfortable she'd ever
sat in.

While she filled out paperwork, he flipped through
magazines, giggling a little bit like a junior-high kid with
the lingerie catalogue. She shot him a dirty look and he
didn't even manage to look contrite.

Thirty minutes later, Andie walked through the doors
of the exam room, alone. Other women had taken their
husbands, the fathers of their babies. Ryder wasn't her
husband. And she couldn't face this with him.

She didn't know how to face it without him. She sat
down on the examining table and waited for the doctor.
And she waited. She glanced at her watch and groaned,
it was way past noon. No wonder she was getting shaky.
Baby needed to eat. An OB should know that.

The door opened. Andie's hands were shaking. She
twirled them in the robe she'd been told to wear by the

nurse who had made a brief stop some thirty minutes earlier.

"Sorry, had an emergency." Dr. Mark looked down at his file. "Good news. You're pregnant."

He said it with a happy smile that faded when he looked at her face.

"That is good news, isn't it?" he asked, pushing his glasses to the top of his head. His hair was blond and thinning, his smile was kind and fatherly. She liked him.

"It is." She bit down on her lip, trying to stop the trembling. "I'm sorry. It's not really a surprise. You can't be sick for days on end and really be shocked by the news that you're pregnant."

"But it isn't something you planned. I'm assuming it is something you plan to keep?"

Heat rushed to her cheeks. She'd never thought of anything other than keeping this baby. Her baby. She blinked a few times.

"Of course I'm keeping my baby."

"Of course." He smiled and sat down. "I'm going to do a quick exam, but first we'll do an ultrasound. If the father is here, he can come back…"

"No, he can't. I mean. This isn't what either of us planned. We're not, we're not in a relationship."

It sounded pathetic. Not in a relationship, but having a baby. She buried her face in her hands and waited for her cheeks to cool to their normal temperature.

"This doesn't have to be the end of the world." Dr. Mark patted her arm. "It's a different path than you probably had planned for yourself. It's going to take some adjusting, to make this work out. But I think you can do it."

Andie looked up, meeting eyes that were kind, with crinkled lines of age and experience at the corners.

"Yeah, I know I can make it."

She wanted to ask him what he thought about God. She had developed a new relationship with God, and then she'd realized she was pregnant. Some people might think the baby pushed her back into church. But it had been her own feelings, her own desire to have that connection that had taken her to that service.

The baby hadn't pushed her there.

"Andie, if you need someone to talk to…"

She shook her head. "I'm fine, really. It's just a lot to adjust to."

She put on a big smile, to prove to him, and maybe to herself, that she was okay.

"Okay then, let's go for that ultrasound. Down the hall, second door on the left. I'll be right there. And we'll take a picture for dad. We don't want him to miss out on everything."

Right. She nodded and hopped down from the table.

"What about activity. I mean, horseback riding? Work?"

"Within reason you can continue activities that you've been doing on a regular basis. Of course you don't want to do anything strenuous, or dangerous."

"Got it." She walked out, down the hall to the room he'd directed her to. Alone.

She was going to see her baby, or what would soon be her baby, and she wished someone was there with her. She wished Etta had come with her. She wished Ryder had insisted. If he had pushed… She shook off that thought, because she shouldn't make him push.

Instead of having someone with her, she walked into a darkened room alone and a nurse helped her onto the bed.

A few minutes later she raised her head and watched the screen, saw the beating heart of her baby and she cried. Dr. Mark handed her a tissue.

"A healthy heart." He removed the ultrasound and the nurse wiped her belly. "Here's your baby's first picture."

Andie took the black-and-white photo, her fingers trembling as she held it up and looked at something that really looked like nothing. Except for that beating heart. Proof that her baby was alive. She couldn't wait to show Etta, and to call Alyson. She didn't want to think about Ryder. Not yet.

"Now remember what I said—make an appointment for one month from today with my colleague near Grove, Dr. Ashford. That'll be a lot easier than driving to Tulsa." Dr. Mark opened the door for her. "And try not to worry. Things have a way of working out for the best."

She nodded and tried not to attach his words of wisdom to the verse that all things work together for good. For those who trust. She had to trust. She had to believe that God would take what she had done on a night when she hadn't been thinking about Him, or trusting Him, and He would work it out for her good.

But one question kept running through her mind. Why should He?

When she walked into the waiting room, Ryder was there. He wasn't relaxed. He wasn't reading a book. He was pacing. She smiled and watched, because he hadn't seen her yet.

He had dressed up for the occasion, wearing jeans that weren't so faded and boots that weren't scuffed. He'd gotten a haircut. For a moment, that moment, he looked like someone's dad. He turned, barely smiling when he saw her. She held up the picture.

Because it wasn't her baby, it was theirs.

Ryder couldn't remember a time in his life that he'd been this nervous. And he had a pretty good feeling it was only going to get worse. For over an hour he'd been watching other women, other couples. A few couples had new babies with them.

That was going to be his life. Andie was going to get a round belly. She would need help getting up from a chair, like a couple of the women who were obviously farther along. Their husbands had helped them up, and held their hands as they walked back to the examining rooms.

He'd never seen himself as one of those men. Man, he'd never even seen himself standing next to a woman, not in his craziest dreams.

He didn't even know how to hold a baby.

Andie walked toward him, her cheeks flushed and that picture in her hand. He'd never seen her so unsure. At least he wasn't alone in his feelings.

"This is our baby." She handed him the picture. In a few months she wouldn't be wearing jeans. He tried to picture her in maternity clothes, pastel colors and with her feet swollen.

She'd hit him if she knew what direction his thoughts were taking. If she knew that he'd been thinking about being there when the baby was born and what they'd name it.

"Is it a boy or a girl?" He held the picture up and tried to decipher the dot that she insisted was their kid. "Are you sure that's a baby? Looks like a tadpole to me."

She laughed. "That's a baby. And we won't know what it is for a few months."

"Wow." He shook his head and looked at the picture again. "We're going to be parents."

"Yeah, we are."

It became real at that moment, with her next to him in a doctor's office. Andie was going to have his baby.

He slipped his arm around her waist and pulled her

close, because how could he not. It felt like what a guy had to do when he found out he was going to be a dad. He hadn't expected it, that jolt of excitement, that paternal surge of protectiveness.

Five minutes ago he'd been full of regrets, full of fear, full of doubt. He still was, but a picture of a heart beating, that had to change something.

"Stop." Andie pulled loose. "You're making me nervous."

"Sorry."

"I forgive you, but you have to feed me."

He got it. And he had to stop acting like she was someone other than Andie. He wondered how they did that, how they acted like they had acted for the past twenty-five years.

"When do we come back?" he asked as they walked out the doors of the clinic, into warm autumn sunshine.

"We don't. I visit Dr. Ashford in a month. She's at the Lakeside Women's Clinic."

"I want to go with you."

"Ryder, please stop. You don't have to do this."

He stopped walking. People moved past them and around them. Andie kept moving so he hurried to catch up with her, to walk across the parking lot at her side.

"I don't know why you're pushing me away." He pulled the keys out of his pocket and pushed the button. "Andie, we have to face this. It isn't going away."

"I know it isn't going away. But I don't want to feel like you're tied to me, knowing you'd rather be anywhere but here. This isn't who you are. This isn't who we are."

"Who are we then?"

"You're you. You're single and you love your life. And I ride barrel horses and live with my granny. That's our lives. This, having a baby, being parents together, this isn't us."

He didn't laugh at her because he'd been reading those magazines in the waiting room and he now knew all about hormones, estrogen, cravings and labor. A few months ago those had been words he wouldn't have even thought to himself. He thought he might have information overload, received after more than an hour of reading prenatal articles.

Stretch marks, whether to medicate during labor or not, natural delivery verses C-section. He wanted the words to go away.

Anyway, he knew better than to laugh at a pregnant woman with surging hormones. She'd either cry hysterically or hurt him. And he wasn't much into either of those options.

He wasn't about to tell her that he'd much rather be at a rodeo than facing her right then. At least he knew what to expect at a rodeo, on the back of a horse, or on the back of a bull. For the time being he had to think that those days were behind him.

That meant he had to come up with something that would placate her until they could deal with this.

Cravings. The word was now his friend.

"What do you want to eat?"

Her blue eyes melted a little and she sniffled. He didn't have a handkerchief.

"Seafood."

"You got it."

That was a lot easier than dealing with the big changes happening in his life, and her body. He shuddered again as he opened the door for her to get into the truck.

As they drove through Tulsa, he glanced at the woman

sitting next to him. The mother of his child. He'd never expected her to be that.

"Andie, we're going to have to talk about this."

"This?"

He sighed. "The baby. Our baby. We have to talk about my part in this."

Her hand went to her belly and she stared out the window. He didn't know if she even realized that she did that, that she touched her belly. He glanced sideways, catching her reflection in the glass. Blue eyes, staring out at the passing buildings and her bottom lip held between her teeth.

"Yeah, I know that we need to talk." She said it without looking at him. "But not yet. Let this settle, okay? Let me get it together and then we'll talk."

"Tomorrow, then, Andie. We'll talk tomorrow." About the future. About them. And about the ring he was still carrying in the pocket of his jeans.

Not that he was planning on proposing again anytime soon. One rejection a year was probably more than enough.

Andie breathed a sigh of relief as she sat down to lunch. It was officially the "tomorrow" that Ryder had talked about yesterday, and he hadn't shown up yet. She'd managed to get a lot of work done at the barn, found her favorite cow just after she'd calved. The new calf had been standing behind her, still a little damp and a little wobbly.

She'd managed to forget, for a few hours, how drastically her life would change next spring.

What Ryder needed to do was go back on the road, rope a few steer, or help Wyatt with the girls. He had to get over thinking she'd let him marry her just because.

When she thought about that, about marrying Ryder, her heart didn't know how to react.

She reached for a magazine off the pile sitting on the edge of the table expecting *Quarter Horse Monthly,* and she got lace and froth instead. One of Alyson's bridal magazines. Andie picked it up and flipped through the pages. She shuddered and closed the magazine.

"What's up with you?" Etta walked into the kitchen. She smiled and laughed a little. "Weddings make you nervous."

"White icing, white dresses, white fluff and white lace."

"It's a special occasion." Etta sat down across from her and picked up the magazine. "It's supposed to be white and frilly. It's supposed to be unlike any other day in a woman's life."

"Right, but couldn't it be white denim and apple pie with vanilla ice cream?"

"I guess it could, if that's what the bride wanted. Are you thinking of getting married?"

"Of course not. Who would I marry? And there definitely isn't any white in my future."

Andie flipped the magazine open and a strange feeling, something like longing—if she'd been giving it a name—ached inside her heart. In high school her friends had planned their weddings. They'd planned the dresses, the flowers, the reception, even the groom and where they'd go on their honeymoon.

Not Andie. She'd saved up farm money to buy the barrel horse of her dreams and the perfect saddle. She'd planned a National Championship win, and she had the buckle to show how well she'd planned.

Etta patted her hand. "You'll have a white wedding, Andie. My goodness, girl, you know that it isn't about what you've done. It's about what God's doing in your heart. This is about the changes that have taken place in your life."

"I know." What else could she say? It wasn't about white. But then again, it was. It was also about dreams she'd never dreamed. "I need to get back to work. What's for dinner tonight? I wouldn't mind taking you out for supper at the Mad Cow."

"I'd love it. I have an order to ship off this afternoon." Tie-dye specialties, Etta's custom clothing line. She and Andie worked together when Andie wasn't on the road.

"Do you need help getting the order together?"

"No, you go ahead with what you need to get done."

Andie took her plate to the sink and walked out the back door. The weather had turned cool and the leaves were rustling in a light breeze. She walked down the path to the barn, whistling for her horses. They were a short distance away and her whistle brought their heads up. Their ears twitched and then they went back to grazing.

Dusty left the herd and started toward the barn. She would brush him first and work him a little. No need to let him get a grass belly. No reason for her to sit and get lazy, either. She'd never been good at sitting still.

For as long as she could remember she'd ridden horses. When she turned six, her dad bought Bell, a spotted pony. That summer she had started to compete in youth rodeos around Oklahoma and Texas. And she'd been competing ever since. For over twenty years.

But this next year would bring changes. She'd seen the women on the circuit with children. But they usually had husbands, too. And they didn't drag little babies from state to state.

Life's about changing—those words were in a song Etta liked.

She snapped a lead rope on Dusty's halter and led him into the barn where she tied him to a hook on the wall. He rubbed his head on the rough wood of the barn and tried to chew on the rail of the nearest stall while she brushed him and then settled the saddle on his back. She reached under his belly and grabbed the girth strap to pull it tight.

A few minutes later she was standing in the center of the arena with her horse on a long, lunge line. This was what she loved. She loved an autumn day and a horse that was so attentive it took barely a flick of her wrist or a slight whistle to command him.

Ryder pulled up the drive as she was settling into the saddle. Not that long ago she would have rode to the fence, glad to see him. But today wasn't three months ago. She blinked away a few tears and she didn't glance in his direction, but she knew he was parking, that he was getting out of his truck.

She rode Dusty around the arena, keeping close to the fence. He was restless and wanted his head, kept pulling, wanting her to let him go. She held him in, easing him from an easy canter to a walk and then she rode him into the center of the arena, taking him in tight circles. He obeyed but she knew what he really wanted were barrels to run.

As she headed back to the fence she made brief eye contact with Ryder. He was walking toward the arena looking casual, relaxed, but even from a distance she saw his jaw clench.

"What are you doing?" He opened the gate and stepped inside the arena.

"I'm working my horse."

"Really?"

"Really." She reined Dusty in, and he didn't want to be reined in. He pranced, fighting the bit, wanting to run.

When he realized it was time to work, he was always ready to go. She held him back though, as her attention settled on Ryder. The new Ryder.

He still looked like the old Ryder. Her gaze traveled down from his white cowboy hat to his face shadowed and needing a shave, and then to the T-shirt and faded jeans. He'd tanned to a deep brown over the summer and in the last few years his body had changed from that of a tall skinny teen to a man who worked cattle for a living.

He had changed. This Ryder didn't seem to get her. Or maybe he wanted to change her? He shook his head and walked toward her and the horse.

"I don't think you should do this."

"Why not?" She held the reins tight and patted Dusty's neck, whispering softly to calm the animal.

"You're pregnant."

"I think I know that." She glared at him, hoping to pin him down, back him off, or make him turn tail and run. He crossed his arms in front of his chest, like he was the law and she was the errant juvenile. He'd never been one to back down from a fight.

Had she really admired that about him?

"Seriously, Andie, you can't do this. It's dangerous."

"No, it isn't. The doctor said I could ride. He said I could do what I've been doing, within reason. I've got to exercise my horse. I can't let him get out of shape. And I'm not going to get hurt."

"Fine, but I'm going to stay here and watch."

"Like I need you to stay and watch. You have better things to do with your time than be my nanny."

"Yeah, I have better things to do, but if you insist on doing this, then I'm staying here."

She pushed her hat back and tried again to stare him

down. "This doesn't make you my keeper. We're not boy-friend and girlfriend. We're not going steady."

"You're right, because we're not sixteen. This is a whole lot more than going steady. This is having a baby."

"Like I need you to tell me." She closed her eyes, be-cause they did sound like kids. She didn't want that.

Ryder stepped closer. "I don't want to fight with you."

She really didn't like change.

"I don't want to fight, either. We've never fought be-fore."

He looked away, but his hand was still on Dusty's neck. He let out a sigh. "I'm sorry."

"You have to stop this." She backed her horse, away from Ryder because she had to take back control, of her-self and her horse. "You have to stop treating me this way, like I'm going to break."

"I'm trying." His features softened a little and he smiled, a shy smile that was almost as out of place as this new, protective behavior of his.

It was sweet, that smile, and her insides warmed a little. She nudged Dusty with her boots and he stepped forward, putting Ryder next to her again.

"Ryder, you have to trust that I'm not going to do something dangerous. I won't put—" she stumbled over the words "—I won't put our baby in danger."

"I know you won't. This is just new territory for me. I've never been anyone's dad. I hadn't planned on it."

"That makes two of us. I hadn't planned on being anyone's mom, not like this." She slid off the back of her horse. "So, what are you doing here so early?"

He looked a little blank, as if he didn't have a real an-swer. Maybe he wasn't sure why he was there. They were both experiencing a lot of that lately.

She was experiencing it at that very moment, because

she wanted him to say things, about them, about the future. And she knew that wasn't them, it wasn't who they'd ever been.

And it shouldn't hurt, knowing those weren't the words he was going to say. He was probably there just to check up on her and nothing more.

She wouldn't let it bother her. She knew what to do—turn and walk away, the way she would have a few months earlier. But nope, she stood there waiting for him to suddenly say the right thing.

Chapter Seven

What was he doing there? Ryder had asked himself that question a few times on the drive over to Andie's. In all the years he'd known her, he'd never had to ask himself that question.

Okay, once, but that's because he'd kissed her the night of her senior prom, a night when she'd decided it would be easier to go with him than to worry about having a date. So he'd headed home from college in Tulsa to be her date.

He laughed a little, thinking back to the two of them in the limo his dad had hired for the night. They'd taken a half dozen of their friends along for the ride and when he'd walked her to the front door at the end of the night, knowing Etta was inside watching, he'd kissed Andie.

The next day they'd made a promise never to complicate their relationship that way again. Their reasons had been good. If a relationship went bad, they knew they wouldn't be able to go back to being just friends. They'd kept that promise until that night when she'd looked vulnerable and he hadn't listened to his good sense and walked away.

He was here now because they were going to have a baby together and they needed to be able to be parents together. So it seemed as if working on a relationship was the best way to start the process. Especially if she was just going to laugh when he handed her a ring and proposed.

Wyatt had laughed, too. No matter what the situation, a woman wanted more from a proposal than some half-hearted attempt at being romantic. Ryder got a little itchy under the collar when he thought about romance in connection with Andie.

"Ryder, what is it you wanted to do?"

"I thought maybe we could go over to the Coopers' arena tonight. A few people are going to get together, buck out some bulls, rope some steers and maybe run barrels."

"You'd let me run barrels?" She grinned and he shuffled his feet and looked away, because her running barrels on Dusty was the last thing he wanted.

"I can't stop you." He stepped back from her horse.

"No, you can't."

She smiled at him, and he knew she was pushing, messing with him. That smile took him back. It was easy to remember being kids, chasing down some dirt road outside of Dawson, doing stuff kids did in the country because going out on real dates took money and a town other than the one they lived in.

They'd built bonfires and sat in groups. Sometimes they found a parking lot in Dawson and parked in a circle, sitting on the tailgates of pickup trucks. In the summer they'd gone to the lake or skiing.

Sometimes the two had dated, but never each other. Andie had dated Reese Cooper. And today that bothered him.

Life had been a lot simpler twelve years ago. But they'd been kids, and kids didn't think about what the future held. When Wyatt had met Wendy in college, he'd never dreamed of losing her too soon. He'd dreamed of having her forever. They'd planned to be youth leaders in a church and save the world.

The irony of that twisted in Ryder's gut and he knew Wyatt had to feel a lot more twisted up over losing his wife. What Ryder wouldn't give to go back to sitting in the parking lot of the Mad Cow with a bunch of kids who had nothing more serious to talk about than the rodeo that weekend and what events they would enter.

"You look like a guy that took a bitter pill," Andie teased as she led her horse through the gate he'd opened.

"Just thinking back." And thinking ahead.

"Yeah, we had some good times, didn't we?"

"We did." He walked on the other side of Dusty, but he peeked over the horse's back to look at Andie. He'd give anything to put a smile back on her face, to make her stop worrying.

"It isn't the end of the world, Ryder."

"I know it isn't." He even managed to laugh. "I'm not sixteen, Andie. When I looked in the mirror this morning, that fact was pretty evident. Most of the people we went to school with have been married for years and have a few kids."

"We're not getting married."

She tied the horse and Ryder slid his hand down the animal's rump, ignoring the tail that switched at flies and a hoof that stomped the dirt floor of the barn. He rounded the horse to the side Andie stood on. She was already untying the girth strap.

"So, do you want to go with me?" He lifted the saddle off the horse's back and ignored the sharp look she gave him.

He opened the door of the tack room with his foot

and walked inside the dark room. The light came on. He glanced over his shoulder at Andie standing in the doorway. She watched as he dropped the saddle on the stand and hung the bridle on the wall. When he turned around, she was still watching.

"Well?" He followed her out of the room, latching the door behind him.

"Yeah, sure, I'll go. I haven't seen the Coopers in a long time." She untied Dusty's lead rope and led him out the back door of the barn. "When do we leave?"

"I have to run home and get a few things done. I'll pick you up at five." He was buying more cattle and a quarter horse with blood lines that would ramp up his herd.

"I'll be ready."

He nodded and for a moment he was tempted, really tempted to kiss her goodbye, to see what it would feel like if they were a couple. Common sense prevailed because he knew how it would feel to get knocked to the ground if he pushed too far too fast.

Instead he touched her arm and walked to the truck that he'd left idling in her driveway thirty minutes earlier. He climbed inside feeling like a crazy fool. When had he ever been the guy who didn't know what to say? He'd been that person a lot lately.

When he first got there, they hadn't been able to carry on a conversation. She had even questioned why they were fighting. He had an answer for that. Couples fought. He didn't want that to be his future with Andie. Their future.

He backed down her driveway, looking into the rearview mirror at what was behind him. Behind him, that was familiar territory. What was ahead, that was a whole other matter.

Kat and Molly were playing in his yard when he pulled

up to the house a few minutes later. Cute kids, still smiling, still able to chase butterflies and blow seed puffs off the dandelions. When he thought about what they'd been through, what Wyatt had been through, he felt like an idiot for crying over his own spilled milk.

Man, life was tough sometimes. Real tough.

Wyatt was leaning against a tree watching the girls, watching Ryder pull up. He waved and stepped away from the tree. As Ryder got out of his truck, Wyatt was there, smiling a little more than he had a few days ago.

How would a guy ever smile again if he'd lost someone like Wendy?

"Some girl named Sheila called." Wyatt watched the girls, but he managed to shoot Ryder a knowing look. "Told her I'd take a message but she said she'd left messages and you hadn't called her back."

"Yeah, I'll call her in a few days. You getting settled in okay?"

"Yeah, you getting in trouble with the women? I think there was a call from someone named Anna, too. She left a message on the answering machine."

"I'll call her, too."

"Keeping them on a stringer?"

"They aren't fish."

"No, but you sure know how to haul them in like they are."

Ryder shoved his hands into his pockets and bit back about a dozen things he'd like to say to his older brother. Wyatt had always made all the right decisions. Wyatt had stayed in church, because he said it wasn't God's fault that people messed up sometimes.

In Ryder's opinion, people messed up a little more often than sometimes.

"Ryder, if you need to talk?"

Right, lay his problems on Wyatt's shoulders when Wyatt couldn't see through his grief to raise two little girls who were still laughing, still smiling. They were chasing a kitten and giggling, the sound picking up in the wind and carrying like the seeds from the dandelion that they'd picked.

"Why do you think I need to talk?"

Wyatt shrugged. "I don't know, just a hunch. You're ignoring women. And you're buying cattle."

"Right."

He was growing up and everyone was surprised. That itched inside him a little. Couldn't he do a mature thing without people getting suspicious? He guessed the answer had to be no.

"Everyone in town still going to the Dawson Community Church?" Wyatt leaned to pick up Kat who had run across the yard to him and was lifting her arms to be held.

"Yeah, I suppose most do."

"You want to go with us on Sunday?"

"No, not really." Ryder rubbed his jaw and shot Wyatt a look. He might as well get it together now. "Yeah, I guess."

Wyatt whistled. "This must be big."

Big. He knew what Wyatt meant. Something big had to happen for Ryder to be thinking about church. So, that's what people thought about him, that he was only going to have faith if God somehow pushed him into it with a big old crisis.

He pulled at his collar because it was tight and the sun was hitting full force now. It shouldn't be this warm at this time of year, just days away from October.

"So?" Wyatt pushed, his gaze darting beyond Ryder to focus on his daughters. Ryder turned to look at the girls. They'd caught the kitten.

"Yeah, it is something big." Ryder picked up a walnut and tossed it. "Andie's going to have a baby and I'm the dad."

It was a long moment and then Wyatt whistled, the way he'd whistled years ago when Ryder was fifteen and had managed to talk a senior girl into taking him to the prom. But it wasn't anything like admiration in his eyes this time. Wyatt shook his head, and he looked kind of disgusted.

"How'd that…?"

"Don't ask. It was a mistake."

"Or something like it." Wyatt watched his girls play and he shook his head again. "Man, Ryder, I just don't know what to say."

Ryder guessed congratulations were out of the question, so he shrugged. "Not much you can say."

"You going to marry her?"

"That makes us sound like we're sixteen."

"You're not sixteen by a lot of years, but she's having your baby and you've loved her since she stepped on the bus her first day of kindergarten and pushed you out of her seat."

"You can't claim a seat on your first day of school, and I had seniority." He smiled at the memory of a little girl with blond pigtails and big eyes. She'd been madder than an old hen at him. She'd been that mad more than once in the past twenty-five years.

"So, marry her, have a family together."

"We're best friends. That isn't love. And she said no."

"She turned you down?"

"Yeah." He laughed a little. "She turned me down."

A smart guy would have let it go. Especially a guy who had always been pretty happy being single. Instead of letting it go, he'd invited her to go to the Coopers'. They had always gone together.

Tonight, though, it was a date. Tonight it was step one in him convincing her to say yes to his next proposal. A couple having a baby should get married.

He repeated that to his brother and Wyatt shook his head.

"Really, Ryder, you think that's the best line to use when proposing?"

"What am I supposed to say? She's Andie."

"Right, she's Andie. But no matter what, she's a woman. Maybe it's time you realized that and started treating her like one, instead of acting like she's one of the guys."

Andie, a woman? It seemed like a good time to end the conversation. He knew Andie well enough to know she didn't want him to start treating her like a girl. She definitely wouldn't want romance and flowery words.

She was Andie. He thought he knew a little something about what she liked and didn't like.

Andie walked into the kitchen and glanced at the clock. That was the last thing she wanted to do, check the time again. She'd been doing that all afternoon, almost as if she had a date.

Ryder wasn't a date.

She walked to the back door and leaned against the wall to shove her foot into one boot, and then the other. She didn't bother to untuck her jeans.

"I think this is a good idea." Etta stood at the kitchen sink. She dried a plate, put it in the cabinet and turned to face Andie.

Andie couldn't agree on the "good idea" part. How

could it be a good idea, for her to show up with Ryder, making the two of them look like a couple?

"What?" Etta poured herself a cup of coffee and held it between her hands, watching Andie.

Okay, she must have made a face of some kind or Etta wouldn't be asking "What?"

Andie met her grandmother's serious gaze, felt the warmth of a smile that had been encouraging her for as long as she could remember.

"Everyone is going to know." Okay, it sounded ridiculous when she said it like that. "That sounds crazy, doesn't it?"

Etta shrugged, her big silver hoop earrings jangling a little. "Oh, maybe it sounds a little ridiculous. I was going to say that you're not fifteen, but I don't think it matters. You're having a baby. You're going to have to face that and face people. I promise you aren't going to be able to hide the fact."

"I know that."

"So, go with Ryder and make the best of things. Make the best of your relationship because that baby deserves for the two of you to act like grown-ups."

"We're working on it."

"I know you are. And, Andie, I know you're working on having faith. I want you to remember that even if folks talk a little, even if they gossip, things will work out and your friends are going to stick by your side." Etta smiled. "And I would imagine even the ones gossiping will stick by you, once they get it out of their system."

"Thanks, Gran." She hugged Etta tight and then Ryder was knocking on the door. "Time to go."

"Have fun," Etta called out as Andie went out the back door.

Ryder stepped away from the porch rail he was leaning

against and tipped his hat back as she walked out the door. She paused, for just a breath of a second, and then let the door close behind her. He even reached out his hand for hers. But she couldn't go there, not yet. She wasn't quite ready for this new relationship, or the new Ryder.

A year ago if he'd grinned and winked at her, she would have told him to peddle his charms somewhere else, to some other female. She walked down the steps and Ryder followed, catching up and walking next to her.

"This is supposed to be a date." Ryder pushed the door of the truck closed when she tried to open it. She glared and he smiled.

"I wanted to open the door for you," he murmured.

"You don't have to. It looks as if you already loaded my horse." Back up, slow down. She took in a deep breath. "Ryder, I've seen you on dates, I know that side of you, the guy who charms and courts. I don't want that. I want my best friend."

"I am your best friend."

"But that guy never opened the door for me. He also didn't try to hold my hand."

"I guess that's the truth." He looked down at the ground and then back up, his dark eyes hanging on to hers. "Do you know how to go back?"

The words bounced between them like a game of pinball gone bad. They just stood there, facing each other and facing reality. And Andie finally closed her eyes and shook her head.

He pulled the truck door open and motioned for her to get in. Andie sat down in the leather bucket seat and Ryder leaned, close enough for her to catch the scent of his soap and to notice that the hair curling under his hat was still damp. She reached, nearly touching those soft curls at the nape of his neck. But she couldn't make that connection because thinking about it stole her breath and made her thoughts turn to being held by him.

That was a lot more complicated than holding his hand.

Ryder backed away, as if his own thoughts troubled him more than he could admit. He winked and closed the truck door.

They rode in silence to the Circle C Ranch, which was owned by the Cooper family. George Strait played on the radio and the breeze whipped in through open windows. Andie loved autumn, had always looked forward to the changing temperatures, the leaves turning colors and the scent of smoke from fireplaces and woodstoves.

This year she looked forward to surviving, to getting past this moment and finding the next path of her future. With a child. She watched out the window, spotting a fox chasing across the field. It distracted her, but just for a moment and then her thoughts went back again.

To faith.

Faith. She closed her eyes and tried to dig up the tattered remnants of what had felt like faith two months ago, before she knew. She'd been seeking a new beginning, thinking she could work it all out, that she'd suddenly not be angry with her mother and that she would immediately forgive. Instead, she was facing a totally different set of problems.

She didn't want her baby to grow up feeling like a problem.

She wouldn't let that happen.

"Cheer up, Andie, we'll get through this." Ryder's easy comment, said with a smile.

"Of course we will." She kept her gaze on the window, at the fields and neighboring farms.

"Or we'll give up, sing about gloom, despair and agony on us, and cry in our oatmeal?"

"Stop being an optimist." She turned up the radio, refusing to smile.

Ryder turned it back down. They were on the long drive that led to the Coopers'. A dozen or more trucks and trailers were parked in a gravel area to the south of the arena and people milled around, leading horses or standing in groups talking.

"I'm going to be an optimist, Andie." Ryder slowed the truck and parked. "I'm going to be the person you count on. I might not pull it off without a hitch, but I'm going to do my best."

"Okay, we'll try this out." She reached for the truck door. "But don't get creepy on me. I want to know that some things haven't changed."

But she knew better. They both knew better.

When they got out of the truck, he met her at the back of the trailer and she could tell that he had more to say. He held onto the latch of the trailer gate, looking inside at their horses.

"Listen, Andie, we've been through a lot together." He pulled up on the latch. "We went through the mess of my pretty dysfunctional family and you stood by me. We were kids, spitting on our hands and shaking, making a deal to forget about church because of what happened."

"It was wrong."

"I know, but it happened and my dad was the reason it happened. I've been thinking a lot about faith, and church. I've been thinking that maybe we should hang tight, stick this out together."

"This, you mean the pregnancy?"

He turned red. "Yeah, the pregnancy."

"You can barely say it."

"I can say it. And I can tell you that on Sunday I'll be picking you up for church."

"I'm holding you to that. But why now?"

"Because I'm not going to be my dad. This kid isn't going to have to worry about what his parents are doing or how messed up his family is."

"It could be a girl."

"I'm okay with a girl."

"That's good, because I think it is a girl." Andie couldn't look at Ryder, not when they were talking about their baby, their future. But they weren't discussing marriage because he didn't love her and she wouldn't marry someone who didn't love her.

What if someday he really fell in love with someone, someone he wanted to marry? What then? Or what if she fell in love? She met his gaze, those dark eyes that she knew so well, eyes she had looked into a thousand times before.

What if she lost him as a friend? She had protected that friendship for years. How did she protect it now, when they were facing the biggest challenge of their lives?

"We should go." He opened the gate and she backed up. "Andie, I mean it. I know my track record is pretty shaky, but I'm in this for the long haul."

Lights came on around the arena and someone whooped out a warning for them to hurry.

"I know you are," she whispered.

Or at least she wanted to hope. But she couldn't dwell on that. This moment, facing friends, people they'd known their whole lives, was going to take all the courage she could muster.

For a brief second his fingers touched hers, grasping them lightly and then letting go. She tried not to think about high school, about how everything had been a new experience and holding hands had been more about belonging to someone and less about really being in love.

And belonging was okay.

He stepped into the trailer and backed her horse out. She took the lead rope and moved out of his way as he backed his horse out.

"Is it too late to change our minds?" She glanced up at him and he smiled.

"I think this is pretty permanent."

"I don't mean about the baby, you goof. I mean about this, about facing people, facing questions."

"I think it's too late. We're okay, Andie."

That was easy for him to say. She'd never felt less okay in her life. But he was getting their horses out of the trailer and if she was going to live her life in Dawson, she would have to deal with looks and whispers.

Ryder tightened the girth strap on his saddle and the big roan gelding that he'd brought with him twitched and stomped his back hooves. The roan was new and Ryder couldn't even get used to the horse's name. Half the time he couldn't remember it. But the name Red worked and the horse didn't seem to care.

"I'm going to tie Dusty and head over to the arena." Andie smiled but he didn't think the look met up with her eyes the way it should.

But he didn't question her. He wasn't going to start doing that. He was the baby's dad, not Andie's keeper. He was having a hard time keeping those two things separate.

"Okay. They're going to put out the barrels later. After steer wrestling and team roping."

"I know, but I'm not sure if I'll ride him tonight. These

are younger riders with younger horses. I'll just give pointers if they want, but…"

"Not be a show-off."

She smiled, this time it looked like the real thing. "Yeah, something like that."

Someone yelled his name. "Gotta run."

She nodded and he almost didn't go. But he had to ride away, to keep this moment normal. He grabbed the saddle horn and swung into the saddle, nearly reaching for her hand and pulling her up with him once he was in the saddle. Instead he held tight to the reins and backed away.

But she hadn't moved. He nudged the red roan forward, close to her and she looked up, questions in her eyes. He didn't have a single answer for her. Instead he leaned and touched her cheek.

"I won't let you down."

She nodded and he rode off, leaving her there alone.

When he got to the arena Reese Cooper motioned him forward.

"You gonna rope with Clay tonight?"

Ryder nodded. "If he needs a partner, I'm the guy."

"He thought so." Reese Cooper was one of the middle Cooper kids. And there were a few of them. Ryder had lost track but he thought there were more than a dozen kids in the Cooper clan. Some were biological, some adopted and a few were foster kids that stayed.

Clay was adopted from Russia years ago. Five years ago he hit about sixteen and every girl in Dawson went crazy over him.

Reese had always been the center of attention.

Ryder wasn't bothered by the fact that the ladies loved the Cooper clan. It meant he could live his life without too many problems from the ladies of Dawson. It did kind of bother him that Andie had dated Reese.

"You gonna ride a bull tonight?" Clay walked up, sandy blond hair and gray eyes. His chaps were bright pink, because Clay didn't care what anyone thought of pink.

"I've thought about it." Ryder settled into the saddle of the roan gelding, holding him steady because the horse hadn't adjusted yet. Obviously the animal had led a quiet life up to this point. Tonight was a real test for him, what with lights, noise and a few rangy bulls bellowing from the pens to the side of the arena.

"Come on, then, we've got bulls ready." Clay spoke with an accent. Ryder tried not to smile because he hadn't figured out if the accent was real, or just something he used as a gimmick. It just seemed that when the kid had been ten or twelve, the accent hadn't been so thick.

Ryder glanced around the arena, finally spotting Andie. She was sitting on the row of risers with Jenna Cameron and the twins. And Jenna's new baby. Funny, thinking about Jenna married to Adam MacKenzie, retired pro football player, and owner of Camp Hope. Adam and Clint, now brothers-in-law, must have brought the bulls over.

That meant they'd be over by the pens on the opposite side of the arena.

"I'll ride a bull." Ryder backed his horse away from the two Coopers. "I'm going to say hello to Clint and Adam. And when you're ready to rope, let me know."

He rode around the back side of the arena, passing a few friends who waved but didn't stop him for a conversation. They looked at him, though, as if they knew. It wouldn't be long before everyone knew.

Clint and Adam were moving the bulls through the pens and into the chutes. Clint waved and then closed a gate between two pens.

"Ryder, good to see you here." Adam MacKenzie walked toward him. "I've been meaning to tell you how much I appreciated the help with fences at Camp Hope."

"It was no big deal."

"Seriously, though, it meant a lot to us." Adam pulled a cola out of a cooler and tossed it his way.

"I didn't mind at all. The camp is a great thing for the kids, and for this community. Gives Dawson something to talk about besides…"

Besides him, for a change.

"How was your season?" Clint had joined them. A few years back the two had ridden to events together. Until Willow showed up in town. And Jenna's boys. The two, Clint and Willow, had fallen in love while taking care of Jenna's boys.

Now that Ryder thought about it, all of their lives had been taking some pretty serious direction changes. These guys didn't seem the worse for wear.

Of course for the last couple of years, Ryder had done a lot of teasing. His friends had all fallen, and they'd all changed their ways. They were family men, now. They went to church and took care of their wives and kids.

He hadn't really envied them.

And now they were staring at him, waiting for him to answer Clint's question.

"Good, really good. Brute turned into a great gelding. I don't know if I told you, but I bought his daddy last week. I needed a good stud horse on the place."

"That sounds like a career choice," Adam interjected with a smile.

"Yeah, maybe." He glanced toward the bleachers. He knew where Andie was sitting, even if he couldn't see her clearly from where he was.

"How's Wyatt?" Clint changed the subject and Ryder

He couldn't think like that.

"Fine." She walked away, slim and athletic, but always graceful. He remembered her in a leotard, forced to take ballet because Etta worried that she was too much of a met his gaze, saw his smile shift. "I saw him drive through town the other day."

Ryder shrugged, and he didn't sit down. "Wyatt's as good as he can be. It's been a long year for him. I don't know how a guy gets over that."

Gets over finding his wife dead and their two little girls in the playpen, crying. How did Ryder convince his brother there were good days ahead? How did he tell Wyatt to have faith, when Ryder had been ignoring God for as long as he could remember?

"Yeah, it won't be easy. But he's got a whole community behind him here." Clint reached for Red's reins. "Want me to hold him while you get your bull rope ready?"

"I guess if I'm going to ride a bull, I'd better get ready. You riding?"

Clint laughed. "No, I don't think so. We've got one little girl and Willow found this little boy in Texas. He's three and hearing impaired."

Ryder nodded because he didn't know what to say. He dismounted and handed Red over to Clint. "You and Willow are pretty amazing."

"Willow's amazing." Clint had hold of the roan and the horse was flighty, more flighty than Ryder liked from a roping horse.

"Ryder, up in two."

Ryder took the bull rope that Adam tossed at him. "Might want to borrow rosin from one of the other guys."

"Got it." Ryder pulled a glove out of his pocket. At least he'd remembered that. As he walked up to the chutes, he didn't look at Andie. Instead he took the Kevlar vest that Clay Cooper offered.

"It's one of Willow's bulls. Think you can handle him?" Clay asked with a grin that didn't do much to im-

A bullfighter, ahead step in front of the bull, giving Ryder a chance to run for his life. That Brahma bull didn't play nice. It was stomping, trying to get his feet, get his legs as he scurried to get away.

As he jumped over the fence, Andie was there. Pale,

press Ryder. Someone needed to take that guy out back and knock some of that vinegar out of him.

"I think I can handle him." Ryder pulled on the vest.

The bull that came through the chute was a big brindled bull with too much Brahma in its DNA. He didn't like to ride Brahma bulls. Not because they were meaner, bucked harder or went after a guy. He didn't like the hump. It knocked him off balance, made it hard for him to stay up on the bull rope.

As he settled onto the bull's back, Clay snickered, like he'd meant to put Ryder on the worst bull in the pen. He worked rosin into the bull rope and then Clay pulled it, tight, so Ryder could wrap it around his gloved hand.

The bull hunched in the shoot and then went up, front legs off the ground, pawing at the front of the chute. Ryder grabbed the side of the chute and pulled himself up, out of danger. The bull went back down on all fours. They started the bull rope process again.

As soon as Ryder had the rope around his hand and the bull was halfway sane in the chute, he nodded and the gate opened. The bull spun out of the chute, nearly falling and then righting himself. Ryder fell forward but got himself back into position when the bull bucked into his hand. Foam and slobber flew from the bull's head. The force of four hooves hitting the ground jarred his teeth.

He kept forward, his head tucked. The bull jerked him to the side and his body flung off the side of the bull, his hand still in the rope. A few jumps, a few hops and then the buzzer. He jerked his hand loose and rolled.

The bullfighter, another Cooper brother, jumped in front

shaking and pretty darned mad. He'd never seen her like that before. He considered going back in the arena with the bull.

He dropped down on her side of the fence and walked away, dragging the bull rope behind him. She followed. He couldn't do this here with everyone watching, wondering what was going on between them.

When he got to the back of the arena, to a spot where they could talk, he waited.

Andie walked up to him, her blond hair short and blowing in the soft, Oklahoma breeze. The air was dry, but still warm, and the sun was starting to set. He didn't know why, but suddenly when he looked at her, he saw someone he hadn't seen before. He saw a woman with soft edges and a look in her eyes that could have sent him running if he hadn't known her better.

They'd gone places together, all of their lives they'd been together. Tonight felt different. Tonight they were one of the couples. He shifted a little and her mouth opened, like she was going to say something, and he was afraid to hear it.

His back hurt and his shoulder throbbed. He didn't need lectures.

"Don't." He shook his head a little and her mouth closed. And he'd hurt her. He hadn't meant to do that. "Not yet, Andie."

Not yet with a rush of female emotions and words, not from Andie. She'd drown him in that stuff and he wouldn't know how to make it work, not with a ton of emotions and hormones hitting him over the head.

tomboy. She'd hated it, but he remembered going to her one and only recital. She punched him in the gut that day, because he told her she looked pretty.

He watched her walk away. Gut punched. Sometimes she didn't even have to touch him. And every now and then, like right at that moment, he wanted to kiss her again. Even if it landed him on the ground.

Maybe later. He let the idea settle in his mind, even imagined holding her close on Etta's front porch.

"Hey, Andie, come back."

She stopped walking, but she didn't turn to face him. "You said not right now."

"I didn't mean for you to walk away. I meant for you to give me a chance to take a deep breath."

She turned, the wind catching her hair. She held it back with her hand and waited for him to walk up to her.

"I didn't know you were going to ride a bull tonight." She bit down on her bottom lip and looked away from him.

Her dad. He wanted to swear but he didn't. She'd seen her dad broken up a few too many times. She'd always disliked it when he rode bulls, said it brought back too many memories that she'd rather forget.

"I didn't plan on it, but Clay…"

"Pushed you into it?" She shook her head, not buying it.

"Yeah, kind of. I can't believe I let a twenty-one-year-old kid get to me that way."

She wiped his face. "Dirt on your cheek."

"Right." He wiped it again, in case she didn't get it all. And because it was a lot less disturbing when he did it.

"Ryder, would you mind if we went home. I really don't feel like I can do this tonight."

"Yeah, we can go home. Stay here while I get my horse."

* * *

Andie waited for Ryder. When he came toward her on the big roan gelding, she smiled. He rode up close and reached for her hand. She looked up, and he winked. Like old times, she thought. And she needed some old times. She took his hand and he moved his foot, giving her access to the stirrup.

He pulled and she settled behind him, her arms around his waist. The horse sidestepped a few times and then trotted a bumpy trot toward the trailer. Andie didn't mind the trot, not when this was the most normal thing that had happened to her in days.

As they rode past the arena and down the drive toward the trailer, Ryder slowed the horse to a walk. Andie leaned, resting her cheek against his back, against the soft cotton of his shirt. She breathed in deep of his scent and then she felt silly, because it was Ryder.

The horse came to a stop at the trailer, but neither of them moved. Andie didn't want to move, to break the connection between them. Ryder glanced back but he didn't say anything. But his hands touched her hands that were clasped around his middle.

"You okay?"

"I'm good. This is just the most familiar place I've been in a while. You know, riding like this with you. Remember when we used to take your old gelding out at night for long rides?"

"Yeah, I remember." His back vibrated with the depth of his voice.

"Those were good times."

"They were. And they aren't behind us, Andie. We're going to have a kid. We can teach him to ride a horse, and to rope a steer."

"Her."

"Right, her." He laughed and she sighed, but then she moved.

Time to leave the familiar for what was real now. "We should go home."

"Give me your hand." He held her hand and she dropped to the ground. "Andie, we'll have more good times."

"I know." She blinked fast to chase away the tears that sneaked up on her.

Ryder landed on the ground next to her. He led the horse back to the trailer and tied it while he pulled off the saddle. Dusty whinnied a greeting because he'd been left behind, tied but not saddled. She untied him and led him to the back of the trailer.

"So, are you okay?" She handed the horse over to Ryder.

"I'll be sore tomorrow. I'm sure everyone will say that I had to leave early because I'm getting soft."

"That's never bothered you before."

"No, and it still doesn't." He led her horse into the trailer. "Go ahead and get in the truck. I'll have them settled and ready to go in a minute."

Andie nodded and she didn't argue. Tonight it was okay to let Ryder do this for her. She climbed into his truck and waited.

A few minutes later he was behind the wheel of the truck and they were easing down the driveway and then turning on to the road that led back to Dawson. It was only minutes before they reached the city limits and tiny Dawson. As they drove past the Mad Cow, Ryder slowed and pulled into the parking lot. There were a half dozen trucks and teenagers sitting on tailgates.

A dozen years ago, they had been the teenagers hanging out in Dawson, not going to Tulsa or Grove on a

Friday night because the drive was too far, the gas too expensive. Dating in Dawson had been cheap and easy; hanging out in town, going to a rodeo, or riding practice bulls from a local stock contractor's pen of livestock.

More often than not they ended up somewhere like the Coopers', where it wasn't for prizes or money, just for fun and practice.

Memories piled up and Andie smiled as Ryder parked his truck next to an old Ford. She understood. For a few minutes he wanted to be that kid again, wanted those easier days back. She got out with him and walked to the front of the truck.

One of the kids had set up practice horns at the outside of the circle of trucks. They were farm kids in roper boots, faded jeans and T-shirts, their girlfriends were hanging together on the back of one truck, girls in tank tops and cutoff shorts. Dawson hadn't changed in years.

The boys grouped around Ryder and Andie leaned against his truck to watch, the way she'd watched years ago. But years ago Ryder had flirted and she'd pretended it didn't matter because they were just friends.

"What are you guys up to?" Ryder took the rope that one of the boys held out to him. He ran it through his hands.

"Just hangin' out and practicing up for next weekend. Ag Days is next Saturday and the Junior Championship Rodeo." A tall boy with straw-colored hair and acne spoke up. Andie recognized him as a kid who had moved with his parents to a neighboring farm. "That sure is a nice stud horse you've got now."

Ryder shrugged off the compliment and Andie wanted to ask the questions, about the horse and when he'd gotten it. He'd never bought a horse without telling her.

She'd seen a load of cattle come in, too. The big trailer

had hauled the livestock down his driveway and turned them loose in his empty pasture, the one he didn't use for alfalfa. The cattle were there, now, grazing around oil wells that pumped a slow steady stream of crude oil into holding tanks by the road.

Now he was roping fake horns, as if he was going through some kind of midlife crisis. Because of her.

Ryder looped the rope again, swinging, letting it go. It slipped through the air, landing effortlessly on the horns. She remembered watching a few minutes of an outdoor program about fly-fishing in the northern states. There had been a beauty and grace to the casting of the line. Roping, effortlessly the way Ryder did it, had the same grace.

After freeing the rope from the horns, Ryder handed it back to the kid and then gave them a few pointers. He watched as they took turns, and then he gave them more advice.

When had they grown up, she and Ryder? When had they become the older people in town? Andie sighed at the thought of how far, and yet not so far, her life had come from the days of high school.

A dozen years ago Ryder had been one of these kids, under these same bright streetlights on the same dark pavement. Like these kids, he'd been dreaming of the future, dreaming of the best horse, the buckle, the money. No, never the money for Ryder, but winning. He'd always wanted to win. He'd won in basketball and baseball. He won in the rodeo arena.

As much as he'd won, she knew he'd lost a lot, too. His life hadn't been charmed. His parents had seen to that. And losing them, he still hurt over that loss. She could see the shadows of the pain in his eyes. There were days that he looked like the loneliest guy in the world.

He had a quick smile, though. It flashed easily, creating that dimple in his chin. It was disarming, that smile. If a person didn't know better, they'd think he'd never felt pain, never been hurt. She knew better.

Two months ago she had seen the lonely look in his eyes.

A quick cramp in her stomach ended the memories. She drew in a deep breath and fought against the knife-sharp pain. Ryder turned, his eyes narrowed and he didn't say anything. He patted the boy with the straw-colored hair on the shoulder and said he'd be back soon.

As he walked toward her, she saw his fear, felt her own. Fear or relief?

She closed her eyes because she didn't want to know, didn't want to recognize the look in his eyes, or look too deep into her own heart.

"You okay?"

She nodded, because the pain had passed. "Yeah, I'm fine. But I think I'm ready to go home."

Chapter Eight

Sunday morning Ryder pulled his truck up the driveway of Etta's house, fighting a serious case of nerves that matched any that he'd met up with on the back of a bull. He couldn't imagine feeling worse on his wedding day, if he'd ever planned on getting married.

Going to church for the first time in over a dozen years was definitely up there on the list of things that were hard to do.

And that thought pulled his attention off the road and drew it to the glove compartment where he'd tossed the ring that Andie had rejected last week. Last week when he'd thought having a baby meant two people ought to do the right thing and get married. Obviously Andie was of a different mind. And that should have cut him loose, should have sent him back down the road and on his way to a team roping event in Dallas.

Instead he was as determined as ever to prove to Andie that he could be a dad, even if she didn't think he could be a husband. A dad did the right thing, even went to church. He was pretty sure that's what an upstanding dad did. No, he took that back. His own dad had gone to church.

He was going to do better than that.

As he parked, the front door opened. Etta stepped onto the porch, a vision in purple and yellow, a floppy straw hat on her head. She waved with a hand that sparkled with jewelry and went on with the green plastic watering pot, tipping it to water plants that turned her front porch into some kind of crazy jungle.

He was lucky if weeds grew in his flower gardens. At least weeds covered up the bare spaces and had blooms that added some color to the place.

He got out of his truck and walked across the lawn, the grass turning brown, but autumn mums bloomed in the flowerbeds. Etta set her watering can down and waited at the top of the steps. He clunked up the steps, his boots loud on the wood.

"What has you up here so bright and early on a Sunday morning?" Etta grabbed her watering can again and moved to a planter overflowing with purple blooms that he didn't recognize.

"I guess I'm here to go to church." He glanced off in the direction of the barn, trying to make sense of the crazy turn his life had taken. A calf was mooing and somewhere a dog barked. He wondered if the animals needed to be fed and how much damage Andie would do to him if he did those things for her.

Etta chuckled a little. "You're going to church?"

"Isn't that what you've been telling me to do for the past eighteen years?"

"I guess I have. But why now?"

"Because it's the right thing to do."

"Oh, I see." She headed back into the house, carrying the green watering can. The open door let out the aroma of coffee and something baked with cinnamon. He followed Etta through the door.

"You don't think I should go?" He followed her down the sunlit hallway.

"Of course you should go." She set the can next to the back door and kicked off her slippers. "Grab a cup of coffee and a muffin. Don't take the chocolate chip muffins, those are for our new pastor."

"Gotcha." He walked into the kitchen, always at home here. He didn't have to search for a cup, didn't have to ask where Etta kept the sugar. He'd been a part of this family for as long as he could remember.

But the idea of going to church had settled in the pit of his stomach like old chili. He'd been talked about his entire life. His family had been talked about. His dad had kept the town loaded with reasons to gossip. He should be used to being a conversation piece for the people of Dawson.

He hadn't worked too hard on his own life, to make himself different. He'd dated women whose names he couldn't remember. He'd spent his teen years chased from fields by farmers who didn't want their hay crops ruined by a kid with a four-wheel-drive truck.

Now it was different. He sipped the coffee that he'd poured for himself and stood at the sink, looking out the kitchen window. Etta's barn needed to be painted. He sighed and set down his cup.

"What are you here for?"

He turned, bumping his cup but grabbing it before it slid into the sink and spilled. He held it as she walked across the room. He'd never looked at her this way, in the early morning, seeing her as a woman and not his best friend. She'd always been his best friend.

Today she was definitely a woman. Her dark blue dress touched her knees and curved in the right places. Her blond hair framed her face, the color of the dress making her eyes more vivid. Her belly was still flat.

"Don't look at my stomach." She grabbed a cup and poured herself a cup of coffee.

He swallowed more emotions than he could name. She was standing next to him, not looking at him. And she was soft and feminine. She didn't smell like leather. Instead a floral scent floated in the air around her. It swished his way when she moved.

When she turned to look at him, lifting a brow and giving him a look that asked what in the world he thought he was looking at, he shrugged. And he took a step closer. That wasn't a Sunday morning thing to do, stepping closer, sliding his arms around her waist.

She wiggled free and pushed him back.

"Back off, cowboy." She moved to the other side of the kitchen and picked up a muffin.

"You aren't supposed to eat the chocolate chip muffins," he warned.

"Why not?"

"They're for the new pastor."

"Well, I'm pregnant and I'm eating it."

He shrugged again. She'd have to deal with Etta. He watched as she took a few bites, closing her eyes as she chewed. And then there were footsteps on the stairs. Andie's eyes flew open. She grinned, a wicked grin that should have been a warning, and tossed the muffin at him.

He barely caught it, and then Etta walked into the kitchen.

"What are you doing eating those muffins after I told you not to?"

Ryder glanced at Andie and her smile was a little

wicked, a little sweet. He had to take the fall for her. "Sorry, I couldn't help myself."

"No, I guess you couldn't. Self-control doesn't seem to be your strongest character trait lately. Well, come on, let's go to church." Etta grabbed the basket of muffins and slid them into a bag. "You can drive."

As they walked out the door, he slid close to Andie. "You owe me."

"I don't think so."

Her voice was soft and her arm brushed his. Everything was changing. Or maybe he hadn't let himself notice before that Andie made everything in his life feel a little better, a little easier.

On the way out the door she paused for a second, closing her eyes and leaning a little toward him.

"Andie, are you okay?"

She nodded. "I'm fine. We need to go or we'll be late."

He hadn't expected to feel this way, as if he needed to protect her, even if he didn't know what to protect her from. But this was the second time in a week he'd seen that look on her face, and the second time he'd felt a stab of fear he hadn't expected to feel.

Andie sat next to Ryder on the third pew from the front of the church. Etta liked to joke that the power of God was down front, so the people in the back were missing out. Andie felt as if the power of two hundred pairs of eyes was in the back and it was all focused on her. And Ryder. It had been eighteen years since they'd been in church together.

His father's actions had pushed them away from God. Her actions had brought them back. Because as much as she'd tried to be angry with God for what had happened to Ryder's dad, she couldn't hide from His presence or her need for this place and faith.

When it had all crumbled in around her, she hadn't wanted to run from God. Instead she'd run to Him. Which was exactly what Etta had always said would happen. And, as Etta liked to remind, she happened to be right most of the time.

"I'd forgotten what it felt like here." Ryder leaned close, his shoulder against hers. She closed her eyes and nodded, because everything hurt too much. Him never loving her hurt. Her stomach hurt. She looked forward, telling herself the pain that had started earlier meant nothing.

"It feels like peace," she whispered, wanting that peace.

"Yeah, that's what it is." Ryder raised his arm and circled her, pulling her closer to his side. The choir sang the closing hymn and Pastor Jeffries smiled out at the congregation. His style of ministry was different than that of Pastor Todd. It was less like a best friend, more like a father.

Final prayer. She needed that prayer. She need for the service to end. As the congregation filed out of their pews, down the aisle, Andie leaned forward, resting her head on the back of the pew in front of her. She took a deep breath and waited for the pain to pass.

"Honey, what's wrong?" Etta's strong voice whispered near her ear. People around her were talking.

"I think I need to leave." She stood up, ignoring Ryder's concern, his hand reaching for hers and Etta standing up behind her. "I have to go."

Panic was shooting through her, making breathing difficult and mixing with the pain that cramped in her lower abdomen. She wiped at tears that slid down her cheeks and tried to smile at the people asking if she was okay, trying to stop her with a cautious hand. Ryder was right behind her, not touching her, but he was there.

As she hurried down the steps of the church toward Ryder's truck, he reached for her arm and pulled her to a stop. Her eyes were blurring with unshed tears and his face hovered close. She wanted to sink into his arms.

"What's wrong?" His voice was hard, but barely above a whisper and his hands held her arms tight, as if she would have escaped. But escape wasn't her plan, not from him, just from the crowds of people in the church, asking questions or staring after her with questions in their eyes.

"I think I need to go to the hospital."

And then Etta was there. Andie drew in a deep breath, breathing past the stress and through the pain. It had been a twinge that morning, but had gotten worse during church.

Etta took her by the arm and led her to the side as people walked past.

"What's wrong?"

Andie drew in another deep breath. "Cramping."

"Then we're definitely going to the hospital." Etta herded them toward Ryder's truck as she talked.

"I don't want to…" *lose my baby.* She couldn't say it.

"Things happen in a pregnancy, Andie. There are different phases and pains. This could be completely normal." Etta pulled the truck door open and motioned for Andie to climb in. "You're going to be fine. The baby is fine."

Andie nodded as she got into the truck, into the seat next to Ryder who was already starting the truck, practically backing out before Etta got the door closed.

"Maybe you could let an old lady get in the truck before you start driving." Etta hooked her seat belt. "Ryder, take a deep breath and just consider this as practice. Lots of unexpected things happen when we have children."

Andie closed her eyes. Prayers slipped through her mind, getting tangled with guilt. Guilt because she shouldn't be having a baby and because, after thinking that she didn't want this, now she was going to ask God to take care of her child?

They drove the thirty minutes to the hospital in twenty. Andie opened her eyes to the flashing lights of an ambulance ahead of them, pulling through the drive in front of the emergency room. This was reality. She touched her stomach and wondered, even though she didn't want to, if she would still be pregnant when she left the hospital.

And if she wasn't… She closed her eyes against the pain that moved to her heart, if she wasn't how would she and Ryder look at one another tomorrow?

Ryder pulled up in front of the door and stopped. He glanced at her as he turned the truck off, his smile strong, the look in his eyes telling her that everything would be okay. And she was a kid again, worried that her dad wasn't coming home. But Ryder was there. Always there for her.

"We're fine, Andie."

"I know."

He was out of the truck and when she tried to step out next to him, he shook his head and scooped her up. He carried her into the building like she was a little girl with a scraped knee and she tried to tell him she could walk. He shook his head each time she opened her mouth.

"I can walk," she finally managed to say.

"I don't want you to talk."

Etta was next to them, breathing fast as she hurried to keep up with Ryder. "Don't argue. For once in your life, don't argue."

"I'm too heavy." She leaned into his neck and he held her closer, tighter. Her doctor met them at the doors to the E.R. That was the great thing about small towns, and switching to a doctor closer to home.

"What's up, Andie?" Dr. Ashford motioned them into an exam room.

"I've been cramping. It was light at first and I wasn't worried, but today it's worse."

"Okay, let's examine you and see what we can find out."

Ryder practically dumped her on the hospital bed. And then he was gone, the curtain of the exam room flapping behind his exit. Andie shook her head. So much for her hero. Her knight in shining armor. The Lone Ranger. No, wait, that was more like it. The Lone Ranger always rode in to rescue the woman and then hightailed it out of town before he could get too attached.

She couldn't let it bother her. She knew Ryder, knew why he bounced from relationship to relationship. She knew him well enough that she should have known better than to attach even the vaguest of dreams to him.

But then, he had just carried her in here. And she wasn't light.

"Andie, I'm going to do an ultrasound and examine you." Dr. Ashford stood next to the bed. "Do you want someone in here with you?"

Andie shook her head. "I'm a big girl."

But her body trembled from shock as reality set in. She was losing her baby. Ryder being with her wouldn't stop that from happening. And if she was going to fall apart, she wanted to be alone.

Chapter Nine

Ryder paced across the waiting room, again. And then he sat down, again. He felt as if he'd been doing that same thing for hours. It had only been one hour, though. He bristled at the idea of waiting without any recognition of his presence here. He wanted a few answers, at least for someone to tell him Andie was okay.

He'd already asked the receptionist, twice, if she'd find something out for him. Or get someone to give him answers. She'd smiled a pained smile that he thought could have been a little nicer and told him to take a seat and she'd see if she could find something out. He'd watched and she hadn't left her desk or picked up the phone.

Etta grabbed his arm when he started to stand up again.

"If you bother that receptionist or pace across this floor one more time, I'm going to knock you down," she whispered. And he was pretty sure she meant it.

She had a magazine in her hand, rolled up. He hadn't seen her open it and read. She kept picking up magazines, flipping through pages and then putting them down. She wasn't much better off than he was, but he wasn't about to point that out to her.

"Well, what am I supposed to do? I can't go back there. No one will tell me what's going on. What else can I do but pace?"

"Sit there and pray."

"Pray?" He drew in a deep breath and brushed his hand over his face. How much was God wanting to hear from him?

"Yes, pray. What else are you going to do in this situation?"

"I guess you're right." It wasn't like he'd ever stopped believing, he'd just had a hard time with church after what happened with his dad. Something like that left a bad taste in a guy's mouth.

The door to the emergency room opened and the doctor walked across the room, smiling. "You can see her now."

"How is she?" Ryder stood up.

"I'm afraid I can't discuss that with you."

"What?" He growled the question, hadn't meant to, but it roared out of him, causing a few people to glance their way.

"I'm Andie's doctor and she has a right to privacy. But you can go back and see her."

He shook his head as he moved past the doctor, past the receptionist's desk and through the door that opened as he got closer. Anger had boiled up inside him, more anger than he'd felt in a long time. He tried to tamp it back down, to get control before he faced Andie. It wasn't her fault.

It wasn't even the fault of that smug-faced receptionist.

"Ryder, calm down." Etta followed him and for the first time, he couldn't listen, couldn't take her advice.

His gut had been tied up in knots and fear had shoved common sense out the door. Fear and a really healthy dose of anger were now tied together in a pretty untidy package.

He pushed back the curtain of the exam room, ready to let Andie know how he felt about not being included in the list of people who had a right to know how she was. He shouldn't have to remind her that this was his baby, too.

When he saw her, he couldn't speak. He couldn't do anything when faced with the reality of Andie curled on her side, the blue of a hospital gown over her shoulders and the white blanket up to her chin. He waited at the foot of her bed and Etta walked into the room. Etta looked at the monitors, looked at Ryder and then took a seat on the edge of the bed. She hitched her yellow purse over her shoulder and sat there for a minute.

"How are you, sugar bug?" Etta patted Andie's shoulder.

Ryder had wanted to do that. He had wanted to offer words of comfort. He hadn't known how. That was Etta's job. Besides that, he didn't know how to comfort when he was the reason she was here. He was the reason she was hurting.

And she didn't want him to know what was going on.

He wanted to throw something. Instead he shoved his hat a little tighter down on his head and waited for Andie to say something, anything.

He'd never seen her so quiet. Never.

"I'm fine." Andie reached up to pat her granny's hand. "The baby..." She wiped her hand across her face. "I still have a baby."

Ryder closed his eyes and said a big "Thank you." That's how two weeks could change the way a guy thought about life. A man could go from living for himself, to being willing to give up everything to keep a baby safe.

On the way to the hospital, he'd had to turn off the radio. A Tim McGraw song about a man on his knees, begging God to "not take the girl" had come on. He and Andie hadn't been able to look at each other, or talk about it. Ryder had turned the song off and Andie had whispered "Thank you."

"What did the doctor say?" Etta smoothed the blankets and waited, patiently. But Ryder knew Etta. He knew patience was something she could show, but he knew on the inside she was ready to push down walls to get answers and get something done.

"Time will tell." Andie whispered the words and her shoulders shook. Ryder started to move forward, but Etta was way more qualified than he was to handle this situation.

"Well, time does have a way of doing that."

"I don't want to lose my baby." Andie turned, pulling the blanket up, avoiding looking at him. Her eyes were puffy and red and her blond hair tangled around her face, sticking to tearstained cheeks.

When she'd lost her dad he'd been the one to hold her. They had always held each other. And now she was avoiding looking at him. Awkward had never been a part of their relationship.

Until now. And it scared the life out of him. He'd made a pretty good show of never needing anyone. And all that time he'd been lying to himself, because he needed Andie. He needed her because she was the most consistent thing in his life.

There were probably other reasons. He knew there were, but right now he couldn't put it all together. He just knew that she had to be safe. She had to be okay. And it wasn't just about the baby.

"I know you don't want to lose this baby." Etta smoothed the hair from Andie's face, as if she was fifteen, not twenty-eight.

Andie sobbed again, shuddering. "I didn't want this baby. This isn't how I would want my child's life to start. This isn't the way a child wants to grow up thinking about itself. But now... Now I can't stand the idea of losing it, of losing my baby."

Their baby. Ryder almost said something, but he bit back the words. He was definitely not experienced at female emotions. He was used to the Andie that threw rocks in the creek and could break about the rankest horses in the county. She knew how to hang on tight through some wild rides. He'd never seen her get thrown.

"Sweetheart, you don't know God's plan. I have to believe, have to pray, that God's going to take care of you and this little one of yours."

Andie covered her face with her hands and Ryder couldn't stand still, couldn't let her hurt that way. There hadn't been a moment in their lives that they hadn't gone through the hard times together.

He wasn't going to let her go through this alone.

He didn't want to go through it alone.

In a few steps he was next to her. When he wrapped his arms around her, she buried her face in his shoulder and he held her close. Etta moved and he took her place on the bed, with Andie's arms around his waist. He leaned, resting his lips on the top of her head.

"I'm not going to let you down." He brushed blond hair back from her cheeks. "I won't let this baby down."

"I know you won't."

"Andie, the doctor wouldn't tell me anything. I really

need to know what's going on." He brushed her cheek with a kiss and kept holding her.

She pulled back, nodding. "I know. I'll make sure she knows that you have to be included."

"Thank you." So, he felt a little better.

The curtain moved and Dr. Ashford walked in, clipboard in hand, glasses on her head. She smiled and pulled the glasses down, settling them on the bridge of her nose.

"Andie, I'm going to release you because there isn't a lot we can do but wait. I know that won't be easy, but that's what we have. The one thing you can do is take it easy and call me if you experience any bleeding." Dr Ashford stepped forward with a tube. "Here's the cream I told you about."

"Thank you, Dr. Ashford."

"Wait a second. I need more information. Isn't there anything we can do?" Ryder reached for Andie's hand and held it tight. Man, this wasn't the way it was supposed to go. He didn't want words like *time* and *waiting*.

"At this point there really isn't anything we can do. I'm sorry to be so blunt, but miscarriages happen in the first trimester. We don't always know why and we can't always keep it from happening. At this point the baby's heartbeat is steady and so we give Andie time. And she rests."

He met the doctor's gaze, and he was mad. She was a doctor. She was supposed to do something. That's why she was there, taking care of them. "She can stay in the hospital."

"Ryder." Andie squeezed his hand.

"Andie, we have to do more than wait."

The doctor put on a patient but slightly pained smile that didn't help him feel better, it just made him feel more out of control.

"If Andie was farther along and having contractions, we could put her in the hospital or give her medication to stop labor."

"So do that." Was that his voice, out of control, unreasonable? Dr. Ashford gave him another of her "poor man" smiles. He wasn't her first time at the circus; he was sure she'd met other clowns like him.

"This isn't a situation where medication will help. This is a situation for…"

"Prayer," Etta whispered.

The doctor nodded. "I would like for Andie to take it easy for a week or two, until the cramping stops. Let's see if we can get her through the third month, make it through the first trimester, and then we'll go from there."

Andie sniffled and her chin came up, because she wasn't giving up. He wanted to feel that strong right now, but instead, he felt like a kid who didn't have a clue.

The doctor kept talking, but when the words headed in the direction of female stuff, Ryder walked to the door. Or maybe hurried. These were words he could handle in connection to a cow or horse, but not to Andie.

He stopped at the curtain.

"I'll be waiting out here. When can she leave?"

"As soon as we get paperwork filled out. Straight home, straight to bed. She can get up to use the restroom and take showers. She can walk to the couch. But that's going to be it for now."

Ryder nodded and walked out. As he walked away he could still hear them talking, still discussing the best chance for the baby. He didn't want to hear about odds. He wanted to know that God was going to do something.

He hadn't expected that, to feel like this so soon, as if he'd push down a mountain to make sure his baby was safe. Baby. He remembered the ultrasound picture that showed something that looked like a tadpole. That was his kid in that picture.

He walked through the E.R., past other curtained cubicles, through doors that slid open as he approached, and then outside into cooler air and a light mist. He took off his hat and stood on the sidewalk with mist turning to rain. The sky was a heavy gray and the wind had died down.

For the first time he knew how it felt to need God so badly he'd bargain. He'd give himself for the life of his unborn child. He knew how it felt to be that man in Tim McGraw's song, begging God to take him, but not the girl, not the baby.

The door behind him opened. He glanced back and it was Etta. She smiled and walked over, looking up at the sky. "It's raining out here, Ryder."

"Yes, ma'am."

"You finding God out here?"

"Trying."

"He's as close as the words you're speaking. So pray hard, boy. And then get that truck and drive it up to the building so we can take her home."

"I'll do that."

She touched his arm. "Ryder, this is going to work out."

He nodded and walked away. He hoped he wasn't going to let them all down. He didn't ever want a kid to feel the way he had. Let down.

When Andie got in his truck fifteen minutes later he was thinking about how he didn't want to let her down, either. He never wanted to find her alone, crying because he'd broken her heart.

Too many times in his life he'd seen his mom that way.

"You okay?" He shifted into gear and pulled away from the hospital.

"I'm not sure."

No, of course she wasn't. He wasn't sure, either.

Andie woke up late the following morning. She knew it was late because she could hear Etta downstairs washing dishes and the sun slashed a bright ray of light across her room. She'd made it through the night. It had been a long night. Ryder had refused to leave until about midnight. That's when Etta finally convinced him that his presence wasn't going to keep bad things from happening and they all needed some sleep.

She touched her belly, because her baby was in there, still safe, still a part of her world. "Stay in there, baby.

"Keep her safe." She looked up, knowing God heard. She tried to hold onto that faith, and not to fear. Every wrong thing she'd ever done flashed through her mind, taunting her as if her mistakes were a reason for God to take this baby, to make her pay. She pushed the thoughts from her mind.

Footsteps on the stairs signaled company. She waited and then there was a rap on her door.

"Come in."

"Are you decent?"

Ryder's voice. She looked down, at the sweats she'd slept in and the ragged T-shirt. "I guess so."

He pushed the door open and she brushed a hand through her hair, hoping to look less like something the cat coughed up and then trying to tell herself it didn't matter. It was just Ryder.

"I brought your breakfast."

He held a tray with a white foam container from the Mad Cow. He put the tray down, sitting it across her lap.

She knew what was in the container. Pecan pancakes. And for the first time she knew she couldn't eat them. Her stomach turned and rolled, the way it had when she'd been ten and they'd gone to Branson for vacation. The more she thought of those curvy roads and the pecan pancakes...

"Move it, quick." Her stomach roiled and she dived as he reached for the trash can and stuck it under her face. If she breathed in, she'd lose it. If she closed her eyes and didn't breathe, that wouldn't be good, either.

"You okay?" He leaned down, a little green.

"Get rid of the pancakes."

"Got it." He grabbed the tray and as he headed out the door, she sat up. He peeked back inside the room. "Sorry about that."

"Not a problem," she groaned and leaned back on the pillows.

"I wanted to do something." He stepped back into the room, without the tray, and leaned against her dresser. He picked up a framed picture of the two of them on a pony she'd had years ago. His gaze came up, connecting with hers. "I feel like I need to take care of you."

"I don't want you to feel that way." She pulled her legs up and sat cross-legged on her bed. "This isn't us. We aren't uncomfortable, trying to figure out where we fit in each other's lives. I don't want you bringing me pancakes and holding the trash can for me. I don't want you to feel like you have to do this."

"But I do. You didn't get this way alone."

She stuck her fingers in her ears and shook her head, juvenile, but effective. "Don't."

He picked up the picture again. "It would have been easier to stay ten, wouldn't it?"

"Yeah, that'd be perfect. But it doesn't work that way."

"No, it doesn't."

"You don't have to stay here and take care of me. I know you have things to do, places to go."

"People to see?" He straightened and moved away from the dresser, a lanky cowboy with faded jeans and a hat that had been stepped on a few times. "I'm here, Andie. I'm in this for the long haul. This is the place where I'm supposed to be."

Etta popped into the room. "You're up. And you don't have to worry about a thing. Ryder fed the horses for you, and he even helped me pick the last of my green beans."

Andie swept her gaze from her aunt to Ryder. "You don't have to feed for me. You don't have to take care of me."

She didn't want to get used to him being there for her this way.

"Before you have this conversation, I wanted you to know that Caroline called. She asked about you and I told her what happened." Etta stood inside the door, not looking as apologetic as Andie would have liked.

"I wish you wouldn't have." The last thing she needed was for Caroline, her mother, to come rushing back to Dawson.

"She asked and I couldn't lie. And she said to tell you she loves you."

This couldn't be her life. Andie rubbed her hands over her face, trying hard to think about the mother who left, and the mother who had finally returned. Caroline had claimed she couldn't do it, couldn't be a mother to both of her daughters. At that moment it was harder than ever to understand how Caroline could walk away.

"It's okay, Gran." Andie smiled up at her grandmother. "Life changes, right?"

"It does change."

Etta slipped back out of the room. Andie could hear her careful steps going down the stairs. Ryder moved to the chair next to Andie's bed and sat down, taking off his hat and tossing it on the table next to him.

"You don't have to be here every day."

"You need to get over this." He raked his hand through his hair and let out a sigh. "I'm here because I want to be."

"You're here because you feel guilty, or obligated."

"No, I'm here because I'd be here no matter what the situation. When have I not been there for you?"

She could have told him that he hadn't been there for her two months ago, when he hadn't answered her phone calls. But then she remembered last night and how he'd held her while she cried, how he'd been there for her when it really counted.

He had always been there for her.

"I know," she whispered. "But this isn't easy, not being able to get up."

"I have a feeling it'll only get worse."

"Thanks." She wiped at her eyes and ignored how he shifted in the chair and fiddled with his hat, not making eye contact.

"How do you feel today?" he finally asked.

"Cagey, kind of angry, and definitely tired of this bed."

He laughed. "You've only been there for about ten hours. Multiply a few times over and maybe you'll have an idea what the next couple of weeks are going to be like."

"Thanks for the optimism."

She leaned back in the bed and tried to push the days and hours from her mind. She could do this for her baby.

Ryder stood up, because he had a lot to get done, but first, he had to try one more time. He reached into his pocket and pulled out the ring that had been his grandmother's. He'd loved her, his grandmother. She had died when he was barely ten, but he remembered her smile, the way she'd listened when he told stories.

Andie focused on the pancakes that he'd set on the dresser. "I'll take those now."

"Okay." He reached for the foam container but he didn't hand it to her yet. She stared up at him, blue eyes rimmed with the dark remnants of mascara from the day before.

"Stop."

"What?" He stopped in the center of her bedroom, the room that hadn't ever changed. It still had framed photos of horses, a quilt made by her great-grandmother and an antique rocking chair near the window.

Some things didn't change. And some did. No use looking in the rearview mirror when you're driving forward. An old rodeo friend had told him more than once. Greg was a rodeo clown and he raised race horses in Oklahoma City. He had a wife and kids, a real family.

People did manage to have families. He knew that. Men managed to stay married and stay faithful. Kids grew up with two parents in a home where they felt loved.

"Stop looking like that." Andie hugged her knees close to her body.

Ryder pulled the ring out of his pocket. He held it in one hand, the box of pancakes in the other and Andie's eyes widened as she watched him. She shook her head a little.

"Andie, please marry me. I haven't done the right thing very often in my life, but I really feel like this is the one time that I'm doing what needs to be done."

She actually laughed. "Seriously? That's your proposal."

He shoved the ring back into his pocket and handed her the pancakes. "What else am I supposed to say?"

"Love, Ryder. Marriage is about love and forever. Not 'doing what needs to be done.' Seriously, that's lame."

Well, thanks for that piece of information. He bristled because she was still smiling and he felt like a stinking fool.

"You'll have to forgive me if proposals aren't my strong suit. This isn't what I expected. I'm pretty sure it isn't what you expected. But we can sure do the right thing."

"I know we can, but this isn't it. I haven't put a lot of thought into marriage, either, but I can tell you one thing for certain, I'm not going to marry someone who doesn't love me."

"Love doesn't have too many guarantees, Andie. I know a lot of divorced couples who claimed to love one another. We've been through a lot together. We could make this work."

"And you'd end up resenting me. You might end up resenting the baby." She glanced up, her eyes were vivid blue and seeking something from him. He didn't have a clue what she wanted him to say.

She'd already pointed out that the proposal had been wrong. If that was the case, then he was pretty close to clueless.

"Fine, if the answer is no, then I'll live with it. But I'm this baby's father and I'm going to be here. I'm going to be a good dad."

"I know you will, Ryder."

Her eyes were soft and she already looked like someone's mom. And he still felt like the guy he'd been a month ago. Maybe she was right, he wasn't ready for this, for fatherhood.

Did other men just come equipped for this role?

"I have to go."

"Where..." She smiled. "I'm sorry, it isn't any of my business."

"I've got some bull calves that need to be taken care of. The vet's coming out this afternoon. Johnny Morgan is coming out to look at that mare I've been trying to sell."

"I wanted that mare."

"I thought you changed your mind."

She looked down and they were both thinking the same thing; he knew they were. She wouldn't be riding for a while.

Finally she smiled, "Yeah, I guess I've changed my mind. Johnny wants her for his daughter. I'm not sure that's a good match."

"I'll try to switch him to another horse then." He started to turn away, and he should have. Instead he leaned to kiss her cheek, just her cheek. "I'll be back later to check on you. Eat your breakfast."

She nodded and he walked to the door. His hand went to his pocket, to the ring that she'd rejected twice. She wanted to marry someone who loved her. He shook his head, not sure what to think about that.

If she didn't marry him, she'd marry someone else. Someday some other guy would know the right words. The thought turned around inside him. He didn't like to think of her married to another man. He tried not to picture it, her with another man's ring on her finger. His kid being raised by some other guy. What if that guy wasn't good to them? He thought if that happened, he'd have to hurt someone.

Or convince her to marry him before it happened. But the way things were going, he was far from convincing her that marriage was the right thing to do.

Chapter Ten

Andie woke up to the sound of footsteps coming down the hall toward her room. Lighter steps, not Ryder's. She blinked a few times and glanced at the clock. It was one o'clock. He'd left hours ago. A light rap on the door and then Alyson peeked in. Andie brushed her hair back from her face and sat up, already smiling.

"What are you doing here?" Andie hadn't seen her sister in weeks because of schedules and because she'd needed time to adjust to having this sister back in her life. Alyson had moved back to the area, but she'd had obligations, concerts she couldn't cancel.

Alyson shrugged, "I heard from a little birdie that you might need to be cheered up."

"You have a concert in L.A."

"Not until next week. And then I'm flying home to finish up the wedding plans. And you'd better get yourself together before the end of October so you can be my maid of honor." Alyson pushed the blankets aside and sat on the edge of the bed. "How are you?"

"Great."

"You're not great. If you were great you'd have something catty to say, or you might pick a fight with me. But you wouldn't have mascara smeared to your chin…"

"Seriously?" Andie rubbed at her cheeks.

"Seriously." Alyson walked to the dresser and picked up a small mirror. She pulled a few tissues out of the box. "You might want to get out of bed and wash your face, maybe brush your hair."

"I'm on bed rest."

"Yeah, but really, you can't go a month without brushing your hair."

Yes, she thought she could. If staying in bed was a way to hide from reality, she could do it. She took the mirror that Alyson held out to her.

Andie held the mirror up and ran her fingers through her hair, untangling it and then wiping away the mascara by method of the age-old spit bath. "I look worse than something that cat of yours would drag in."

"Not even close." Alyson sat back down on the edge of the bed. "Do you want to talk?"

"About what? About making a huge mistake? About being pregnant? Or about the possibility that I could lose the baby?" Andie closed her eyes. "Do you know how guilty I feel? I told myself this baby is a mistake. I was upset about being pregnant. I resented what this would do to my life." She sighed. "If you notice, all three problems were about me, about how I would be affected. And now this is happening and the only thing I can think of now is how can I keep my baby safe."

"I think every single emotion you've had is probably realistic in your situation." Alyson pushed her over a little and scooted up next to her so that they were side by side on the bed, backs against the headboard.

Etta had told them they shared a crib when they were

babies and when they moved to toddler beds they had refused to sleep alone.

And then they'd been ripped apart.

"I'm worried that I have too much of Caroline Anderson's DNA," Andie whispered. "What if I have a baby and then realize that I can't do this? What if I'm the type of mom who can't handle it?"

"You aren't our mother."

"I don't know that."

Alyson leaned close and their heads touched. "I do."

Andie nodded because she couldn't get the words out, couldn't tell her sister about Ryder's proposal, about him wanting to marry her, but not loving her.

"Let me help you with the wedding."

Alyson laughed. "You want to plan a wedding?"

"I can do something. I can at least keep you from making a frilly, lacy mistake."

"Okay, I'll get the books and you can help me. I need to pick out flowers. Oh, and your dress. I'm thinking pink."

"You're not."

Alyson laughed again. "No, I'm not. The wedding is going to be fall colors."

Andie sank back into her pillow as her sister left the room, her feet light on the stairs as she went down, calling for Etta. One sister happy, and one trying to be happy.

What if she said yes to Ryder? What would their wedding be like? Would it be a quick trip to a judge? Or something quiet on a weekday afternoon, just them, Etta and Pastor Jeffries?

As much as she'd never planned her wedding, Andie couldn't imagine either scenario. She groaned and covered her face with her hands. She suddenly wanted white lace and a man looking at her like she meant everything to him.

The way Jason looked at Alyson, not the cornered way Ryder looked at her. He hadn't ever looked at her this way, as if she was a stranger, or a problem he had to fix.

A cramp tightened around her stomach and she rested her hand there, praying the baby would stay safe, stay inside her where it could grow and be hers someday. Changes, life was definitely about changes.

She closed her eyes and thought about bargaining with God. But it wasn't about a bargain, it was about faith, about God's plan. She knew that and yet… She rested her hand on her stomach and fought against fear.

"You okay?"

Andie opened her eyes and smiled for her sister. "Yeah, I'm good."

"You don't look good."

"Pain. It isn't the same as yesterday. I think resting has helped. And the doctor prescribed some cream that is supposed to do something with my hormones."

"I'm glad." Alyson put down the pile of magazines. "You know I'll be here for you."

"I know you will." A year ago that wouldn't have been the case. But now, Alyson would be just down the road. Nothing ever stayed the same, Etta's song said. It was a bittersweet message of loss and gain.

"Ryder was down at the barn when I got here earlier."

"That's good." Andie wanted her sister to forget stories about Ryder. She pointed to the magazines as a direct hint.

"He's pretty sweet about all of this. When Etta mentions the baby, his eyes get damp. Cute."

"Right. Cute is what you want when coupled with,

'Hey, sweetie, let's get married. It's the right thing to do.' Isn't that cute?"

"What do you want him to say?"

Andie fiddled with the soft, worn edges of the quilt. Etta had threatened to get rid of it, but Andie loved it because it was familiar and comfortable.

"You want him to say that he loves you?" Alyson set books on the table next to Andie's bed. "Because you love him?"

"I don't really want to talk about it."

Alyson giggled and it wasn't like her, to giggle. Or to push. "So that's the way this is working out. You, the person who gave me advice to be careful with my heart, has lost yours."

"I haven't lost my heart."

But hadn't she? Wasn't it splintering off into tiny pieces, breaking apart each time he proposed with silly words about friendship and doing the right thing?

And as much as she didn't want her thoughts to turn that direction, she thought about what would happen to them if they lost the baby. What would happen if she said yes and then there wasn't a baby to hold them together?

The sight that met Ryder when he walked into his living room nearly undid him. He didn't need this after dealing with Andie and then working thirty head of rangy bull calves that weren't too partial to what the vet had to do with them. He stood in the doorway of his living room and stared. He counted to ten, reminding himself that they were little girls. But the little girls in question were sitting on his living room floor with sidewalk chalk, drawing pictures on his floor and his coffee table. He loved that table.

"What are you guys doing?" His voice roared a little, but he couldn't help it.

"We aren't boys." Molly stopped drawing long enough to inform him. "We're girls and we're drawing."

"That's sidewalk chalk." He scooped up the box and the chalk they weren't holding. "Sidewalk, as in outside, on concrete. Not inside on floors."

"We can wash it off." Molly kept doodling something that looked like a cat.

"Where's your dad?" Ryder held out his hand and they handed over the chalk they were still using.

Be a dad, he told himself. Be a dad. He knew what his dad would have done if he'd caught Ryder and Wyatt doing something like this. It would have started with a belt and ended with the two of them not being able to sit down for a week.

That parenting example wasn't going to work so he had to think of something on his own. He looked down at the girls. They were staring up at him, two brown-eyed little angels with smudges of pink, green and yellow on their cheeks. Kat rubbed at her nose and left a dot of orange behind.

"I need for the two of you to come with me. We're going to clean this mess up and you're not going to do this again." Ryder motioned for the two girls to head for the door.

"What happened?" Wyatt asked, looking a little frazzled. His hair was too long and he hadn't shaved since he rolled into town with that moving truck.

How did a guy go from dating, rodeoing, living his own life, to this? He wasn't Mr. Family Guy. He didn't *do* baby wipes, diapers and cleaning up kid messes. At least that didn't used to be his life.

He sure wasn't going to raise his older brother on top of everything else.

Get used to it, big shot. His good self smirked at his bad self, as if there had been a major victory of some sort. Rip the good life right out from under a guy and then be happy about it.

"We're cleaning up a mess," Ryder answered and he glanced back over his shoulder, at what was obviously a zoo of chalk-drawn characters on his floor and table. "Where were you?"

Wyatt shrugged. "I had to figure out what to feed them for supper. I was in the basement going through the freezer."

"Yeah, well, feel free to go to the store."

"I'll do that." Wyatt took the chalk.

Ryder walked down the hall to the kitchen, his brother and nieces following. He dug through the cabinet under the sink and pulled out wipes that promised to clean kitchen cabinets, woodwork and bathrooms. All purpose, of course. He handed it to the girls.

"What do we do?" Molly stared at the container.

He smiled, because she was little and trying to act so big. And not once had she backed down when faced with his anger. He stayed on the floor, at eye level with her.

He wanted to hug her, not punish her.

"We're going to clean up the chalk. And I'll help you." Molly's eyes lit up a little. "Okay."

He wasn't such a bad uncle. He stood up and Molly took his hand. Kat grabbed his leg so he picked her up.

"How's Andie?" Wyatt followed him into the living room.

"I thought you were looking for something to cook?"

Wyatt took Kat from his arms. She had a wipe in her hands and she struggled to get down. Wyatt set her free to start cleaning. He stepped back, watching. Ryder lifted his gaze to meet his brother's.

"We'll just have Mad Cow again." Wyatt sat down next to Molly and showed her how to rub the chalk off the floor. "What about Andie?"

That was fine, Ryder didn't do family meals. He could slap some microwaved something on a plate, but the whole nutrition pyramid wasn't in his diet. He glanced back at the girls because they probably needed some of the stuff on that pyramid. At least Vera had vegetables at the Mad Cow.

Wyat cleared his throat, reminding Ryder of the question about Andie.

"She's doing good. I guess."

"You guess?"

"I proposed again. She turned me down again."

Wyatt moved from the floor to the sofa. "Well, how did you propose?"

"Are you the proposal expert?"

"No, but I've had more experience than you. At least with a real relationship."

"Yeah, well…"

"If you want her to say yes, you have to show her how special she is to you. You have to do more than pull out a ring and say, 'Hey baby, how 'bout we get hitched.'"

"Andie isn't about romance."

Wyatt laughed. "Have you been under a rock? She's a woman. She's having a baby, your baby. She wants romance."

"Chocolates and flowers?" Ryder hadn't ever bought a woman flowers.

"Do what you've always done. But maybe this time, mean it."

"She knows she's my best friend." Ryder showed

Molly a spot on the floor that still had the smudged outline of a snake. She wiped it up with dimpled, pudgy hands. He looked at her hands and suddenly those hands meant everything. His baby would have hands like that, soft and pudgy. His kid.

But maybe his kid would have blond hair like Andie. Maybe she'd have his eyes, or his curls. He blinked and looked away from his niece, to the brother that was trying to give him advice.

"Ryder, I don't know how long you're going to tell yourself that Andie is just a friend, but there's something you ought to think about."

"What's that?" He was still thinking about Molly's hands and he wondered how Wyatt felt the first time he held his daughter. But he didn't want to ask.

"You might ought to think about the fact that she's the longest relationship you've ever had."

His longest relationship. He brushed his hands down the legs of his jeans and smiled at Molly, whose wide eyes clued him in to the possibility that wiping dirt on clothes was bad.

"Yeah, I guess you're right, she is." He leaned and kissed Molly on the top of the head. She smiled up at him and then she went back to scrubbing.

"You think I might be right?" Wyatt got down on the floor to help his girls. "That's a huge change."

Ryder stood up, still holding the container of wipes. Yeah, huge change. But he'd had a lot of changes in his life. Not all bad. He watched the girls as they finished scrubbing his table. Change wasn't the worst thing in the world.

"I don't want to be like our dad. I don't want to mess up a kid the way we were messed up. Did you ever feel that way? Were you afraid to have kids?"

Wyatt looked at the girls. "Yeah, I was. I learned something though. If you're worried about being like him, that means you know what he did wrong. You can make changes."

Ryder wondered about that. He wondered about Wyatt and the past year, trying to get his life back.

"Take my word for it, you can do this, Ryder. But first you have to make Andie feel like you love her, like she's your sweetheart, not the woman that lassoed you and dragged you down the aisle against your will."

Make her feel like his sweetheart? He had a feeling flowers and chocolate weren't the key to Andie's heart. And he had bigger problems than that. How did he go from thinking of her as his best friend to turning her into the person he loved?

He might not have all the answers, but he did know the way to her heart. And it wasn't chocolate.

It was dark outside when headlights flashed across the living room wall. Andie glanced out the window, but she couldn't see who it was. Alyson walked to the window and shrugged.

"I don't know who it is. It's a truck and a trailer." Alyson shot Andie a knowing look. "It's Ryder."

"Why can't he give me a break?"

"Because he's worried about you?" Alyson left the room and Andie knew she was letting Ryder in, and she imagined the two would share secretive little looks, maybe whisper something about her mood.

Staying down was not easy. She kicked her feet into the couch and screamed a silent scream of protest. When the footsteps headed her way she managed a calm smile.

"What are you doing here?" She flipped off the television when he walked into the room. He stood in the doorway, his hand behind his back. His jeans had pastel pink stains down the front.

Alyson peeked in, screwing up her face. "That's nice."

Andie drew in a deep breath and exhaled. "Fine, I can play this game. Ryder, it's nice to see you."

He smiled and stepped into the room, dark hair and dark eyes, and all cowboy. Except the pink stain. Her gaze kept straying to the pink blotch. But then his hands moved.

He had flowers and a sheepish grin as he held them out to her. She wanted to laugh. He actually had flowers. Her heart did something strange, because he'd never done that before. No one had ever bought her flowers. He hadn't even bought her flowers when he took her to the prom. Not even a wrist corsage.

"I wanted to check on you. I thought I'd see if there was anything you needed." He shrugged a little and he looked cute in jeans that had dirty smudges on the knees and a T-shirt that was a little threadbare. He didn't smell good.

"What have you been doing? You stink."

"Sorry, I worked with calves all day and then I had to go pick something up."

"You have pink on your jeans."

"Sidewalk chalk."

She pictured him on a sidewalk drawing hearts and flowers. He wouldn't have liked that image of himself.

He walked across the room with the flowers that were a little smushed and slightly wilted. She took them and held them to her nose. The rose in the bouquet flopped to the side with a broken stem. She peeked over the top of the flowers and smiled because his cheeks were ruddy from the sun and embarrassment.

"What did you have to pick up? The flowers?" She

scooted up so he could sit on the couch next to her. He didn't sit down.

"No, I bought the flowers at..." He looked down, at boots covered in mud. On Etta's glossy wood floors. "I bought them at the convenience store."

They both laughed. At least they could still do that. "I love them."

"I bought you something else. I know you can't get up right now. But if you could sneak over to the window, I'll show you."

"Oh, okay."

And then he was gone. She waited a few seconds to see if he would come back. When he didn't she hurried over to the window and looked out. He was opening the back of the trailer. Her heart hammered a little harder than before.

It was dark but the light in the backyard glowed in the night and bugs buzzed around the front porch light. Andie leaned close to the screen and waited for Ryder to walk out the back of the trailer. When he did, she laughed.

He stopped in the yard, looking up at the window, at her. He motioned to the creature standing behind him. She pushed the window up.

"How do you like her?"

"A llama?"

"An alpaca." He sounded a little offended. "You said you wanted one."

"And I do. And she's beautiful. I love her."

"Etta can knit blankets with her wool."

"For the..." She bit down on her lip for a second. "For the baby."

He nodded and then he gathered up the lead rope of the animal. "Yes, for the baby. I'll put her in the corral with hay for tonight. Tomorrow we can see how she does with horses."

She watched until he was out of sight and then she hurried back to the couch. But Etta caught her. Etta, a dish towel in her hands and a frown on her face.

"What are you doing up?"

"Ryder had a surprise for me. I just slipped over to the window to see what it was."

"And it was what?"

She laughed. "An alpaca. Can you believe he got me an alpaca?"

"I think that's about the sweetest thing I've ever heard. Now, stay on that couch and I'll make hot cocoa."

An alpaca. Andie hugged her pillow and she couldn't stop smiling. The flowers were on the table, wilted but fragrant. And Ryder had bought her an alpaca.

She'd always known that sweet side of him. He'd always done the silliest things. The sweetest things.

And she'd never been able to think about falling in love with someone else, because she'd always loved him. She had dreamed of him someday loving her, someday asking her to marry him. But the dreams had been different.

The dreams hadn't included mistakes and this wall between them. The dreams had included words of love and forever, not the words *have to*.

She'd loved him forever and no one knew her secret but her. And probably God. The two of them knew how it had hurt to be his best friend while he dated, and never women like her. Ryder had dated women from Tulsa. He had dated the kind of woman she would never be, the manicured kind who always knew how to put outfits together, always looked stylish and beautiful.

His footsteps, minus boots, alerted her to his presence.

She looked up as he walked through the door of the living room, without his hat, without boots. She smiled at his bare feet and he shifted a little, like he couldn't handle bare feet in her presence.

"Etta made me take my boots off."

"It's okay, you have cute feet."

He sat down on the coffee table facing her. "My feet aren't cute. I have long toes."

"My toes look like little clubs. Etta says because I went barefoot when I was a kid. I should have worn shoes." She stopped herself from rambling more. She looked up at him. "I love the alpaca."

"Nothing says I care like an alpaca." He winked and her stomach did this funny thing that felt like flips. How often had she watched him wink at girls, and then watched those same silly females follow him, not knowing that he wasn't good for much more than one date?

One night.

But they'd done everything together. They'd gone everywhere together. She'd been his comfort zone. He'd been safe with her. Maybe too safe, she decided.

"You're right about that." She couldn't look at him, her heart ached and it hurt to take a deep breath.

"Andie, I'm sorry. This isn't the way we planned our lives, but we can make it work. I'm going to be a good dad. I'll figure out how to be good at this."

"I know you will." She met his dark brown gaze and her heart thudded, her face warmed. "I know, because I know who you are, that you're good and kind."

"I'm not, Andie. I've never been good or kind. I've been shallow and selfish just about all of my life."

"Not to me."

He reached for her hand and she held her breath as he slid his fingers between hers. "No, not to you."

His eyes narrowed a little as he stared at their hands, and then he leaned. He leaned and he slid his free hand to the back of her neck, cupping it with a gentleness that made her heart melt. His lips touched hers, leaving behind the sweet taste of cola. Time slowed down and he held her close, keeping his lips close to hers. He moved, kissing her hair right above her ear and still holding her. He whispered but her brain didn't connect words that sounded as if he meant to hold her forever.

And then Etta cleared her throat. "Hot cocoa anyone?"

Ryder scrambled back away from her, leaving her alone and cold on the sofa. He stood up, looking sixteen and ashamed of being caught necking in the parlor. Andie smiled at this side of him, the soft and vulnerable side.

"I should go." He coughed a little. "I'll be back tomorrow. To check on the alpaca, and on you."

Andie nodded and then he was gone. From her seat on the sofa she watched his truck go down the road, back in the direction of his house.

He'd bought her an alpaca, and he'd kissed her goodbye. As much as she wanted to go back to being "just friends" she knew that could never happen.

Chapter Eleven

Ryder hadn't gone home the night before. Instead he'd left Andie's, driven past his house and straight to Tulsa. He hadn't been sure what he was going to do once he got there, but as he'd driven past a home store, it had hit him. He was going to have a kid, and that kid needed a room. A nursery.

Kids had rooms. Babies had nurseries. He'd learned a lot last night while he'd been shopping.

Two pots of coffee later, he stepped back and looked at the wall he'd been painting. It wasn't what he'd expected, but it wasn't bad. It was pretty good considering he didn't have a clue what he was doing. This was a far cry from painting a wall white, or beige.

"What are you doing?" Wyatt walked up beside him. "I guess I know what you're doing, but isn't it a little early?"

"If a guy's going to have faith—" the word wasn't easy to get out "—then he has to have faith. I'm going to be a dad and my kid is going to have the best nursery I can make."

"Green?"

"Yeah, green. For a boy or a girl." Ryder didn't look at

his brother, he kept looking at the walls and he explained what the girl at the all night home store had told him. She'd said this was some shade of antique pastel green. And it would look great with cream trim on the woodwork. That's what the girl at the store had said.

He'd taken her word for it because he would have painted the room pink if it had been up to him. Pink because he couldn't stop thinking about having a little girl. As much as he'd ever wanted anything, the idea of that little girl in his arms had become the biggest dream ever.

Wyatt stepped over to the box Wyatt had placed on top of an old dresser. He started pulling out stuff that Ryder had bought on his late-night shopping trip. A train, a picture of a pony, a porcelain doll and a clown. Ryder still didn't like the clown. It looked too creepy for a baby's room. Wyatt shot him a look.

"That's the creepiest clown I've ever seen." Wyatt dropped it back in the box. "So, trains, stuffed animals and butterflies?"

"It could be a boy or a girl. We won't know for a couple of months." We, as in he and Andie. He figured it would get easier to deal with, eventually.

But he thought most people planned these things and had time to adjust, to deal with it. He was going to be a dad and that hadn't been on any of his to-do lists.

He tried not to think of Andie losing the baby because he didn't really want to think about how that would make him feel. It didn't make sense that something he hadn't wanted, hadn't planned to have, could mean so much to a guy in a matter of weeks. It felt like something he wouldn't be able to handle losing.

His kid.

The whole nursery thing had happened after he'd kissed Andie earlier. Or had it been the night before?

He glanced at his wrist, but his watch was on the counter downstairs. And none of that took his mind off that kiss. If a kiss, if holding a woman could make a man change his mind about having a woman in his life forever, that might have been the moment.

"What about a bed?" Wyatt finished rummaging through the box and looked at him.

"Our old cradle and crib are in the attic. I thought I'd sand them down."

"Wow, seriously?"

Anything for his kid.

"Yeah, a baby has to have a place to sleep."

Wyatt walked over to the rocking chair Ryder had bought last night. Every time he looked at that rocking chair he pictured it next to the window and he could see Andie in it, holding their baby. For that to happen, she'd have to marry him. She'd have to live here with him and make a home with him.

That didn't seem likely because she was pretty stuck on their "best friend" relationship. He had to take the blame for that.

"You're right—a baby has to have a place to sleep." Wyatt touched the rocking chair and his smile faded. Ryder thought Wyatt probably had images in his mind that were a little harder to face. Images of Wendy holding their girls.

Ryder slapped his brother on the back. "I think we need to go break a horse or something. All of this paint is starting to get to me."

"Wish I could, but the girls are waking up. I'm going to drive over to Grove. Do you need anything from town?"

"I was in Tulsa until three in the morning. What do you think?"

"Probably not. How did it go with Andie?"

"I bought her an alpaca."

Wyatt shook his head. "Okay, maybe you don't know what you're doing."

"What? She liked it."

"Yeah, she probably did."

Ryder grinned. "I bought her flowers, too."

Wyatt shook his head and walked out of the room. "You'll never get it."

Ryder dipped the brush in the paint and finished up a small section of wall that he didn't want to leave undone. Green, for a boy or a girl. The clerk at the home store had asked him all the details, like when was the baby due and did they have a name picked out. And he'd tried to think up answers because he didn't have any.

He tossed the brush into the tray and walked out of the room. A guy who was having a baby should have answers. By the time he pulled up to Etta's he'd managed to cool down.

Etta answered the door, motioning him into the kitchen and then looking at him like he'd dropped off the moon.

"Do you want a cup of coffee or a shower?" Her nose wrinkled and she stepped back. "Take your boots off."

"I guess I look pretty bad." He looked down. The pink chalk had faded but he had specks of paint on his shirt and arms.

"Not too bad. She's in the living room."

"Has she had breakfast? I could take her a tray."

"You might lose your head. She's already sick of staying down. She made Alyson drag that alpaca up to the window, right up on my front porch."

He laughed picturing that in his mind. Alyson was about the prissiest female he'd ever met. If she and Andie didn't look so much alike, he'd say there wasn't any way they could be twins.

"She'll be glad to see me." He took the cup of coffee from Etta. "Do you think she wants anything?"

"No, she can't have more coffee. One cup a day and she had eggs for breakfast."

He nodded and walked down the hall to the living room. He knew this house as well as he knew his own and as a kid he'd probably spent more time here than at home. He peeked around the door of the living room and Andie smiled. She didn't look mean. Or angry.

"Come in." She grimaced and looked him over, top to bottom. "You look horrible."

"Thanks." He sat down in the rocking chair, still holding his cup of coffee.

"You're wearing the same clothes you had on last night."

"Yeah, I am."

"And you haven't shaved."

He rubbed his hand across his cheek. It had been a couple of days since he'd shaved. "Andie, about the baby. What do you think we'll name her?"

She smiled and curled back into the couch. "Name her? I don't know. I mean, we don't know if…if she'll be a girl."

"But she might be."

"Yeah, she might be." Her eyes softened and she looked out the window. "I like the name Maggie."

"We could call her Magpie."

"Yeah, we could. And buy her a pony when she's three."

Andie looked at him and her smile faded. "Ryder, I don't want to do this."

"What, have the baby?" He could barely get the words out, but she was shaking her head.

"I don't want to plan. I don't want to think about names when I might lose her."

"That isn't going to happen." He wouldn't let it happen. The idea of this kid had settled inside him. The idea of Andie as the mother of his child was settling inside him, taking root. He tried to smile, for Andie's sake. "What happened to faith? What happened to trusting God?"

"I'm trying…I'm really trying, but I didn't expect this to be so hard." She bit down on her bottom lip and he'd never seen her like that—vulnerable. Her blue eyes were huge and her lips trembled.

Andie had always been the strongest woman he knew. She hadn't ever really seemed to need him, or anyone else. He always said she rolled with the punches.

But a baby changed everything.

He left the rocking chair and went to her side. She looked up, blue eyes swimming in tears that didn't fall. "I'll have enough faith for both of us. I can do that for you. I can do that for her."

And he meant it.

Step one in being a dad, trusting someone other than himself. Trusting God. He hoped God was still in the forgiving business because if Ryder was going to work on faith, he had a lot to confess to the Almighty. He had a lot of work to do on himself.

Andie leaned against a shoulder that was strong and wide and Ryder held her close. She sniffed into his shirt and pulled back.

"You really have to take a shower."

"Sorry, I should have done that before I came over, but I had to know. Last night someone asked me what we were going to name her, and when she'd be born, and I didn't know the answer."

"Where were you last night?" Ick, was that jealousy? Andie shrugged it off. "I mean, you left here and…"

"I went to Tulsa to buy a few things for the house. And then I stayed up all night working."

She ran her hand down his arm, touching small spatters of green paint. She didn't want to take her hand off his arms. They were suntanned and strong. "Were you painting?"

"Yeah. You know, the girls are living at the house, and Wyatt."

"Oh." And it shouldn't have hurt. She should have been glad that he was doing something for the girls.

"Hey, let me get you some books. Or lunch. Would you like some chocolate?"

"Ryder, I don't need anything." She glanced out the window. "Except up from here."

"Yeah, I can't do that for you. What about Dusty?"

"I miss him. He probably thinks I've abandoned him." She wiped at her eyes. "Could you go out and check on him?"

"You know I will. But I wanted to check on you, first."

His voice was gentle but deep and he was still sitting on the coffee table, facing her. She brushed at her eyes again.

"Ryder, I'm so afraid."

"Why?"

She pulled back, looking at him, at a face she knew as well as she knew her own. She knew that dimple in his chin, the way his hair curled when it got a little too long, and the way his brown eyes danced when he was amused. And she thought he should know her, too.

"Because I don't know what's going to happen. I don't

want to lose this baby. It was the most unexpected thing in the world, but now…" She wiped at her eyes. "She's a part of me. She's a part of us. As afraid as I am of raising her, I'm afraid of losing her."

"I'm not going to let you raise her alone." He grinned. "Or him."

That wasn't what she wanted him to say. She wanted him to say that he was afraid. But telling her she wouldn't be alone in this, maybe he was doing his best, the best a cowboy who had never planned on settling down could do.

It wasn't like he was going to suddenly pledge his undying love to her. She was lucky he'd agreed to go to church. He had promised to have enough faith for both of them. That was good, because her faith was pretty shaky at the moment and at least he was strong.

"I know you won't." She looked out the window. A car drove down the road, a rare thing for their street at this time of day. It didn't stop.

It went on down the road, the distraction ended. And her heart was still aching because she was going to have a baby and she wanted more than anything to hear Ryder say he loved her.

"You should go. I know you have a lot to do today." She didn't want him to feel like he had to stay and take care of her.

She wanted to get up and take care of herself. She'd thought about it earlier, before anyone was up. She'd considered sneaking out of the house and going outside to check on her horse and see the alpaca. And small twinges of pain had convinced her otherwise.

As hard as it was to stay in bed, she didn't want to take chances.

"I don't have a lot to do, Andie. I've been getting things taken care of. Today I'm here to take care of you."

She squirmed a little. "I really don't think that's a good idea."

"Why?"

"Because that isn't us."

"It's the new us." He sniffed his own shirt. "But I do need a shower."

"Ryder, really, you don't have to stay here and take care of me. I have Etta and Alyson. They'll take care of me."

Ryder stood up. "This isn't just about you, Andie, this is about our baby. I'm taking care of you and our baby."

"I don't need to be taken care of."

"Of course you don't, you stubborn female." He walked to the door. "I'll be back in an hour."

The front door slammed and then she heard him backing out of the driveway and then shifting as he headed back down the road. She picked up one of the wedding magazines that Alyson had been looking at.

White and frilly. Couldn't a wedding be practical? She was practical. She wouldn't want a dress she couldn't wear again. She wouldn't want cake that looked beautiful but tasted like dust.

If she was to get married she'd want daisies and denim. She'd want to ride off into the sunset on her horse and camp in the mountains for her honeymoon. With her baby next to her. But who was the groom in this little dream? The guy who wanted to take care of her?

Her hand went to her belly and she whispered, wondering if it was true that babies could hear from inside the womb. But a baby the size of a shrimp? She really didn't like that image.

She preferred picturing the full-sized baby, with

brown hair and brown eyes. Her imagination fast-forwarded her ten years and she was still living with Etta, raising her daughter. But in the dream, Ryder was a visitor and a woman waited in his truck as he picked up his daughter for the weekend.

That wouldn't do. But neither did the other version of the dream, the one where she and Ryder were together but he resented her, resented their child because the ring on his finger kept him tied to them.

As she drifted on the edge of sleep she told herself that wasn't fair. It wasn't fair to Ryder that she was putting him in the role of villain. Ryder had always been honorable. He had always been there for her.

But having a baby, neither of them knew how to approach this mountain. She had made mistakes in her life, mistakes that she knew God had gotten her through, helped her to overcome. As she lay there she thought about her baby and she couldn't call a child a mistake.

The baby was a choice they had made. It might not have been the right choice, but it was one they would work through. And it would never be the baby's fault. She would never let that happen.

A truck door slammed and she jumped but then settled back onto the couch. She listened to boots on the wood front steps, a rap on the door and then Ryder walked into the living room. He had shaved and his hair was damp and curled a little.

"Wake up, sweetheart, you're going outside."

"What?" She sat up, but she didn't reach for the flip flops on the floor next to the sofa.

"I'm going to work Dusty, but I thought you'd like to go. You can sit on a lawn chair out there."

"You think that would be okay?" She reached for her shoes.

"Don't stand up."

"What?" She held her shoes and then he was standing in front of her, leaning to pick her up.

"I'm going to carry you." He scooped her up and she grabbed quick, wrapping her arms around his neck.

"I'm too heavy."

"You're not heavy." He laughed and jostled her, shifting her. "No, you're not heavy. I've picked up bales of hay that weigh more."

"Thanks, I'm a bale of hay." She leaned and he did smell better. Soap, aftershave and the minty smell of toothpaste. He turned a little and they were face-to-face, practically nose to nose.

"You're not hay," he whispered. He touched his forehead to hers and then looked away, his arms tensing, holding her close.

What was she to him? Okay, she got it, she wasn't hay. But if she asked, what would he say? Best friend, pain in the neck, or was she now just extra baggage that he wasn't sure how to handle?

Andie wasn't heavy. She held him tight, her arms around his neck, and her head close to his. He carried her down the hall and into the kitchen. Etta was sitting at the table with a basket of yarn, knitting needles in her hand and something partially made. She looked up as they walked into the room.

She set the knitting needles and yarn on the table and stared for a moment before shaking her head. "What do you think you're up to?"

"Going outside." He stopped at the screen door and waited for Etta to tell him he was crazy and why he shouldn't do this. But the more he thought about Andie stuck in the house, the more he knew he had to get her outside.

"She has to stay down," Etta warned.

"I'm not going to let her walk, just letting her get fresh air. We can't keep her locked in the house for nine months."

Andie moved in his arms. "I don't think I'll be on bed rest for seven months."

"Well, probably not, I'm just saying that you could use some fresh air."

Etta shook her head again. "I think the two of you were meant for each other."

Meant for each other.

Ryder couldn't respond to that. He pushed the screen door open with his hip and slid through. Andie pushed to keep the door from hitting them on their way out. She was easy in his arms, and he'd never thought of the two of them as a couple. As "meant for each other."

Or maybe he had. Maybe he'd pushed it from his mind because it was easy to be her friend and the idea of breaking her heart had been the thing that scared him the most. He'd never let himself think about the two of them together. She had always been his best friend.

He'd picked safe.

"What?" she quizzed as he sat her down in the lawn chair, cradling her close as he settled her in the seat.

"Nothing."

"Whatever. I think I've known you long enough to know when nothing is really something. Your jaw is clenching because you're grinding your teeth. You do that when you're mad about something."

"I'm not mad."

"Are too."

"Not right now, Andie. I can't have this conversation with you right now."

"Yeah, I guess we're talked out."

No, he thought they probably had plenty to talk about, just nothing they wanted to talk about. "When's your next doctor's appointment?"

"Next week." Her hand went to her belly and she looked away from him.

"Are you—" he squatted next to her "—are you having pains?"

She drew in a deep breath. "Some twinges, but nothing too bad. Sometimes I'm afraid..."

He'd never heard her admit that before. "I know, me, too. But I'm praying."

"You're praying?"

"Every time I take a breath." He couldn't stop looking at her belly, because his baby was in there. He'd never thought it could change him like this, that child and Andie needing him.

"One of us has to be strong, Ryder."

"You can count on me." He stood and she was staring up at him. "What do you need me to do with Dusty?"

He backed away, hoping she'd let the conversation end.

"I think lunge him in the arena. He doesn't like it when you ride him." She pulled her sweater closer around herself.

"Yeah, I seem to remember the last time I rode him. I think I still have the scar on my arm where he dumped me."

She smiled at that and picked up the cat that had left the barn and was circling her chair. When her smile faded and her eyes clouded over, he knew he should have left when he had the chance.

"Ryder, what if I lose the baby?"

How was he supposed to answer that? Two months ago having a baby was the farthest thing from his mind. And now she wanted to know what they'd do if she lost it? Having that baby meant changing his life in ways he hadn't planned.

Now, not having it felt like the change he didn't want to face.

"We're not going to lose the baby." He bent and kissed the top of her head. "I'm going to catch Dusty."

She might have whispered "chicken" as he walked off. He couldn't be sure of that, and he wasn't positive it wasn't just his own thoughts calling him names.

But yeah, he was a chicken. That was something he was just now figuring out about himself. He was a big old chicken. He was afraid of conversations with obstetricians. He was afraid to talk about having kids with Andie.

He was not afraid of a horse. He whistled and Dusty didn't even lift his head. That horse was not going to make him walk out into the field and catch him.

Chapter Twelve

The house was quiet. Andie hated the quiet. She hated being inside. She hadn't been out since the day Ryder had carried her outside to watch while he worked Dusty. He'd meant it to be a good thing, but instead it had ached inside her, watching him work her horse.

At least she'd gotten to go out.

Since then it had been daily visits. He showed up with food from the Mad Cow or movies for her to watch. He'd sat with her while she dozed. He constantly asked how she was and if she needed anything. Her heart was getting way too used to him being around.

Today it was raining, a cold rain that blew leaves against the windows while thunder rumbled in the clouds. And everyone was gone. Alyson was in Tulsa with Etta, getting the finishing touches on her dress. Ryder was selling off a herd of year-old steers. She'd promised she would stay on the couch. She had food. She had a thermos of cold water.

She had cabin fever like nobody's business.

Somewhere in the distance a dog barked, the sound getting swallowed up by thunder and rain beating on the roof of the porch. Andie strained to listen. She heard it again and then a cow.

Normal farm sounds, she told herself. Dogs barked and cows mooed. The only thing that wasn't normal was her, and the fact that she couldn't go check and see what was going on.

The barking got louder, more frantic.

"Okay, I can't sit here." Andie picked up her cell phone and slipped her feet in tennis shoes by the door. She grabbed a jacket off the hook on the wall and walked outside. For a moment she stood on the front porch, protected from the rain. Of course the dog stopped barking when she walked outside.

Andie walked off the porch and headed across the yard, in the direction of the most pitiful mooing she'd ever heard. Her stomach twisted, because she didn't know what she'd find, and because she shouldn't be up.

But she hadn't had pains for two days. That had to be a sign that things were getting better. She was close to finishing her first trimester.

She scanned the fence, looking for the cow and the dog. They were quiet for a minute and then it started again. The dog barked an excited bark, not angry. Picking up her pace, she headed for the clump of brush and stand of trees near the corner of the fence. The dog barked again. And then she saw the cow on the ground. It bellowed, low and pitiful, sides heaving. The dog was crouched on the ground, tail wagging. It turned to look at her, tongue hanging out. It didn't leave the cow.

Now what?

Andie slid between two rows of barbed wire and approached the cow, talking quietly to calm the poor heifer. "I know, it's scary, isn't it? Poor thing, you don't know what's happening to you."

The cow looked up, her eyes huge, her mouth opening in a pant that became a low moo. Andie squatted next to her, running her hands over the animal's heaving sides. Cows never picked good weather or good conditions to calve. And if they were going to have problems, which they often did, it always happened at the worst possible time.

Andie had pulled a calf two hours before her senior graduation. That's how life worked on the farm. She'd pulled a calf, and then she graduated from high school.

But this was different. A cow in distress, but Andie's baby, needing a chance, needing to be safe.

One hoof was out. Andie couldn't begin to guess how long the cow had been down or how long she'd been trying to push this baby out.

It was her first calf and she was obviously going to be like her mother, having difficult deliveries. But Andie couldn't help her. Any other time, but not today. It wasn't a difficult decision to make. It really felt like the only decision.

Etta had ordered her to call Ryder if anything happened, or if she needed anything. He had his cell phone on and was just minutes away. This qualified as an emergency, as needing something. She let out a sigh, because she hated having to call him away from what he was doing. To take care of what she needed to have done.

But this wasn't about her. It was about the baby.

She stood up.

The dog, a stray that had showed up in town a year or so ago, hurried to her side, wagging his entire back end. He hadn't run the cow, she was sure of that. He'd just been sending out his own alert. He sat down next to her, proud that he'd done his job.

Andie pulled out her cell phone and dialed. Ryder answered after a few rings.

"Andie?"

"Ryder, I have a cow in labor. I think the calf is going to have to be pulled."

"Are you outside?"

"Yes, I'm outside." She wiped rain from her face but it kept coming down, soaking her hair and clothes. "I had to see what was going on."

A long pause and then he spoke. "Andie, get back inside."

She could hear sounds in the background. Laughter, conversations and dishes rattling. It riled her that he was ordering her back into the house. When had he ever done that?

"I can't leave the cow."

"You have to leave her." His voice got loud, firm. "I'll be there in five minutes."

"Fine." She slid the phone back into her. "Help is on the way, girl."

The cow mooed and raised her head. "You're right, I'm not going to leave you alone."

No one wanted to be alone in a situation like this.

Andie backed up to a tree that was just a few feet away. It gave her a little protection from the rain, a little shelter. But the whole time she stood there, waiting, she felt mad and guilty. She didn't want to feel, either.

Ryder grabbed the ticket for his lunch at the Mad Cow and reached into his pocket for his wallet. He was trying to look casual, as if this was something he did every day, getting calls from Andie and leaving in the middle of lunch.

But lately, nothing was what he'd been used to doing

every day. He looked at the guys he'd had lunch with—Clint Cameron, Adam Mackenzie, Reese Cooper and a couple of others. They were all taking their lunch break at the Mad Cow. A few of them were getting ready to go to the livestock auction. Reese was getting ready for the rodeo finals in Vegas. They were all still living the lives they were comfortable with.

Without warning, Ryder's life had become something so upside down he didn't recognize it. Church yesterday with Wyatt and the girls and afterward he'd taken lunch to Andie. A couple of weeks ago he'd found out he was going to be a dad. And each and every day he was climbing up the biggest mountain of his life, trying to find his way back to God and his way forward in this situation with Andie.

For a while it had been like wearing someone else's boots. But he was adjusting. And everyone at the table was looking at him like they thought maybe he was going to lose it if they didn't hitch him to an anchor.

Clint reached for the ticket Ryder was still holding.

"You go on, that sounded like something that needs to be taken care of. I'll buy your lunch."

"Andie has a cow down." He picked up his burger to take it with him.

"Do you think you'll need some help?" Adam Mac-Kenzie grabbed the ticket from Clint and pulled out his wallet. "I'll get lunch."

Clint laughed. "Will he need help with what, Andie or the cow?"

Ryder threw money on the table for the tip. "You guys are hilarious. I don't think I'll need help with either."

Reese, chair tilted back on two legs, was grinning. And Ryder kind of wanted to hit him, because Reese had dated Andie back in their college days. He'd dated her and cheated on her. It had mattered then, it mattered more now.

"I never thought you'd be the guy falling like this," Reese finally commented. Clint jerked his chair back and Reese scurried to get his feet back under him as the chair went to the floor with a crash that had people staring and Vera running from the back.

The owner of the Mad Cow glared at them and then she headed toward Ryder with foam containers. "Are you heading out?"

"Yeah, Andie called." He shot Reese a look. "She has a cow down. I need to run but Adam's buying lunch."

"I wasn't worried about you skipping out on a bill, Ryder. I was worried about Andie. I saw you here and I know Etta's in Tulsa, so I made Andie up some of my special cashewed chicken. Take this to her. And let me have that." She grabbed a napkin out of the holder on the table and reached for the burger he was about to take a bite of. Before he could object she opened the foam container and put the burger inside. "There, now you're all set to go. And you'd better hurry or she'll be hooking up a pulley to her truck and pulling that calf on her own."

"I know." He kissed Vera on the cheek. "You're the best.

He pulled into Andie's a few minutes later. She was sitting on the porch, out of the rain. She didn't stand up when he pulled up to the house. Worry knotted in his stomach. He should have ignored her when she said she didn't need him here. He could have found someone to do his work at home and he could have sat with her while Etta was gone.

He jumped out of the truck, grabbing the container of food before he shut the door. Andie crossed her arms

over her front and glared as he hurried toward her. She
was mad. He guessed that was a plus.

"What took you so long?"

"Had to get our food." He felt the need to defend himself. "And it didn't take that long. Here's your lunch. Vera
made you some of her cashewed chicken."

She took the container from him. "The cow is over
there, near the corner post and that clump of brush."

"She'll be fine, Andie. Why don't you go inside?"

"I couldn't sit in there. I'll sit on the porch. This isn't
walking around. This isn't doing something." Her hands
clenched into the sleeves of her sweater.

"I know." He took a few steps back to keep from holding her when he knew being held was the last thing she
wanted. He knew her, knew she was close to tears that
she was fighting hard against. There were times to hold
a woman and let her cry. He knew this wasn't one of
those times.

"I'm so tired of this." She brushed her hands over her
face and didn't look at him. "I'm so tired of not being
able to take care of things. And having to call someone
to take care of things I can usually take care of. And then
there's the guilt because I got up to see what was wrong."

"It's okay to be sick of this, you know."

"But the baby..." she began.

"Is going to be fine. You're going to be fine."

"You don't know that," she insisted.

Now was when a man held a woman and let her cry.
He sat down next to her on the wicker bench that always
creaked with his weight and she leaned into his side. He
heard the cow mooing and tried to ignore it.

"Andie, we're almost to the three-month mark. What
have we got, another week or two?"

"Yeah."

"So, we're going to make it." He held her and felt her tense and pull away.

"You have to go deliver that calf. I can't lose that calf."

"I'm going."

He hurried out to his truck and found rope, a coat and some old towels. He kept the metal toolbox on the back of his truck stocked with just about everything he might need in an emergency. As he dug around inside the box he found a rain poncho that he'd never taken out of the package. Now that was prepared.

The dog greeted him as he walked across the yard. The scruffy looking terrier cross was mud-caked but happy. He'd never seen a dog like this one, one that always looked as if it was grinning. He guessed if everyone in town was feeding him, he'd be pretty happy, too.

The cow was still laboring. He climbed the fence and eased toward her. The wild look in her eyes warned that she wasn't going to be pleasant about dealing with him. Good thing she was nearly worn out. That was a bad thing, too. It meant she wasn't going to be a lot of help pushing this calf out.

"How is she?" Andie had moved to another seat on the porch and she leaned out. He knew it was killing her, this inactivity, and not taking care of her farm.

"She's having a baby, Andie. Now give me a minute." He looped the rope around the tiny hooves that were trying to poke out.

It wasn't the worst case he'd ever seen. It wasn't going to be the easiest. He probably should have taken Adam up on his offer to help.

"Do you want me to call for help?" Andie asked.

He shook his head and she'd have to deal with that answer for now. The cow tried to get to her feet but couldn't.

Oh man, that wasn't what he needed. He turned back to Andie and she was still leaning out, still watching.

"Call Clint."

He got the calf delivered before Clint got there, but the cow was still down. "Momma cow, we need you to get up and take care of this baby."

It happened sometimes, a cow got down, got sick and that was just the end of it. He couldn't look at Andie, sitting on the porch. He knew she'd be out there fighting to save that heifer if she knew what he suspected.

Clint's truck pulled into the driveway and Adam was right behind him. Ryder had never had a sentimental day in his life, but right at that moment, it was a pretty good feeling to be from his hometown. It was good to be where people knew him and where he didn't have to go far to find a helping hand.

The two were armed with calf starter in a bottle for the calf, several bottles of medication and a needle to give the cow the necessary shots. They climbed the fence as Ryder dried off the calf. It was the most pitiful looking little black baldy calf he'd ever seen. Black with a white face, its sides were caved in from dehydration and it kept coughing from the gunk in his lungs.

"That's a shame." Clint had lowered himself next to the cow and he injected her with antibiotics. "She's a good little heifer."

"Yeah, and if we don't do something, Andie's going to be down here trying to get her on her feet." Ryder took the bottle that Adam carried and pushed it into the little calf's mouth. It moved away a few times and then finally started to suck. It didn't take long for the little guy to put down the two liters of milk.

"Let's see if we can get her on her feet." Adam grabbed

the rope that Ryder had used to pull the calf. It was soaked and muddy. "What do you think?"

Ryder shrugged, so did Clint. Clint took the rope and put it around the cow's neck. Ryder was dealing with a calf that now thought he must be mommy. It was sucking at his jeans and at the hem of this T-shirt. It would have been cute if buckets of rain hadn't been falling on them and the momma cow hadn't been on her side in a puddle of water.

They were heaving on the cow when Andie came traipsing across the yard again.

"What are you doing up?" Ryder was in the process of sliding a rope under the cow's middle.

She stopped at the fence and watched. "I had to check on her because I know you aren't going to tell me everything."

"Andie, you have to get back on the porch. If Etta comes home and you're standing down here in the rain…" He stopped. "You know, it doesn't matter what Etta is going to say. You're an adult and you know better."

"Tell me how she is."

"She's going to die if we don't get her up."

"Ryder." Clint's voice was a little softer and Ryder thought that had to be Willow's influence. When had Clint Cameron ever been the guy with the soft touch? "Andie, we'll get her up and if we can get her in the trailer on my truck, I'll take her home and work with her. We'll get her back on her feet. You might have to bottle feed that calf, though."

"Thanks, Clint." Andie shot Ryder a smug smile. "Now I'll go sit back down. Just consider this my shower for the day."

Ryder watched her go. Rain was pouring down, and a crack of thunder gave him the motivation he needed to kick it up a notch. He had no desire to be standing under this tree when lightning hit.

Clint pulled on the rope, heaving and out of breath and Adam helped Ryder push the back end of the cow as she fought to get up.

She was finally on her feet.

"Let's take her out this corner gate right to the trailer." Clint leaned to catch his breath.

"We can take her to my place." Ryder didn't have his trailer, but they could put her in Andie's.

"Ryder, you have enough going on right now with Wyatt at your house and Andie needing you here. Let us do this one for you."

"I can manage."

"I didn't say you couldn't." Clint pounded him on the back. "But I'd say you've got your plate pretty full right now. And the next few months aren't going to get any easier."

"That's great to know."

Clint laughed, but he was still working, still moving the cow and working with her. "Yeah, well, that's how life is. When you think you've got it all figured out and think you know your next move, God surprises you with something huge. But seriously, it's about time you and Andie realized what the rest of us have known forever."

"Known?" He'd never had such a hard time forming sentences.

"Yeah, known." Clint shot him a look like he really should be getting it. "You and Andie haven't been far from each other's side in years. And when you thought Reese hurt her, you broke his nose."

"He deserved that."

"Yeah, he probably did." Clint led the cow a few wobbly steps toward the gate that Adam had opened. "But most guys wouldn't bust their buddy's nose for just any girl."

"She's…" He wasn't going to get baited into this conversation. Clint and Adam shot one another knowing looks and Ryder decided to ignore them. The odds of him taking the two of them were pretty slim, so it made sense to load the cow and forget this conversation.

He walked away from Clint's trailer telling himself that this was just part of his new life. Every guy in town was dating, getting married or recently married. And they didn't want to suffer alone.

Andie reheated Ryder's cheeseburger up while he changed out of his T-shirt into a button-up shirt he found behind the seat of his truck. When she heard him coming down the hall she poured a cup of coffee and sat it next to the plate.

Domestic. She'd never been one of those females, the kind that loved to cook and clean. She could make a decent burger or pancakes, she could brew pretty terrific coffee, but she had never seen herself as June Cleaver or Martha Stewart.

Ryder walked into the kitchen, stopping at the door. He eyed her, eyes on the meal and the coffee, and then back to her. She ignored him and poured herself a glass of milk, because she'd had her cup of coffee already.

"You should be sitting down. I could have done this. I could have made coffee." He didn't sit down.

"I wanted to do something for you. You've been doing everything for me for the past couple of weeks."

"That's because you've needed me to be that person, Andie. There's been plenty of times you've taken care of me."

"Yeah, but this is just not right, all of this sitting and letting people wait on me."

"You're not doing it because you're lazy. You're taking care of our baby. And I'm taking care of you." He pointed to the hall and she knew what that meant. "Back to the parlor, sweetie."

She grabbed her milk and walked past him down the hall. He followed a few minutes later with his coffee and plate of food. When he walked through the door she was back on the couch, her feet up, the pillow over her face.

He had the nerve to laugh.

She tossed the pillow at the end of the sofa. "You think this is funny?"

"I think you're suddenly a drama queen and you're not very good at it."

"How's my cow?"

"Clint thinks he can save her. You know how it is, Andie. She's in bad shape. The calf drank, though. We got some colostrum for him and added it to the milk replacer in the bottle."

"Thank you." She hugged a pillow to her stomach. "I'm sorry I had to call you."

"I'm not." He finished his burger and set the plate down. "Now, tell me what I can get you? Chocolate? Books? Something to drink?"

"Nothing." She pointed to the obvious. "I have books. I have magazines. I have the TV remote. The only thing I don't have is my life. I shouldn't resent that, should I?"

"I think it's probably natural."

"I don't want this baby to feel resented. What if she can feel it now, that I'm sick of sitting. I don't blame her, though. This is my fault. This whole pregnancy is my fault. You didn't ask for this to happen to you. If it wasn't for me, you'd be on your way to Vegas to the finals."

"Andie, I'm not blaming you. And this pregnancy isn't your fault. We, I think that's how this works. I made a decision to stay here. This is where I need to be. The finals aren't that important."

"Right. And you'll never resent that a night with me changed your life? This is exactly what we were worried would happen. We can't go back to being friends. I'm not even sure if we can go back to being us."

He moved to the table, the place that had become his in the past couple of weeks. She met his gaze, the dark eyes that always looked at her as if he knew her better than anyone else knew her.

"Andie, we'll make this work. We'll deal with it."

"Right, that's what we'll do, deal with it." She leaned back away from him, against the cushioned arm of the sofa and she closed her eyes. "I need to take a nap. That's one of the symptoms of the first trimester of pregnancy, being tired."

"I'm not leaving."

He got up and moved to the cushioned rocking chair a short distance away. He looked out of place in Etta's parlor and in that prissy chair. She smiled, watching him try to get comfortable. He stretched jean-clad legs in front of him and crossed his legs at the ankles. His hat was low over his eyes and he crossed his arms in front of him.

She was the one needing a nap and he'd probably be asleep long before her. If she even fell asleep. Mostly she wanted an excuse to stop talking about their lives and how everything had changed.

One thing hadn't changed. She loved Ryder. But Ryder thought she was nothing more than his best friend.

And the mother of his baby.

Chapter Thirteen

Something woke Andie up. A bad dream? A bad feeling. She turned and she was on the edge of the sofa. She moved back to keep from falling off. It took her a minute to put it all together, to remember that it was Tuesday and Etta was in Tulsa with Alyson. She sought the person who had been there with her when she fell asleep.

Ryder was still in the rocking chair. His head was bent forward, his hat covering his face. Soft snores drifted across the room. She smiled and curled back into the blanket that hadn't been on her when she fell asleep. And she tried not to think about it, about him hovering over her, covering her with the afghan that had been folded at the other end of the sofa.

Pain slid through her abdomen, catching her by surprise, taking her breath.

That's what had awoken her. It hadn't been a dream. It hadn't been just a bad feeling. She rubbed her belly and waited for it to end. It didn't. The cramping wrapped around her lower abdomen and held on.

"No," she whispered but it woke Ryder.

"What?" His voice was groggy his eyes a little foggy from sleep.

She needed a minute, just a minute to get her thoughts straight.

"I'm cramping again." She met his gaze and his brow furrowed. "It's my fault for going out to check on the cow."

"We left you here alone. I should have stayed with you." He stood. "We aren't going to sit and talk about this being someone's fault. We don't know what this is, or even if there's something that could be done to stop it."

"I know." Her heart tightened with dread, because she knew that there was nothing a doctor could do, not at this stage in her pregnancy.

He grabbed her shoes and a jacket that she'd left on the other chair. "Come on, let's go."

"Go?"

"To the E.R. Andie, we're not going to sit here and do nothing. We'll call Etta on our way."

"I don't want to call Etta. Alyson deserves to have this day without me interfering."

"Alyson would want you to interfere if…"

If she lost the baby. Andie slid her feet into the shoes he set on the floor for her and then she let him hold the sweater for her to slide her arms into the sleeves. They felt like a couple. She closed her eyes against another sharp wave of pain, and a similar one that invaded her heart that asked her what became of them tomorrow.

"I don't want to lose my baby." She looked up at him, not wanting to need him, but she did.

He sat down on the sofa with her. He touched her cheek and turned her to face him. "I know."

His kiss was sweet, gentle, and it made her feel strong. It made her feel loved. And she knew that wasn't what he meant to do with that kiss. She sighed into his shoulder and he hugged her close.

"Let's go, Andie."

She walked out the door at his side, her hand on her belly, her baby still safe inside her. And thoughts invaded, because she knew that when she returned to this house, everything might be different. The last thing she saw was the pile of clothes on the table next to the door, the little baby clothes that Etta had found in the attic, and an afghan that Andie's mom had tried to crochet years ago—when Andie was a baby.

The E.R. was bustling with late afternoon activity. Rush hour in Grove always resulted in plenty of minor fender-benders, the nurse informed them as they got Andie settled in a bed.

"You can't leave me this time." Andie waited until the nurse left and then she grabbed Ryder's hands. "Don't leave me."

"I'm not going anywhere."

"Please, don't be angry with me."

He sat down on the edge of the bed. "I'm not angry, Andie, I'm worried. This is my baby, too."

"I know."

"Do you? Because sometimes you act like you're in this alone. And you're not. We were both surprised by this, but I'm no less invested in this pregnancy than you are." His voice cracked. "That's my kid. It isn't something I planned, but after a couple of weeks, a guy starts to get used to the idea."

"I'm so afraid that this is God's way of punishing me."

He rubbed his thumb over her fingers. "Andie, you thought being pregnant was punishment. Now you think God's punishing you with problems. Why? Do you think God is sitting up there waiting for you and you alone to mess up so He can come up with new ways to punish you?"

"Consequences?"

"Yeah, okay, consequences. But you're wrong about this." He leaned close, touching her cheek. "Your whole life you've worried about being good enough. That's your mom's fault. And your fault for blaming yourself for her skipping out on you."

"If I'd been easier…" She choked on sobs that came in waves and Ryder grabbed her up and held her close.

"She messed up, not you."

"How does a mom walk out on a kid?" She leaned into his shoulder and all of the pain of her childhood came out, all of the feelings of being defective. Ryder held her tight, rubbing her back.

"You're not your mom."

"No, I'm not." She wiped at her eyes and moved away from him. "But if I lose the baby, you're off the hook."

"Oh, so now I'm your mom?"

"I don't know, Ryder. I don't even know what I'm feeling right now." More tears rolled down her cheeks and this time Ryder didn't hold her. "This could be the last day that I'm pregnant."

"I choose to have some faith, Andie. So, I'm not going to play this game with you."

The curtain opened and Dr. Ashford walked in. Ryder moved off the edge of the bed as the doctor washed her hands and pulled gloves out of the box on the table next to the bed.

"When did this start?" Dr. Ashford glanced at the curtain and motioned a tech into the room with a portable ultrasound.

"An hour or so. I woke up and was cramping then."

"Have you been staying down?"

"As much as possible. I had a cow get down today."

"She called me." Ryder shot her a look. "Andie, you

walked out into the yard and then back to the house. This isn't your fault."

Dr. Ashford smiled at him and then turned her attention back to Andie. "He's right. Now isn't the time to blame yourself. Now is the time to see what's going on. Any bleeding?"

Ryder stood up. "I'll wait outside."

"No. And, Ryder, stay. I don't want to be alone."

He sat back down. "I'll stay for the ultrasound."

Dr. Ashford slid a heart monitor over her belly and smiled.

"There's that heartbeat." She paused, frowned and moved it again. "Oh."

"What?" Andie's heart squeezed painfully and she watched, waiting for Dr. Ashford to smile, to say something.

"Let's get that ultrasound in here before I make any big announcements."

Andie leaned, waiting. And praying. Because she needed faith. And she needed God. She wasn't going to believe lies that she was being punished or tossed aside because she wasn't good enough. Old wounds. She tried to tell herself it was time to let them heal. It wasn't easy.

Dr. Ashford squeezed cold gel on her belly and reached for the ultrasound. The tech stood back as the doctor moved the gizmo over her belly, finding the baby, settling on the heartbeat. The doctor nodded and moved the ultrasound a little to the right.

Another heartbeat.

"You're a twin, aren't you?"

"Yes." Her heartbeat was echoing in her ears, beating in unison with the two heartbeats on the ultrasound.

"Andie, you're having twins."

"But there was only one."

"Yes, well, there wasn't only one, but we didn't hear baby number two the last time we checked."

"But they're okay?"

"Andie, they seem to be very okay. I want to do a blood test and keep you here tonight."

"Here, in the hospital?"

"For the night, yes."

Andie's body trembled and she reached for Ryder. His hand tightened around hers.

"Andie, we're having twins." His voice shook a little.

Two babies. Her life had changed, and then changed again. She looked at Ryder, and to her, he looked a little cornered. And that wasn't what she wanted.

She didn't want him stuck somewhere he didn't want to be, including in a relationship he never planned to have.

Dr. Ashford left them alone. She was going to arrange for Andie to have a room for the night, and she thought they might need to catch their breath. She made the last comment with a smile as she walked out the door.

Ryder whistled a low whistle. "Wow. Not only are we going to do this, but we're going to have twins."

"I'm sorry."

"Why are you apologizing? Andie, we've talked about this. I'm a part of this. I'm the dad. You aren't having a baby, we are having a baby. Two babies."

"Exactly. The guy who didn't want to get married or have kids is now going to have two."

"I know." He sat back in the chair and tried to think about that. "You're going to be on bed rest for a big part of the next seven months."

"Dr. Ashford didn't say that."

"No, but that's the way it works."

"Stop."

He stopped. He knew when a woman was at the end of the emotional rope swing and about to go off. Andie was dangling.

"We have to get married." He said it with as much conviction as he could, because it was going to take conviction to convince her.

"Excuse me?"

"Married, Andie. We can let Alyson and Jason have their day, but I think we should plan on a Christmas wedding."

"Haven't I already told you no, twice?"

"Yeah, but..."

"But we don't even know yet that the babies are okay. Have you thought of that? Have you thought about putting that ring on my finger and then..."

She could lose the babies.

Of course he hadn't let his thoughts go there. He was a little upset that she would. And he told her so as he stood up.

"Andie, you're emotional. I guess I'm pretty emotional right now, too. But this is crazy. Those babies deserve for us to be married."

"I don't want a proposal that's prefixed with 'this is the right thing to do.' Ryder, just go."

"Go?"

Dr. Ashford walked into the room. "Problem, kids?"

"No, no problem." Ryder grabbed his hat. "Her grandmother will be here in an hour."

"Oh, okay."

As Ryder started his truck, his better self told him to go back and wait. But he couldn't. He was so mad at Andie, he knew he'd say the wrong thing if he stayed.

She didn't need that right now. He didn't know what she needed. Definitely not anything he could give.

He'd done his best. He'd proposed three times.

He should have at least stayed to make sure everything was okay after the blood test. But he'd seen the babies, seen their hearts beating. Two of them.

That took a guy some time to adjust to. Two beds. Two ponies. Two frilly pink dresses and two infant carriers in the back of his truck.

Maybe she was right. He wasn't ready for this. He'd been doing the right thing, or what he thought was right, by proposing. But was that really the best thing for them, and for the babies?

Andie was in a darkened hospital room alone when Etta walked through the door, smiling like summer sunshine. Andie looked up, trying to smile back. She'd never felt less like smiling in her life.

She'd chased Ryder out of her room and she was afraid she'd chased him out of her life. But it was for the best. She didn't want him tied to her by guilt.

"Sugar bug, what in the world is going on? I went to the E.R., but they said you'd been moved up here and they didn't know anything."

"Dr. Ashford wants me to stay a night or two, just to keep an eye on the, on the…" she sobbed "…babies."

"Babies?"

"As in two. I was barely adjusting to the idea of one, and now there are going to be two. Two heartbeats, two little babies growing inside me."

"Which explains a lot. Where's Ryder?"

"Home." Andie pushed the button and raised the back of the bed.

"Now, I didn't expect that. He told me he'd wait with you, that he wouldn't think of leaving you alone."

"Yeah, well."

Etta set her yellow purse on the table next to the bed and poured a glass of water that she drank without offering it to Andie. Her lavender-and-gray hair was windblown and her red lipstick was smudged.

"Well, explain to me why Ryder went back on his word. Because Ryder usually keeps his word."

Yes, Ryder did keep his word. And if he promised to be at her side forever, he'd be there. Even if it wasn't where he wanted to be.

"I told him to leave. I am not going to keep him hooked to my side this way. I'm not going to use this as a way to force him into my life."

"Well now, that's new. I didn't know you wanted him in your life."

"Not like this, I don't. I don't want proposals that start with 'the right thing to do.' I want love." Tears streamed down her cheeks. "I want frilly stinking dresses, fluffy dry cake with jam stuck between the layers and a lot of people crying and wiping their eyes with lace hankies."

"Hormones."

"Probably." Andie took the hankie her granny dug out of her purse.

"You love Ryder. Andie, that's nothing to be ashamed of. It's been as clear as the nose on your face for as long as I can remember. It's just that you've spent a big part of your life playing it safe and pretending you were just his best friend."

Because she kept him in her life that way. The one way to run Ryder off would have been to let him know how she felt. Ryder had always run from females who were looking for forever. He had good reasons, she told herself, even though she knew he was nothing like his dad. He was nothing like his mom.

And now he'd be in her life as the father of her babies. They'd share weekends. They'd share school pictures. And her heart would break someday when he found someone he loved and wanted in his life forever, someone who got a real proposal.

"Andie, you're going to have to work this out. You're going to have to tell Ryder. Because I'm a pretty good judge of things, and I think he loves you, too. He's just afraid to love anyone."

"I know." She knew about his fears, not about his feelings for her.

"The other thing you have to work out is your relationship with your mother. She called and Alyson told her what is going on. She's flying in tomorrow."

"To help Alyson with the wedding?"

Etta shook her head. "No, to be with you."

Dr. Ashford knocked lightly on the door and stepped into the room. "Etta, did Andie tell you her news?"

"She did. We're so excited."

Dr. Ashford's gaze landed on Andie. "Are we excited?"

"Scared to death is probably more like it." Andie flipped off the TV because it was just noise.

"I think that's probably normal. Andie, a pregnancy like this can be hard on relationships."

Andie shook her head. "There isn't a relationship."

"Oh, there is one, whether the two of you want it or not. You're going to be parents and you're going to start out with double the joy, and double the work. That's a relationship."

"It isn't the end of the world." Etta patted her arm, her smile big, like she meant what she said.

All Andie knew for sure was that she felt sick.

Dr. Ashford touched her arm. "Andie, if you need anything, don't hesitate to call. I know things look a little frightening right now, but I promise you'll adjust. You have months to get used to this. And babies have a way of helping us to grow into parenthood."

"Yes, in most cases." Every single time Andie thought of parenting, she thought about her mother. And she didn't want it that way, with that memory hanging over her head.

Her mother would be there tomorrow. For her. The same woman who walked away, and now she was trying to walk back into Andie's life. She closed her eyes and breathed deep, fighting the sting behind her eyelids as tears tried to push through. She wouldn't cry.

Etta touched her arm and Andie opened her eyes.

"You'll be a good mother. And you're going to have plenty of help." Etta smiled in a way that said she understood.

"Andie, let me know if you need anything." Dr. Ashford patted her foot and walked out the door.

"Alyson is with Jason." Etta sat on the edge of the bed. "She wasn't with me when Ryder called. But I called to tell her what is happening. After that your mother called and Alyson explained the situation to Caroline."

"Call Alyson and tell her she doesn't have to come over. She and Jason have so much to do in the next month."

"I'll tell her, but I can't guarantee she won't come over."

The door opened a few minutes later. Andie's heart jumped a little, expecting it to be Ryder. Because he wouldn't stay gone. He'd never stayed away for long. It wasn't him, of course it wasn't. She had told him to go. It was a nurse's aid with a dinner tray. The young woman set two covered dishes on the table and opened the container of milk.

"Dr. Ashford told me to bring food for you and for your grandmother."

"Thank you." Andie raised her arms and the aid moved the table across the bed.

She was hungry, but she didn't know if she could eat. Her heart was still breaking, because she hadn't expected to want the person walking through her door to be Ryder. She hadn't expected it to hurt this much when he left.

Etta sat down in the chair next to the bed. She thanked the aid for their food and waited for the young woman to leave.

"Andie, I don't know what is going on with you and Ryder, but I know the two of you will work this out. You'll find a way to be parents to these babies. And I think you'll both do a good job at it."

"I hope you're right."

"Oh, honey, when have I ever been wrong?" Etta winked and then her smile faded. "Goodness gracious, what kind of food is this?"

Andie managed a smile, but it was hard to smile when she didn't know when Ryder would be back. She wouldn't let herself think the worst—that he wouldn't come back.

Chapter Fourteen

Ryder Johnson didn't run. Or at least he'd been telling himself that for the past few days. But it really felt like running. He'd taken his cue from Andie, and he'd run. It wasn't sitting too well with him. He'd called himself things like "yella" and "coward." But it was hard to shake off pretty serious changes to his life, and to Andie's.

He was going to be a dad—to twins. Every single time he thought that, which was often, it felt like a punch to the gut. But it wasn't all bad. He was adjusting. And it was starting to feel a little better, the idea of those two babies in this house.

Since he'd left the hospital, he'd been working on the nursery. The room was painted, all but the trim around the door, and he'd ripped up the carpet. Antique green with antique ivory trim. He didn't get all of these antique colors. His mom had worked hard to make this house look French country and anything but antique.

Ryder stepped back, wanting to see how the room looked from the door, as a first impression. He wasn't very creative, and he wasn't much of a painter, but he thought it looked pretty good. He wondered what Andie would say.

Not for the first time in the past couple of days he thought about calling her. But he wasn't going to push. He'd said what he had to say and now she had to come to terms with things, with life, and with them as parents.

When he left the other day he'd decided they both needed a few days to adjust and think. He had to admit to being knocked on his can with everything that had happened. First the pregnancy, and now twins. He shook his head and looked at the room he had meant for one baby.

Now he thought about how it would be to have the babies here part-time.

He put the brush down and walked around the room, trying to picture it with Andie here, and babies in that crib he was sanding down out in the garage. A room, a crib, a rocking chair and babies. He told himself not to put Andie in this room, not even in his imagination. Babies, yes; Andie, no. But he couldn't stop thinking about her in this room, in this house and in his life.

Floorboards in the hallway creaked. He turned and Wyatt walked in. He stopped just inside the door and nodded what Ryder hoped was his approval.

"You got it done. I guess that's why you've been up here with the door closed for the past two days." Wyatt wiped a streak of green off the trim at the door.

"Yeah, almost done. Still have to do the trim around the door."

"Word around town is that Andie Forester is having twins."

Ryder hadn't talked to his brother much since the night he came home from the hospital. He'd come home, went out to the barn and knocked around the old punching bag they had in one of the stalls. That was one thing their dad had done for them. He'd taught them to box. He'd given them an outlet. So after his fight with Andie he'd come home and put on boxing gloves.

"Yeah, we're having twins."

"Wow, that's huge."

"Thanks." Ryder put the cap on the paint.

"Is she going to marry you?"

"Nope. She says I have to say something other than 'I think we should.' I'm not sure what she wants from me."

Wyatt laughed, really laughed. "You can't figure it out? You know, everyone in this town thinks you're the ladies' man. But you're really just the guy who dated a lot of women. You know, to be honest, I've never figured out why you didn't date her."

"Because we're friends. I didn't want to mess that up by dating."

Wyatt had said it best; Andie was the longest relationship Ryder had ever had.

But he had messed it up. Instead of dating, he'd taken advantage of her when she needed him the most. He'd done a lot of praying about that, and he'd needed a lot of forgiveness.

"This isn't about protecting your friendship." Wyatt picked up the brush and stroked it across an area that looked smudged. Now that Ryder looked a little closer, maybe it was. He'd never said he was a painter.

"Well then, oh wise one, what do you think it is?" Ryder was about to get those boxing gloves again. It wouldn't be the first time he and Wyatt had settled something in the backyard under the security light.

Wyatt shrugged. "I guess I'd say you're selfish. You didn't want to lose your best friend so you never put yourself out there to see what other kind of relationship you could have with her."

"I asked her to marry me." Ryder growled the words

and then he took a deep breath and made his words come out a little quieter. "I asked her to marry me and she said no."

"You asked her like it was a solution to a problem."

"Yeah."

"Yeah? You're an idiot if that's all you can say. You're a clueless idiot and you don't deserve her."

"I'm not clueless… I know exactly what I feel." He stopped, shocked by his own words, and not surprised that Wyatt was smiling.

"Really, what do you feel?"

"I'm not going to hurt her." Ryder looked away from his brother. "I don't want her to be Mom. I don't want to start out thinking we can conquer the world and then someday realize we don't even like each other."

"I guess if you start out thinking someday you'll fail, or things will go south, then you're probably doomed."

"Yeah, I guess we are, but I love her too much to have her hurt that way."

"You love her too much to marry her and be a dad to those babies of yours. Like I said, idiot. You're not our dad. You're the guy who has been in this room for two days, painting it some prissy looking shade of green. You're the guy who has been down in the garage sanding a crib by hand."

Wyatt tossed the brush in the bucket and walked out of the room. Wyatt was getting it together. He'd even taken the girls to church. Ryder would have gone after him but he figured his older brother was figuring out his own life.

He had proposed to Andie by telling her it was the right thing to do. No wonder she was ticked off. And he'd left her in the hospital alone.

It would take a lot of paper to list the mistakes he'd

made in his life. And now, at the top of the list was the way he'd treated Andie.

Somehow he'd make it up to her. He'd find a way to show her that he loved her and that he wasn't going to let her down. He wasn't going to be the man who walked away from her. He wasn't going to walk out when things got tough.

But those were words he had to share with her. As soon as he got this room ready. He wanted to show her that he hadn't walked away and forgotten about her. This room was for her.

All this time working up here and he hadn't really thought about it that way. He'd been fixing a room for the babies. That meant having those babies living here, with him. And that meant Andie.

He couldn't picture this room without seeing her in it. And it was that image, man, that image of her, with her blond hair and the sun shining through the window, that made him want to have her in this house forever.

Because he loved her. He hadn't ever, not once in his life, let himself think those words about Andie. But he'd selfishly kept her tied to his side in the place of best friend.

Now he was going to find another way to keep her in his life. And he wasn't going to use the words that had gotten him thrown out of her hospital room.

Andie walked out to the barn. It was great to be able to come and go again. She'd tried not to overdo it, but it had been hard to remember that she still needed to take it easy. She wanted to go everywhere and do everything. She wanted to buy baby clothes in matching sets and pretty pictures for the walls.

The thoughts were pretty out of place in her life. Etta

called it nesting and said it would get worse as she got closer to her due date. She shuddered to think about it, about how bad it could get.

She'd had the same bedroom furniture, the same quilt, the same pictures on her walls since as far back as she could remember. And why? Because a girl didn't plan her wedding, or talk about children, when she was in love with her best friend and she knew that he had no intention of ever settling down.

She wondered how much he resented her for taking away his freedom.

Dusty whinnied when he saw her. He trotted up to the fence, his gold coat glimmering in the evening sun. He pushed his head at her, demanding attention and a treat. She pulled baby carrots out of her pocket and held them out to him. He sucked them off her hand, barely moving his lips.

And then she saw the alpaca. She laughed and tears slid down her cheeks. She touched her belly. "That's your dad's idea of romantic."

It wasn't chocolates or roses, although he had brought wilted flowers with the alpaca. But it showed how well he knew her, and how much he cared. He'd bought her an alpaca, a silly thing she wouldn't have bought herself.

"I can't believe he bought you an alpaca." Alyson walked across the yard, pretty and feminine.

Andie tried not to compare herself to her twin. But she did look down at her faded jeans tucked into worn boots. Two peas in a pod, they weren't. But they were connected. Andie should have hunted her sister down. It wasn't fair, that Alyson didn't know about them, but they'd known about her. They should have found her.

But Andie had been too stubborn. She'd decided, without any proof, that Alyson knew about them but didn't want to see them.

She was bad about that assuming thing. She had assumed for a lot of years that her mother didn't care about her. She was learning now, since Caroline's arrival the previous day, that maybe more connected them than Andie had thought.

Last night they'd talked about how it felt to be Caroline, leaving her life in the city, trading it for life in Dawson. And then having twin girls.

Last night Andie learned that her mother suffered from chronic depression. And she learned, from her mother, that the biggest difference between them was that Caroline had never felt like a part of Dawson. She had been the wrong fit for Andie's father.

But Andie and Ryder had always been here, always loved their lives here. They knew each other. They knew one another's dreams and goals.

Caroline had helped Andie see that. In a conversation that had been a little stiff, a little formal, Andie had learned about herself from her mother.

"Yeah, an alpaca." She finally answered Alyson's question. "What did you say Jason bought you, a baby grand?"

"Yeah, but Jason knows that I wouldn't have appreciated an alpaca. I think Ryder probably knows how much you'd love one. And you do, right?"

"He's the cutest, sweetest thing in the world."

"The alpaca or Ryder?"

Andie laughed at her sister's very obvious attempt at bringing the conversation back to Ryder. "The alpaca."

"Yeah, of course." Alyson leaned across the fence and scratched Dusty's neck. The alpaca walked toward them, a little slow, hesitant. "How do you feel?"

Andie shrugged. "Good, really. No more cramping. For now, no bed rest. I'm not looking forward to that last trimester. But Dr. Ashford assured me that if I take it easy now, maybe the last trimester won't mean a lot of bed rest."

"That's good to hear. You aren't a good patient."

"Thanks for that." Andie reached to pet the alpaca she'd named George. "I guess I need to try on my dress this week."

"That would be good. The seamstress says she can leave a little room. In case you've gained weight by the end of the month."

"I don't plan on doing that."

Alyson touched Andie's belly. "I have bad news for you. There's a little pooch here now."

"That's water weight."

"Of course it is. But about Ryder..."

"This had to come up, didn't it?" Andie turned away from the alpaca and they headed toward the house. "Did Etta send you out? She's been after me for three days. Your...our mother has been after me."

"The two of you not talking isn't going to solve anything."

"I never said that I'm not talking to him. He left. He didn't come back." Okay, she'd kind of wanted him to leave at the time, but he didn't have to stay gone.

"Tell him you love him. Give him the opportunity to do the right thing." Alyson said it with such conviction, looping her arm through Andie's as they walked back to the house. "He deserves that honesty from you if you're going to be good parents together."

"Yes, he deserves to know." That she loved him. But once the words were between them, what happened then? She had no idea. She didn't think it would change anything, though. There were some realities that mattered and wouldn't change. The fact that they were going to have twins was a big reality. He was going to be a dad. She was going to be a mom.

But the two of them together? She wondered if maybe she was being stubborn. She had been called stubborn once or twice. Maybe loving him was enough?

Maybe him loving the babies and being a good husband, being her best friend, was enough? Her heart picked up speed because she'd never felt more like God was showing her something, as if He was really showing her an answer to her prayers for herself and Ryder.

There were starting places in life. Most of those starting places had a lot to do with trusting God, even with a situation that you didn't know how to tackle, or how to face.

"I have to go." She walked through the back door of the house and grabbed her purse off the kitchen table.

"You have to what?" Caroline had walked into the kitchen. Andie paused in the doorway, because it still took her by surprise to see her mother in this house.

"I have to go talk to Ryder."

"Really? Are you done with the silent treatment?"

"I'm done. We have to come to an understanding. I think the understanding is that we're going to be parents and maybe 'I think we should' is a good enough reason to get married. For our babies."

"Oh." Caroline walked to the coffeepot.

"What?"

"Well, I'm glad you're putting the babies ahead of yourself." She poured her coffee and turned.

Andie stood at the door, not sure how to have another conversation with her mother. They'd never discussed the important things in life. They'd barely discussed more than the weather in the three times that they'd met. Except last night, when they'd gotten to know each other a little.

But it still felt like a new pair of boots. She wondered if that would always be their relationship?

Andie guessed probably so if that's all she expected. She breathed a little and let go. Because Caroline wasn't going away anytime soon.

"I love him." Andie slid the strap of her purse over her shoulder and she wondered if her mother saw the parallel between their lives, the way she was seeing it.

"I know you do." But Caroline had never approached anything with faith. Andie was holding fast to hers.

"I know you believe I'm doing the wrong thing. But in my heart I know that going right now and talking to Ryder is the right thing to do. I know that we have to stop being stubborn and be parents."

Caroline smiled. "You're doing the right thing."

Andie nodded and left. She hadn't needed to hear that from her mother, she already knew it. But it shifted things. A small empty space in her heart closed up a little.

Ryder carried the sanded cradle into the nursery. He planned on painting it that same ivory color. He thought that'd be the right color. First he had to figure out what kind of paint to use. Babies chewed on things. He knew that. Even toddlers chewed on stuff. He'd found Kat chewing on the kitchen cabinet.

He turned at a noise and smiled. Kat was sitting in the doorway, watching. She had a paintbrush and was pretending to paint the door. Fortunately she didn't have paint.

"Good job, Kat."

"Ryder, you have company," Wyatt shouted up the stairs.

Ryder had thought he heard a car come up the drive a few minutes earlier. He brushed his hands down the front of his jeans and wiped dust off his shirt. It might be Andie. Or it might not.

He wondered just how bad a guy could look after getting just a few hours' sleep over the last few days. He raked a hand through his hair and hoped for the best. When she came up the stairs, he was waiting for her. Kat was still sitting in the doorway, smiling at her pretend paint job.

"Hi." Andie stopped in the hallway, smiling, looking from him, to Kat, to the open door.

"You look good. I guess it feels good to be out of the house."

"Really good." She shrugged. "It might not last long."

He let his gaze slide to her belly. In a few months he'd be a dad. To twins. Andie was going to be the mother of his kids. And she'd never looked more beautiful. He wanted her to know that.

He took a few steps and when he was close enough, he ran his fingers through her hair, and pulled her closer to him, holding his hand at the back of her neck.

"You look beautiful." He whispered words that he'd never said to her before. And he should have. His teenaged attempts at being cool had included phrases like, "You look hot."

But she was beautiful.

"I'm beautiful?" She blinked a few times and shot a look past him. He turned, smiling at Kat who watched with all of the attention she typically focused on her favorite princess cartoon.

"Yeah, beautiful. I've been meaning to tell you that."

"When you were stumbling over words like, 'Hey, babe, how about you and me get hitched?'"

"I should have told you that you're beautiful and then said 'Hey, babe, how about if we get hitched.'"

"Not much better." She touched his cheek. "You look beautiful, too."

She stole his breath with those words and that moment. He had too much to say to stop now and hold her the way he wanted to hold her. If he didn't back up he'd never get the words out.

"Ryder, I'm here because I've had time to think, and I want to marry you. I want to raise our babies together." She bit down on her bottom lip. "You don't have to love me, but I love you. I've loved you for as long as I can remember, but I didn't want to lose you by saying something that would push you out of my life."

He hadn't expected that. She could have said almost anything and he'd have been fine, but he hadn't expected love. Or that she'd marry him. And he didn't even have to love her back.

He'd done that to her. All of his macho words about staying single and never falling in love had put these ideas into her mind.

Kat was giggling and she couldn't understand their conversation. He shot her a look and it didn't quell her two-year-old joy an ounce. She was beating on the door, grinning her kind of toothless grin.

Ryder turned back to Andie. "That's it, you love me? And now we can get married?"

Andie hadn't expected that reaction. She swallowed the lump that lodged in her throat. Maybe it was too late for those words. Maybe he'd changed his mind after her third rejection. Not that she blamed him.

And then he smiled. That smile that shifted the smooth planes of his face and took a girl by the heart, holding her tight so she couldn't escape if she wanted to. Andie didn't want to escape that smile or what it did to her heart.

"Andie, I want you to see what I've been doing." He took her by the hand and led her into the bedroom, past the very smiley Kat.

Andie had felt like crying a few times since she'd walked up the stairs and saw Ryder for the first time in three days. But this room, it undid her emotions. Emotions that were raw and close to the surface overflowed when she stood in the center of a room he had planned out and painted.

For their babies. He didn't have to tell her that this was a nursery. The colors and the box of nursery items said it all.

"This is beautiful." She walked around the room, stopping at the rocking chair next to the window. She pictured herself in that chair with her babies.

In this house.

She pictured late night feedings and a lamp glowing softly in the dark. She was holding her babies and Ryder was standing in the doorway, watching. He was leaning against the door frame, his hair a little messy and his feet bare.

She liked him like that. And she liked images of herself in this house.

"Why are you smiling?" Ryder had walked up to her and he leaned in, slipping his arm around her waist and pulling her close.

"I love the room." She touched his shoulder, sliding her hand down to his. "I love you."

He leaned, resting his forehead against hers. "I want you to marry me."

Okay, that was better than his earlier proposals.

"I'll marry you." She swallowed all of her fears, emotions that could become regret and she said it again. "I'll marry you. I want us to raise these babies together, to give them a home where they feel loved and protected."

"What about you?" He was still standing close.

"I'm sorry?"

"What about loving you?"

"You're my best friend."

Ryder reached into his pocket and pulled out the same ring he'd tried to give her three other times. But this time he held onto her hand and sank to one knee. He raised her hand to his lips and kissed her palm. He turned her hand over and slid the ring into place.

"Marry me, Andie. Marry me because I love you so much I can't breathe when you smile at me like that. I want to be more than the father to our babies. And I plan on having a bunch of them. I want to marry you because I love you."

"You love me." She dropped to her knees in front of him and cupped his cheeks in her hands. "You're not just saying that?"

"I'm not just saying that. I love you. It was easy, being your best friend and not worrying about hurting you or losing you. But I love you and I was hurting you. I hurt you by not being honest with you or myself."

"We're both pretty stubborn."

"We are." He lifted her hand and his ring glinted on her finger. He brushed a kiss across her knuckles and then he pulled her close and kissed her again.

Andie closed her eyes, letting her heart go crazy with his words. He held her close and his lips brushed hers again and again and then moved to her ear.

"We have an audience." He motioned toward the door with his head.

Andie glanced that direction and smiled. Kat was

standing at the door, holding it and watching, her thumb in her mouth.

"That's going to be our lives," she whispered.

"Yeah, I think I'm going to like it a lot."

She was going to like it a lot, too. She was going to love living in this house, being his wife and loving him as he loved her back.

Epilogue

Ryder woke up, wondering why Andie wasn't next to him in bed. It didn't take him long to find her. She was sitting in the rocking chair in the nursery. Her foot was on the cradle in front of her, rocking lightly. But one of his daughters slept in her arms. Both of the girls must have woken up.

He stepped into the room and peeked into the cradle at the sleeping, month-old baby girl. Her hair was blond, like her mother's hair. She slept on her side, her fist in her mouth.

The other baby was her identical sister. They were both blond with eyes that might turn brown. Or maybe blue. He'd insisted on matching pink sleepers.

"Which one is eating?" He peeked but couldn't tell.

Andie looked up at him, her features soft in the dim light of the lamp. She smiled and he would have done anything for her. He would do anything for her. Every moment since she'd married him and moved into his house, their house, had been better because she was part of his life.

And they were a family. In this house they were a family. With Wyatt and the girls in their own place—but always around, at church when they sat on the pew with Etta, Jason and Alyson, they were a family.

"They're your daughters and you can't tell the difference?" she teased.

"No, Mrs. Johnson, I can't. So, who is this?"

She lifted the baby girl and handed her to him. "This is your daughter who needs to be burped while I feed her sister."

He peeked at the tag inside the sleeper. "Ah, my darling Annette."

"Exactly. And Amelia is about to get her midnight snack."

"This is actually her 3:00 a.m. snack."

He pulled the second rocking chair next to Andie's. That had been a necessity when they'd found out they were having twins. Two rocking chairs. Two cradles. One crib because Andie and Alyson insisted the babies sleep together. And stay together.

These two little girls would never be split up. They would be protected and they would have parents who raised them with love and security.

Ryder was working hard to keep that promise to his wife and to his little girls.

"I love this room," Andie whispered into the quiet of the room.

"Me, too. I love waking up and having you here. I've never loved this house more than I love it right now."

"Do you know what I love?" Andie shifted her nursing daughter and turned to look at him. "I love looking up and having you standing there, watching me. I dreamed about that the day you proposed. I dreamed of seeing you standing there, your hair messy and your feet bare."

"Really, Mrs. Johnson, I had no idea."

"No, you have no idea." They leaned close together.

The kiss was sweet and a promise of something wonderful and lasting.

"I've always loved you, Andie." She cuddled her baby close and smiled, because nothing in the world felt better than being loved by her best friend and knowing that their children would grow up in a family where two parents loved them and they were there for them. Twenty years ago she had pulled petals off a daisy and prayed the last petal would tell her that he loved her. And he did.

* * * * *

THE COWBOY'S FAMILY

To my readers.
And especially to Julie, for your prayers,
your thoughtfulness and your insight.
To Stephanie Newton, for those
last-minute critiques!

Chapter One

Why had she thought this was a good idea, cleaning house for Wyatt Johnson? Rachel Waters cut the engine to her car and stared up at the big, brick home that Wyatt had built over the winter. She pushed her sunglasses to the top of her head as she mulled the reasons for being here. First of all, she'd agreed to this as a favor to Ryder and Andie. Second, she struggled with the word *no*.

There were plenty of reasons not to be here. She didn't need the money. She didn't need the headache.

She especially didn't need the heartache.

And Wyatt Johnson had heartache written all over his too-handsome face. Heartache was etched into his eyes. It was the whisper of a smile on his lips. It hovered over his lean features when he picked up his girls from the church nursery, hugging them but saying little to her or the other nursery workers.

So what had she gone and done? As if she didn't have enough to occupy her time, Rachel had agreed when Ryder Johnson asked her to clean the house his brother, Wyatt, had built on land across the road from the original Johnson ranch house, the house Ryder and his wife, Andie, now called home.

Rachel eyed the brick, French country-style home. The windows were wide, the porch was brick and stone. The landscaping was professionally done, but the flowers were being choked out by weeds.

It was a far cry from the parsonage she'd shared with her parents for the last year; since her dad took the job as pastor of the Dawson Community Church. Their little house could fit into this one five times. But the parsonage was immaculate. If her father could get hold of these gardens, he could do wonders with the place.

Oh, well, she couldn't put it off forever. She hopped out of her car. A border collie bounded toward her, tail wagging. The animal, black-and-white coat clean and brushed, rolled over at her feet. Rachel leaned to pet the dog's belly.

"So, at least you get some attention, huh, girl?"

That wasn't fair. Wyatt tried, she was sure he tried. But his girls often came to church with ragged little braids and mismatched clothes. Not that the girls seemed to mind. They smiled and hugged him, and then waited for him to pick them up again.

Rachel cast a critical gaze over the lawn and the house. The barns and fences surrounding the place were well-kept. The horses grazing in the fields gleamed in the early spring sunshine. She'd spent a lifetime dreaming of a place like this.

She walked up the patio steps and knocked on the back door. She stood there for a long time, looking out over the fields, talking aimlessly to the dog. She knocked again. From inside she heard children talking and the drone of the television.

She knocked a third time.

Finally footsteps headed her way and a male voice said something about the television show they were watching. She stepped back and the door opened. Wyatt Johnson stared at her, his dark hair longish. His brown eyes with flecks of dark green were fringed with long lashes. Gorgeous eyes and a gorgeous man. She nearly groaned. He stared at her and then looked down. Two little heads peeked out at her. Molly, age three, and Kat, age two. Molly had told her that she'd be turning four in a few weeks.

"Can I help you?" Wyatt didn't move, didn't invite her in. He just stared, as if he didn't have a clue who she was. Six months he'd been home. Six months she'd held his girls and read them stories. Sundays had flown by and each week he'd signed the girls in, signed them out and she'd asked how he was doing.

She was the invisible Rachel Waters. He was probably trying to decide where he knew her from.

"I'm here to clean," she explained, and she managed to smile.

"Clean?"

She held up the bucket she'd taken from her car and the tub of cleaning supplies. "Clean your house. Ryder hired me."

"He didn't say anything to me."

"No, he probably didn't. Surprise!" She smiled at the girls. They giggled. At least they thought she was funny.

Kat, hands pudgy, her smile sweet, pushed against Wyatt and slipped outside. Rachel wasn't invisible to Kat. Or to Molly.

"We have crayons."

"That's wonderful, Kat. Are you coloring a picture?"

Kat nodded. "For Mommy. Daddy said we could mail it to heaven."

"That's a lovely idea." That was the heartache in his eyes. Rachel didn't look up because she didn't want to see his pain. His story was his, private, that's how he'd kept it. She understood. She had her own stories.

Molly remained behind Wyatt, but she moved a little and peeked out from behind his legs. "I like coloring flowers."

"I think flowers are one of my favorite things, Molly. It's April, we'll have lots of flowers blooming very soon."

Rachel glanced up. Wyatt hadn't moved. He just stared for a long minute and then he shook his head and let out a long sigh. It sounded a lot like someone giving up. It didn't seem as if he'd changed his mind about her, though, because he didn't move an inch.

"I don't think we need help with the house."

Rachel peeked past him and her nose wrinkled. "I disagree."

He glanced back over his shoulder and shrugged. "It isn't that bad."

"It is bad." Molly waved a hand in front of her nose. "It's smelly bad. That's what Uncle Ryder said when he came home last week from the rodeo circus."

"Circuit," Wyatt corrected and then his gaze was back on Rachel. "I don't need help with the house."

He leaned against the door frame, faded jeans, bare feet and a T-shirt. She took a step back, putting herself out of his personal space and back into her own.

"Ryder already paid me." And she didn't like backing down. "I have a few hours free today, no time tomorrow. I'm not going to take his money and not do the job."

"Ryder should have checked with me. The girls and I were about to clean."

"After Daddy traces our hands and then does bank stuff." Molly supplied the information with all the innocence of an almost-four-year-old.

"Sounds like fun." Rachel stood on the porch, sun beating down on her back. Wyatt continued to stare and she felt fifteen and overweight. She wasn't, but that look took her back about fifteen years to a place in her life that she really didn't want to return to.

"Honestly, Rachel, we don't need a housekeeper."

"Sorry." She smiled and took a step forward. Ryder and Andie had warned her that he'd be stubborn about this.

"Yeah, I'm sure."

"So, I can come in?" Rachel glanced at her watch. She really didn't have all day.

Wyatt, tall and cowboy lean, shrugged and stepped back. He waved her in and she was pretty sorry she'd ever agreed to do this. Dishes covered the counters and the sink overflowed. Toys were scattered across a floor that hadn't seen a mop in, well, it looked like a long time.

"I guess it's a mess." Wyatt smiled a little and scooped up Kat to settle her on his shoulders. "We haven't really paid much attention."

She wanted to ask how he could not pay attention but that insult piled up on top of a dozen other things she wanted to say to him. His daughters were still in their pajamas and he hadn't shaved in days. This wasn't a life; this was hiding from life.

Wyatt had been home for more than six months and from what she'd seen, he hadn't done a thing to step back into life here, other than church on Sundays and meals at the Mad Cow. Oh, and he'd bought horses. He always had his girls in tow, though. She had to give him credit for that.

He couldn't match an outfit for anything, but he loved Molly and Kat.

So this was how his brother planned on pushing him back into the dating world. She was probably clueless and really thought this was about cleaning the house. Wyatt planned a few choice words for Ryder as Rachel Waters stepped away from him and leaned to talk to Kat, dusting his daughter's hands off in the process. The back of Rachel's shirt came up a little and he couldn't look away.

He must have made a sound because she straightened and shifted her shirt back into place. Her face was a little pink and she glanced away from him as she pulled her dark, curly hair into a ponytail. She continued to ignore him and he couldn't stop thinking about a butterfly tattoo at the waist of her jeans. Did the church nursery worker have secrets?

A little late he remembered to be resentful. His younger brother had a habit of pushing his way into people's lives and shoving his ideas off on them. Rachel cleaning the house was Ryder's idea.

Wyatt kept his own ideas to himself, the way he'd been doing for the last few months. He didn't have time or energy to worry about Rachel or what Ryder was up to.

"I guess if you're here to clean, have at it." He nodded in the direction of the kitchen. He'd put a lot of thought into building this house. Granite countertops, stainless steel appliances and tile floors. It should have gleamed. Instead it looked like a bunch of teenagers had ransacked the place.

He hadn't meant to reminisce, but he remembered his parents' kitchen after it had been ransacked by Wyatt, Ryder and their friends. He and Ryder hadn't been easy to raise. Not that their parents had done a lot of raising; more like they'd just turned them loose and told them to do whatever, as long as they didn't land in jail.

Rachel looked around the kitchen, her mouth open a little. Yeah, it was pretty bad. He didn't have time to do everything. The girls came first, then the farm, then business. Last, and probably least, the house.

"Need anything?" he asked, turning his attention back to Rachel Waters.

"No, thanks. If you don't mind, I'll get started." She smiled, a wide smile that settled in dark brown eyes.

"I don't mind. I'll be in the office with the girls. Don't worry about upstairs."

"Seriously? Wyatt, your brother paid me a lot. I really don't want to do a halfway job."

Kat was tugging on his hand, wanting him to help her finish drawing a pony. He glanced down at his daughter and then back to the woman standing a short distance away. She was already moving around the kitchen, picking up trash and tossing it, putting dishes next to the sink. Long curls were held in a ponytail and she wore flip-flops with her jeans.

The shoes made a flap-flap sound on the tile floors that distracted him for a second, until she cleared her throat.

"Upstairs, Wyatt?"

He glanced up, meeting brown eyes and a hint of a strawberry-glossed smile. Molly's hand slid into his and he squeezed lightly, holding her close, grounded by her presence and shifted back to reality by her shoulder against his leg.

Eighteen months of holding it together, just trying to be a dad and trying to make sense of life, and now this. This, meaning Rachel Waters and the sudden realization that he was still a man. He blinked a few times, surprised that he'd noticed anything other than the broom she held in her hand. When was the last time he'd noticed a woman's lips? Or her hair?

He'd seen her at church every Sunday, though. It wasn't the first time he'd noticed her, her smile, her laugh. It wasn't the first time she'd taken him by surprise.

"Yeah, sure, go ahead. The bedrooms are fine, though. The girls clean their own. Kind of." He grinned down at his daughters because that cleaning part was an exaggeration. "Anyway, there are a couple of bathrooms up there."

"Good, I'll clean those, too." She grabbed a broom and swept at his feet. "Scoot, now."

Scoot. Molly was already pulling him toward the hall. He glanced back at Rachel. She had turned on the CD player hidden under the upper cabinets and in moments Sara Evans was singing about a runaway teen leaving the suds in the bucket and the clothes hanging on the line.

As his daughters led him down the hall to the office, he could hear the chorus of the song and Rachel singing along. Her voice got a little louder on the line about wondering what the preacher would preach about on Sunday. He shot a look back in the direction of the kitchen, but the wall blocked her from sight.

Kat was dragging him into the office, jabbering about ponies and wondering when she would get one of her own. She was two. He considered reminding her of that fact, but she'd been reminded more than once.

For the next couple of hours the girls colored pictures and he went over farm accounts and receipts for taxes that had to be filed. The vacuum cleaner rumbled overhead. Rachel was still singing. She was always singing. Even when he picked the girls up in the nursery at church he could hear her singing to them.

He should be glad about that, that someone sang to them, someone soft and feminine. And she laughed, all the time. At least with the kids she laughed. He tried to remember the last time he'd really laughed. He watched his daughters trade crayons and he remembered. Kat had done something that made him laugh. They laughed more than they had six months ago. Far more than they had a year ago.

He shook his head and glanced back at numbers blurring on the ledger he'd been staring at for the last hour. Ryder had just about let the ranch run into the ground. Not financially, just upkeep, the things that required sitting still.

His cell phone rang and he reached for it, distracted. Wendy's mom's voice said a soft hello. Mother-in-law? Did he still call her that? She was still grandmother to his girls. A week didn't pass that she didn't call to check on them. More than once a month she and William, her second husband, drove up from Oklahoma City to visit.

He didn't want to sound paranoid, but he thought it was more like spying. It was Violet's way of making sure he was surviving and that her granddaughters were being taken care of. He didn't really blame her. There had been a few months when he hadn't been sure if he was going to make it.

"Violet, how are you?"

"I'm fine, of course. The question is, how are you?"

The Southern accent should have been sweet and maternal. Instead it held about a dozen questions pertaining to his sanity.

Which was just fine.

"Good, Violet. The girls are coloring pictures and we're getting ready to eat lunch." He glanced at his watch and winced. It was past time for lunch.

"Isn't it a little late for lunch?" She never missed a thing. He smiled.

"A little, but we ate a late breakfast." That probably didn't sound better, but he wasn't going to lie to her.

"Right. Well, I thought I'd come up this week, just to…"

"Check up on us?"

"Of course not. Wyatt, you know we love you and the girls. I miss…"

Broken sentences. He held back the sigh. In the last eighteen months they'd talked in broken sentences, half-finished thoughts and unspoken accusations.

"I miss her, too." He finished the sentence for her.

"So, about this week?"

It wasn't a good week for a visit. He leaned back in his chair and stared out the window at the overgrown lawn. He needed to hire a lawn service. "Sure, Violet, I'll be here."

The vacuum cleaner stopped.

"What's that noise?" Violet asked.

"Ryder hired a housekeeper."

"Oh. Well, that's good."

"I guess it is."

"And a cook?"

Of course it came back to cooking. He smiled a little. "I don't need a cook."

She didn't respond for a minute. "Okay, Wyatt. Well, I'll call and let you know what day I'll be up."

No, she wouldn't. He slipped the phone back in his pocket knowing full well she'd launch a sneak attack when he least expected it.

He leaned to kiss Molly on the top of her head. "You girls stay here for a second. I'm going to talk to Miss Rachel and then we'll blow up our balloons. Later we'll go to town."

To the store for groceries and a cookbook for dummies. Maybe he could learn to cook before Violet showed up.

Molly shot him a narrow-eyed look. Kat ignored him. The girls were like night and day. Molly was her mother all over, but she looked like him. Kat looked like Wendy. They both had dark hair, but Kat's was a little lighter and she had Wendy's light brown eyes. It was getting easier to stare into eyes that reminded him of his wife.

He hurried up the stairs and met Rachel in the hall-way. She picked up her bucket of cleaning supplies and then smiled at him. Perspiration glistened on her brow and her hair was a little damp. But the upstairs smelled clean for the first time in a long time.

The windows gleamed at either end of the hall and there were no cobwebs clinging to the ceiling. Maybe a housekeeper wasn't such a bad idea. It might be a great idea. But he didn't know if Rachel Waters was the one he wanted. She wore faded jeans and had the tiniest butterfly at the small of her back. Shouldn't a housekeeper wear something more…housekeeperish?

He pictured Alice from *The Brady Bunch*. Or the robot maid from *The Jetsons*. Yeah, that's what a house-keeper should look like. A housekeeper should make

PB and J sandwiches and smell like joint cream, not wild-flowers.

"Is there anything else I need to do?" She stood in the center of the hallway, the bucket in her hand, and he'd lost it for a minute.

"No, nothing else." He glanced around. "It looks great, though."

"I'm glad you approve. Listen, I know this isn't what you wanted, but if you ever need me to come over again, just call. I can even watch the girls if you need time away."

Time away from his girls. He needed that less than anything. He needed them with him, all the time. He didn't ever want them to be alone and afraid again. She didn't know that, though. There were details that no one knew but Ryder, Andie and a few others. He'd left Florida to escape those memories. Florida, where he and Wendy had been in youth ministry after college.

"Thanks, I appreciate that. I don't usually leave them, other than in the church nursery. But I do have to head out in a few minutes and I wanted to make sure Ryder paid you enough."

"He did." She brushed strands of damp hair back from her face. "Are you sure you don't want me to stay with the girls?"

"No, I'll take them. I'm just going to the store."

Because he had separation anxiety and so did they. It was about the least manly statement he could think of to make, so he didn't. He glanced out the window, which gleamed and the fingerprints the girls had put on the glass were gone.

She smiled. "Okay, but the offer stands."

"Thanks."

Rachel headed down the stairs with the bucket. He followed. Her shirt stayed carefully in place. He kind of hoped…and then again, he didn't. He shook his head and worked hard to pull it together.

She stopped at the bottom of the stairs. The girls ran out of the office, pigtails and sunshine. His sunshine. He hugged them both close. But they broke out of his arms and ran to Rachel. She didn't hesitate, just pulled them close and hugged them as she kissed the tops of their heads.

His phone rang again, not a moment too soon because he needed the distraction from the scene in front of him. Rachel walked away with his girls. He watched them as he raised the phone to his ear.

"Wyatt, how did you like your surprise?" Ryder laughed from five hundred miles away.

"Thanks."

"Is she done cleaning?"

"Yeah, the house looks great. I'm going to think of a nice surprise for you when you get back."

"You should be more appreciative. You have a clean house and a pretty woman to clean it."

"I wouldn't talk like that in front of my wife if I was you."

"She knows I only have eyes for her. But you, on the other hand…"

"Ever heard of the word *subtle,* little brother?"

Ryder laughed, louder, longer. Wyatt held the phone away from his ear.

"I guess subtle has never been my thing," Ryder admitted.

"Listen, I have to go shopping. Remind me that I owe you for this. And the payback won't be pleasant."

Rachel walked toward him, the laughter gone from her dark eyes and he didn't even know why. He couldn't let that be his problem. He had enough girl problems. One was two and the other was almost four. They were more than enough to keep him busy and keep him guessing.

"I'm going now." She stared straight at him, her gaze unwavering. She had a few freckles on suntanned cheeks.

"Okay, well, thank you." He didn't have time for this. "Look, I appreciate what you did. The place looks great. I just…"

"Don't need a housekeeper?"

He shrugged off the sarcasm in her tone. They both knew that he needed a housekeeper. What he didn't need was that little smile of hers making him feel as if he needed a housekeeper and an intervention.

"Yeah, I don't need a housekeeper." It hadn't been what he'd planned to say, but it worked.

What he really didn't need was someone who smelled like spring and who reminded him of everything he'd lost.

Chapter Two

Rachel drove away from the Johnson ranch and she was pretty glad to see it in her rearview mirror. She wanted to be a good distance away before the girls released the balloons with messages to their mother. It wouldn't have done anyone any good to have Rachel crying by their side.

She really should have known that she wouldn't be able to do this, spend more time with them, and stay detached. After years of considering herself a real pro at detachment, two little girls and a cowboy were going to be her downfall. The signs had been pretty obvious. The girls had been in the nursery and her preschool Sunday school class for six months and it had been way easy to fall in love with them.

Of course Wyatt wasn't included in those emotions. She felt sorry for him, nothing else. After hearing his conversation with Ryder, she knew he felt about the same for her.

It shouldn't matter to her what he thought. At twenty-nine, when she finally knew who she was and what she wanted out of life, Wyatt Johnson's opinion shouldn't matter. But old feelings of inadequacy didn't care what she thought of herself now. Those old emotions had a way of pushing to the surface when she least needed them.

So what? She would never be homecoming queen and guys like Wyatt Johnson always laughed behind her back.

It didn't matter anymore. She wasn't the fat girl in school or the rebel in the back of a police car trying to prove to people that she wasn't the good little preacher's kid.

She knew who she was, and who God wanted her to be. She worked in children's ministry, helped when her mother's lupus flared, and she loved her life in Dawson.

All of those pretty sermons to herself didn't take away a sudden desire for a big, fat chocolate bar. Or brownies with ice cream. She reached for her purse and dug her hand through the side pocket for a pack of gum. As she drove she managed to get a stick of peppermint gum out of the package.

She shoved the gum in her mouth and chewed, trying to pretend it helped the way chocolate helped. It didn't.

Forget Wyatt, she had other things to do. She was supposed to work for Etta Forrester that afternoon. Etta designed and sewed a line of tie-dye clothing that she sold to specialty boutiques around the country. Etta made sundresses, skirts, pants, tops and even purses. Rachel worked for her a couple of days a week, more if Etta needed. With Etta's granddaughter, Andie, married to Ryder Johnson and Andie's twin, Alyson, married to Jason Bradshaw, Etta had more need for help these days.

She drove down the road and pulled into Etta's driveway. The bright yellow Victorian with the lavender wicker furniture on the wide porch managed to lift Rachel's spirits. Etta stood on the porch with a watering can in her hand and a floppy hat covering her lavender-gray hair. She waved as she poured water on the flowers. Last week she'd made a trip to Grove and she'd come home with a truckload of plants for the baskets and flower gardens.

Rachel parked under the shade of an oak tree and stepped out of her car. As she walked up the wide steps of the porch, Etta put down the watering can and pulled off her gardening gloves. Her nails were long, painted purple and never chipped. It was a mystery how Etta could take care of this farm, make her clothing and always be perfectly manicured.

The one time Rachel asked how she did it, Etta laughed and said, "Oh, honey, life teaches those little skills."

Rachel doubted it. She always felt about as together as a pair of old shoes falling apart at the seams. She couldn't paint her nails without smudging at least one. And her hair. The only good thing that had ever happened to her hair was a ponytail holder.

"Good to see you, honey." Etta slipped an arm around Rachel's shoulders. "I thought we'd have tea out here before we get started on those T-shirts."

"Tea sounds wonderful."

"You look about wrung out. Did you clean Wyatt's house today?"

Rachel nodded and picked dead blooms off the petunias.

Etta lifted her sunglasses and stared hard. "Well, tell me how it went."

"The place was definitely a mess." She shrugged and

kept plucking blooms, tossing them over the rail into the yard. "And so is Wyatt."

"Oh, he isn't such a mess. He just needs a little time." Etta lifted the little watch she wore on a chain around her neck. "Goodness, speaking of time. I'm going to keep watering. Do you want to bring the tea out?"

"I can do that."

Etta had lowered the sunglasses. The big rhinestone encrusted frames covered half her face. "And try not to look so down in the mouth, honey. You're going to depress me and you know I don't depress easily."

Rachel smiled. "Is that better?"

"Not much." Etta laughed and went back to watering. "I'll be back in a few."

"I'll be here."

The dog that had been sleeping under a tree started barking as Rachel fixed the tea tray. She picked up the wooden tray and headed down the hallway to the front door. The door was open and a breeze lifted the curtains in the parlor. Voices carried on that breeze.

"So you think you're going to learn to cook something more than canned spaghetti and hamburgers?" Etta laughed and said something else that Rachel didn't hear.

She stopped at the screen door and looked out. Etta was standing on the sidewalk and Wyatt stood next to her. Etta's skirt flapped in the breeze. Wyatt had taken off his hat and held it behind his back. They were both facing the opposite direction and didn't see Rachel.

"It can't be that hard to learn, Etta. I've got to show Violet that I'm capable."

"Of course you're capable." Etta turned and waved when she saw Rachel. "There's Rachel with my tea. Well, have a seat and while you have tea, I'll look for a cookbook."

"I appreciate it, Etta, but I don't have time for tea. The girls are waiting in the truck. We're going grocery shopping."

Etta argued, of course she did. "Well, get the girls out."

Wyatt laughed, white teeth flashing in a kind of hot smile. He shook his head. "I'm not getting them out of the truck. If I do, I'll never round them up and get them back in the truck. I just thought rather than taking my chance with any old cookbook I found in the store, I'd see if you had one that spelled it all out."

Etta held the rail and walked up the steps, Wyatt following. "I'll see what I have. Something with casseroles would be best."

"If I can throw the whole meal in one pan, I guess that would be the best thing."

"You ought to know how to cook, Wyatt. It isn't like you're a kid."

"I never thought much about it, Etta." His neck turned a little red. "I guess I always thought…"

Etta's eyes misted and she patted his arm. "I'll be right back. I'll pick you out a couple and you'll be cooking us dinner in no time."

After Etta walked away, Rachel didn't know what to say. She hadn't been at a loss for words in years. Probably about twenty-eight of them. Her mom liked to tell people that she was talking in complete sentences when she was two and that she'd been talking ever since.

But at that moment she was pretty near speechless and so was Wyatt Johnson.

"My mother-in-law is coming to visit." He had placed

the cowboy hat back on his head. He leaned against the rail of the porch, tall and confident. His boots were scuffed and his jeans were faded and worn in spots.

How many people would guess that the Johnson brothers had part ownership of a bank in Tulsa and subdivisions named after their family? She only knew those things because Andie, Wyatt's sister-in-law and Etta's granddaughter, had told her. Andie had married Ryder Johnson before Christmas and their twin babies were due in a month or so.

"I see." She nearly offered to help, and then she didn't. She'd already told him she'd clean or watch the girls. He'd rejected both offers.

"She's worried that I'm not coping." His smile lifted one corner of his mouth and he shrugged. "I guess it won't hurt me or the girls to have a home-cooked meal once in a while."

"I imagine it won't." Rachel poured her tea. "Do you want a cup?"

"No, thanks. I like my tea on ice and out of a glass that holds more than a swallow."

She smiled and listened for Etta's footsteps. Etta would give him a long lecture if she heard him demean her afternoon tea ritual.

It was a few minutes before Etta appeared, her arms holding more than a few cookbooks. "Here's a few to get you started."

"That's a half dozen, Etta, not a few."

"Well, you can find what you really like this way."

He took the books from her arms. "Thanks, Etta. Rachel, see you at church."

He nodded to each of them and walked down the steps.

The truck was pulling down the driveway when Etta laughed a little and whistled. "That's tension you could cut with a knife."

"What?" Rachel nearly poured Etta's tea on the table.

"The two of you, circling like a couple of barn cats. I'm no expert, but I think it's called chemistry."

"I think it's called, Wyatt knows that everyone, including his brother, is trying to push me off on him."

"And would that be such a bad thing?" Etta sat down on the lavender wicker settee.

"I'm not sure, but I think he believes it probably would be."

"What about you?"

Rachel sipped her tea and ignored the question. Etta smiled and her brows shot up, but Rachel didn't bite. No way, no how was she chasing after Wyatt Johnson or any other man, for that matter. She'd done her chasing, she'd had her share of fix-ups, and she'd learned that it worked better to let things happen the way they were supposed to happen.

Or not. But she had decided a long time ago that being alone was better than pushing her way into the life of the wrong person.

It had been two days since Rachel cleaned and his house still looked pretty decent. Wyatt stood in the kitchen with its dark cabinets, black granite countertops and stainless steel appliances. A chef's kitchen for a guy who had to borrow cookbooks because he couldn't make mac and cheese. That was pretty bad.

He hadn't planned it, but Rachel was front and center in his mind again. She was a strange one. First glance and he would have thought she had all the confidence in the world. But the other day on Etta's porch, there had been something soft and kind of lost in her expression, in those dark eyes of hers.

Not that it was any of his concern.

He dropped bread into the toaster and started the coffeemaker. Excited voices and little feet pattering overhead meant the girls were up. His day was about to start.

At least he'd had fifteen minutes to himself. That didn't happen often these days. It hadn't happened much in the last eighteen months. Since Wendy left him.

He stopped in front of the kitchen window and looked out. For a minute he closed his eyes and remembered that he used to pray. He used to believe that with Wendy he could build a life far from this ranch and the chaos of his childhood. He opened his eyes and shook his head. Prayer these days was abbreviated. It went something like: *God, get me through another day.*

That would have to do for now. It was all he had in him, other than anger and guilt.

Eighteen months of trying to figure out what he could have done differently. He was still trying to come to terms with the reality that he couldn't have done anything more than he'd done. Wendy had made a choice.

The choice to leave him and their daughters. She wrote a note, opened a bottle of sleeping pills and she'd left them for good.

Eighteen months of wondering what he could have done to stop her from going away.

He breathed in deep and it didn't hurt as much as yesterday, even less than a month ago. He was making it. He had to make it—for the girls. He had to smile and make each day better for them. And he calculated that he had about two minutes before they hit the kitchen, ready for breakfast. Two minutes to pull it together and make this day better.

On cue, they rushed in, still in their pajamas. Man, they made it easy to smile. He leaned to hug them and pulled them up to hold them both. He brushed his whiskered cheek against Kat and she giggled.

"What are we going to do today, girlies?"

"Get a pony!" Kat shouted and then she giggled some more.

"Nope, not a pony." He kissed her cheek.

"Let Miss Rachel clean again." Molly's tone was serious but her smile was real, her eyes shining. She knew how to work him.

He sat both girls on the granite-topped island that sat in the center of the kitchen. "Miss Rachel? Why do you want her to clean?"

He liked the idea of a clean house, but he was determined to find a nice grandmotherly type. He wanted control top socks and cookies baking in the oven. It sounded a lot less complicated than Miss Rachel I've-Got-Secrets Waters.

Kat sighed, as if he couldn't possibly be her dad or he would understand why they picked Rachel. She leaned close. "She hugs me."

"She draws pictures and sings." Molly crossed her arms and her little chin came up. "She has sheep."

"I'm sure she does. But she's really busy with church and helping Miss Etta."

"She doesn't mind cleaning." Molly was growing up and her tone said that she had a handle on this situation.

"Look, girls, she just cleaned for us that one time. Uncle Ryder hired her." He reached into the cabinet under the island and pulled out a cereal box. Add that to his list for the day. He needed to go to the store again. Even though he'd had a list, he'd forgotten a lot. "How about cereal?"

"And a pony?" Kat grinned and her eyes were huge.

A pony. Would it work to buy himself a break from this?

"Maybe a pony." He was so weak. "But first we have to eat breakfast and then we need to go outside and feed the horses and cows we already have."

He lifted them down from the counter and sat them each on a stool at the island.

"You girls are getting big."

Molly. He shook his head because she wasn't just big, she acted like an old soul, as if she'd had to learn too much too soon. And she had.

Most of it he doubted she remembered. If she did, the memories were vague. But she remembered being afraid. He knew she remembered that.

He took bowls out of the cabinet and set one in front of each girl and one for himself. He opened the cereal cabinet door again and looked at the half-dozen boxes. "Chocolate stuff, fruity stuff or kind-of-healthy stuff?"

The girls giggled a little.

"That does it, you get kind-of-healthy today. I think you've had way too much sugar because you're both so sweet." He grabbed the box and then reached for the girls and held them, kissing their cheeks. "Yep, sweet enough."

Normal moments, the kind a dad should share with his daughters. Eighteen long months of going through the motions, but they were all coming back to life. They were building something new here, in this house. They would have good memories. He hadn't expected to have something good for his family here, in Dawson. His own dad hadn't provided that for him and Ryder.

But he wasn't his dad. He guessed he learned something from his dad's mistakes. Like how to be faithful. And how to be there.

His phone rang and he answered it as he poured cereal into three bowls. Two partially filled and his to the top. He talked as he poured milk and dug in a drawer for spoons. When he hung up both girls were looking at him.

"I have to go pick up something for Uncle Ryder." He ate his cereal standing across the counter from the girls.

"A pony?" Kat giggled as she spooned cereal into her mouth. Milk dribbled down her chin and her brown eyes twinkled.

"No, a bull."

"We can go?" Molly didn't touch her cereal and he knew, man, he knew how scared she was. He was just starting to get over it, *he* hadn't been a two-year-old kid alone with a mommy who wouldn't wake up.

That kind of fear and pain changed a person. Molly was watching him, waiting for him to be the grown-up, the one who smiled and showed her that it was okay to be happy.

"Of course you can go." He took a bite of cereal and she followed his example. She even smiled. He let out a sigh that she didn't hear.

Fifteen minutes later he walked out the back door with them on his heels. Today they'd slipped back into the old pattern of leaving dishes on the counter and dirty clothes on the floor in the bedroom. He didn't have time to worry about it right now. He'd barely had time to pull on his boots and find his hat.

Horses saw him and whinnied. The six mares in

the field closest to the house headed toward their feed trough. He whistled and in the other field about a dozen horses lifted their heads and headed toward the barn, ready for grain.

A quick glance over his shoulder confirmed that Kat and Molly were close behind him. They weren't right on his heels now, but they were following, grabbing up dandelions and chasing after the dog.

He turned away from the girls and headed for the fence. He watched for a chestnut mare. She walked a short distance behind the others. Her limp was slight today. She'd gotten tangled in old barbed wire out in the field. Sometimes a good rain washed up a lot of junk from the past.

This mare had stepped into that junk one day last week after a gully washer of a rain. He'd found her with gashes in her fetlock and blood still oozing from the wound. She headed for the fence and him, the extra attention over the last week had turned her into a pet.

A car driving down the road honked. He turned to wave. The red convertible slowed and pulled into his drive. The girls hurried to his side, jabbering about Rachel's car. He had worked hard at building a safe life for his girls.

What was it about Rachel that shook it all up? He glanced down at his girls and they didn't look too scared.

He tossed the thought aside. Rachel was about the safest person in the world. She was a Sunday school teacher and the preacher's daughter.

So what part of her life had been crazy enough for butterfly tattoos?

Rachel had meant to drive on past the Johnson ranch, but the girls waving dandelions had done it for her. She had seen them from a distance, first noticing the horses running for the fence and then spotting Wyatt and his girls. She had slowed to watch and then she'd turned.

As she pulled up to the barn she told herself this was about the craziest thing she'd done since... She had to think about it and one thing came to mind. The tattoo.

She'd thought about having it removed, but she kept it to remind herself to make decisions based on the future and not the moment. So what in the world was she doing here, at Wyatt Johnson's? He probably wanted her around as much as she wanted to be there.

This was definitely a spontaneous decision and not one that was planned out. Stupid. Stupid. Stupid.

The girls dropped the dandelions and raced across the lawn, the dog at their heels. As she pushed her door open, Molly and Kat were there, little faces scrubbed clean and smiles bright. No matter what, he'd done a great job with the girls, even if he did seem to be color-blind. That had to be the reason the girls never seemed to have an outfit that matched.

This time they were in their pajamas.

"What are you girls up to?"

"We're going with Daddy." Molly held tight to her hand.

Wyatt had disappeared. Into the barn, she decided. She could hear him talking and heard a door shut with a thud. He walked back out, his hat pulled down to block the sun from his face. He had a bag of grain tossed over his shoulder, his biceps bulging.

She let the girls tug her hands to follow him. He stopped at a gate and unlatched it with his free hand. Cattle were at a trough, waiting. From outside the fence she watched him yank the string on the top of the bag and pour it down the length of the trough. He walked back with the empty bag. After closing the gate he tossed the bag into a nearby barrel.

And then he was staring at her. The hat shaded his face, but it definitely didn't hide the questions in his dark eyes. And she didn't have answers. What could she tell him, that her car suddenly had a mind of its own? But she'd have to think of something because the girls were pulling her in his direction.

"What are you up to today?" He pulled off leather gloves and shoved them in the back pocket of his jeans.

She didn't have an answer. The girls were holding her hands and she was staring into the dark eyes of a man who had been hurt to the deepest level. And survived. Those eyes were staring her down, waiting for an answer.

She was on his territory. She'd never felt it more than at that moment, that territorial edge of his. He protected the ones he loved.

"I saw the girls and I realized you might not know about our church picnic Wednesday evening. Instead of our normal service, we're roasting hot dogs and marshmallows."

It wasn't a lie, she had forgotten to remind him. He seemed to need reminding from time to time. He had a degree in ministry and yet church seemed to be something he forced himself to do. She got that. She had done her share of avoiding church, too.

He'd actually been in youth ministry until eighteen months ago.

"Sounds like fun." He glanced at his watch.

"I should go. Listen, if you need anything, any more help around here…"

"Right, I'll let you know."

She should have known better than to think he'd want to talk. A momentary glitch in her good sense had made her believe that he might want a friend. But then, he probably had friends. He'd grown up here.

"See you two Wednesday." Time to walk away.

Kat grabbed her hand. "Come and see my frog."

"Kat, you don't have a frog." Wyatt reached for her but Kat pulled Rachel the other direction and two-year-olds were pretty strong when they had their mind set on something.

"I have a frog." She didn't let go and Rachel didn't have the heart to tell her no. She went willingly in the direction of an old log.

"Is that where your frog lives?"

"There are millions of frogs." Kat dropped to her knees and pushed the chunk of wood. Sure enough, little frogs hopped out. Actually, they were baby toads. She didn't correct the toddler.

"Wow, Kat, there are a bunch of them." Rachel kneeled next to the child. "Do you have names for them?"

Kat nodded. "But I don't 'member."

"I think they're beautiful. I bet they like living under this log."

Kat nodded, her eyes were big and curls hung in her eyes. Rachel pushed the hair back from the child's face and Kat smiled. A shadow loomed over them. Kat glanced up and Rachel turned to look up at Wyatt. He was smiling down at his daughter. The smile didn't include Rachel.

He had a toe-curling smile, though, and she wanted her toes to curl. Which was really just plain wrong.

"Kat, we have to go, honey." He got hold of Molly's hand. "I have to finish feeding and you two need to be getting ready to jump in the truck."

"We're getting a pony." Kat patted Rachel's cheek with a dirty hand that had just released a toad back to its home under the log.

"Are you?" She looked up and Wyatt shook his head.

"We're picking up a bull."

"I see." Rachel stood and dusted off her jeans. "I could stay here with them, Wyatt."

She had offered the other day and he'd said no, so why in the world was she offering again? Oh, right, because she loved, loved, loved rejection. And to make it better, she loved that look on his face when his eyes narrowed and he looked at her as if she had really fallen off the proverbial turnip truck.

He took in a breath and she wondered why it was so hard for him to leave them. "No, they can go with me."

"But we could stay, and Miss Rachel could help us draw pictures." Molly bit down on rosy lips and big tears welled up in her eyes. "I always get carsick."

"I'm sorry, I shouldn't have said anything."

"That's a thought." Wyatt picked up his little girl. "Molly, you're going with me."

She nodded and rested her head on his shoulder.

"I'll see you later." Rachel brushed a hand down Molly's little back.

Yes, driving up here had been the wrong thing to do. She leaned to kiss Kat's cheek and then she walked away. She had a life. She had things to do today. She definitely didn't need to get tied up in the heartache that was Wyatt Johnson's life.

She made it to her car without looking back.

* * *

Wyatt put Molly down and he held tight to Kat's hand because he had a feeling that if he let go, she was going to run after Rachel. Molly was looking up at him, as if she was wondering why in the world he wasn't the one running after her new favorite person.

He needed this as much has he needed to hit his thumb with a hammer. If God would give him a break, he'd get the hammer and hit his thumb twice.

He wasn't going to run after a woman, not one who made more trouble in his life. And that's what she was doing. She was causing him a lot of trouble. She was upsetting the organized chaos of his life with her sunny personality and cute little songs.

She was getting in her car and Kat was next to him, begging him to stop her. He stared at the preacher's daughter in jean shorts and a T-shirt. Not for himself, for Kat. Man, he didn't need this. He let go of his daughter's hand and went after Rachel. Yelling when she started her car. Waving for her to stop when she put it in Reverse.

The radio was blasting from the convertible. She loved music. He shook his head because today she was listening to Taylor Swift and a song about teen romance gone wrong. He really didn't need this.

She had stopped and she turned the radio down and waited for him to get to her. This was proof that he'd do anything for his girls. He'd even put up with Miss Merry Sunshine for a couple of hours if it made Molly and Kat smile.

When he reached the car she turned and lifted her sunglasses, pushing them on top of her head. He realized that her eyes were darker than he'd thought, and bigger. They were soft and asked questions.

"The girls really want you to go with us. I thought it might help. They'll be bored if this takes too long."

She just stared at him.

"I'll pay you," he offered with a shrug that he hoped was casual and not as pathetic as he imagined.

She laughed and the sound went through him. "Pay me?"

"For watching them."

She was going to make him beg. He shoved his hat down a little tighter on his head and then loosened it.

"You don't have to pay me. It would be kind of fun to see that bull. Is it one they'll use for bull riding?"

"Yeah, probably."

"Fun. Where should I park?"

He pointed to the carport near the barn. "That'll keep it a little cooler. I have to finish feeding and the girls have to get dressed."

"Can I help?"

Hadn't she helped enough?

"No, I can do it." He walked away because it was a lot easier than staying there to answer more of her questions. He knew it probably seemed rude, but she didn't have a clue.

She didn't know that he was rebuilding his family and that it took every bit of energy he had. Everything he had went to his girls, into making them smile and making their lives stable.

As he walked into the barn he glanced back. She leaned to talk to Kat. Curls fell forward, framing her face, but a hand came up to push her hair back. She smiled and leaned to kiss his daughter on the cheek. And then the three of them, Rachel, Kat and Molly, headed into the house.

He walked into the shadowy interior of the barn and flipped on a light. He breathed in the familiar scents. Cows, horses, hay and leather. He could deal with this. He couldn't deal with Mary Poppins.

Chapter Three

If it hadn't been for Kat and Molly she wouldn't have climbed into this truck and taken a ride with Wyatt. But the girls, with their sweet smiles and tight hugs, they were what mattered. Little girls should never hurt. They shouldn't hide their pain in cheesecake or think their self-worth depended on the brand and size of their jeans.

Oh, wait, that had been her, her childhood, her pain.

"You aren't carsick, are you?" Wyatt's voice was soft, a little teasing. Yummier than cheesecake. And she hadn't had cheesecake in forever.

She glanced his way and smiled. "I don't get carsick."

"Good to know. The girls do. Not on roads like this, fortunately."

"We keep a trash can back here," Molly informed her with the voice of young authority. Rachel heard the tap, tap of a tiny foot on plastic.

She looked over her shoulder at the two little girls on the bench seat behind her. Kat's eyes were a little droopy and she nodded, her head sagging and then bouncing up. Molly looked as if she had a lot more to say but she was holding back.

Poor baby girls. Wyatt loved them, but there was an empty space in their lives that a mom should have filled. And they wouldn't even have memories of her as they grew older. They would have pictures and stories their dad told.

If he told stories. She chanced a quick glance in his direction and thought he probably didn't tell stories about the wife he'd lost. He probably had a boatload of memories he wished he could lose.

"Here we are." He flipped on the turn signal and smiled at her as he pulled into a gated driveway. "Can you pull through and I'll open the gate?"

"I can open the gate." She reached for the door handle and opened it, ignoring his protests. It was a lot easier to be outside away from him. A soft breeze blew in warm spring air and she could hear cattle at a nearby dairy farm.

She loved Oklahoma. Growing up she'd lived just about everywhere, but mostly in bigger towns and cities. She'd never felt like she belonged. Maybe because she had always been the pastor's kid, poor in wealthy subdivisions, trying to fit in. Or maybe because deep down she'd always wanted to be a country girl.

She had wanted to jump out of trucks and open gates. She had studied about sheep, wool and gardening. Pitiful as it sounded, she'd watched so many episodes of *The Waltons,* she could quote lines. She couldn't think about it now without smiling.

The truck eased through the gate and stopped. She pushed the gate closed and latched the chain. When she climbed back into the truck, Wyatt wasn't smiling.

"I said I'd get it." He shifted into gear and the truck eased forward again.

"I don't mind."

"No, you don't."

Oh, no, he hadn't! She shot him a look. "I'm not five. I don't mind opening gates. I really don't have to *mind* you."

His brows went up. He reached for the hat he'd set on the seat next to him and pushed it back on his head. The chicken wasn't going to comment. She glanced back at the girls and smiled. Kat was sleeping. Molly stared out the window, her eyelids drooping.

Wyatt parked next to the barn, still silent. But when she glanced his way, she saw the smile. It barely lifted the corners of his mouth, but it was there.

"This shouldn't take long." He opened his door and paused. "I think you and the girls can get out and look around."

"Thanks, we'll do that. If you think I can handle it. After all, I'm five."

"You're not five. You're just…" He shook his head and got out of the truck. He didn't say anything else. He opened the back door of the truck and motioned for the girls to get out. He set each of them on the ground and then glanced back in at her. "Getting out?"

"Yeah, I'm getting out."

She'd been crazy to stop at his house. She was still trying to figure it out. He smiled at something Kat said. Oh, that's right, now she remembered. It was that smile. She wanted him to smile like that at her.

"Wyatt, good to see you."

She turned to face the man who'd spoken. He stood outside the barn and everything about him said "rancher." From his dusty boots to his threadbare jeans, he was a cowboy. His skin was worn and suntanned, making deeper lines around his mouth and crinkles at his eyes. His hair was sun-streaked brown. He winked at her.

"Jackson, I'm surprised to see you here. I thought your brother was meeting me." Wyatt stepped toward the other man, hand extended.

"Yeah, he's at the bank. You know, he's Mr. Work-aholic."

"Got it. So what are you doing these days?"

"Oh, trying to stay away from trouble. But most of the time, trouble just seems to find me." He smiled at Rachel. "Hi there, Trouble."

Heat climbed her cheeks.

"Jackson Cooper, meet Rachel Waters. Her father is the pastor of the Dawson Community Church."

If Wyatt had used that introduction to put the other man in his place, Jackson Cooper didn't look at all embarrassed. "If our pastor's daughter looked like you, I might just get right with God."

Wyatt wasn't smiling. "Okay, let's look at the bull."

"You gonna ride him?" Jackson laughed.

"I doubt it."

"Chicken?" Jackson Cooper obviously didn't know about backing down. She thought it might be a family trait; not backing down. She had heard about the Coopers. There were about a dozen of them: biological and adopted.

"Nope, just smarter than I used to be. I haven't been on a bull in a half-dozen years and I don't plan on starting again."

"There's a lot more money in it these days," Jackson continued, his smile still in place.

"Plenty of money in raising them, too." Wyatt turned

to his daughters. "You girls stay with Rachel and I'll be back in a few minutes."

The men left them and Rachel smiled down at the girls. "I think we should make clover chains."

One last glance over her shoulder. Wyatt picked that moment to stop and watch them, to watch his girls. Rachel turned away.

"Nice bull." Young, but definitely worth the money the Coopers were asking. Wyatt watched the young animal walk around the corral. He was part Brahma, long and rangy with short legs. He'd been used in local rodeos last year and was already on the roster for some bigger events.

"Want me to get a bull rope and chaps?" Jackson leaned over the corral, a piece of straw in his mouth.

"No, I think we know what he'll do. And we know where you live if he doesn't."

"He'll go out of the chute to the right for about four spins and then switch back and spin left. He's got a belly roll you won't believe."

"Your brother Blake told Ryder that he isn't mean." Wyatt continued to watch the bull. The animal pushed at an old tire and then stomped the dusty ground.

"He's never hurt anyone. But he's a bull, Wyatt. They're unpredictable, we both know that."

"Yeah, I know we do." They'd lost a friend years ago. They'd been teenagers riding in junior events when Jimmy got killed at a local event.

"That was a rough one, wasn't it?" Jackson's sister had dated Jimmy.

"Yeah, it was rough." He brushed away the memories. "Do I write you a check?"

"Sure. So, is she your nanny?" Jackson nodded in the

direction of Rachel Waters. She was in the large yard and the girls were with her. They were picking clover and Rachel slipped a chain of flowers over Molly's head.

Wendy should have been there, doing those things with their daughters. He let out a sigh and refocused on the bull. It took a minute to get his thoughts back on track. Jackson didn't say anything.

"No, she isn't." Wyatt pulled the checkbook out of his back pocket. "I like the bull, Jackson. I don't like your price."

Jackson laughed. "Well, now, Wyatt, I don't know that I care if you like my price or not."

"He isn't worth it and you know it."

"So what do you think would make him worth it?" Jackson's smile disappeared. Yeah, that was the way to wipe good-natured off a guy's face, through his bank account.

"I've been thinking of adding Cooper Quarter Horses to our breeding program. I'd like one of your fillies." His gaze swept the field and landed on a small herd of horses. One stuck out, but it wasn't quite what he'd planned to ask for. "And that pony."

"You want a pony. Shoot, Wyatt, I'll throw in the pony. We'll have to talk about the horse, though. This bull's daddy was Bucking Bull of the Year two years in a row. He isn't a feedlot special."

"Okay, let's talk." Wyatt let his gaze slide to where the girls were still playing with Rachel. Kat was sitting on the grass, a big old collie next to her. Molly and Rachel were spinning in circles.

They needed her. The thought settled so deep inside of him that it ached. His girls needed Rachel. Maybe more than they needed him. He couldn't make chains with clover or even manage a decent braid in their hair.

"Do you think she'd go out with me?" Jackson walked over to the gate and tugged it open. "I mean, if you're not interested."

"I'm not interested." Wyatt walked through the gate, sidestepping a little snake that slid past. "I'm not interested, but I think maybe you're not her type. Shoot, I'm probably not her type either."

"Yeah, well, I always had this idea that when I settle down it'd be with a woman like her, the kind that goes to church on Sundays and probably makes a mean roast." Jackson shot him a smile. "Yeah, a guy would live right with a wife like her."

"Right." He'd had enough of this talk. "Let's take a look at the pony first. How old?"

"Ten. He was my niece's. But Tash is getting older and Greg bought her a bigger horse."

"I don't want to take someone's pony."

"He's just eating grass and getting fat."

Wyatt stopped in front of the paint pony. It was a pretty thing, brown and white spotted with a black mane and tail. The pony lifted its head from the clover that it was munching on and gave him a look.

"He isn't mean?"

"Never seen him be mean."

Wyatt knew all about horse traders and lines like that. He wasn't about to take Jackson Cooper's word for it. He patted the fat pony and leaned against him, holding his mane to keep him close.

"Yeah, but I want a little more reassurance than that, Jackson. This is for my kids."

Jackson walked up and lifted a leg to settle it over the

pony's back. His normal smile had disappeared and he was all serious. "Wyatt, I might be a lot of things, but I can tell you this: I wouldn't get a kid hurt. This pony is the safest one you'll find. I broke him myself and I wouldn't be afraid to let my own kids on him. If I had a kid."

Wyatt nodded and he didn't take his eyes off the pony. Even with part of Jackson's weight on his back, the little pony hadn't moved, hadn't been distracted from the clover he was tugging at. He didn't even startle when shouts from the gate meant that he'd been spotted by the girls.

The girls were on the gate, standing midway up, waving. Rachel stood next to them, her smile as big as theirs. He wondered if she was still dreaming of having a pony someday? He'd known girls like her his whole life. Wannabe cowgirls. He used to like them. They were fun on a Friday night at a rodeo in Tulsa. They were easy to impress and soft to hold.

That had been a lifetime and another Wyatt Johnson ago. Before. His life fell into two slots. Before Wendy, and after. The first half had been full of hope and promise. The second was about getting it back.

He was just standing there, staring, when Jackson waved them into the field. They yelled and before Rachel could open the gate, they were running toward him. The little pony looked up, watching, dark ears pricked forward. Yeah, he'd do for a first pony.

Rachel caught up with the girls halfway across the field and spoke to them. He watched them settle and reach for her hands. One on each side of her.

Jackson whistled and shook his head, laughing a little. Wyatt shot him a sideways glance and shoved his hands in his pockets.

"Keep it to yourself, Jackson."

"I'm just saying…"

"Yeah, I know what you're saying." He wasn't blind.

And then the girls were there, Rachel standing quietly behind them. They were all hands, reaching for the pony, saying it was the prettiest pony ever. Jackson Cooper looked as if he had created the thing himself and set it in front of them with a ribbon.

"Be careful, girls." Rachel moved closer and her hand went out, reaching to brush through the pony's mane.

"What do you think, girls? Would this be a good pony?" Wyatt wanted to be the hero. He'd been fighting the pony conversation for a while. They were still little, still needed to be held and couldn't brush their teeth alone. He'd been on horses his entire life, but that was different. When it came to his girls, it was different.

Molly nodded. "This is a perfect pony named Prince."

"Actually, his name is…" Jackson grinned. "His name is Prince."

Rachel smiled at him. Wyatt lifted his hat and settled it back in place. "We'll take him. And a filly."

"Let's talk price." Jackson looped a bit of rope around the pony's neck. "Can you girls lead Prince back to the barn so we can load him in the trailer?"

Molly was nodding, her hands moving in anticipation, but Jackson handed the lead rope to Rachel. Wyatt started to tell them to be careful, but he clamped his mouth shut. He hadn't been real good at letting go lately. It wasn't easy, letting someone else take care of Molly and Kat. It wasn't easy watching them with someone who was not their mother.

But they needed this. They needed to let go of him once in a while.

His good intentions almost came undone when half-way to the gate Rachel stopped, picked up Molly and then Kat and placed them on the back of that pony. Kat was in front and Molly wrapped her arms around her sister. Rachel stood close to them.

"Might as well breathe and let it go, Wyatt." Jackson laughed and slapped him on the back. "Two things are going to happen. They're going to grow up, and that woman's probably going to get under your skin."

Wyatt didn't smile. He watched as Rachel led the pony with his girls on it through the gate and then he settled his attention back on Jackson Cooper and the filly he wanted.

And he repeated to himself that Rachel Waters wasn't going to get under his skin.

Chapter Four

Stupid moment number twelve. Or maybe twelve thousand? That's what Rachel thought of volunteering to ride along with Wyatt and the girls to get that bull. And it was even worse standing in the shade watching Wyatt unload the pony from the trailer. He had hauled the pony and his new filly home. He'd left the bull for Jackson Cooper to trailer for him.

The girls stood next to Rachel, waiting for their dad to give the all clear. They fidgeted in one spot because they knew better than to run at the pony.

Wyatt led the filly, a dark bay two-year-old, into the barn. The horse pranced alongside him, her black tail waving like a banner. The filly dipped her head a few times and whinnied to horses in the field who answered back with shrill whinnies to the new girl in town.

Wyatt walked out of the barn a few minutes later. The filly was still inside, her shrill whinny continued. Wyatt pulled off his hat and swiped his brow with his arm. The girls were tugging on Rachel's hands, but she didn't let go. Somehow she managed to stand her ground.

He had told them to wait. She was more than willing to do what he asked. She was content to stay in one spot and watch as he stepped back into the trailer to retrieve the pony.

The second he stepped out of the trailer with the pony the girls started to jabber. Kat was pulling on her hand. Rachel leaned and picked the child up. When she looked up, Wyatt watched, his smile gone, his expression unreadable. He turned away and led the pony to the small corral next to the barn.

He closed the gate and tied the lead rope to the pole fence. "Come on over."

She put down Kat and the girls ran toward him. He held up his hand and they slowed to a walk. Rachel followed because it was time to say goodbye. It had been a good day. The girls were wonderful. Wyatt was a wonderful dad who loved his daughters.

He probably thought Rachel could be a decent friend.

She'd had a lifetime of being the best friend, the girl that guys called when they wanted a pal to hang out with. Funny that when she lost weight all of those best friends started looking at her in a different way.

Wyatt untied the lead rope. "If you want to hold her, I'll get the bridle and saddle."

"I can do that." So much for the quick escape. She took the rope and their fingers touched. She looked up, into dark eyes that held hers for a long moment. She looked away, back to the girls. Things that were easy.

Kat and Molly had climbed up on the bottom pole of the fence. They reached through and little fingers found the pony's mane.

"I'll be right back." Wyatt glanced from her to his daughters and then he walked away, disappearing through the side door of the barn.

And she should do the same. She should tell him she had things to do today. She needed to clean her room or weed the garden. There were plenty of things she could have been doing.

It might be a good idea for her to go home and spend time in prayer.

When he came back with the tiny saddle and bridle, she opened her mouth to explain that she should go. But he smiled and she stayed.

She stayed and held the little pony as Wyatt lifted Kat and Molly onto his back. They rode double the first time, so that neither of them could say they got to ride first. Rachel stood by the gate watching as he led them around the corral. Kat was shaking the reins she held in her little hands, trying to make the pony run. Molly had her arms wrapped around her sister's waist and her smile was huge.

Wyatt lifted Molly off the saddle and put his hat on Kat's head. The black cowboy hat fell down over the child's eyes. She didn't mind. She had a pony.

Molly trudged across the arena and stopped next to Rachel. The little girl watched her sister ride the pony around the arena and as they got close, Molly started to bounce up and down.

"Might want to stand still, sweetie. We don't want to startle the pony," Rachel warned.

"Daddy said he didn't think a train going through would make him scared."

"He's a pretty special pony."

Molly looked up, her smile still splitting her little face. She nodded and continued to bounce as Wyatt headed their way with Kat in the saddle.

As he pulled one daughter down and lifted the other,

Rachel stood close. "I should go now. Thank you for letting me go with you today."

Wyatt took the hat off Kat's head and placed it on Molly's. He turned to Rachel, his smile still in place. The hair at the crown of his head was flat from wearing the hat.

"Thanks for going. Are you sure you don't want a turn?" He teased with an Oklahoma drawl and a half smile.

"No, I think probably not. My feet would drag on the ground and the poor pony would need a chiropractor."

"I doubt that." He handed the reins to Molly. "Hold tight, kiddo."

"Have fun with the pony." Rachel leaned to kiss Kat's cheek and she waved to Molly the cowgirl. "See you at church Wednesday."

She turned to walk away, but Wyatt touched her arm, stopping her. She smiled because he looked as surprised as she did. His hand was still on her arm, warm and rough against her skin.

"All joking aside, I really do appreciate you going with us today. I know the girls loved having you along."

She shrugged and his hand slid off her arm. "I enjoyed it as much as they did."

And then she stood there, unmoving. The moment needed an escape route, the kind posted in hotel rooms. It should read: In case of emergency, exit here.

Wyatt remembered the Wednesday evening bonfire fifteen minutes before it started. He pulled into the parking lot of the church and the fire was already going, and people were gathered around in lawn chairs. He killed the engine on his truck and glanced in the backseat.

"Oh, man, we really should have done something with

your hair." But the girls' hair had been the last thing on his mind as they rushed out the door.

He'd spent the day working the new bull, bringing it into the chute and bucking it out with a dummy on its back. He knew that it would buck, he just wanted to see for himself what they'd gotten themselves into. In the next week or two he'd take him over to Clint Cameron's and let some of the teens that hung out over there give him a try.

But the bull aside, he'd also had to put out a fire in the kitchen. A cooking experiment had gone very wrong. Good thing he'd remembered the Wednesday evening bonfire. He smiled at the girls. Both had dirty faces, pigtails that were coming undone and boots with their shorts. He was pretty sure this was a real fashion catastrophe.

At least they were at church. He got out and opened the back door for the girls. They clambered down from the truck, jumping off the running board and then heading off to join Rachel and the other kids.

She was the pied piper of girls, big and small. Teenagers followed her around, talking as she worked. Sometimes she gave them jobs to do. As he stared she glanced quickly in his direction.

"She's our bonus."

He turned and Etta smiled at him.

"What does that mean?" He shoved his keys in his pocket and walked across the big lawn with Etta. He thought to offer her his arm, but she would have laughed and told him she was able to walk on her own steam.

"I mean, we got a great pastor and pastor's wife and Rachel is the bonus. She does so much in the church. Our youth and children's ministries have doubled. That's why Pastor Waters is thinking of hiring a youth minister."

"I'm not interested."

"In Rachel you mean?" Etta smiled and headed in the other direction.

"You know what I mean," he called out after her. She turned and waved, ornery as ever. And he loved her. He thought back to the hard times in his life. She had been there, getting him through every one of them. She'd even flown down to Florida after Wendy died. She'd stayed a month, helping with babies, helping him to breathe.

"Wyatt."

This time it was Jason Bradshaw and his wife, Alyson. The happy couple headed is his direction. There was too much romance going on in this town for his comfort.

"How are you two?"

"Good. I'm glad to see you here. We're going to have music after we eat. We can always use another guitar, if you have yours."

"I left it here last week." Wyatt scanned the yard for his girls.

He saw them in the playground. Molly had just gone down the slide. Kat had her arms around Rachel's neck and was being carried to the swing.

"Then I'll find you when we're ready to get started." Jason followed the direction of his gaze and smiled.

"Sounds good. I need to check on the girls."

"Right, check on the girls." Jason laughed and shot a pointed look in the direction of Rachel Waters.

Wyatt ignored the insinuation. He headed across the lawn toward the playground. Rachel sat on a bench, Molly in front of her. She had ponytail holders in her mouth and a brush in her hand. When he got close enough she looked up and smiled.

"Do you mind?"

He shook his head. "No."

But he did mind. For reasons he didn't get, he minded. It might have been about her, or about himself, maybe it was about Wendy, but he minded.

She scooted and he got that it was an offer. He could sit down and let people say what they wanted or he could walk away. And people would still talk. It wouldn't be malicious, the talk. No, it would be pure Dawson. Everyone would be hoping to fix him.

Option one seemed like the best bet. He sat down next to her. Kat hurried to him and climbed on his lap. Her hair had already been fixed. He hadn't noticed from across the lawn.

Molly sat quietly. She never sat that still for him. Rachel talked about their pony, talked about s'mores and ran the brush through his daughter's tangled brown hair. When it was smooth she pulled it back, brushed it smooth again and held it tight. She had placed the ponytail holders on her wrist and she took them off, wrapping them around the ponytail, holding it firm at the crown of Molly's head.

"There you go, sweetie." Rachel kissed her cheek.

"You make it look easy."

She smiled at the comment. "It takes practice. You'll get the hang of it."

He wasn't so sure.

After cooking hot dogs and marshmallows in the fire, Rachel sat with the kids, making a circle around Jason, Wyatt and some others. The men started with a few praise songs and then switched to contemporary Christian music. The teens clapped and sang along.

Molly and Kat climbed into her lap, both of them snuggling close. She held them tight and pretended it didn't hurt. But it did. The other children had gone off to their mommies.

Molly and Kat had turned to her while their daddy sang. She wrapped them in an extra blanket her own mother had brought and the two dozed in her lap. Firelight flickered. The songs were softer, sweeter. She closed her eyes and listened.

When she opened her eyes her gaze sought another, connecting, holding. Wyatt looked away first, shifting his gaze down, to the strings of his guitar.

Etta moved from her chair and joined Rachel on the ground. She lowered herself onto the blanket and reached for Kat.

"Let me help you with that little sweet thing." Etta held the child close. "I do love these babies."

"Me, too." Rachel exhaled and a chill swept up her back. The night was getting cooler, the air was damp. The fire was burning out and the heat no longer reached where she sat.

"We should wrap this up." Jason Bradshaw put his drum down and looked around. The crowd had seriously disappeared. "Wow, where'd everyone go?"

"It's almost ten o'clock," Alyson informed him, smiling, her eyes revealing that she adored him.

"Wow." Jason leaned to kiss his wife.

Wyatt stood up, putting his guitar back in the case. He carried it to where she sat and leaned it against a chair. He towered over her and she breathed easier when he knelt next to them.

"Thank you for watching them for me."

Rachel held Molly close. "They were watching me."

"Let me get her and then I'll come back for Kat."

"I have an idea. You take her, I'll take Kat from Etta and carry her over for you."

He stared down at her and after a minute he nodded. But he had that look on his face, the same one as the other day when she'd opened the gate.

He took Molly from her arms, leaning in, his head close to Rachel's. She waited for him to move away before she stretched her legs and then stood. Etta smiled up at her, brows arching. But she didn't comment. Rachel loved that the other woman knew when to keep her thoughts to herself. Sometimes.

Rachel took Kat and held her in one arm. She extended her free hand and Etta took it, pulling herself to her feet.

"That ground isn't as soft as it used to be." Etta kissed Kat's cheek and hugged Rachel. "See you in a few days, Rachel Lynn."

"Let me know if you need me sooner."

"Will do, honey." And then Etta headed for Alyson.

Rachel headed toward the parking lot with Kat. When she reached Wyatt's truck Molly was already buckled in and his guitar case was in the front seat. He opened the driver's side back door and reached for Kat. His hands slid against Rachel's arms. He caught her gaze, held it for a second and then moved away.

Rachel backed up a few steps. "They're easy to love."

He smiled at that. "Yeah, they are."

She took another step back, trying not to think too much. He leaned against his truck, always the cowboy in his faded jeans and worn boots. He had on a ball cap tonight, though, no cowboy hat.

Time to make her escape.

"I'll see you in a few days." She backed up, tripping over the curb.

A hand shot out, grabbing her arm, steadying her. He laughed a little and winked. "You might want to work on that walking thing."

"Yeah, I might."

He let go of her arm. "Good night, Rachel."

She watched him drive away and then she hurried back to the leftover embers of the fire.

Chapter Five

Wyatt never would have imagined that one little pony would be so much trouble. But a few days after they brought Prince home, Wyatt was starting to see what he'd done. The night before, the girls had ridden the poor little animal until sunset. Wyatt had finally insisted they go inside and eat something quick before they crashed.

This day had been more of the same. The sun wasn't going down, but it was suppertime and the girls were hungry and beat. He wasn't too far behind them. Wyatt herded them into the laundry room, trying to ignore the massive pile of laundry that needed to be done. He kicked off his boots as the girls sat on the floor and pulled theirs off.

"What are we gonna eat?" Molly sat on the floor, her arms crossed over her raised knees. "Are you gonna cook?"

The cookbooks. He bent to help Kat get her left boot off. Her cheeks were a little pink from the sun and her hair was tangled from the wind. They needed a bath and an early bedtime.

"I can try another recipe. I have hamburger."

Molly covered her face. "Not hamburgers."

Kat imitated her sister. "Not burgers."

"I don't mean hamburgers. I'll cook something *with* hamburger." He picked them up and walked into the kitchen. He put the girls down and Molly looked around, her face nearly as pink as her sister's. She opened the cabinet with cereal.

They'd had cereal the night before. And the night before that they'd eaten at the Mad Cow. He'd never been much of a cook. For the first year or so it hadn't seemed to matter. He'd been numb and food had just been food. Ryder had shaken him out of that way of thinking.

He really needed a housekeeper. He needed someone who could cook. He glanced at his girls sitting on the stools where they were waiting for him to cook something wonderful. Molly's braids were coming undone. She pulled it loose. They needed someone who could put ribbons in their hair.

Rachel Waters's image interrupted his thoughts and he pushed it aside as he reached into a drawer for the apron he'd bought a few days ago. He tied it around his waist and winked at his girls. They giggled and Kat covered her eyes.

Rachel Waters was not on the short list of people he could hire. He wasn't going to let her do this to him. She wasn't going to be traipsing around the place, smelling it up with her perfume, invading his peace and quiet.

"Okay, we need food."

"We need Rachel," Molly said, the voice of reason. He wasn't convinced. He had an apron. He could cook.

"Why do we need Rachel?" He stood next to his oldest daughter. Her arms wrapped around his waist and she held him close.

"She sings."

"Right, she sings." He didn't know if that qualified her to be their housekeeper. They needed a grandmotherly woman who knitted scarves. Yeah, that would be perfect.

"I'm hungry." Kat rubbed sleepy eyes with her pudgy fists.

"Right, and I'm cooking." Something quick and easy. He opened the casserole cookbook and found a recipe that included Tater Tots, soup and hamburger. Man, what could be easier than that?

Molly stared, her expression skeptical as he tossed the thawed hamburger into a heated pan and then turned on the oven to preheat. He glanced at the cookbook. To four hundred degrees.

"I can do this, Mol, I promise."

"Promise?" Kat covered her eyes again and peeked between her fingers.

"Kat, it isn't going to be that scary. Why don't you go wash up and it'll be ready soon."

Kat was drooping like some of the plants in the den. He guessed he had about ten minutes to get something in her before she crashed. They'd been having so much fun on the pony he hadn't paid attention to the time.

Eighteen long months of trying to make the right decisions. Eighteen months of wondering what he could have done to change the course of their lives. He should have noticed something that day when he left Wendy and the girls for a youth retreat.

He stirred the hamburger until it turned brown.

Instead of noticing the look in Wendy's eyes, he'd kissed her goodbye and wondered why she held him so long before he walked out the door. Even now, eighteen long months later, the memory shook him. He started to slam his fist into the wall, but the girls were there, watching. They kept him sane. They kept him being a dad and living his life.

They kept him in church when he would have liked to walk away. They kept him from being so angry that he couldn't go on.

"Hey, you girls going to go clean up?"

He turned and Kat's head was on the granite top that covered the kitchen island. A chef's kitchen for a guy who could barely manage a bowl of cereal. Pretty crazy.

When he talked to the contractor last fall, he had this idea that a great kitchen would inspire him to cook. Instead, it inspired him to spend as much time as possible in the barn.

Molly stared up at him, her dark eyes seeing too much. She wasn't even four years old. She needed to chase butterflies and ride ponies, not spend her days worrying about her dad or what they'd feed her little sister. He hugged her.

"We can have cereal, Daddy," she whispered in his ear.

"No, we're not going to have cereal. We're going to have a casserole. Kat can nap while I cook." He glanced at the clock. It was almost seven. "Let's go wash your hands and I'll put your sister on the couch. We'll straighten up while the casserole cooks."

"You're a bad cleaner, Daddy." Molly leaned her head on his shoulder. "And you even burned our grilled cheese."

"I know, pumpkin, but tonight will be better. I have a cookbook."

Fifteen minutes later the smoke detector was going off

and Kat was screaming the house down. He ran down the hall to grab a broom and he knocked the offending alarm off the ceiling. Smoke filled the kitchen and someone was banging on the back door.

Just what he needed. No reason to call and warn a person that you planned to visit.

"Come in." He could hear the girls crying. The upstairs smoke detector was now going off and the backdoor banged shut.

"Do I need to call the fire department?"

He was pouring baking soda on the flaming hamburger meat when his mother-in-law appeared at his side and set a lid on the fiasco that was supposed to be dinner. His baking soda had already worked to put out the flames. He'd remembered that much from something he'd read years ago.

"Grandma." Molly and Kat in unison ran to Violet and hugged her legs. She hugged them back.

"Girls, get your shoes on, we're going to the Mad Cow." He ignored Violet and smiled at his daughters. And he hated ignoring Violet. She'd been more of a parent to him than the two he'd been stuck with at birth.

"This was their dinner?" Violet stood and flipped on the exhaust fan before opening the window over the sink. "Honestly, Wyatt, this isn't what I wanted to see when I showed up here."

"Well, Violet, I'm not sure what to tell you. Accidents happen."

"Of course they do."

Okay, so she was making him feel like a ten-year-old kid who had gotten caught writing on the bathroom wall. He jerked off the apron and tossed it on the counter. "Look, Violet, we're fine. The girls are fine."

"I know you're fine." She fiddled with the diamond rings on her left hand. "I'm not here to grade your progress. I'm here to see you."

"I didn't know you were going to be here today."

"I wanted to surprise the girls." Her arms were around his daughters again.

"I see." It felt like some kind of snap inspection.

"Let's take the girls to the diner and later we can talk."

"Talk about what, Violet?" He shot a look past her, to his daughters and he smiled a little softer smile. "You girls go find shoes and wash your hands and faces before we go."

Molly took Kat by the hand and led her out of the kitchen, down the hall. He could hear their little girl jabber and once they were out of earshot, he turned his attention back to Violet. He hadn't noticed before that she had dark circles under her eyes and more gray in her dark hair than the last time he'd seen her.

But then, he wasn't the most observant guy in the world.

"What is it we're going to talk about?" he reminded her when she didn't say anything.

"About the girls coming to spend time with me."

"Violet, I'll bring the girls to see you. Maybe in a week or two. We'll spend a couple of nights." He knew that wasn't what she wanted.

He pretended it was as he walked out the door to the laundry room and slid his feet into his boots. Violet followed him. She didn't belong here. She wore designer dresses and diamonds. Wendy had worn jeans and T-shirts.

A jacket on the hook next to his hat caught his attention. Not his jacket. He closed his eyes and remembered

Rachel taking it off and hanging it there. Man, for a minute he almost felt at ease.

He glanced away, not wanting Violet to notice that jacket. It didn't mean anything, but it would imply a lot. He didn't want that hornet's nest opened, especially when there was nothing to know.

"You know that isn't what I mean. I don't want a day visit, Wyatt." Violet was a small woman with a will the size of Mount Rushmore. "I want to take the girls, maybe for the summer. I think you need time to get your head on straight. You can't do this, taking care of them, the house and the ranch, alone. I know you're trying, but you need help."

Anger simmered and he couldn't look at her. If his head hadn't been on straight, as she'd implied, he would have lost it right at that moment. He reached for his hat and shoved it down on his head. What he really wanted to do was walk out the door. If it hadn't been for his girls he might have.

"I'm together, Violet. I'm not a perfect parent. My cooking skills are pretty limited, but I'm doing what counts. I'm here every single day taking care of my girls. I'm the person making their breakfast and the guy who tucks them in at night."

Tears welled up in Violet's eyes. "I know you're a good dad. But I also think that maybe you're suffering and that isn't good for my granddaughters."

He turned away from his mother-in-law and rested a hand on the door, sucking in deep breaths, trying to keep it together before she had a real case against him.

"I'm not letting you take my girls."

"Wyatt, I didn't say I wanted to *take* them. I want to give you a break. Maybe you can find a housekeeper, someone to help with cooking and laundry? They're my granddaughters and I'm worried, that's all."

His daughters. He started to remind her of that fact, but footsteps in the hallway stopped him. He looked past Violet and smiled at Kat and Molly.

Molly's nose scrunched and her eyes narrowed as she looked from her father to her grandmother and he wondered how much she'd overheard, or if she'd heard any of it. Maybe she sensed the problem. Either way, he wasn't going to let her be a part of this.

Violet picked up her purse. She opened her mouth and he shot her a look that stopped her from saying more.

"Let's go, girls. We're going to the Mad Cow and I bet Vera will cook us up something special."

"Fried bologna sandwich?" Molly's eyes lit up and Violet gasped.

Wyatt picked up his two girls, one in each arm, and walked through the back door, leaning against it to hold it open for his mother-in-law. She wasn't smiling and he didn't know if it was because she'd given up or was planning a new strategy. Maybe she was still trying to get over the idea of fried bologna?

A housekeeper, she'd said. As if he hadn't given it a lot of thought. But the one person that kept coming to mind was the last person he needed in his home on a daily basis.

Violet stood there for a moment, not walking through the door. He didn't have a clue what she expected from him. Maybe she wanted him to promise to send the girls with her, or maybe she expected him to cave on the subject of a housekeeper.

She walked out the door and he made the worst decision he figured he'd made in years.

"Okay, Violet, I'll hire a housekeeper." He let the door close and he followed her down the steps to her car. She'd won. He didn't know how, but he did know that this was a victory for his mother-in-law.

A warm breeze whipped the sheets on the clothesline. In the bright light of the full moon, Rachel unpinned the clothes she'd hung up earlier and pulled them down. She folded the crisp sheets, holding them to her face to breathe in the outdoor scent. They smelled like clover and fresh air.

The clip-clop of hooves on the paved road caught her attention. She looked into the dark and wondered who was lucky enough to be riding tonight. It was a beautiful evening with a clear sky and a light breeze that promised rain, but not yet.

She stood in the dark holding a pillowcase she'd pulled down from the line and whispering for her dog to stay still. The German shepherd stayed at her side but he growled low, a warning for anyone who came too close.

The horse stopped and then the clip-clop continued. Instead of going down the road it was coming up the drive, hooves crunching on gravel. She grabbed the dog's collar.

"Laundry this late at night?" Wyatt's voice called from the dark shadows.

"Riding this late at night?"

He rode closer and the moonlight caught his face and the big gray that he rode. She shivered and felt the chill of the breeze against her arms.

"I had to get out of the house."

"Who's with the girls?" It came out like an accusation. She hadn't meant that. "I'm sorry, that's none of my business."

"No, it isn't." He sat steady on the horse that shifted a little and pawed the ground. "My mother-in-law."

"Oh, I see." But she didn't. She didn't know Wyatt, not really. She didn't know his life, other than caring about the girls and hearing about his wife's death. He didn't really share personal details.

She got that, because neither did she. Too many times in the past when she'd shared, it had been recycled and used against her.

"She showed up this evening." He swung down off the horse, landing lightly on the ground and holding the reins as he stood there.

Unsure. She was surprised to see him unsure. He should have looked confident standing there next to that horse. She wondered if it was about his mother-in-law. His hand went up, catching hold of the horse's bridle. The big animal pushed at his arm and Wyatt held him tight.

"I'm sure the girls are happy to see her." She held on to the laundry basket with one arm and with her left hand she kept hold of the dog that growled a low warning.

"They were. Unfortunately I was in the process of burning the house down when she showed up." Wyatt reached up and pulled something off his saddle. Her jacket that she'd left at his house. "I thought you might need this."

He dropped it in the laundry basket on top of the sheets she'd just folded. And then he stood there. She looked up, caught him watching her. It was hard to breathe when he did that.

"Would you like to go for a ride?" He said it so easy

and nothing was that easy. No word fit him better than complicated. Everything about him fit into that box.

His mother-in-law was at his house and he was riding in the dark. That meant something other than "nice night for a ride."

But a moonlight ride with Wyatt Johnson seemed to trump the fear of complications and whatever was going on with him. Her gaze shifted to the tiny parsonage that she shared with her parents. Her mom was inside knitting. She'd had a rough day, a rough month. Rachel's dad was working on Sunday's sermon.

"We won't be gone long." Wyatt moved a little closer.

"I shouldn't. I have more laundry to do."

He laughed a little. "Are you always the good daughter?"

No, she wasn't.

Cynthia was the good one. That fact didn't hurt the way it once had. Life changed. Cynthia was married and had a family. Rachel lived with her parents, making sure their mother stayed healthy. It was an easy choice to make. Stay with her parents, help with their ministry and take care of them. Leaving wasn't an option, not when her brother and sister both lived on the other side of the country.

Her gaze landed on Wyatt's dusty boots and slid up. When she reached his face, he was smiling. And he winked. She nearly dropped the laundry basket and in her shock, she let go of the dog. Wolfgang jumped away from her. His tail wagged and he made a beeline for Wyatt.

"Hey now, you're a big old dog." His hand went out and the dog dropped on his belly. "And he's friendly."

"He isn't supposed to be."

"Oh, you want him to attack me?" Wyatt grinned again.

"No, but I don't want him to lose his edge. He's a guard dog."

"Right." Wyatt continued to rub the dog behind the ears. "So, you want to go? I can't be gone too long."

Rachel bit down on her bottom lip and then she nodded.

"Okay, let me take Wolfgang in and I'll put on boots."

"Flip-flops are okay."

"Right, so you can laugh at the city girl who wore the wrong shoes to go riding."

"Okay, I'll stand out here and hold on to Gatsby."

She laughed. "Gatsby."

"Oh, laughter from the woman with a dog named Wolfgang?"

She whistled and Wolfgang trotted to her side. "I'll be right back."

As she walked through the back door, letting it bang softly behind her, Rachel heard her dad on the phone. She glanced at the clock, surprised that he'd have a call this late at night. Hopefully no one was hurt or sick. Late calls were almost never a good thing. She peeked into the living room. Her mom was still sitting in the recliner next to the window, the lamp glowing soft light and her hands working the knitting needles as the scarf in her lap grew.

"Hey, I'm going riding with Wyatt Johnson." Rachel set the basket of laundry on a chair and used what she hoped was a casual, it's-really-nothing voice.

Her mom glanced up. Gloria Waters always looked serene. Rachel envied that about her mother. She envied that her mom and sister could eat cake and never gain an ounce. And yeah, she knew that envy was wrong. But there were days she could really use a piece of cake.

Or maybe the whole cake. And that was the problem.

"Riding with Wyatt?" Gloria put her knitting down. "Okay, well, be careful."

What had she expected her mom to say? That she couldn't go? Rachel smiled. She was a dozen years past the time when her parents made decisions for her. And yet she still checked with them.

Her father's voice carried from his office. "I'm not sure if we're interested, Bill. I know we've talked about that. Let me pray on this…"

His voice faded. Rachel couldn't breathe for a second because she'd heard similar conversations in the past. She hadn't expected it now. She shifted her gaze to her mom and got a shrug, nothing more.

"What's going on?"

"I'm not sure. Your dad missed a call from Bill and he called him back."

Rachel nodded.

Her mom picked up her knitting again as if it didn't matter. Maybe it didn't. Maybe it was another door opening, another one closing. But she didn't want this door closed.

"I should go. Wyatt is waiting."

She walked out the back door still wearing her flip-flops. It wasn't cold but the air was damp and the breeze blew against her bare arms. She shrugged into the jacket that Wyatt had given her before she went inside.

"Ready to go?" Wyatt looked down at her feet. "I was kind of joking about shoes. Do you have boots?"

"I do. I'm sorry." She glanced back at the house.

"It isn't a big deal. You can wear those." His booted

foot went into the stirrup and he swung into the saddle. He reached for her hand. "Come on."

She hesitated and then she grasped his hand. Strong fingers wrapped around hers. It felt like a lifeline.

Chapter Six

Wyatt grasped Rachel's hand and her fingers wrapped tight around his. It was easier to think about riding than to think about the lost look on her face when she walked out of the house. She had looked pretty close to shell-shocked.

"Put your foot in the stirrup." He moved his left foot and she slid her foot into the stirrup. "And up you go."

He pulled and she swung her right leg up and over, landing behind him. The horse sidestepped and then settled. Her foot was out of the stirrup. He slid his foot back into place and glanced back at her.

"Ready?"

She nodded but didn't say anything. Three minutes in the house shouldn't have done this to her. Maybe she'd had a day like his?

Gatsby headed down the road at an easy clip, his gait smooth, his long stride eating up the ground and putting distance between them and the parsonage. Rachel was stiff behind him, holding the saddle rather than wrapping her arms around his waist.

"Where are we going?" Her voice trembled a little. She was close to his back but didn't touch him.

"Nowhere, just riding. I haven't done this in years. Since Violet is at the house I decided to get out and clear my head."

He was taking steps. The girls were with Violet. They were fine. He was fine. Rachel Waters was sitting behind him, and he thought he could hear a quiet sob as the horse's hooves pounded the pavement.

"We've got land down here. I'm going to cut across the field and hit a dirt road that will take us back to your place."

She didn't answer.

The gate was open and he rode Gatsby through the entrance. They hadn't put livestock on this place since last fall. The grass was growing up and in a month or so they'd cut it for hay.

The moon was almost full and the silver light that shone down on the field was bright. The grass blew and the moonlight caught the blades, turning them silvery green. Wyatt slowed the horse to an easy walk. Behind him, Rachel sighed. He hoped she'd relaxed a little.

They rode through the field. Wyatt felt the presence of the woman behind him, even though she hadn't touched him. He'd been impulsive in his life, but this one had him questioning what in the world he'd done. He'd planned on taking a ride and clearing his head. It wasn't often that he had a few minutes alone. Instead of being alone, he had Rachel Waters on the back of his horse.

Out of the corner of his eye he saw a flash of something running through the grass. The horse must have seen it at the same time. The animal jumped a little, knocking Rachel forward. Wyatt held the reins steady and tightened his legs around the animal's middle.

"Easy there, Gats. It's a nice night for a ride, but I'm not looking for a big run."

Rachel's arms were now tight around his waist. He smiled and remembered high school, pretending a car had died or run out of gas on a back road. He kind of figured he could spur Gatsby just a little and send the animal running across the field, and keep Rachel Waters holding tight.

Instead he eased up on the reins but kept the horse at a steady walk. "He's fine, just startled. I think that was a coyote."

"I think so, too." Rachel's cheek brushed his back and then was gone. But her hands were still at his waist.

"So what happened back at the house?" He eased into the conversation the same way he eased his way into the saddle of a green broke horse.

"Why don't you tell me what happened with your mother-in-law?"

He glanced back and then refocused on the trail that was overgrown from years of neglected riding. Rachel readjusted behind him. Her arms slipped from his middle and her hands grabbed the sides of his shirt.

"Okay, rock, paper, scissors." He turned sideways in the saddle and held his hand out.

She shook her head but she smiled and held her hand out.

"Fine. One, two, three." She cut his paper with scissors.

He groaned. "Me first. Great. My mother-in-law isn't positive I'm fit to be a parent right now."

She didn't respond.

"You still back there?" He glanced back, pushing his hat up a little to get a better look at the woman behind him.

"I'm here." And then a sweet pause with her hands on his waist. "She's wrong."

"Thanks." He spurred Gatsby a little and the horse picked up his pace. "He'll be a good horse when we're done breaking him."

"Done breaking him!"

"Yeah, he hasn't ridden double before tonight. In a few weeks we're going to start him on roping."

"Great, I'm practice."

No, not practice, he wanted to tell her. But she was a soft, easy way to slip back into life. He hadn't thought about dating too much, about any other woman taking Wendy's place. It still wasn't the direction he planned to take, but life was pulling him back in.

"You're not practice. You're helping me," he assured her, smiling as the words slipped out, meaning more than she would understand.

"Oh, so I can add horse trainer to my résumé?"

That's right, they were talking about the horse being broke to ride double, not about his dating life.

"Yeah, and since I spilled it, I think it's your turn to talk."

No answer. They rode for a few minutes in total silence. No, not total silence, tree frogs sang and a few night birds screeched. Her arms slid around his waist again. Her chin brushed his shoulder.

"I really can't talk about it. It has to do with my dad and the church."

The years in Florida doing youth ministry weren't that far behind him. He got that she couldn't talk. But whatever had happened, it'd upset her. He leaned back a little, turning his head. It caught him by surprise, that she was so close. His cheek brushed hers and she moved back.

A Justin McBride song filled the night air. Wyatt groaned and reached into his pocket for his phone. It was Violet. He answered and in the background he could hear Molly crying. He'd been wrong, to take off like this, to leave them.

"I'll be home in five minutes." He spoke softly to his mother-in-law, offered more assurances and slid the phone back into his pocket. "Mind going back to my place?"

She shook her head, but he wondered. If he was her, he'd probably mind. Man, even he wasn't crazy about going back. It wasn't about his girls. It was about not wanting to face Violet, not with Rachel on the back of his horse.

It took less than five minutes to get from the field to the dirt road and back to Wyatt's house. Rachel held tight as the horse covered the ground in an easy lope. She tried hard not to think about falling off at the pace they were going.

Falling off or facing Wyatt's mother-in-law? She had to wonder a little about which one would be worse. Falling off would leave more marks. She wasn't that stupid.

"You okay back there?" Wyatt's voice was raspy and way too sexy.

"I'm good." Ugh, she was horrible.

He chuckled, his sides vibrating under her arms. "Of course you are. I promise, Violet isn't dangerous. She's overprotective of the girls. I guess I am, too. Maybe that's why we clash on a regular basis."

"They're your girls, of course you're protective. I don't think you're over…" She sighed.

"I'm overprotective." He glanced back at her. "It's okay, I can handle it. There are reasons, Rachel."

"But sometimes…"

"No, not sometimes." He reined in the horse. "Okay, sometimes. I know Molly needs to be able to separate from me. The hour or so a week that she's in the nursery has helped."

"I can see that she's doing better." Without knowing all of the reasons why Molly was afraid, it was hard to help her.

She held on as he cut through a ditch and up the driveway to his house. It looked as if every light in the house was on.

Nerves twisted a funny dance in her stomach as he pulled the horse to a quick stop next to the back door. He didn't wait for her to slide off. Instead he swung his right leg over the horse's neck and jumped off, leaving her sitting on the back of the saddle.

The door opened as she was sliding forward into the saddle, grabbing the reins as the horse started to sidestep. He calmed the minute she held the reins. Wyatt took the steps two at a time and met his mother-in-law and Molly as they walked out the back door. Molly held her arms out to him, no longer crying, just sobbing and hiccuping a little into his shoulder.

"I'm here." He spoke softly to his daughter.

"She woke up and you were gone." Violet, a woman with soft features and hair that framed a face that was still young.

"I shouldn't have left."

His mother-in-law shook her head. "Wyatt, there are going to be times that you have to leave."

Rachel sat on the horse, waiting for them to remember her. She didn't want to be the witness to their pain. She didn't want to be the bystander who got in the way. Violet remembered her presence and turned to stare.

Emotions flickered across the woman's face. Anger, sorrow, it was difficult to tell exactly what Violet thought about Rachel's presence.

"I should go." She didn't really mean to say it out loud. She slid to the ground, still holding the reins. "It isn't far. I can walk."

Wyatt, still holding Molly, came down the steps. "Don't be ridiculous. I'll drive you home, Rachel. Molly and I can drive you home."

"Rachel?" Violet walked to the edge of the porch. "Are you the Rachel that my granddaughters talk about nonstop?"

"I'm Rachel."

"Wyatt said you cleaned his home last week. Are you interested in the job on a permanent basis?"

Rachel shot Wyatt a look and she wondered if that was what this night ride had been about. Had his mother-in-law put him on the spot and he'd used Rachel as his get-out-of-jail card because she had cleaned one time?

"She makes the house smell good," said Molly, suddenly talkative. Rachel smiled at the little girl.

"Well, that sounds perfect to me." Violet smiled at her granddaughter. "Do you cook?"

Rachel nodded because she had no idea what to say. She avoided looking at Wyatt because he probably looked cornered. She knew that she felt pretty cornered. Cleaning Wyatt's house once did not make her a housekeeper and nanny.

"Perfect." Violet looked from Rachel to Wyatt. "When do you want her to start?"

"Violet, this is something Rachel and I need to discuss."

"Well, the two of you talk and I'll go check on Kat."

Rachel thought about reminding them that she was still there, still a grown-up who could make her own decisions, but the conversation ended and Violet went inside looking like a woman who had solved a national crisis.

"That went well." He walked down the steps, still holding Molly, toward Rachel. Wyatt took the leather reins from Rachel. "Let me unsaddle him and I'll drive you home."

"I can walk. Or call my dad." She hugged herself tight, holding her jacket closed against the sudden coolness in the wind.

Wyatt turned, pushing his hat back. He shook his head. "You aren't walking. You're not calling your dad. I'm driving you home. Right, Mol?"

Molly nodded against his shoulder. She looked so tiny in her pink pajamas and her dark hair tangled around her face. The security light caught her in its glow and her little eyes were open, a few stray tears still trickling down her cheeks.

"I'm sorry that Violet put you on the spot."

"I understand." She stepped closer. "Do you want me to take her while you unsaddle Gatsby?"

He dropped a kiss on his daughter's brow and nodded. Molly held out her arms. Rachel didn't know why it mattered so much to her, but it did. In her heart it mattered that this little girl would reach out to her. It changed everything.

It even changed that truck ride home, sitting with Molly between them and the stereo playing softly. It changed the way she felt when Wyatt said goodbye and then waited until she was in the house before he backed out of the driveway, the headlights flashing across the side of the house.

And then she refocused because her parents were still up, still discussing something that could change her life forever.

Wyatt turned up the radio as he headed down the drive and back to his house. Molly was in the seat next to him, curled over against his side. Her breathing had settled into a heavy pattern that meant she'd fallen back to sleep.

When he pulled up his driveway he could see Violet in the living room, watching for him to come back. His house. His life. His kids. Violet was their grandmother. As much as he cared for her, he didn't care for facing off with her tonight.

He definitely didn't like her trying to make decisions for him. Decisions such as hiring Rachel Waters to be his housekeeper. There were plenty of women out there who could do the job. Women with loose housedresses and heavy shoes. That seemed pretty close to perfect.

He stopped the truck and got out, lifting Molly into his arms and carrying her up the back steps. Violet met him. She pushed the door open and he stepped into the laundry room, kicking off his boots, still holding his daughter tight.

"You're dating her?" Violet followed him through the kitchen.

Man, he needed peace and quiet, not this. He needed to put his daughter to bed and think before he got hit with twenty questions. He wasn't dating.

He'd gone for a ride to clear his head and for whatever reason he'd let that ride take him straight to Rachel. It wasn't like he'd planned it.

"I'm going to put my daughter in bed, Violet."

He glanced back and she stood in the hallway, her eyes damp with tears but she wasn't angry. He let out a sigh and walked up the stairs to the room Molly and Kat shared. Twin beds painted white, pastel quilts with flowers and butterflies. It was the perfect room for little girls to grow up in. Until they started fighting like barn cats and needed their own space.

That wasn't something he wanted to think about, their growing up. He hoped they would always be close. He didn't want to think about them in their twenties, having one major fight and pulling away until…

He didn't want to go back and he wasn't going to let his girls be him and Ryder.

He put his daughter in her bed and pulled the quilt up to her chin. She opened her eyes and smiled softly, raising a hand to touch his cheek. Sleepy eyes drifted closed again and he kissed her cheek. "Love you, Molly."

"Love you, Daddy." She smiled but her eyes didn't open.

"I'm downstairs if you need me." He walked to the door. "I'm not going anywhere."

As he walked downstairs, he felt as if he was about to face the judge. Violet was waiting in the den. The TV was turned off. She put down her book, a book he knew she hadn't opened. He took off his hat and shoved a hand through his hair. And he stood there in the middle of the living room, unsure.

"What's going on, Wyatt?"

"There's nothing going on, Violet. I'm being a dad to my daughters and I'm raising horses with Ryder." He sat down on the couch and rubbed a hand over his face because he was a grown man and he really didn't feel the need to answer her questions. But he owed her something. "I'm not dating Rachel Waters. She's the pastor's daughter and she takes care of the girls when they're in the church nursery. She teaches their preschool Sunday school class."

"I see. Well, she's very pretty."

"Right." Was that a trick statement?

"Wyatt, someday you'll want to date again. You'll move on. That's okay."

He closed his eyes because it seemed like a real good way to avoid this discussion. Instead he got smacked upside the head with a vision of Rachel Waters. Facing Violet was easier than facing the image taunting him behind closed eyes.

Never in his wildest dreams would Violet have been the person telling him to move on.

"Hire her, Wyatt. She'd be perfect for the girls. They need someone like her in their lives."

"They have me." He twisted the gold band on his finger. Someday he would have to take it off. "No one can replace Wendy."

"She was my daughter, Wyatt. I think I know that no one can replace her. But I lost a husband once and I do know that we can't stop living."

"I haven't stopped living." Okay, maybe he had for a while.

He hadn't expected it to hurt when the grief started to fade and life started to feel like something he wanted to live again. Moving on felt like cheating.

"Wyatt, you're a good dad. You were a good husband."

He had wondered for a long time and never been able to ask if she blamed him. He sure blamed himself. He still couldn't ask.

"It's the hardest thing in the world, moving forward. But…" What else could he say? Moving forward meant accepting.

She leaned and patted his arm. "Don't beat yourself up too much for having good days."

She had lost her husband years ago. Wendy's dad had died at work. A sudden heart attack that took them all by surprise. A few years ago Violet had remarried. He admired her strength, even if she did try to run his life from time to time.

"If you don't hire Rachel, do you have any thoughts on who you would like to hire?" Violet picked up her purse and dug through it, pulling out a small tablet and pen.

"Someone capable." He pictured Rachel and brushed the thought aside to replace it with a more suitable image. "Someone older."

Violet laughed a little and wrote down something about unattractive older woman. Now she was starting to get it.

Chapter Seven

The new lambs frolicked next to their mothers. Rachel leaned against the fence and watched, smiling a little. And smiling wasn't the easiest thing to do, not after the previous evening's conversation with her parents.

This was her place, Dawson, this house and the sheep she raised. Working for Etta, that was another place where she fit. Finally, at twenty-nine she fit.

That meant something because growing up she'd been the misfit, the overweight rebel always compared to her older sister. Cynthia had been the pretty one, the good one. Rob, her older brother, had been the studious one.

Rachel had set out to prove that she had a mind of her own.

"Thinking?" Her dad appeared at her side.

She glanced at him, wondering when he'd gotten those lines around his eyes and that gray in his hair. As a kid, she'd always imagined him young and capable. She'd never imagined her mother in bed for days, fighting a lupus flare-up that attacked her joints and caused fatigue that forced her to rest more often.

Parents weren't supposed to age.

"Yes, thinking."

"Rachel, if we get this church, you don't have to go."

She stepped back from the fence and turned to face him.

"If you go, I go."

"I know that's how you feel, but we also know how you feel about Dawson. In all of the years of moving, there's never been a town that became your home the way this town has. We want you to be happy."

"I'd be happy in Tulsa."

"No, you won't. But we will. We love the city and we need to live closer to the hospitals and doctors. We're not getting any younger."

She didn't want to have this conversation. She turned back to the small field with her six ewes and the three babies that had been born so far this spring.

"You're not old."

Her dad laughed. "No, we're not, but there are things we need to consider. Promise me you'll pray about this. I don't want you to make this decision based on what you think we need."

"I'll pray." She sighed and rested her arms on the top of the gate. "When do they want you to take the church in Tulsa?"

"Six weeks. And remember, nothing is set in stone, not yet."

"But that isn't a lot of time for the church here to find a pastor."

"It isn't, but there are men here who should pray about stepping into the role. Sometimes God moves us so that others can move into the place where He wants them."

"True." She turned to face him. "But then I question why He brought us here just to move us."

"To everything there is a season, a purpose. God doesn't make mistakes, Rachel. If we're here for a year, there's a purpose in that year."

"I know you're right." She stepped away from the gate. "I have to run into town to get grain. Do you want lunch from the Mad Cow?"

"No, we're going to have sandwiches." He kissed the top of her head the way he'd done when she was a kid. He hadn't changed that much. He still wore dress slacks and a button-up shirt. He still parted his hair, though thinning, on the side.

He was still the person she turned to when she needed advice. And sometimes she recognized that her parents were a crutch. They were her safe place. This was easier than getting hurt again.

She drove the truck to town. Not that she couldn't put feed in the back of her convertible, but she liked the old farm truck her dad had bought when they moved to Dawson. When she'd thought this would be the last move.

She'd been moving her entire life. From place to place, in and out of lives. She'd learned not to get too close. Either the friends would soon be gone, or they'd find out she was human, not at all the perfect preacher's kid.

But she was no longer a kid. And this time she'd gotten attached.

She parked in front of the black-and-white painted building that was the Mad Cow Café. It was early for the lunch crowd. That meant time to sit and talk to Vera, the owner. Maybe they could have a cup of coffee together.

A truck pulled in next to hers. She glanced quick to the right and nearly groaned. Wyatt Johnson in his big truck. He saluted with two fingers to his brow and grinned. That cowboy had more charm than was good for him.

Or anyone else, for that matter.

She guessed it would be pretty obvious if she backed out of her parking space and went on down the road, so she opened the door and grabbed her purse. Wyatt met her at the front of the truck. The girls weren't with him.

"How are you?" He pulled off the cowboy hat and ran a hand through hair that was a little too long. Dark and straight, it looked soft. She thought it probably was soft.

"I'm good. Where are the girls?"

"Andie and Ryder are home after a trip to the doctor in Tulsa. Andie is on the couch for the next month or so till the babies come, and she thought the girls could keep her entertained."

"That'll be good for all three of them."

"Yeah, it is."

"And your mother-in-law?" She walked next to him, his stride longer than her own.

"Interviewing housekeepers."

"Oh."

It shouldn't hurt, that he was going to pick someone else. Of course she didn't want a full-time job as anyone's housekeeper. She didn't even know that they'd be here for her to take such a job.

"It will make things easier," he explained in a way that made her wonder if he wanted to convince himself.

"Of course it would."

"Do you have any suggestions?" He opened the door to the Mad Cow and she stepped in ahead of him, brushing past him, trying hard not to look at him, to look into those eyes of his, to not see the faded jeans, the scuffed boots or the buckle he'd won at Nationals back when he team roped. Before marriage, before horse training. He still roped in local events.

A few weeks ago she had watched from the bleachers. She had watched him smile and avoid the women who tried to get his attention. Those women rode horses and they understood his world.

She was still breaking in boots she'd bought when they moved to Dawson. And now she'd have to put them back in the closet like most forgotten dreams. She'd pack them up with childhood books, love letters she'd never sent and pictures of ranch houses she'd dreamed of owning.

Wyatt was a cowboy. He was the real deal. He even held the door open and pulled out a chair for her when Vera pointed them to a table in the corner.

And he did it because it was what men in Dawson did. It was the way they lived. Her heart ached clean through and she told herself it wasn't about him, it was about leaving.

"You know, I'm not used to seeing you without a smile on your face." He drew her back with that comment and she managed a smile. "Oh, that's not better."

She laughed. "Sorry, just a lot on my mind. What about Ernestine Douglas?"

"What? Ernestine's smile?"

She laughed at the pretend shock on his face. "As a housekeeper."

"I hadn't thought about her. Yeah, I might give her a call."

"She'd be great with the girls. Her kids are grown and gone."

Vera approached, dark hair shot through with silver, knotted at the back of her head and covered with a net. She wiped wet hands on her apron and pulled an order pad out of the pocket.

"What can I get you kids today?"

Wyatt laughed, "Vera, I wish I was still a kid. If I was twenty again I'd ride a few bulls and then take Rachel off to Tulsa for a wild night."

Vera tsk'd. "Wyatt Johnson, you're talking about our preacher's daughter. She teaches Sunday school and watches over your babies in the nursery."

"Yeah, but in this dream, we're still young and crazy. Remember?" Wyatt winked at Rachel and picked up the menu. "What's special today?"

Vera pointed at the white board on the wall near the register. "My special cashewed chicken, and the pile of nothing you're trying to feed us."

"Vera, Vera, I guess you won't give a guy a break."

"Not a chance."

He laughed and ordered the cashewed chicken. Rachel ordered a salad. But she wanted that cashewed chicken. She had always wanted what she shouldn't have, the things that weren't good for her. Fried chicken, chocolate and the cowboy sitting across from her. The last was new on the list of things she shouldn't want and couldn't have.

Wyatt watched Rachel pick at the salad she'd ordered. Lettuce with chopped-up turkey and ham and barely a dab of dressing. He felt kind of guilty digging into the plate of fried chicken chunks over rice that covered his plate, the special gravy oozed over the side and dripped onto the table. Cashews and chopped green onions topped it off.

The way he looked at it, skinny women ought to eat something fried every now and then. He grabbed the saucer from under her coffee cup and scraped some of his chicken onto it.

"What are you doing?" She put her fork down and wiped her mouth.

"Feeding you. If you haven't got the sense to eat some of Vera's cashewed chicken, I'm going to help you out."

"But I don't want it."

"Oh, yes, you do." He grinned, hoping she'd smile and look a little less cornered. Man, what was it about this woman? She didn't eat. She had a butterfly tattoo. She had secrets.

He had two little girls who needed him to stay focused.

He reached for his iced tea and the band on his left hand glinted, a reminder. And guilt. Because he still wore a ring that symbolized forever with a woman who was gone.

But her memory wasn't.

He sighed and Rachel lowered her fork. Her eyes were dark, soulful. She didn't smile but her eyes changed, softened. "You okay?"

"I'm fine. So, are you going to try the cashewed chicken?"

Rachel picked up her fork and took a bite. Her eyes closed and she nodded.

"It's as good as people say." Her eyes opened and she flashed him a smile. "And you Johnson boys are as wicked as they say."

"We're not really wicked." He wanted to hug her tight because she was dragging him past a hard place in his life and she didn't even know it. "We're just on the edge a lot of the time."

"Temptation."

"Reformed."

The door opened. The lunch crowd was piling in. While they'd been talking the parking lot had filled up with farm trucks, a tractor or two and a few cars. He knew about everyone in Dawson and he figured Rachel did as well.

"We're about to get caught."

Rachel shrugged. "Yeah, that's life in Dawson. I love it here."

She sounded as if that meant something.

"You know, if you need to talk, I know how to keep a secret."

Her smile was sweet. She wasn't a girl from Dawson, but she fit this place, this world. From her T-shirt to her jeans, she was fitting in. But maybe that's what she did. The life of a preacher's kid wasn't easy. They moved a lot, changed towns, changed schools and changed friends.

Maybe she knew how to become the person each town or church expected her to be? Did that mean she wasn't who he thought she was? That left him kind of unsettled.

"I need to go. I don't want to leave the girls too long. They..." He stood up and dropped a few bills on the table for their lunch and Vera's tip. "The girls worry if I'm gone too long."

Rachel stood up. "Wyatt, if you need anything, I'm here."

Man, he could think of a list of things he needed. He needed to keep his life together. He took a step back. He really wasn't ready for this.

The Johnson brothers weren't the only temptation in town.

Trouble was looking him in the eyes and it was about time he made the great escape. He and Ryder had done a lot of that in their younger days. They had experience. They knew how to race through a hay field to escape an angry dad. They knew how to escape the county deputy on a dirt road. Not exactly life lessons he was proud of.

He touched the brim of his hat. "Thanks for recommending someone. I'll call Mrs. Douglas."

"Right, that's a good idea."

"Or you could take the job? The girls would love that."

"I don't think so."

"Yeah, of course."

He bumped into a chair as he backed away from her and a few of the guys called out names and other things he didn't really want to deal with.

The only good idea right now was to escape Rachel Waters, maybe spend some time at Ryder's knocking the tar out of the punching bag still hanging in the old hay barn. Their dad had put that thing up years ago. He had taught them one decent lesson in life, other than how to make money. He'd taught them the art of boxing.

And right now felt like a pretty good time to go take a few swings at an inanimate object.

There were a list of reasons why. Wendy's memory, tugging him back in time and pushing him to think about how he'd let her down. His girls hurting and needing their mom. Rachel Waters with brown eyes and a butterfly tattoo, offering to be there for him but rejecting a job offer to take care of his girls.

Thoughts of Rachel felt a lot like cheating.

Thirty minutes after he left the Mad Cow he was in the barn behind Ryder's house. He had spent fifteen minutes in that hot, dusty barn slamming his fists into the frayed and faded bag that hung from the rafters.

"Trying to hurt someone?"

Wyatt punched the bag and then grabbed it to keep it

from swinging back at him. He turned, swiping his arm across his brow. Boxing in boots and jeans, not the most effective form in the world.

Ryder stood in the doorway, sunlight behind him. They'd taken a few swings at each other over the years. The last time had been about something crazy, a woman that Ryder had hurt. It shouldn't have mattered to Wyatt—he hadn't known her. But Ryder had left a trail of broken hearts in his reckless wake.

They hadn't talked for over a year after that fight.

"No, just exercising." Wyatt stepped away from the punching bag.

Ryder grinned and shook his head. "Right, and that's why you were in town having lunch with Rachel Waters."

"That's why I don't like this town." Wyatt walked past Ryder, into the warm sunlight. At least there was a breeze. He didn't put his hat back on but stood there for a minute, cooling down.

"Yeah, people talk. Most of the time they're talking about me. Or at least they used to. Kind of nice to have you being the target of the gossip."

Wyatt walked on, toward his truck. "How's Andie?"

"Itching to get out of bed. The church brought a truck-load of frozen meals for us and a few of the ladies cleaned the house. Rachel came over yesterday and brought a pie."

"Of course she did."

"Want a glass of tea or a bottle of water?" Ryder had stopped and that forced Wyatt to stop and turn around.

"Nope, I need to get home to the girls. Violet is trying to find a housekeeper-slash-nanny for us. I'm leaving it up to her, but I want to keep an eye on things."

"Wyatt, I know you're still angry or hurt. I know this messed you up, but it's time…"

Wyatt took a step in Ryder's direction. "Don't tell me when it's time, little brother. You think because you're married and finally getting it together, you have it all figured out. You don't have a clue how I feel."

Man, *he* didn't even know how he felt. So being angry with Ryder, wanting to shove him into the dirt, probably wasn't the right reaction. He sighed and took a step back, tipping his hat to shade his face.

"I'm sorry, Ryder. But let me figure this out, if you don't mind."

"Got it. But I wanted you to know." Ryder looked down and turned a little red. "We're praying for you."

That was a change for his brother. Ryder was now the one with the stronger faith. That was another thing Wyatt was working on getting back. He'd walked away from the ministry and spent a long year blaming God. He'd spent the last six months working through that and trying to find peace.

"Ryder, I appreciate that."

Ryder grinned. "Yeah, do you appreciate how hard it was to say?"

They both laughed.

"Yeah, cowboys from Dawson don't have a lot of Dr. Phil moments."

"Ain't that just about the truth?" Ryder slapped him on the back. "See you later. If I don't get in there, she'll be climbing the curtains."

Wyatt watched his brother walk away and then he headed for his truck. He sat behind the wheel for a minute, letting things settle inside him and watching as Rachel Waters jogged down the driveway and away from his house.

Now what in the world was that all about?

Chapter Eight

Friday night lights had a different meaning in Dawson, Oklahoma, than it did in Texas. Friday nights in Dawson meant the local rodeo at the community arena. Trucks and trailers were scattered in the field that served as a parking lot and cars parked in the small lot that used to be gravel, but the rain had washed it out last fall and so now it was dirt, grass and some gravel.

Wyatt's truck and trailer were parked near the pens where livestock were ready for action. There were a half-dozen bulls, a small pen of steers and a few rangy horses. Someone had dropped off a few sheep for the kids' mutton bustin' event.

The youth group from Community Church was busy cooking hamburgers on a grill as a fundraiser for their trip to Mexico. Pastor Waters had asked him to think about going as a counselor. He wasn't ready for that but he'd agreed to pray.

Maybe soon, though.

He watched the crowds file in, taking seats on the old wooden bleachers. His girls were with Violet. She should be there by now. She'd stayed at home to make more calls to prospective housekeepers. He had thought about stopping her. He had managed just fine all this time, so why did he need someone now?

He wasn't sure he liked the idea of a stranger in his home, taking care of his kids, cooking their meals. The one thing about Violet, she was determined. She'd informed him she had one woman that seemed to be perfect for the job. Great.

"Hey, are you competing tonight?" Ryder walked through the pen of steers, his jeans tucked into boots that were already caked with mud.

The rain they'd had that morning had cooled the air and left the arena pretty soupy. It had also brought a lot of rocks to the surface inside the arena.

"I'm going to rope with Clint Cameron. How's Andie?"

Ryder shuddered. "Not a good patient. You know she doesn't like to sit still. But she'll do it for the girls. Etta is with her tonight."

Twins. Wyatt shook his head and laughed a little. In less than a month his brother was going to be daddy to not one, but two babies. It had taken Andie and those babies to settle Ryder.

"She'll survive it. I'm not sure about you." Wyatt slapped his brother on the back. "You getting on a bull tonight?"

"Andie said if I get on a bull and break my leg, she'll break my neck. Think she means it?"

"Yeah, she probably does."

He glanced toward the bleachers again, looking for his girls. He spotted Violet, but not the girls. He scanned the area around her and didn't see Molly or Kat. Ryder was still talking, but Wyatt held up a hand to stop him.

"I have to go find the girls."

"Aren't they with Violet?"

"They were supposed to be." Wyatt stepped around his brother. "I'll be back."

"Do you want me to help you look?"

"No, I've got it. You stay here in case they show up over here. Maybe they gave her the slip."

He walked on the outside of the arena, ignoring a few people who called out to him and sidestepping puddles left behind by the downpour.

A child yelled. He glanced toward the refreshment stand and his heart hammered hard. Molly and Kat, each holding a corn dog. And Rachel Waters standing next to them. He stopped and then moved quick to get out of the way of a few riders about to enter the arena for the opening ceremony.

The horses moved past him and he had to search again for Rachel and the girls. They were standing a short distance away. Molly laughed and Rachel wiped her cheek. Kat was shoving fries in her mouth. Ketchup had dripped down the front of her plaid shirt and her jeans had dirt on the knees. Her pink boots were almost brown from dirt and mud. His little girl.

Rachel looked up and her smile froze when she saw him. He headed in their direction with anger and some other emotion having a doggone war inside him. Why were his girls with Rachel, not Violet?

Man, seeing her with his girls, seeing them smile like that. Come to think of it, he wasn't even sure he was angry, just confused.

"You have my girls." He spoke as softly as he could, not raising his voice, but it wasn't like he was happy.

"I do." Rachel touched each of their heads. She wasn't eating a corn dog. "I pulled in right after they did. When we got inside the gate, the girls asked Violet for something to eat. I was heading this way, so I told her I'd get them something. Is that okay?"

"Of course it is." He said the words like it was easy and didn't matter.

Rachel remained a few feet away, shifting back and forth on city-girl boots, her jeans a little too long. Her T-shirt said something about joy. A few curls sprang rebelliously from the clip that held her hair in a ponytail.

"I'll take them back to Violet."

"Let them finish eating and I'll take them back with me. They want to see the calves and the sheep."

"Okay." She bent and dropped a kiss on the top of Molly's head and then she hugged Kat. "I'll see you later."

"Why don't you come with us? I'll show you the horse I traded for this morning." He didn't know if she cared about a horse. But he did know that he wanted to keep his daughters smiling.

And the smile he got in return, her smile, kind of shattered his world a little. It also made him regret not thinking this through more carefully.

The girls finished their corn dogs and tossed the sticks in the trash. Rachel wiped their hands with a napkin and then their mouths. Wyatt stood back, like a bystander, observing. She made it all look so easy.

But nothing was simple, not even the way she twisted his emotions. She had somehow hijacked his life and he didn't think she even knew it.

"Let's go." She smiled at him, her hands holding tight to Kat and Molly.

The girls led Rachel as they followed Wyatt back to pens on the north side of the arena. Cattle mooed low and a few sheep bleated their dislike of the muddy pens. A horse whinnied and someone laughed loud. Rachel followed that sound to the source.

The source happened to be tall and wiry with sandy brown hair that curled just a little and a big smile that flashed in a suntanned face. Black framed glasses somehow made his angular features look studious.

He was one of the Cooper brothers, she couldn't remember which. It surprised her to see him at a local event. He was a bullfighter for the professional bull riding events across the country. Tall and wiry, he made his living jumping in front of bulls and taking the shots to keep the bull riders safe.

She knew a daredevil when she saw one. And a flirt.

He lived up to his reputation, jumping one of the fences to land in front of her. Wyatt turned, his smile dissolving when the unknown Cooper took off his hat and bowed in front of her.

"Pleasure to meet you, ma'am." His accent was a little heavy. Andie had told her that she thought he used his Russian heritage to woo the ladies and that his accent hadn't been as heavy a few years back.

She smiled because he was cute and she wasn't interested.

Wyatt appeared at her side. She shivered a little because he didn't appear to be in a great mood. Nor did he appear to be too patient.

"See you later, Travis." He nodded curtly.

The younger man laughed and mumbled something about striking out before he climbed back over the fence to finish saddling his horse.

"He's always up to something." Wyatt led them through a crowd of men and then to his truck and trailer.

A pretty chestnut, deep red with white socks, was tied to the back of his trailer.

"He's beautiful." Rachel ran a hand down the horse's sleek neck.

"I thought so. I bought him at the auction the other night. People are dumping horses like crazy."

"I heard that they're being abandoned on government land."

Wyatt nodded. "This guy belonged to some folks over by Grove. They had to sell all of their livestock."

"I had planned on getting a horse." She stroked the fine boned face of the gelding. His ears pricked forward and he moved to push his head against her arm.

"Planned. You still could. If you decide to get one, I can take you to the auction and we can find you a good deal."

"Thanks, but…" She sighed and focused on the horse, much easier than looking at the cowboy leaning against the horse's saddle where he'd placed his two little girls. His arm was around Molly's back, holding her in place.

"But?"

"But I think right now isn't the right time for me to buy a horse." She smiled and pretended it didn't hurt. "I should go. Do you want me to take the girls back to Violet?"

"First name basis with my mother-in-law?"

"She took me to lunch today," she admitted with a fading sense of ease.

"That's great. Well, I do love to know that my life is being arranged for me." He lifted the girls down and then he put them in the back of his truck. "Stay there and don't get down. There are too many hooves back here and not enough people paying attention."

When he headed her way, Rachel shivered a little. She'd seen that stormy look on his face before. His dark eyes pinned her to the spot where she stood. He untied his horse, still staring at her.

"Rachel, I take care of my girls. I might not be the best cook in the world and maybe my house gets messy, but I haven't let them down. I hope you know that."

"Of course I do." She wanted to touch his arm, to let him know that she wasn't the enemy. She kept her hands to herself. "Violet knows you're a good dad. She's only trying to help. Maybe it's misguided, but…"

"I get that." He led the horse away from her. "I have to get in the arena to ride pickup. Can you take the girls back to Violet?"

"I can. And for what it's worth, I'm sorry."

He tipped his hat and rode off, the horse splattering mud as his big hooves bit into the ground. She stood there for a minute and then she turned to the girls. They were sitting on the tailgate of the truck, waiting. They knew better than to get down. She smiled at them and the two smiled back. They looked sweet in their plaid shirts, jeans and little boots.

Violet must have dressed them. She smiled and reached for their hands. "Let's head back to Grandma and watch the rodeo."

Rachel led the girls back through the crowd of cowboys. A few were zipping up their Kevlar vests in preparation for the bull rides. Bulls moved through the pens and a couple of the big animals were being run into chutes.

Adam MacKenzie stood next to Jason Bradshaw. They were watching one of the bulls, a big gray animal that snorted and when he shook his head, he sent a spray of slime flying through the air.

Kat giggled and wiped her cheek.

"Hey, girls." Jason lifted his hand and Molly high-fived him. "You having fun with Miss Rachel?"

Kat nodded big and smiled. "She could live with us."

Heat crawled up Rachel's cheeks. Jason and Adam laughed but they were definitely curious, she could see it in widened eyes and raised brows.

"Wyatt is thinking about hiring a housekeeper," she explained. "I'm *not* applying for the job."

"Oh, then that makes perfect sense." Jason was married to Etta's granddaughter, Alyson. Ryder's wife, Andie, was Alyson's twin.

Rachel smiled at Jason and kept walking, a little girl on each side of her.

A person didn't have to go far in Dawson to find people who were somehow related. Andie had told her it made dating in Dawson a real challenge. The reason Andie had explained that to her was because she wanted Rachel to know that she shouldn't have a difficult time finding someone to date in Dawson. At least she wasn't anyone's cousin.

At the time it had been funny. Now, not so much. If the church in Tulsa called, she would be gone by the end of June. Once again she had been smart not to get too attached.

Of course, she was just lying to herself. The two little girls holding her hands as they headed for the bleachers happened to be proof that she had gotten attached. The fast beating of her heart when she turned to watch Wyatt rope a bull that refused to leave the arena could probably be called serious evidence.

When they reached Violet, she smiled at the girls and patted the bench next to her. "Come on, girls, time to sit and watch."

A rider was already flying out of the gate on the back of a big white bull. The ride didn't last three seconds. The bull twisted in a funny arc, jumped and spun back in the other direction. Rachel held her breath as the rider flew through the air and landed hard on his back.

"Who was that?" Rachel leaned to ask Jenna who sat on the bench in front of her.

"I think it was one of the Coopers. I can't keep them all straight."

It must have been because Travis Cooper hopped in front of the bull, distracting it while Jackson ran through the gate to the fallen rider. Rachel bit her lip hard and watched, waiting for the rider to move, waiting as the medics hurried into the arena.

A leg moved, then an arm. The cowboy sat up. Rachel released her breath. The crowd erupted in applause. The cowboy lifted his hat as he stood, but then he went limp and his brothers lifted him and carried him from the arena.

"I have a love–hate relationship with this sport," Jenna MacKenzie said. She looked back and shook her head as she made the quiet comment. "I know why they do it. And then I wonder why they do it."

Rachel's gaze traveled to the back of the arena, to the rider holding his horse back from the fray, waiting for the next rider out of the chute. His rope was coiled, ready in case of emergency. He was all cowboy in a white hat, his button-up shirt a deep blue. She remembered the silver cross dangling from a chain around his neck.

If she didn't care, it wouldn't hurt to leave.

But she did care. Kat cuddled close, leaning and then curling on the bench to rest her head on Rachel's lap. Violet handed her a blanket. Kat carried that blanket everywhere, even to the nursery on Sunday.

Rachel dropped it over the little girl who dozed, thumb in her mouth. Molly was still bright-eyed, watching another bull being loaded into the chute. A rider on the catwalk prepared to settle himself on the animal's back.

But it all lost importance because Kat was curled next to her asleep. Rachel stroked the child's hair and Kat cuddled closer. By the time saddle broncs were run into the chutes for that event, Kat had climbed into her arms.

Nothing had ever felt as sweet, or hurt so much. It reminded her of waking up with the tail end of a wonderful dream still fresh on her mind and realizing it had just been a dream.

The cowboy who owned that dream was on his horse, taking the part of pickup man for the saddle bronc event. He glanced up at them, nodding and touching the brim of his hat. Molly waved big. He waved back, grinning. Oh, that grin. In his dark tanned face it flashed white and crinkled at the corners of his eyes. She didn't have to see the details because it had been imprinted in her mind.

His gaze settled on Rachel and Kat. She smiled and nodded. But then his attention returned to the task at hand.

Tension knotted in Rachel's lower back. Maybe due to the child in her arms, having to sit so straight, or the stress of watching men take risks on wild animals. Or maybe because Wyatt Johnson unraveled her a little, making her feel undone and kind of crazy.

She tried to remember the last time a man had made her feel that way. It had to have been when she was fourteen and Andy Banks was the star football player who lived next door. He had been nice when they walked to school together. But one day she'd heard him in the hall talking about her weight and how he thought she had a crush on him. It had turned into a big joke for him, something to laugh about behind her back.

It no longer hurt, but it was something she still remembered. That kind of pain left a scar.

It made it hard to believe in a smile.

But that girl was long gone. That girl had learned to eat healthy and exercise. After losing fifty pounds she'd seen Andy again and he hadn't recognized her. He'd actually smiled and flirted.

Rachel pushed back against those old feelings because she was the person God had created her to be. Fat or skinny, she was His. She knew who she was, and where she was going. She wasn't the person those kids had teased or the girl who had rebelled trying to find herself.

Instead she was the person who had taken control of her life. She had started believing in herself, who she knew she was and stopped believing the lies that were whispered behind her back.

Jenna reached back and touched her hand. "Wyatt's sweet."

Rachel nodded but she didn't know what to say, not when her own thoughts were still in a chaotic jumble and his mother-in-law had just left for a few minutes to stretch her legs.

"Yes, he really loves his girls."

Jenna laughed a little, "Okay, sure, that's what I meant."

Rachel knew what Jenna meant but she didn't comment. Instead she watched Wyatt ready his horse to run it up alongside the saddle bronc as the cowboy on the bucking animal made a leap and landed on the back of the pretty chestnut gelding Wyatt had bought at the auction. The cowboy immediately slid to the ground and headed back to the gate as the judge called out his score.

She was way too old for crushes. When Violet returned, Rachel made up an excuse why she had to leave. It wasn't really an excuse. She had a lot to do tomorrow and she didn't want to get to bed too late.

She kissed the girls goodbye and eased down the bleachers to the ground. Wyatt turned, nodding when he saw her on the grassy area next to the arena. She smiled back, trying to pretend the moment meant nothing to her.

The choir had taken their seats when Wyatt walked through the back doors of the church Sunday and found a seat near the front of the sanctuary. He'd taken the girls from the preschool Sunday school class to the preschool nursery. No Rachel in nursery this morning. His gaze scanned the front of the church, remembering she was in the choir.

She had taken her seat on the left side of the stage with the other altos. Her choir robe was red and white. She stood as the song leader hurried onto the stage. Her hands were already clapping the beat of a fast-paced song. As he stood there like an idiot, her gaze shifted. She smiled big and waved a little.

He hadn't felt so completely tongue-tied since seventh grade and Cora Mason, a ninth grader, had thought he was pretty cute. She had teased him for a couple of weeks and then informed him that he was too young. He wasn't twelve anymore.

And the preacher's daughter wasn't too old for him or

a flirt. She laughed and sang a song about joy. He had to refocus, from Rachel to the music. The music invaded his spirit, pushing the darkness from the corners of his soul.

It was easy to find faith here. This church, Pastor Waters, it all worked together to make a difference in a heart that had been ready to turn itself off to anything other than anger and bitterness. There were moments when he started to feel alive again, as if he could turn it all around. He had been thinking about the teens in this church, not having a youth leader. Everyone scrambled to find activities that kept them out of trouble and gave them options on weekends when there wasn't much to do in Dawson other than get in trouble.

As the choir switched to a more worshipful song, Wyatt closed his eyes. He sang along, listening for one voice. But another spoke to his heart, this one said to trust.

When he opened his eyes the choir was walking off the stage. Rachel hurried out the side door. He smiled because he knew that she would be going back to the nursery. No one could ever accuse her of sitting by, waiting for someone else to do the work.

Her mother, often fighting sickness, sat behind the piano. She had days when she couldn't make it to church, but when she did make it, she played the piano and taught a Sunday school class.

People made choices every day, how to deal with pain, what to do with anger. He remembered back to being a kid in church and the anger over his dad's affairs. He had been angry when the affairs were made public, but he hadn't blamed God. He'd blamed the person responsible, his father. Ryder had blamed God.

Eighteen months ago, Wyatt had been the one blaming God.

He leaned back in the pew and listened to the sermon. It took concentration to hear the words, but as he listened something in that sermon sounded like goodbye. It had to be his imagination. By the time the sermon ended, he was sure of it. It was just a sermon about moving on in life, making choices, following God. That wasn't a goodbye.

The congregation wasn't in a hurry to leave, but Wyatt had two girls waiting to be picked up from the nursery. He shook a few hands and moved past a crowd that seemed like it might pull him into a long conversation. When he reached the back door, Pastor Waters stopped him.

"No church tonight, Wyatt, but I wanted to talk to you if you have time."

"This evening?"

"If that's okay."

Wyatt glanced at his watch. Violet had stayed home to fix a roast and he had a horse that needed one more day under the saddle before his owner picked him up.

"Seven o'clock okay?"

Pastor Waters nodded. "Sounds good. I'll meet you here."

"Good. I'd better get my kids."

Wyatt hurried down the hall to the nursery. He peeked in and his girls were the last to be picked up. Rachel leaned to tie Molly's shoes. Wyatt waited, not saying anything. He watched as she made the loop and then hugged his little girl. Kat turned and saw him.

"Daddy!"

"Hey, kiddo." He leaned over the half door and picked

her up. Little arms wrapped tight around his neck. "Did you have fun?"

Kat nodded. "We made Nose Ark."

"Noah's ark! Cool beans!"

"And there were lions and they roared," Kat continued. "And fish."

"Fish on the ark?"

Kat nodded, pretty serious about the whole thing. "And Rachel said we could fish."

He glanced over his daughter's head and made eye contact with Rachel. She bit down on her bottom lip and shrugged a little. Nice way to look innocent.

Chapter Nine

Rachel smiled at Molly. The little girl stood next to her, looking first to Wyatt and then back to Rachel, her eyes big. Rachel smiled at Wyatt, too, ignoring that he looked a little put out. "You can go, too."

"Where are you going fishing?" He leaned against the door frame, still holding Kat.

She knew this had to be difficult. For the last six months he'd kept them pretty close. Now Violet was pushing him to get a housekeeper and Rachel wanted to take them off fishing.

"To the lake. I have permission to fish off a dock that belongs to one of our church members. It's a pretty day and…"

She was rambling. He did that to her, and she really resented that he managed to undo her ability to hold it together. He was just a man. A man in jeans, a dark blue polo and boots. His hair was brushed back from his face, probably with his hand. And he'd shaved for once. His cologne drifted into her space, a fresh, outdoorsy scent.

Right, just a man.

So why couldn't she focus and act like the adult she

was? He was leaning, hip against the door frame, watching her, his dark eyes a little wicked, sparkling with something mischievous; as if he knew that she wanted to step closer.

One of the Sunday school teachers appeared behind him, opening her mouth to say something. Maria, just a few years older than Rachel, looked from Wyatt to Rachel and then she scurried away mumbling that she'd catch up with her later. That left her, Rachel, stuck in a quagmire of emotion she hadn't been expecting.

She climbed out of the emotional quicksand and got it together.

"If it isn't a good day…" She had been so sure of herself that morning when the idea hit.

So much for the butterfly on her back serving as a reminder to think before acting. If she'd followed that rule she would have allowed him to sign his girls out, and she'd have driven on to the lake alone. Alone was much less complicated than this moment with Wyatt.

"It actually is a good day." He glanced out the window, and she followed his gaze to blue skies and perfectly green grass. "It's a perfect day. I have a young horse that I need to work before his owner picks him up. I think Violet is leaving so it would be good to work him without the possibility of little girls racing across the yard."

"Good, then this works for both of us." She felt a funny sensation in her stomach. "I'll pack a lunch and we'll make a day of it."

"Is it Frank Rogers's dock?"

"It is."

"Good, I just like to know where they are."

"We can go?" Molly jumped up and down. "And take our swimsuits?"

"If your daddy says it is okay. I'll go to our house and make sandwiches while you take them home to get play clothes. Swimsuits, if you don't mind them getting in the water."

"If you keep them in the shallow water."

"I think we can manage." She watched him leave with the girls and then she packed up her bag and headed out. This felt good, spending time with the girls. She had wanted to do it since they showed up in Dawson, but up till now he hadn't looked as if he would agree to let them go.

But today she would teach them to fish. And she wouldn't think about not being here at the end of the summer.

Two hours later, although fishing was her plan, she realized fishing was the last thing the girls wanted. Try as she might, Rachel couldn't get them settled down next to her on the dock's wooden bench. Instead they were running back and forth, sticking their feet in the water.

Kat wrestled with her life jacket, wishing, over and over again, that she could take it off. Finally she sat down next to Rachel, her little head hanging as she fiddled with the zipper.

"Leave it on, Kat," Molly lectured in a voice far older than a three-, almost four-year-old.

"I'm big enough."

Rachel smiled and shook her head at the statement.

"I tell you what, girls, let's skip rocks. And maybe we can wade." She looked around, spotting the perfect way to kill time. "Or we could take a ride on the paddleboat!"

Both girls let out squeals of delight. Who needed to catch fish, when there was something as fun as a paddle boat? She tightened the life jacket that Kat had managed to loosen and lifted her into the boat. Molly went in the seat next to her. Rachel untied the fiberglass boat and settled into the empty seat next to the girls. She started to peddle and the little boat slid away from the dock.

Waves rolled across the surface of the lake making it rough going for one person pedaling against the wind. But the girls didn't mind. Rachel looked down at the two little girls, their faces up to the sun and eyes closed against the breeze.

They were quite a distance from shore when she turned and headed them back toward the dock. Kat leaned against her, groggy, her thumb in her mouth. Rachel leaned back, her arms relaxed behind the two little girls.

It was moments like this she ached for a child of her own. She wanted to be someone's wife, the mother of their children.

A few years ago she had started to doubt that dream.

Her sister, Cynthia, had chided her for martyrdom. She said Rachel was giving up her life to take care of their parents. Rachel shrugged off that accusation. It wasn't martyrdom, not really. It wasn't even guilt, not anymore. It had started out that way, but over the years, when no handsome prince appeared, she stopped believing that there would be one for her.

Cynthia had a house in the suburbs. Rachel had boxes that she kept in the closet for the next move.

She didn't want to think about moving again, not now with the girls next to her. If they moved, it would hurt in a way that no move had ever hurt before. She leaned to kiss Kat on the top of her head.

Time to push these thoughts from her mind and enjoy this day. She didn't know for certain that her dad would take a new church. He never made a decision without prayer. And Rachel was praying, too. Because she didn't want to leave Dawson.

The horse stood stiff-legged with Wyatt in the saddle. He really didn't want to get thrown today. He should have stopped when he finished working the other horse, but this one couldn't be put off. He gave the horse a nudge with his heels. The leather of the saddle creaked a little as the horse shifted. Wyatt settled into the saddle and the gelding took a few steps forward. He pushed his hat down a little because he wasn't about to lose a brand-new hat.

A car pulled up the drive and honked. Great.

The horse let loose, bucking across the arena, jerking him forward and then back. Wyatt tightened his legs around the horse's middle and held tight. Man, he really didn't like a horse that bucked.

Eventually the animal settled and Wyatt held him tight. The horse stood in the center of the arena, trembling a little and heaving.

"Sorry, Buddy, I'm still back here. You aren't my first trip to the rodeo." He nudged the horse forward and they walked around the arena.

They did a few laps around the arena, the horse jarring him with a gait somewhere between a walk and trot. Wyatt nodded when his mother-in-law approached the fence. He'd thank her later for the ride he hadn't really wanted to take.

At least the horse had calmed down and they would end this training session with the gelding remembering that Wyatt had remained in the saddle. Horses kept those memories. If they got a guy on the ground, they remembered. If you gave up on them, they remembered. If you stuck, they remembered.

He rode up to the gate and leaned to open it. A little more of a lesson than he'd planned, but the gelding didn't dump him. Instead he backed and then slid through the open gate with Wyatt still in the saddle.

"I'm so sorry, Wyatt." Violet smiled a little and shrugged. "I didn't even think."

He swung his leg over and slid to the ground. "Normally it wouldn't matter. He's just greener than most. The people bought him as a yearling and kept him in the field for the next two years. He hadn't been trailered or had a halter on until we brought him over here."

"And you're already riding him?"

"We've done a couple of weeks of ground work to get him to this point."

"I see." But she didn't. Violet wasn't country. She had never been on a horse. A half-dozen years ago Wyatt had still been hitting rodeos and Violet had seen it as a waste of time.

He'd quit after that year, the year he won the buckle he'd always wanted. He quit to focus on ministry, on his wife and family.

The dog ran out of the barn and barked. Another car was coming up the drive. He groaned a little. Just what he needed, Violet and Rachel here at the same time. Rachel pulled up and his girls climbed out of her car.

"She took them fishing," he explained, because Violet had been gone when he got back from church. She'd left a note that she'd be back in the afternoon and she'd spend another night before going home.

"That's good, Wyatt." Violet didn't cry, but man, her eyes were overflowing.

"They love being around her."

"Yes, they do. And she's a lovely young woman." She

smiled at him as if that statement meant more. She was making a point he really didn't want pointed out.

"Violet, she isn't…"

Rachel was too close and the girls were running toward him with a stringer of perch. He shook his head and let it go. Violet could believe what she wanted. He let his gaze slide to the woman in question, to a smile that went through him with a jolt. Her hair was pulled back in a tangled mass of brown curls and her eyes sparkled with laughter.

Violet could believe what she wanted, he repeated in his head as his attention slid back to his girls, to what really mattered.

"Did you girls have fun?" He took the string of fish and hugged the girls close. Molly and Kat wrapped their arms around him.

"We fished and waded and paddled a boat." Molly smiled a big smile. Her wounded spirit was healing. He smiled up at Rachel, knowing she was partially to thank for that. Rachel and time were healing their hearts. Kat's and Molly's, not his.

His didn't feel quite as battered, but he thanked time, not Rachel. Oh, and the faith that he'd held on to, even when he hadn't realized he was clinging to it like a life raft.

"They had lunch and on the way home took a short nap."

"Thank you." Wyatt straightened from hugging the girls, a little stiff from the wild ride he'd taken a few minutes ago. "I guess I should get inside and get cleaned up. I'm supposed to be at the church this evening to meet with your dad."

Rachel glanced at her watch. "I have a meeting, too.

But first I'm going to drive up and see if Andie needs anything."

He nodded and watched her walk away. The girls were telling him all about fishing and the lake. He shifted his focus from them for just a moment to watch Rachel get in her car. She waved as she drove away, the top down on her car.

"Wendy would have liked her." Violet spoke softly and he couldn't meet her gaze. His mother-in-law liked Rachel Waters.

So where did that leave him? It left him staring after a little red convertible. The dog had come out of the barn and chased her down the drive. At least Wyatt had more sense and dignity than that.

Rachel pulled up the long drive to Andie and Ryder's house. She did a double take when she spotted a plane parked near the barn. What in the world?

She got out of her car, still looking at the plane and ignoring the border collie that ran circles around her, barking and wagging its black-and-white tail to show that the barking was meant to be friendly. She reached to pet the dog and then walked up the sidewalk to ring the doorbell.

Etta opened the door before Rachel could actually push the bell. The older woman looked beautiful as always with every hair in place and makeup perfectly applied. Today she wore jean capris and a T-shirt, no tie-dye.

"Hey, girl, what are you doing out here?" Etta motioned her inside.

"I took Molly and Kat fishing, then thought I'd stop and see if Andie needs anything."

Etta laughed. "She needs something all right. She

needs off that couch. She's driving us all crazy. It's spring and she can't stand being inside."

"I hear you talking about me," Andie yelled from the living room.

Etta's brows shot up and she smiled a little, then motioned Rachel inside. She walked to the wide door that led into the living room.

Poor Andie, pregnant with twins, flat on the couch. The other option was the hospital. She waved Rachel in.

"Contrary to popular belief, I don't bite." Andie rolled on her side. "And do not call the media and tell them there is a whale beached in Dawson."

"You look beautiful."

Andie growled a little and sighed. "Right."

"It'll be worth it…"

Andie waved her hand. "I know, I know."

"And it won't take you long to get back to your old self. With babies, of course."

"It's frightening." Andie's eyes shadowed. "Honestly, Rachel, it really is scary. Ryder and I are just learning to be responsible for ourselves, and we're going to be responsible for two little people, for making sure they grow up to be good adults. We're going to be responsible for their health, for their well-being, for their spiritual life."

"I'm sure God is going to have a little hand in it."

"Of course. And hopefully He'll get us past the mistakes we're going to make."

Rachel sat down in the chair next to the couch. "Train up a child in the way they should go."

"And when they are teens they'll rebel and give you gray hair." Andie laughed and the shadows dissolved.

"Right. I think I gave my parents more than their share of gray hair during my rebellious years."

"I can't picture it, you as a rebel."

Rachel sat back in the chair and thought about it. "I don't know if it was rebellion or just trying to find a place where I felt included."

"You?"

"Me. My sister, Cynthia, was the pretty cheerleader. Rob was studious. I was overweight and never felt like I fit in. I was always the poor pastor's daughter in second-hand clothing, lurking at the back of the room."

"I'm sorry, Rach. I wish you could have grown up here."

"Me, too. But I went through those things for a reason. I can relate to feeling left out, afraid, unsure of who I'm supposed to be. When I tell the kids at church that this stuff is temporary, they believe me."

"I love you, Rachel Waters." Andie reached for her hand. "The girls at church are lucky to have you. And before long maybe we'll also have a new youth minister?"

"Dad has interviewed a few people but he hasn't landed on the right person." Actually, her dad believed the right person was in their church and just not ready for the job. Not yet. Not until his own heart healed.

"What about Wyatt?"

"I'm not sure if he's ready."

"No, I mean, what *about* Wyatt?" Andie's smile changed and her eyes twinkled with mischief. "He's pretty hot."

"He's pretty taken and your brother-in-law."

"Taken?"

Humor and laughter faded. Andie's head tilted to the side and she waited.

"He still wears his wedding band."

"Of course. I think he hasn't thought to take it off."

Andie grimaced a little. "These two are really doing the tango in there."

"Do you need me to get Etta or Ryder?"

Andie shook her head. "Nope, not yet. It's just occasional kicks and a few twinges. When the contractions really hit, I won't be this calm."

Rachel left a few minutes later. As she drove down the drive and turned back in the direction of Dawson, her thoughts turned again to Wyatt Johnson.

He was a complication. She smiled because it was the first time she'd found the perfect label for him. Complication.

How did people deal with a complication like that, one that made them forget convictions, forget past pain, made them want to take chances?

It seemed easy enough. Stay away. That was the key to dealing with temptation, resist it. Turn away from it. Not toward it.

She'd learned to resist the lure of chocolate cake, so surely she could learn to resist Wyatt Johnson. After all, she really, really loved chocolate cake.

Chapter Ten

It felt pretty strange, walking out of church with the sun setting, and his girls not with him. Wyatt reached into his pocket for his keys. He waved goodbye to Pastor Waters and headed for his truck.

Slowly, little by little, he was getting back to his life. Or at least the life he now had. That included faith. He could deal with life, with being alive.

Pastor Waters had helped him through the anger part of his grief. Wyatt had been working through the questions that had haunted him, kept him up at night.

Why had God allowed Wendy to take those pills? Why hadn't God stopped her from getting them, or stopped her from taking them? Why hadn't God sent someone to keep her from doing that to them? To herself?

Wyatt exhaled, but it didn't hurt the way it once did. He stopped at his truck but didn't get in. Instead he walked to the back of the truck and put the tailgate down. A few minutes alone wasn't going to hurt him. The girls were good with Violet.

He sat on the tailgate.

God hadn't stopped Wendy from breaking his heart.

He closed his eyes and man, the anger still got to him. It was easier to be mad at God than to be mad at Wendy. She had made a choice. She had gone to a doctor who hadn't known about her depression, got pills Wyatt hadn't known about and had taken those pills.

After counseling. After prayer. After it seemed that she was doing better.

She'd made a choice to ignore the voice that probably tried to intervene, telling her to stop, to call someone, to give God a chance. God had been there the day she took those pills, probably pleading in His quiet way, trying to get her attention. And she'd made a choice.

Wyatt had to let go of blaming himself and God. He had to let go of blaming her. She'd been far sicker than any of them realized. She'd been hurting more than he knew.

A voice, real, clear, fresh, carried across the lawn of the church. He opened his eyes and listened to her sing. Rachel. He couldn't see her but he saw her car on the other side of the church. He hadn't realized she was still there.

He listened carefully to words that were far away. She was singing about falling down in the presence of God.

After a few minutes there was silence. The door of the church thudded closed. He watched as she walked down the sidewalk, away from him, not even realizing he was watching. He smiled a little because when no one was watching, she had a fast walk, almost a skip. She had changed from shorts and a T-shirt to a dress and cowboy boots.

A few minutes later he listened as she tried to start her car. The starter clicked but the engine didn't turn over. So much for casual spying without getting caught.

He hopped down from the back of the truck and headed her way.

She sat behind the wheel of the convertible, the top down. When she spotted him she looked surprised and a little smile tilted her mouth.

"Problem?" He leaned in close and her scent wrapped around him. Oriental perfume, peppermint gum and wild cherry lip gloss.

"No, not really." She turned the key again.

"Really?"

She bit down on her bottom lip and shook her head. "The alternator has been making a funny noise. Dad said it was about to go."

"Oh. That isn't something I can fix."

"Really?" Sarcasm laced her tone and he laughed.

"Really." He opened her car door. "But I can give you a ride home."

"Thank you." She stepped out of the car. Up close the dress had tiny flowers and she was wearing a jean jacket over it. He was used to seeing her in jeans. She reached into the back of the car for her purse and the bag she carried each week. He knew it usually contained cookies and craft projects for the nursery. On Wednesdays she worked with teen girls. She was always busy.

He took the bag from her hands. "Let me carry that for you."

She smiled and let him take it. "I didn't expect you to still be here."

"I had a meeting with your dad."

"Oh, that's right."

He wondered if she knew, but he doubted she did. Pastor Waters wasn't the type to talk, not even to his family, about church business or counseling sessions.

"Have you had dinner?" He opened the passenger-side truck door for her and she climbed in.

"No."

"I would take you out, but the only thing open is the convenience store. How about a slice of pizza and a frozen slush?" He stood in the door of the truck, waiting for her answer.

She finally nodded. "Sounds good."

No, it sounded like trouble. But he'd offered and now he had to follow through. He shut her door and then he whistled low and walked around to climb in on his side.

He started his truck and backed out of the parking space. A quick glance right and Rachel was staring out the window, her hands in her lap, fingers clasped. He smiled because he hadn't expected her to be nervous.

The smile faded pretty quickly when he realized he felt a little like wringing his own hands. What was he, sixteen? Not even close. He was double that and then some. But when was the last time he'd been alone with a woman who wasn't his wife? Other than his mother-in-law or Andie, when he drove her to the doctor once a couple of months back, it had been a long time.

At least he still knew the basics. Open the door for her. Buy her a nice dinner. Or the closest thing to a nice dinner. Walk her to the door when he took her home.

Kiss her goodnight?

He shifted gears and cruised down the back road that led the few blocks to the convenience store. The evening was warm and humid. He rolled down the windows and wind whipped through the cab of the truck.

Rachel continued to stare out the window. She reached up to hold her hair in place as it blew around her face. They passed a few houses and people in their yards turned to wave. Well, at least everyone in town would know tomorrow that he'd been spotted with Rachel Waters.

Good or bad, it would get around.

"Want me to roll up the window?"

She shook her head and finally turned to look at him, smiling a little. She had a dimple in one cheek, and he noticed for the first time that her hair glinted with hints of auburn. He was a man, he wasn't supposed to remember details.

"I love this time of year."

He downshifted and turned into the parking lot of Circle A convenience store. "Yeah, me, too."

The timbre of his voice was low and husky, reminding her of fingers in her hair. Rachel swallowed at a thought that felt a little dangerous to a woman who had always been pretty happily single.

The metal building that housed the Circle A was lit up inside and out. Cars were lined up at the gas pumps and several trucks were stopped at the edge of the paved lot; teenagers hanging out on a Sunday night.

"This town never changes." Wyatt shook his head as he made the observation.

"Is that bad?"

"No, not really. I guess it's good to find a place that isn't moving too fast." He pulled the key from the ignition. "Do you want to eat at one of the booths inside?"

Orange plastic seats and bright fluorescent lights. That would just draw attention to them. "I'd rather eat out here."

"I guess we could be like the kids and sit on the tailgate."

Why that appealed to her, she didn't have a clue. But it did. She dug around in the handful of teenage memories she'd held on to and not one of them included sitting on the tailgate with a cowboy. Every woman should have that memory.

"Sounds like fun."

He shot her a look and smiled. His eyes were dark and his skin was tanned from working in the sun. He pushed the white cowboy hat back a little, giving her a better view. Who needed the Seven Wonders of the World if they could sit in a truck with Wyatt Johnson?

"So, are you coming in?"

She nodded and reached for her door handle. This was getting ridiculous, getting lost in daydreams that should have faded when she was sixteen, wanting things she'd thought she'd never have, with a man who clearly wasn't looking.

Butterfly, don't fail me now. She smiled a little as she closed the truck door and met him on the sidewalk. They didn't hold hands and he didn't put a guiding hand on her back. This wasn't a date, just two people having pizza.

Because her car hadn't started. She reminded herself that he was just being kind. When they circled the building and walked up to the sliding glass doors on the front of the building, their reflection greeted her. A man in jeans and a cowboy hat, a woman in a dress and boots. They looked like a nice couple, she thought.

Reminder—not a couple, just a nice guy who offered to take her home. Handsome, sweet and just a friend.

The cool air of the convenience store and the aroma of convenience foods greeted them as they walked through the doors. A few kids stood around the soda fountain, talking, laughing and being kids. Wyatt's hand touched her back and he guided her to the counter where food warmed beneath lights and pizza circled on a display wheel.

"Pepperoni or sausage?" Wyatt asked, too close to her ear. She shivered a little and shrugged. He smiled at the girl behind the counter. "Three slices of each."

She started to object but kept her mouth closed. The girl in the red apron smock opened the plastic door and slid slices of pizza into a box.

"I can get our drinks," Rachel offered. "Do you really want a slushy?"

He grinned, the way Kat grinned when she was up to something. And a slushy wasn't exactly an act of rebellion. But on him, it appeared that way. His grin was a little lopsided and his dark eyes flashed.

"I want all three flavors."

She grimaced. "For real?"

"For real."

It sounded disgusting to Rachel, but if he really wanted to do that to himself, more power to him. She held his cup under each nozzle and grabbed a bottle of water for herself. When she returned he was at the register. He eyed her water but didn't comment.

Not until they were back outside sitting on the tailgate of his truck.

"Water, seriously?"

"I like water." She took a slice of pizza from the box.

And then there was silence as they ate and watched teenagers horsing around. One girl tried too hard. Rachel sighed because she remembered trying too hard. She remembered chasing the boys, grabbing them, laughing too loud.

"Another slice?" He held out the box but she shook her head.

"Two is enough for me."

He set the box down next to him and nodded at the teenagers. "That really takes me back."

"Yeah, me, too." Rachel leaned against the side of the truck bed. "But I bet we have different memories. You were that boy, the one with the swagger and the grin."

A boy in jeans, a T-shirt and boots, with the big truck and the bigger smile.

He grinned and tipped his hat back. "Yeah, I guess I was."

"I was that girl." She pointed to the girl who was grabbing the boys and staggering just a little. Rachel wanted to rescue her, to pull her out of the crowd and tell her to love herself.

Closing her eyes, it was too easy to be that girl, to feel so insecure, to want so much to be loved and not getting that it really did have to start with accepting herself. She really hadn't gotten it, that she couldn't force people to love her.

"You okay?" The words were soft and a hand touched hers.

Rachel opened her eyes and smiled. "Just remembering."

"What's wrong with that girl?" Wyatt didn't look at the girl. He watched her instead. She shrugged and avoided what she knew would be a questioning look, but she felt his gaze on her, felt his intensity. "She looks like she's having fun."

"She isn't having fun. She's trying to find someone who will love her."

He didn't respond. She turned to look at him, smiling because she hadn't meant to delve that deeply into the past.

"That was you?"

"That was me."

"I can't imagine."

"I've gone through some changes since then." Another reason for the butterfly, a reminder that life has a way of changing things. Every season brings something new.

She hopped down from the back of the truck. "We should go."

He nodded, agreeing. Instead of commenting, he grabbed their trash and carried it to the barrel at the corner of the store. Rachel opened her door to get into the truck, but she shot one last look back at the kids. They had a beach ball, bouncing it in the air from person to person. Another truck pulled in. More kids got out. The young girl she had watched raced around the crowd, frantically trying to be a part of something.

A deep ache attached itself to Rachel's heart, remembering that person she'd left behind. But when Wyatt got behind the wheel, she questioned if she really had, or was that insecure girl still hiding inside her, wanting the love that Rachel insisted she really didn't need.

The lights of the parsonage glowed a soft yellow from behind gauzy curtains. A motion light in the backyard came on as Wyatt pulled the truck to a stop. He shifted into Neutral and set the emergency brake. Rachel was already reaching for the door handle.

He should let it end that way, with her getting out, him letting her walk up to the door. But a butterfly tattoo and the hurt look that had flicked across her features as they'd sat eating their pizza kept him from listening to common sense.

Later he would regret this moment, he knew he would. He would regret not listening to the part of him that wanted to remain detached. Instead he got out of the truck and met her as her feet hit the ground.

"I can help you get your car to the garage tomorrow."

"Dad can take care of it." Her eyes were huge in the dusky night.

Another moment that he'd have to think about later: looking a little too long into those eyes. But looking into her eyes didn't begin to compare to the need to hold her. His hands were shoved into his pockets and he fought the part of himself that didn't want to get back in that truck and drive away.

She sighed and her lips parted, not an invitation, he didn't think. No, she was probably going to say something. She probably should tell him to back off or hit the road. Either of the two would work.

A thinking man would have given her a chance to say one of those two things. An idiot cowboy like him didn't always think things through. Sometimes guys like him just had no sense at all and they acted.

That's what he did, he acted, freeing his hands from his pockets and tangling them into masses of brown curls that smelled like wild flowers. He breathed deep as he leaned toward her. He hovered for a second, giving her one last chance to send him packing. When she didn't, he touched his lips to hers.

For a long second she didn't react, but then she moved and her hands touched his arms. He drank her in, steadying himself with one hand on the truck door behind her.

Man, she was sweet. The kiss was sweet. Her hands moved to his back, holding him close. That was sweet.

He pulled back, resting his forehead against hers because he couldn't really breathe. Or think.

And then reality came rushing back in, hitting him full force with a load of guilt and remorse. Those shouldn't be the emotions a man felt after a kiss. She deserved more than a guy tied to the past.

"I'm sorry," he whispered close to her ear, wanting to pull her back into his arms. Instead of giving in, this time he stepped back.

"Yeah, I knew you would be." Pain flickered across her features, hard to miss, even in the dark.

"What do you mean?" He jerked off his hat and swiped a pretty shaky hand through his hair.

Her expression changed to compassion. She reached for his hand. "I just kissed a married man."

He pulled his hand loose from hers, too aware of the wedding ring he'd never taken off, and aware of the message it sent. He shoved his hat back on his head and took a few smart steps back.

It hurt to breathe and hurt worse to think about her words. She hadn't moved away from his truck until that moment and as she stepped past him, she paused to touch his cheek, her smile was soft and sweet.

"I know you loved her. You really don't have to explain or apologize."

"Yeah, I do." He said the words too late. She was halfway to the house and he was standing there like a fool. Her dog ran out of the house, past her to him. The big shepherd circled him a few times, growling. Her whistle called the animal off.

The drive home didn't take near long enough. He had

two minutes to get it together. He felt like he needed two hours. Or two days. A man didn't kiss a woman like that and just walk off.

Rachel was the kind of woman looking for forever, not stolen moments at the end of the night. And Wyatt didn't know if he'd ever want to do forever again. But he did have to think about the future and about the ring still on his finger.

As he parked, lights flashed off in the upstairs room that belonged to his girls. He sat in his truck and watched as other lights came on. Violet waiting for him to come home.

He needed to get his act together. He leaned back in the seat and stared at the barn, at the glimmer of moon peeking through the clouds. At stars glittering in the clear patches of sky.

For eighteen months he'd been asking himself the question he had wanted to ask Wendy. Why had she left them? He let out a tight sigh that came from so deep inside him that it ached. Had she stopped loving them? Had she been unable to love them? He rubbed a hand across his face, clearing his vision.

It was wrong to blame her. He'd even come to terms with the fact that he couldn't blame himself. Now he had to come to terms with the fact that she wasn't coming back. Guilt, accusations, anger—none of that would bring her back.

He put his hands on the steering wheel and the gold band on his left hand glinted. He raised his hand and shook his head. Maybe it was time to let her go, to move on with his life.

Or maybe it wasn't. He'd deal with one thing at a time. It took a minute to get the ring off, twisting and sliding it over his knuckles. His finger felt bare. His heart felt even worse. He slipped the ring into his pocket and opened the door of the truck.

Violet walked out the back door. He walked across the yard, his vision blurred. He took in a deep breath and let it go.

When he walked up the steps of the porch, Violet gave him space. She followed him inside and instead of asking questions she started a pot of coffee. Good thinking, because it looked like it might be a long night.

When she turned, her eyes were misty and her smile trembled on her lips. "Are you okay?"

"I am. Thank you for staying with the girls while I helped Rachel out."

"Where else would I be? Wyatt, you didn't stop being my family when…" She bit down on her bottom lip and blinked a few times. "You're my kid. Those are my sweet granddaughters up there. You're all I have left of Wendy, and I don't ever want that to end. No matter what happens in the future, I hope to always be your mom."

He hugged her and she eventually pulled away and reached for a tissue, pulling it from the box on the counter. She wiped her eyes and smiled.

"Violet, I thank God every single day for you and you'll always be in our lives."

"That's good to know because I can really be a pain sometimes and I need people who will put up with me."

He laughed, and pulled two cups from the cabinet over the coffeepot. Violet sighed a little and he turned.

"You took off your ring."

He looked at his left hand and nodded. "Yeah, I did." Because of Rachel Waters. He didn't have to explain that to Violet. He guessed she probably knew. She probably understood better than anyone else in his life. Maybe even better than he understood it himself.

Chapter Eleven

The dog slid through the door ahead of Rachel. She kicked off her shoes and pushed them up against the wall. She dropped her purse next to them. She hadn't come in right away. After that moment in the yard with Wyatt, she had needed a few minutes to clear her mind and get it together before she faced her parents.

As if she was still fifteen and trying to hide something.

She was twenty-nine and really not a child.

In reality she was a long, long way from childhood and innocence. She sat down at the kitchen table and moved a few pieces of the puzzle that had been there for days, unfinished. The painted faces of kittens on cardboard were scattered, unrecognizable. She found an edge and slid it into place.

Her life was just as scattered, just as in pieces, as that puzzle. She had kissed Wyatt Johnson. Her parents had decided to take the church in Tulsa and she couldn't tell anyone until the formal announcement. She had to bury the pain of moving and leaving this place behind.

She had to leave Wyatt and the girls. She hadn't expected that to be the part that hurt the most. She hadn't expected to feel anything for Wyatt other than sympathy.

Surprise. The feelings were unexpected after years of holding back and waiting for God to bring someone into her life. She moved another puzzle piece and a ring on her own finger glinted in the soft light of the kitchen. A purity ring that she'd put on after some very bad relationship choices.

She had made a promise to wait for God to bring someone into her life. She had made a promise to herself to stop pursuing and to wait for someone who loved her enough to pursue her. She figured the fact that she was nearly thirty said it all.

"Hey, kiddo, how's your car?" Her dad stood in the doorway, the tie from earlier in the day gone, but he still looked like Pastor Waters. She smiled and pushed the other chair out with her foot, an invitation.

"It'll have to go to the garage. The alternator finally gave up and died."

"I'll have it towed to Grove tomorrow."

"Thanks, Dad."

"What's up?"

"Nothing."

Robert Waters crossed the room and sat down across from her. She smiled up at him because this was a scene that had played out a lot in their lives, the two of them together with a puzzle between them. He started moving pieces and she did the same.

"This move isn't what you want, is it?" He looked up, smiling a little. "You don't have to go."

"I know that. I want to go."

He pushed a piece of the puzzle into place and they

finally had an entire kitten. She was allergic, so this was the closest she got to fuzzy felines.

"Rachel, promise me you'll tell us the truth. If you don't want to leave, you shouldn't. You know that Etta would gladly let you stay with her."

"I know that, but Etta isn't my family."

"No, she isn't." He piled up gray puzzle pieces that went to the gray kitten she was working on. Rachel reached and took one that might fit.

"Dad, I'm okay with this." She smiled because she was okay. It wasn't her first move and she knew that moves were never easy. But she was okay. She would adjust.

She was used to leaving places, leaving people. Doing the right thing didn't always mean the right thing felt good. Sometimes doing the right thing was difficult.

Her dad stood up. Before he walked away, he leaned to kiss the top of her head. "Your mom said to tell you goodnight and she loves you."

"Right back at her." She reached for his hand to stop him from walking away. "Don't worry about me."

"I always do. That's part of being a parent. We want our children to be happy."

She nodded but this time she didn't answer. She didn't know how to respond to being happy. Her heart had gone into rebellion and suddenly wanted something she knew she couldn't have.

The best way to get her heart into check was to explain to it that she had just experienced something that everyone experiences: a goodnight kiss. It had been nothing more and nothing less, just a kiss at the end of a sweet evening with a man who might possibly be a friend.

To make it anything more than that was a mistake. Like telling him he was still wearing his wedding ring.

She cringed a little because it wasn't her place to point that out to him, not a man who had been kindness itself. He had kissed her goodnight. It wasn't as if he'd proposed.

Wyatt Johnson was sweet and gorgeous. He wasn't looking for long-term.

She moved another piece of puzzle into place and got up to go to bed. Tomorrow she'd apologize.

The crazy gelding jumped sideways and lurched. Wyatt held tight, wrapping his legs around the animal's belly. If he'd been paying attention instead of thinking about holding Rachel last night, maybe he wouldn't have been in this position. The horse beneath him shook his head and hunched again. Wyatt held tight, waiting. The horse settled into a jarring trot across the arena.

He'd be glad to send this one back to his owner. If it wasn't for the fact that he liked to tell people he'd never met a horse he couldn't break, he'd probably send the horse back today.

He glanced to the side, making sure the girls were still on the swing. They were. As he watched, Molly jumped up and started waving. He caught a glimpse of an old truck. Molly waved and ran.

The horse unleashed on him, bucking across the arena. Hooves beat into the hard-packed dirt of the arena. Wyatt pushed his hat down and held tight, his teeth gritted against the jolt that set him a little back in the saddle. The horse lurched again, this time nearly getting him off the side.

He barely made it back into the saddle when the crazy animal's head went down and his back end went up. Wyatt felt himself leave the seat and go airborne over the horse's head. He heard Molly scream and then he hit the ground.

Pain shot through his back and head. He rolled over on his back and worked to take a deep breath. He bent his knees and blinked a few times to clear his brain.

This couldn't be happening.

Rachel yelled his name. Good way to be calm, Rachel. He shook his head. The girls were screaming. He rolled to his belly and made it to his knees. Oh, yeah, he'd been here before, sucking in a breath that hurt like crazy.

"I guess this is a bad time to tell you I saw a few of your cows out on the road?"

The voice came from his left. He rolled his head that way and tried to smile. But smiling hurt, too. He was way too old for getting thrown.

"Yeah, this might be a bad time."

"Want help?" Rachel reached for his arm. He gritted his teeth and pushed himself to his feet with her hand holding him steady.

"Daddy?" Molly's voice trembled. He blinked and focused on her face, just behind Rachel.

"I'm okay, sugar bug." He drew in a deep breath. "Wow."

"Should I call…" Rachel bit down on her bottom lip and shrugged a little.

An ambulance. Good not to say it around the girls and panic them more than they were. He shook his head and regretted it because it felt like it unhinged his brain a little.

"You can call Greg Buckley and tell him to come and get that crazy horse of his. I'm done with that animal." He'd been fighting that crazy buckskin every time he got in the saddle.

"You think?" She smiled and his girls followed her example. "What about those cows?"

"Daddy, are you broke?" Molly stared up at him, eyes full of unshed tears.

"Nah, of course not."

Violet headed their way, picking through the dirt and rocks with high heels that he would have laughed about if he'd been able to laugh. "Do you want me to drive you to the hospital?"

She'd been packing her stuff, getting ready to go home. Now he had other concerns.

The girls. He sucked in a breath that hurt like crazy. And *crazy* wasn't the word he really wanted to say. A lot of other words came to mind. He leaned on the fence, draping his arms over the top rail. The girls.

He shifted to look at Rachel.

"Could you stay with the girls?"

"Of course I can. Or I can drive you."

"No, Violet can take me." What he didn't need or want to do was lean on Rachel. Literally. He didn't want to be in pain in front of her. It didn't do a guy's ego any good to have to lean on a woman to make it to the car.

"Daddy?" Molly stared up at him, brown eyes wide.

"I'm fine, Mol. You stay with Rachel and I'll be home later."

"Do you need help?" Rachel had stayed next to him, smelling soft and sweet. And she was asking if he needed help.

Even if it killed him, he wasn't going to lean on anyone.

"I'm fine." He touched Molly's cheek and she smiled. "Be good."

She nodded and grabbed Kat's hand. "We will."

He never had a doubt. But would she be afraid?

"Okay, let's go." One last deep breath, and then he headed for Violet's car with steady steps that said he would be fine.

Violet walked next to him. "You're such a tough guy."

"Yeah, well, we wouldn't want the girls to see me cry." He gritted the words out from clenched teeth.

"Are you really going to cry?" Violet teased as she opened the passenger-side door.

He waved at Rachel and the girls. "Not on your life, Violet."

"You cowboys think you're so tough."

Yeah, that's exactly what he thought.

Violet slid behind the wheel of the Cadillac and turned the key. As she shifted into Reverse, she glanced his way. "How badly are you hurt? No lies this time."

"I haven't lied yet." He leaned back into the soft leather seat. He wished his truck felt this good. "Maybe ribs, maybe my back."

"How are you going to take care of the girls when I leave? You've vetoed every applicant I've interviewed. What do we do now?"

"I can take care of my girls, Violet."

"I know you can, but this changes things."

"You have me in the ICU and I haven't even made it to the E.R."

"I'm thinking of all the possibilities."

"Well, I'm not. I'm fine and I'll be home by dinner. I have a birthday party to plan. Molly will be four next week."

"I know. I had planned on going home to get a few things done and coming back before then."

"And you can still do that." He closed his eyes and counted to twenty.

As he counted he heard her phone dialing. He opened his eyes and waited.

"Rachel, this is Violet. Oh, no, honey, we haven't made it to Grove. No, but I need a favor. I'm taking John Wayne to the E.R., but he's probably going to need help when I leave. I haven't hired anyone because he's picky. I know you have a lot going on, but if you could take the job temporarily." Short pause and he wanted to jerk the phone out of Violet's hand. "Just for a month or until we can find someone."

"Violet." He whispered what she should have seen as a warning. She smiled at him and kept talking.

"That's great, honey. I'll write you a check when we get back. Or when I get back. Right, just keep the house clean, cook some meals and make sure the girls have clothes that match."

"I can dress my kids." He pushed the button to recline the bucket seat. "Women."

Because of a woman he'd taken his ring off last night. It was all connected: the kiss, her words and removing his wedding ring. He just didn't want to draw the lines, not at the moment.

Maybe it was just about letting Wendy go. Maybe it was about Rachel. Right now he needed a shot of something and a lot less thinking going on in his scrambled brain.

Chapter Twelve

"What do we do with that horse?" Rachel looked down at the girls. The two of them shrugged. Of course they didn't know. They were two and four. Or almost four.

Molly was about to have a birthday. Rachel worried her bottom lip thinking about that special occasion and the possibility that Wyatt would stay in the hospital. Okay, horse first, cows in the road second. Or maybe the cows should be first.

She pulled the phone from her pocket and called Ryder.

"Ryder." He answered with his name and he sounded stressed and frazzled.

"Ryder, it's Rachel. Listen, Wyatt got thrown and Violet is taking him to the E.R."

"Oh, that's just what I need."

Okay, not the response she expected. "Ryder, you guys have cows out, just a few hundred feet down from your drive. And I have this horse here, the one that dumped him, and…"

"Rachel, I'm sorry, I can't. Andie's having contractions. I'm flying her to Tulsa."

In the background she heard Andie yell that she wasn't getting in a plane with him. Rachel smiled and waited for the two to argue it out and remember that she was on the phone.

"Rachel, I'll call Jason and see if he can put those cows in. Can you handle the horse?"

"I don't know. I can try."

She looked at the horse in the arena. The buckskin stood at the far corner. He needed the saddle and bridle removed and he needed to be put in the field. Or maybe a stall. She wondered which one.

"If you can't get him, call Jason or Adam."

"Okay. Is there anything I can do for you and Andie?"

"Pray."

The conversation ended and she was on her own. Rachel looked at Molly and Kat. No help there. They both looked pretty nervous. Molly's dark eyes overflowed with tears.

"I want my daddy."

"I know, honey." Rachel squatted in front of the girls. "I know you're worried about your daddy. He's fine. Remember when he left, he was talking. He even walked to the car. He's fine."

"He'll come home." Molly sobbed and rubbed her eyes.

"Of course he will." This wasn't normal fear. Rachel hugged the girls close. "He'll be fine. And while he's gone, we'll be fine. We'll get that silly horse taken care of and if we need to, we'll put the cows in. We can do that, can't we?"

Keep them busy. That's all she knew to do.

But it meant walking into the arena with a horse she didn't trust. She straightened, trying to look taller, and gave the horse a look. As if that would do any good. A hand tugged on hers.

"You aren't gonna ride him." Molly wide-eyed and maybe a little impressed.

"No, honey, I'm not. I'm going to unsaddle him and—" she bit down on her bottom lip "—I'm going to put him in a stall."

Molly grabbed her hand and with her other hand she grabbed hold of Kat. "We'll go with you."

"I appreciate that, Molly, but I think I should go in alone."

It sounded like a movie, as if they were going into a house with monsters, or some horrible villain. It was a horse, a tan horse with a black mane and tail. Just a small little horse. Well, maybe not so small.

"You girls wait out here." She handed Molly her phone. She didn't say to call 9-1-1 if something happened. Instead she smiled as if she was brave and not shaking in her shoes.

She whistled, kind of. The horse shot her a disinterested look. Okay, she was used to that look. He must be a man. She smiled at her joke and kept walking. The horse didn't move.

"Buddy, it would help me out if you'd play nice."

The horse reached his nose under the bottom rail of the fence and nibbled at a few blades of grass. Rachel walked up to him, talking softly, saying a few prayers under her breath. Did horses smell fear? She really hoped not.

She reached for the reins that had been dragging on the ground. The horse snorted and raised his head. He jerked away from her but she held tight.

"Listen, horse, I'm not a cowgirl like Jenna and Andie,

but I do know how to hold on tight. I am not going to let you win."

The buckskin edged close and snorted, blowing grass and grain all over the front of her shirt. "Oh, that's real nice."

She held both reins and led the horse back to the barn. He plodded along behind her as if he was Kat's little pony. She rubbed his neck as they walked.

"So now you're going to be nice?"

For a brief moment she relaxed but then she remembered how it felt when she watched Wyatt go flying from the horse's back. She didn't want to remember how it felt to watch him hit the ground and stay there, motionless.

From across the arena she heard her phone ring. She glanced back. Molly held it up.

"Go ahead and answer it. Tell them I'll call back." She didn't want to yell, to startle the horse.

She had decided the best course of action was to un-saddle him, take off his bridle and leave him in the arena. She could get him a bucket of water and hay.

First, the saddle. She wrapped the reins in a hook on the wall of the barn and the horse stood perfectly still. She pulled the girth strap loose and eased off the saddle. He moved away from her and she thought about how easy it would be for him to turn and kick.

Instead of thinking about that, about possibilities, she unbuckled the strap on the bridle and pulled it over his ears and off his head. The horse stood for a moment, a little unsure. Finally he backed away from her and turned to trot to the other side of the arena.

She had done it. Now to take care of the girls. She turned as a truck pulled up the drive. Jason Bradshaw.

He hopped out of the truck and headed her way, his big smile making things feel better.

"You got him unsaddled." Jason opened the gate for her. "I'll put him in a stall and feed him for you."

"What about the cows in the road?"

Jason picked up Kat and tickled her until she laughed. "I put them back in and fixed a loose section of fence. Have you heard anything yet?"

"Not yet. I don't think they've had time." She glanced at the girls because she didn't want to have this conversation in front of them.

Jason sat Kat on the back of Rachel's truck. He motioned for her to walk with him. Rachel followed. The cowboy, his red hair cut short, had a smile that made everyone feel better.

"Rachel, do you know about the girls?"

"I'm not sure what you mean."

Jason rubbed his jaw. He glanced from her to her truck where the girls were waiting. "This should be up to Wyatt, but there's something you should know. In case Wyatt doesn't get home tonight, you need to understand that Molly gets pretty upset when he isn't here."

"I'm not sure if you should tell me something that Wyatt hasn't told me."

"He'd want you to know. For the sake of his girls. Molly and Kat were with Wendy. They were alone until he got home that afternoon and found them."

And she got it in a way that ached so deep inside her she didn't know if she could draw in a breath. She thought about those two little girls alone with their mother. But Wendy wouldn't have been with them. She took the pills and left them alone.

Rachel turned away from Jason because it was too

much to know this secret about the wife that Wyatt had loved. Still loved.

But he'd taken off his wedding ring. She'd noticed it as she'd helped him up. She wondered if it had been about the kiss or what she'd said. Or had it been something he'd been working up to and he finally realized it was time?

"I should take them inside and fix their dinner."

Jason walked with her back to the truck. "He doesn't tell people because it's Wendy's memory. He doesn't want that to be what people think about when they remember her."

"I understand."

Jason lifted Molly and Kat out of the back of the truck. He gave them each a hug as he set them on the ground. "You girls help Miss Rachel. She's going to stay with you until your daddy gets home."

"Will he come home tonight?" Molly held on to his hand.

"I'm not sure, Molly. He might come home tonight. Or maybe tomorrow. Either way, he'll be fine and so will you. Rachel is going to stay with you."

She was staying. She smiled at the girls. They looked at her, both wide-eyed and full of trust. Of course she was staying.

It was after midnight when Wyatt walked through the front door of his house. He had eased up the front steps because two steps were easier than five or six when a guy had a few cracked ribs and a couple of pulled muscles. Oh, yeah, and a concussion.

He didn't remember, but the horse must have landed a good kick in his side as he went down.

Violet walked behind him. Poor Violet, he guessed

she really wanted to go home after a week of the drama in Dawson. He smiled because she hadn't said too much. She'd actually been pretty terrific, fighting with the doctor when they wanted to keep him overnight.

No way could he leave his girls overnight. He knew the look of terror in Molly's eyes when she thought he wasn't coming home. He remembered eighteen months ago walking through the front door and finding her in the playpen with Kat. The two had been red-faced, eyes swollen from crying and nearly breathless from sobbing. That memory would never leave him.

"Wyatt, you have to let your mind rest." Violet touched his arm. "I know that look on your face. I know what you're thinking. The girls are fine. I've never seen them better."

"I know." He took careful steps into the living room. He'd sleep on the couch tonight instead of climbing the stairs.

But the living room was occupied. He stopped in the doorway. Molly and Kat slept on the couch. Rachel slept curled up in the chair near the couch. A fire, only embers, glowed in the fireplace. It felt good and smelled good. The temperature outside had dropped after a late-evening storm rolled through. The fire was pretty inviting.

Yeah, right, the fire.

"This is sweet." Violet touched his shoulder. "Now where are you going to crash?"

"The sofa in my office." He didn't move, though. Either because it hurt too bad or, he looked at the girls and at Rachel Waters, it hurt too bad. He smiled at Violet. "What about you?"

"I'll stay up with you."

"You should get some sleep." He nodded toward the stairs. "Go, Violet, I'll be fine."

"I'll stay up with him." A sleepy voice from the living room interrupted their conversation. Rachel stretched and sat up. "I've been sleeping for a few hours. You go to bed, Violet."

He really didn't need a babysitter. He considered arguing, but he didn't have the strength and he knew he'd never win against two women. Rachel was already on her feet, a blanket around her shoulders.

Blame it on painkillers or a concussion, but he wanted to say things he wouldn't be able to take back in the morning.

"He has to be woken up every hour." Violet explained what the doctor had told them. He kept his mouth shut, glad she'd stepped in and kept him from making a complete fool of himself.

"I can do that." Rachel stood, folding the blanket that she'd had over her.

"I really don't need a keeper. This isn't my first concussion or the first time I've cracked a few ribs." What he didn't want to admit was that it hadn't hurt as bad as this the last time.

"Right." Rachel smiled at Violet who said goodnight and then retreated up the stairs. He watched her go and then he was alone with temptation itself. She smiled at him, completely unaware of how beautiful she was standing in that spot with just a sliver of moonlight coming through the window and the warm embers from the fire reflecting the auburn highlights in her hair.

Yeah, guys weren't always clueless.

"I'm not sure if this is right or wrong." He eased a step in her direction and braced a hand against the doorway.

"What?"

"This." He reached for her hand and pulled her close. She stood in front of him, unmoving, unblinking, staring at him as if he'd lost his mind. Maybe he had. Maybe the horse had knocked him silly. Maybe it had knocked sense into him. Whatever it was, he didn't want to think too deeply, not yet.

"This." He whispered it again and leaned, touching his lips to hers. She was so sweet, like cherry soda on a hot summer day. She was his first time driving alone, the first horse he owned, the first time he'd ever felt free. She was everything and more.

She healed his heart with that kiss. She made him feel things he hadn't expected, had never felt.

And she scared the daylights out of him. He moved his hand from her arm to her back and he held her close, trying to breathe, trying to get it right and trying to convince himself to let her go.

Eventually she stepped back. Her lips parted and she shook her head. "No."

"No." Did he want to argue with her or agree? He wasn't sure.

"This isn't what you want." She smiled a little. "This is about feeling vulnerable and alone. This isn't about us. This is something you have to work through, on your own."

He looked a little deeper and saw her pain. It shimmered in her eyes and he remembered the other night on the tailgate of his truck when she'd talked about girls trying too hard to be loved.

Her story. Man, he wanted her stories.

"You should lie down." She swallowed and looked away.

"I should." He laughed and it hurt like crazy. "I think I might need help."

"The sofa in the office."

"Yeah." Cowboy up, Wyatt, he told himself. A guy couldn't impress a woman if he had to lean on her just to make it to a chair. Casual would work. He draped his arm around her shoulders.

"That's a lame move." She left it there, though.

"It's all I could think of right now." He walked next to her, pretty thankful for a strong woman who felt soft and smelled sweet.

"Stop sniffing my hair." She whispered the warning as they walked through the office door.

"Sorry."

She laughed and shook her head. "My dog has more manners."

"Not possible."

"I'm sure of it." She stopped in front of the couch and slid out from under his arm.

With her hands holding his arms, she held tight while he lowered onto the couch, trying hard not to groan. He gritted his teeth instead. She smiled, not the kind of smile that meant sympathy.

He really wanted sympathy. A nice pillow, a soft blanket and maybe a glass of water. She didn't look as if she planned to play nursemaid. More than anything she looked like someone about to escape.

He was the guy who needed to let her go because that made sense. Getting tangled up in this didn't. He'd seen tangled up before. He'd doctored a horse for a week because it hadn't had the sense to stay out of barbed wire.

Yeah, he had more sense than that horse.

Chapter Thirteen

He looked pitiful, miserable actually. His dark hair was a mess, hanging across his forehead. The top two buttons of his shirt were gone and he still wore the jeans he'd been wearing when he hit the ground. Rachel stood for a moment, unsure of what to do next. Her internal alarm sounded, telling her to find the nearest exit and leave him to his own devices. But she had promised to stay with him, and Violet looked worn out. The girls were sleeping in the living room.

"You should take your boots off and I'll find a pillow and blanket." Good first step.

He grinned and shook his head, "Honey, I'd love to take off my boots, but I don't think I can lean down."

Okay, she didn't need this. Instead of discussing, she knelt and reached for the heel of one boot. She slid it off and reached for the other. "Your feet stink."

He laughed a little, but she heard the grimace of pain. "Yeah, I bet they do. Thank you for taking one for the team."

She looked up, mid-pull. He was watching her. She looked away quickly and finished the second boot. As she stood up, he wrapped his legs around hers, right at her knees, and held her in front of him.

His smiled changed from soft to rotten, lifting at one corner. No, no, no. Rachel didn't want this thin strand of emotion connecting them. She didn't want to get tied into this when he was having fun, or using her to get past something.

She'd been used before and it wasn't going to happen again.

"I'm going to get you a pillow." She stepped out of the circle of his legs and moved to the door. "Ice water?"

He nodded and she left the room, walking down the darkened hallway to the kitchen. Her heart hammered in her chest and she worked to get a deep breath.

"Okay, God, give me strength." She pulled a glass out of the cabinet and instead of heading for the fridge, she looked out the window, watching trees blown by a south wind and paper fluttering end over end across the lawn. Another storm was blowing up. Clouds were eating up the dark sky, blotting the moon and the twinkling stars.

Give her strength. More than that, help her find peace. Help her to not rush into a relationship with someone who was emotionally tied up and working past his grief.

She filled the glass with ice and water. Now to find a pillow and blanket. She had seen them the day she cleaned, in a closet off the main bathroom. She flipped on the light, dug around in the closet and headed back down the hall.

He was sleeping when she returned to the office. Stretched out on the couch, one foot on the floor and his arm flopped over his face. It would be good if he stayed asleep. She put the glass down and unfolded the blanket.

"I'm not cold." He moved his arm and there was no

smile. His chest expanded with a heavy sigh. "I'm scared to death."

"Why?"

She couldn't have this conversation standing. She pulled a chair close to the couch and sat down. He reached for her hand, holding it, looking at it, running his fingers over hers. He had rough, warm hands. The hands of a cowboy, a rancher.

"Wyatt, it's just a concussion. Right?"

He smiled up at her, still holding her hand. "I'm not afraid of that. I'm afraid of you. I'm scared to death to feel what I feel. I'm not ready."

Slam. She drew in a shaky breath and pulled her hand from his. Be afraid of death, she wanted to tell him. Be afraid of the dark. Be afraid of anything, but not her.

But wasn't she scared to death of him, of being used, of being rejected?

She looked up, gathering strength and trying to find God. All of those words and then to hear that he wasn't ready. She reached for the pillow.

"You'll want this." She waited for him to lean forward and she slid it under his head. "And now, I should go."

"But…"

"I'm not leaving. I'm going in with the girls. These are not the words I want to hear in the middle of the night." She felt wrung out, exhausted, run over. "I'll be back in an hour. If you need me, I'm across the hall."

"Rachel?"

She shook her head as she walked out the door and back to the living room where the girls were sleeping. She couldn't respond, instead she brushed away tears and buried her face in the pillow she'd been using earlier in the evening.

Nothing had ever hurt this bad. He wasn't ready. She wondered if he would ever really be ready. The awkward teenager she had been taunted her, telling her she'd never be the person he moved on with.

Tonight she fought back. God hadn't made her an awkward teenager. She was more than that. She knew that He didn't create mistakes. Every inch of her was designed by God.

The young girl who had wanted nothing more than to stay in one house was designed by Him. The teenager who had turned to chocolate and cheesecake, later to a reckless crowd of friends, and the twenty-year-old who had finally gotten it right, they were all the same person, His creation, fearfully and wonderfully made. It had just taken her a while to figure it out and to stop fighting who she was. It had taken her a while to trust Him with her life.

It had taken her a while to be comfortable in her own skin and to love herself enough to stop punishing herself.

Tonight the girl who wanted to be loved was fighting tooth and nail, wanting to believe a cowboy like Wyatt Johnson could really, really love her someday.

And maybe her parents' plan to move had come at just the right time. Maybe this move was designed to protect her heart.

Wyatt cracked one eye and saw two little girls leaning close, whispering for him to wake up. After a long night of hourly wake-up calls, this time waking up felt great, even if he didn't know how to take a deep breath and his head ached as if he'd been hit with a sledgehammer. At that moment it was all about Molly and Kat leaning over him, studying his face with worried little expressions.

"Daddy, are you awake?" Molly leaned, her nose close to his. "Because we didn't know if you would wake up."

He wrapped them both in one arm and pulled them to him. "I'm definitely awake. And I love you both."

"Grandma left." Kat kissed his cheek. "And said you had to be good and listen to us and to Rachel."

"Rachel?"

Molly nodded, all serious and wide-eyed. "Rachel told Grandma she'd be our nanny and clean our house. And she already cooks good."

"Really?" He smiled, even though it hurt.

"She doesn't need books to make pancakes. They aren't even frozen first."

"Really?" He growled and pretended to get her arms. "Can she do that?"

Molly shook her head. "She doesn't have whiskers, Daddy."

Now that was something he did know. "You're right about that. Now help me up and we'll go see about that bad ol' buckskin."

"Rachel unsaddled him."

"That's good." They each had hold of a hand and he groaned as they pulled him to a sitting position. "Man, I'm sore."

"Grandma said you've been run over by a truck, but it was just a horse."

"She meant I feel like I've been run over by a truck."

Kat held on to his hand. "Mean old horse."

"Yeah."

They led him down the hall. The aroma of bacon lingered in the air. He hoped there was some left for him. On top of that, the house smelled clean. He glanced at the clock. It was just after nine in the morning. A clean house and breakfast. Not too shabby.

Rachel walked out of the laundry room carrying a mop bucket. Her hair was braided and she had changed into shorts and a T-shirt. He knew now that she jogged nearly every day. He'd seen her a few times in the last couple of weeks.

"Seems like I might be Rip Van Winkle. Everything changed while I was sleeping." Including her, his feelings and his house.

He ambled into the kitchen, working on casual when he felt as cagey as a penned-up cur dog. He poured himself a cup of coffee and took a piece of bacon from the plate near the stove. When he turned around she was in the kitchen, taking up space, moving around as if she belonged there.

It shouldn't bother him, that Violet had hired her, but it did. He wanted to choose the person who came into his home. He wanted to choose someone who didn't smell so stinking good and who didn't look prettier than a rodeo queen, even in those faded shorts and a T-shirt.

"I'll make you pancakes." She had the fridge door open, blocking her from his view. Molly, not even four, was sitting on a stool smiling at him as if she knew way more than he was saying.

He shot his daughter a look and she giggled. The fridge door closed and Rachel's eyes narrowed as she stared at him. It took him a second but he worked up to innocent and shrugged, as if he didn't know what his kid was all about.

"Sit down and I'll fix your breakfast."

He pulled out a stool next to Kat. Okay, maybe this

wasn't so bad. What could possibly be bad about sitting here watching her in his kitchen?

"I should feed the animals before I eat breakfast."

She turned, a spatula in her hand. "I took care of it."

"You fed?" He didn't feel like smiling now.

"No, I called Ryder. Of course he's in Tulsa with Andie, but he sent Jason over to take care of things. And Jackson Cooper..."

He raised a hand to stop her. She flipped the pancakes and he had to wait a second for her to get back to him. This was getting a little crazy. He was feeling pretty crazy on the inside.

Emotions should be gradual, not wildfire, spreading every which way. But he didn't think emotions came in gradual increments. Pain—Bang. Grief—Bang. Anger—Bang. Now this—Bang. He didn't want to put a name on it.

Oh, wait, maybe jealousy. He lifted his coffee cup and took a few drinks. She flipped pancakes onto a plate and set it in front of him with butter and syrup.

"Jackson doesn't need to come over here. I can manage things myself." He jabbed a knife into the butter and spread it over the tops of the pancakes.

"Right."

"Yeah, right. Cracked ribs and a concussion, that's it, Rachel. I really don't need all this help." He wasn't some namby-pamby sissy. He'd been bucked off more bulls than he could count. He'd been thrown by horses. He'd been run over and stepped on.

"Fine, you can call Jackson and tell him you can do it yourself."

Okay, that made him sound like a three-year-old tackling a flight of stairs by himself. He chewed on pancakes that were so good he forgot to be mad.

Instead of anger, he felt a big urge to hug her. Molly giggled again. He looked down and she laughed harder.

"What's so funny?"

She giggled more. "You're funny, Daddy. You're not mad, you're happy."

Well, that just about beat all.

He kissed her cheek. "You're right, Molly Doodle, I'm happy."

As he finished the plate of pancakes, he watched Rachel move around his kitchen. He was happy. Bang. Just like that.

Being happy should have been something he grabbed hold of and thanked the good Lord above for. Instead he questioned it, a lot like the Israelites had questioned everything God did for them in the wilderness.

And on top of that, he felt guilty. The bad thing about guilt is that it undid happy.

He finished the pancakes and got up to carry the plate to the sink. Rachel took it from his hands with a smile.

"I can get it."

She rinsed it off and put it in the dishwasher. "So can I."

"Fine. I'm going to go outside and check on that buckskin. Did Jason call to see if they would pick him up?"

"I think they're getting him this evening."

He nodded and then he backtracked to the fact that she'd mentioned Ryder and he hadn't really paid attention. He blamed it on the concussion.

"What was that about Ryder?"

"Andie was having contractions. Ryder flew her to Tulsa yesterday. They called earlier and she's resting.

The contractions slowed down, but they think it will be in the next day or two."

"Ryder, a dad. That's going to be fun to watch."

"He's ready for it. He has you."

Now what did he say? He stood there, aching from the inside out thanks to cracked ribs and some deep bruises. He tried for casual and leaned hip against counter, arms crossed in front of him. Rachel's narrowed gaze went from his chest to his face. She cocked her head to the side.

"I'm going outside." He eased across the kitchen.

"Don't do too much too soon," she warned softly.

"I'm not. I can't stay in the house."

"I know." She picked up the bottle of pills he'd left on the counter and tossed it. He caught it.

"I don't need these. I don't want to feel sleepy all day."

"If you're sleeping you won't be doing something you shouldn't do."

He laughed because what he was thinking and what she was thinking were two different things. Maybe she had a point. Maybe drugging him was the best thing for both of them.

"Rachel, I'll take a few aspirins, not these. And I am going outside to check on things."

She shrugged and walked away. "Suit yourself."

Right, he would suit himself. Kat and Molly were sitting on their stools watching him and watching Rachel. He brushed a hand through his hair and smiled at his girls.

He'd pick getting thrown from a horse every single day of the week over the mess Violet had made of his life by hiring Rachel Waters.

* * *

Rachel started her car and leaned back in the seat, catching her breath while the top went back on the convertible. She reached for her sunglasses to fight the sun. She was going home for a few hours and later she'd return to Wyatt's to fix dinner for him and the girls.

One last glance back at the house and she pulled onto the road and headed home. She had chores to do there, too. She had her sheep. Her mom would need help with laundry. There was plenty to keep her busy.

Including packing. As she pulled into the garage she thought about that, about packing things up again. This time she really didn't want to go. And what would she tell Wyatt? What would she say to the girls, to Molly and Kat?

Complicated. Life was very complicated. She closed her eyes and thought about that, and she tried to grab hold of God's perspective. To Him it wasn't all that complicated. She had to trust His plan.

He hadn't opened all of these doors and brought her here for no reason. Maybe He had planned for them to be here just to help Wyatt and the girls through this difficult time. And when she left, there would be someone else to help.

Maybe Wyatt would find his way back to faith and take a job in the church.

The door to the house opened and her mom smiled.

"How was the first day?"

Rachel rolled her eyes heavenward. "Not easy. A sick man is a difficult man."

"That's how they are. And he just called."

"Called here? Is he okay?"

"I think your cell phone battery must be dead. He said it went right to voice mail."

"Oh, it might be." She pulled it from her pocket. Sure enough, dead. "What did he want?"

"Andie's having the babies. He wondered if you would ride with them to Tulsa. He didn't say it, but I wonder if he isn't supposed to drive?"

"Probably not, but he isn't going to give up that information." She didn't want to go. Her emotions were wrung out and what she really wanted was to stay home and be safe. Home with her parents, no pressure, no difficult thoughts to sort out.

"Do you want your dad to drive them?"

"No, I can do it. It's just that I know we need to start packing. I planned on helping you for a few hours."

Rachel's mom stopped her, putting a hand on her arm. "Rachel, I can pack. Your dad has already started. We've done this so many times, I think we know how to get it done."

"But you need my help."

"Tonight Wyatt and the girls need you."

More people needing her. She didn't really know if that's what she wanted for her life. And when she left, what then?

Not that he couldn't replace her with someone just as capable, maybe more so. There were plenty of people looking for jobs and several in the area who would be great with the girls.

"I'll call him and see what's going on. But I need to change clothes and get cleaned up." She'd been cleaning and cooking all day. No one would want to sit in a truck with her for an hour.

Cooped up in a truck. With Wyatt.

Not exactly the thought she needed while trying to convince herself that she needed to do this. Of course she wanted to, though. Andie might be having the babies. That was something Rachel didn't want to miss out on.

Thirty minutes later she parked next to Wyatt's garage, under the carport. He walked out of the barn as she got out of the car and reached in for her overnight bag. She watched him walk toward her, limping a little, a tiny bit stiff. He pushed his hat back and smiled.

"Nice to see you again."

"Yes, again. Do I need to get the girls ready to go?"

"I think probably. Molly is upstairs packing a bag. She's going to be four this weekend, so she's positive she can do it. I'm sure she'd let you help out, though." He pulled off his hat, smiling. "She said I can't help."

She knew he wasn't a lot of help in the clothing department, but he probably didn't need to hear that from her. But the birthday, that definitely needed to be discussed.

"Her birthday. Have you ordered a cake?"

"No, I planned to do it tomorrow." He rubbed his cheek and half smiled. "I'm not good at birthdays. Worse at buying their clothes. I really stink at the girl stuff."

Slow, steady breath. "I can help. I can even bake the cake, if you'd like."

"I'm keeping you from your life. What about Etta? I know you've had things to do that haven't gotten done because of us."

"Etta is having a slow period. She calls when she needs help."

"So this isn't taking you away from something else?"

"Not really." Just packing and telling this life goodbye. That happened to be something else she wasn't ready to tell him. Her dad would share the news with the congregation Sunday. She planned on telling Wyatt before then. She didn't want him to hear it from the pulpit, from her dad.

"Rachel, if you have other things to do, I really can do this alone."

She smiled. "I don't mind. And while we're in Tulsa we can shop for birthday presents and summer clothes for the girls."

"Now that's a good idea. You probably know how to match things."

"Maybe a little better than you."

He leaned against her car, smiling.

"I should go inside."

He edged away from the car that she thought had probably been holding him up. "We'll leave as soon as I get finished feeding. Adam is going to feed tomorrow."

"I'll make sure things are closed up inside the house."

He flashed her another smile. "Thanks."

Leaving had never been easy. This time it would feel like tearing her heart out. She watched him walk away, a little slower but still with that confident cowboy swagger.

He would never know what these weeks meant to her or how much it hurt to go. What difference would it make if he did?

She only had to remind herself what he'd said last night. How could she forget? He'd kissed her silly and then said he wasn't ready.

Chapter Fourteen

Wyatt stared through the window into the NICU at the two little girls, Ryder and Andie's babies. They were close to five pounds each, but Amelia needed oxygen and they were watching Annette. Two more A names. He shook his head, a little in awe over the whole situation.

His little brother was a daddy.

Molly and Kat stood on a stool and watched their little cousins. He couldn't help but think about their births. Molly's had been a happy occasion. But Kat's birth... He wrapped an arm around a little girl who had never really had her mother. Wendy had tried. He knew she'd tried. What a rough few years.

And lately? Things were changing. The weight on them wasn't as heavy. The girls smiled more.

The common denominator happened to be in the other room with Andie, hugging her, praying with her. He'd said his own prayers on the drive here, that the babies would be safe and healthy.

He tugged down on his hat, because he wasn't about to cry. But man, his eyes burned. Little babies did that to a guy. A hand slapped his back. He grimaced, cringing a little.

"Oh, sorry about that." Ryder grinned and pointed to his little girls. "Aren't they something?"

"Yeah, hard to believe you could make something that pretty."

"Don't make me have to take you outside and whoop you, not today." Ryder draped an arm over Wyatt's shoulder. "They look like Andie. Ain't that something?"

"Yeah, funny how that works." He glanced down at his own girls and saw their mother in them. He still had her, in them, in their smiles, their eyes. In Kat's spunky nature. In Molly's laugh.

"We're going to have to get busy and have some boys to protect these girls." Ryder smiled into the NICU window. "Yep, I'm starting to see why the Coopers had all them kids."

"I guess having the boys is up to you."

"Ah, come on, you could have a little boy in the next year or two."

Wyatt shook his head and gave his brother a look. "Ryder, I don't even know where you're going with this conversation. But let's just stick with the idea that you're married and before you know it, you'll have a son. Poor kid."

"I think Andie isn't going to want to have another one for a while." Ryder's smile softened. Andie had done that, turning him from a boy to a man. "Wendy's gone, Wyatt."

"I think I know that." He looked around. The girls had wandered back to the sitting area and weren't paying attention to their uncle Ryder.

"I know you do. No one knows it better than you. But seriously, Wyatt, it's okay to find someone else."

"Right."

Heels on the tile floor. He turned and smiled at the woman walking toward him. Her hair hung in loose curls that framed her face. She smiled a little, her eyes misty and her lips trembling. She bit down on her bottom lip and blinked a few times.

Babies did that to people. Not to him, of course. He turned back to the window, the babies that were wiggling and scrunching up those wrinkled little faces. He'd always said babies weren't really as pretty as people said. He was rethinking that.

"Aren't they beautiful?" Rachel peeked over his shoulder, her chin touching, resting on him.

"Yeah, they sure are." He caught her reflection in the mirror. She backed away but she still stared at those babies. Twin girls with downy soft, blond hair.

"You guys staying the night in Tulsa?" Ryder glanced from Wyatt to Rachel, smiling. Wyatt shot him down with a look.

"Yeah, we've got a couple of hotel rooms. Molly already informed me she's staying in the room with Rachel."

Kat was hugging Rachel's leg. He figured he'd lost her, too. And it was okay. He was fine with that. He was kind of losing himself, too.

"We're going shopping tomorrow," Molly piped up, smiling big with tired eyes. Wyatt picked her up and she wrapped her arms around his neck. Man, this was what life was all about.

"I'm going to have that." Ryder had the look of a man who had just gotten it.

"Yeah, this is it, Ryder. Good times and bad, it's all

about this." Wyatt hugged his daughter and rubbed his cheek against hers. "This is what makes it all worth it."

"I have to go see Andie." Ryder blinked a few times.

Wyatt slapped him on the back and then he turned to Rachel. Ryder was already down the hall, turning the corner. Wyatt slipped an arm around Rachel's waist and, as if she knew, she took Molly.

He took a good deep breath and kept his arm around the woman at his side. Sometimes it just felt good to have someone to lean on. He remembered last night, holding her, teasing her.

"What now?" He didn't really know what he meant by that. "Something to eat? Shopping?"

Rachel held Molly and Kat walked next to her. Both girls were dragging. "Both, if they don't fall asleep in the car."

"Right." He held his arms out to Kat. "Come on, Kat, I can carry my girl."

She grabbed his hands and he picked her up. Rachel smiled but she didn't say anything. Yeah, fine, it wasn't as easy as it should have been. But Kat's arms clung to him and she buried her face in his shoulder.

Yeah, it was all worth it.

After shopping with two toddlers, Rachel's feet hurt and she was ready for a cup of coffee on the balcony of her room. She kissed Molly and tucked the blanket in close. The child wrapped sweet arms around Rachel's neck and smiled.

"I love you, Molly."

"I love you."

Rachel's heart melted. She leaned to kiss the little forehead again. Kat, next to Molly in the queen-size bed, slept soundly. She'd fallen asleep as soon as they got her into her jammies and tucked her in.

"Go to sleep." She tucked Molly's blankets again. "I'll be sitting on the balcony and I'll leave the door open a crack."

"You won't leave?"

"I won't leave. Promise. I'll be on the balcony and I'll be here with you in the morning."

Molly nodded and smiled.

One last kiss on the cheek and Rachel walked away. She poured herself a cup of coffee and stirred creamer and sugar in it. When she turned, Molly's eyes were closed. Sleeping already. Rachel smiled and walked quietly past the bed toward the glass doors that led to the balcony.

A movement on the balcony caught her attention. Wyatt. They had separate rooms but shared a balcony. He stood at the wrought iron railing, leaning against the support post that ran from the floor to the upstairs balcony. When she opened the door, he turned.

"It's a nice night," he commented as he turned back to the view of the skyline.

She nodded, but he probably wasn't paying any attention. It had been that kind of day, the kind that wrung a person out and left them empty. The babies, the memories and she was positive he was in more pain than he let on. It hadn't been an easy day.

"Coffee?"

He shook his head. "No, thanks, too late at night."

She sat down and held the cup in her hands. Tulsa evenings were beautiful. It was a little warm, a little humid and traffic honked on the city streets. She put her feet up on the chair next to the one she sat in.

Wyatt left the rail and sat next to her. He moved slower but broken ribs didn't seem to be something that slowed him down. He told her it wasn't the first time he'd cracked a few ribs and probably wouldn't be the last.

She sipped her coffee and he rubbed his shoulder and neck. Try as she might, she couldn't ignore him, couldn't avoid watching him. His profile was dark, his expression impassive. Rachel sighed and set her cup down on the table. She moved her chair closer to his, her heart catching a little.

No going back.

But did she really want to move forward? She closed her eyes and waited for common sense to return, to drag her back to sanity. She had made so many reckless decisions when it came to relationships. Worse, she had tried to make people love her.

Her hand was on his shoulder, the knotted muscles were tense beneath her touch. She opened her eyes and he turned, his expression questioning. The words from the other night came back, that he wasn't ready.

After a long moment he reached for her hand and pulled it forward. With her pulse fluttering at the base of her throat, he brushed the back of her hand with a sweet kiss. "Good night, Rachel."

"Good night?"

"Yeah, time for you to go." He smiled at her. "I think we both need space and maybe fresh air. Alone."

She couldn't move.

"Rachel, this is me being a gentleman and not a rogue cowboy. This is me making the right choice for both of us. I'm not sure what to feel right now and I don't want to hurt you."

"Not sure?"

He shrugged. "Until recently I still felt married to a woman who isn't coming back. I still have a lot to work through and I don't want to hurt you."

"I'm not going to get hurt. I'm a big girl."

He smiled at that. Her hand was still in his. He squeezed her fingers lightly and let go.

"I know you are, but I'm not willing to be the one who hurts you."

Rachel picked up her cup but she didn't move from her seat. He was telling her to go, but the look in her eyes said something else. She knew, of course, to back off, to not take things where they shouldn't go. She moved her chair away from his, giving them both space.

"Wyatt, what was she like?"

He stared off into the night and didn't answer right away.

"I'm sorry, I shouldn't have asked."

"No, it's okay, I'm just surprised." Wyatt sighed. "I can talk about her. For a long time I couldn't, but now, it's been eighteen months and I can talk. I can tell you that she loved our girls. Man, when we had Molly, Wendy glowed. She loved that baby."

"I'm sure she did."

"She loved her, but..." He stared out at the night, away from her. "She left us. She held Molly, she fed her and sometimes she laughed. When we had Kat, Wendy disappeared inside a shell. She stopped taking care of herself. She didn't take care of the girls. I took her to doctors, to counseling..."

"I'm so sorry."

He nodded. "Yeah, me, too. I had some pretty wonderful years with a woman that I thought I'd spend my life with."

"I think she probably wanted the same thing." Rachel didn't know what else to say. She had seen his pain, but hearing it made it all the more real.

It put everything into perspective.

She stood and he looked up, smiling. Her hand trembled as she reached to touch his cheek. His eyes closed and he leaned into her touch. Her heart couldn't decide if it should fast-forward or pause.

"Good night, Wyatt."

As she walked through the door she heard him sigh and she echoed the gesture. Walking away was something every girl, every woman should know how to do.

And sometimes, she knew from experience, it wasn't easy. Sometimes there was a cowboy on the other end of the emotional tightrope.

She closed the door and bolted it. She pulled the curtain closed and locked the connecting door between their rooms.

The phone rang. She picked it up, glancing quick at the girls. Kat slept on, Molly's eyes fluttered a little.

"Hello?"

"It's me." His voice was soft, not sweet, not this time.

"I kind of knew that."

He laughed. "Yeah, well, I wanted to apologize. I just wanted to say that I'm trying not to lead you on."

"I'm not going to let you." She sat on the edge of the desk and held the phone with her shoulder. "Wyatt, I'm…"

"Rachel?"

"I was a really wild teenager and I made a lot of mistakes, mistakes I regret and that I've worked to get past. I'm almost thirty years old. I know what I want. I know what I'm waiting for. I'm not chasing you."

She closed her eyes and told herself how stupid that sounded. She'd spent the last few years thinking that God would send someone if there was someone for her. And now she was telling this man she wasn't going to chase him. Stupid, stupid, stupid.

"Rachel?"

"Yeah?"

"I think you're amazing." She could hear his smile.

Amazing. Right. He didn't know that she was trembling from her head to her toes. Fear?

"Thanks. Good night, Wyatt."

She put the phone in the cradle, her hand on it, waiting. It didn't ring again.

Wyatt pulled up the drive to his house. The girls were sleeping in the backseat of the truck. Rachel hadn't said much on the drive home. He hadn't pushed her. After last night it seemed like a good idea to keep quiet.

Breakfast had been a quiet affair on the balcony of their hotel. The girls had eaten cereal from room service, Rachel had eaten fruit and yogurt. He'd felt pretty guilty eating biscuits and gravy. They'd had lunch at the hospital cafeteria.

The twins were doing great. Amelia was breathing on her own now. Wyatt breathed a sigh of relief over that situation. At least that, if only that, was going right. He, on the other hand, had a big mess to clean up. He had a woman sitting next to him and he didn't have a clue what to say to her or how to fix things.

How did a man move on when, until eighteen months ago, he'd planned on spending his life with one woman, raising their children, growing old, serving God? And then it had all changed. Yeah, move on. That's what people were telling him. Time to move on, Wyatt.

He stopped the truck and just sat there. Rachel opened her door but she didn't get out. He shot her a look and she didn't smile. Of course she didn't. He hadn't given her a lot to smile about. He really wanted her to smile.

He really wanted to explain to her how it felt to try this moving on stuff. It hurt like crazy, deep-down hurt. It hurt the way it had when people had tried to tell Wendy to just get over it, take a shower, go for a walk. And she hadn't been able to do those things.

He sat there for a second, thinking. Maybe it didn't hurt as much as he'd thought it should? The thought hit like a ton of bricks, the knowledge that getting over his pain could hurt, too. He sure hadn't planned on that.

"I'll carry the girls in for you." She stepped out of the truck and looked back in at him.

Oh, no way was she doing this.

"I can take the girls in, Rachel." He got out and opened the back door to reach for Molly. She woke up enough to crawl into his arms. "Come on, kiddo, you can take a nap inside."

"I want a pink cake for my birthday," she whispered close to his ear.

"A strawberry cake?" He held her close, his ribs hurting like crazy.

"No, just pink. A pink cake." He carried her up the back steps. Rachel followed with Kat.

"Well, then, we'll find you a pink cake."

"I can make her a cake." Rachel had opened the other door and reached in for Kat. "If you want."

"I think she'd like that. We usually buy one from the store."

Last year they hadn't had much of a party. It had been the three of them and a store-bought cake. Her third birthday and he'd put candles on her cake and later, after the girls had gone to bed, he'd stood outside and bawled like a baby. He'd had a fight with God, then he'd shifted his anger to Wendy.

The dog ran around the side of the house, wagging his tail, glad to see his people home. Wyatt carried Molly up the back steps and into the house. Rachel was behind him with Kat. He opened the door and nodded for her to enter first.

"Do you want me to fix something for dinner?" Rachel asked as she carried Kat through the house to the living room.

"No, I'll take the girls to the Mad Cow. Why don't you go on home? I'm sure you have a life that doesn't include us."

She shifted her arms and placed his daughter on one end of the sofa. When she turned, her smile was vague. He placed Molly on the other end of the sofa. Her eyes opened and she smiled.

"I'm not tired, Daddy."

"You don't have to sleep, honey." He turned and Rachel had found an afghan and was covering Kat with it. "Seriously, though, if you have things to do…"

"I actually do. My mom needs help with some things."

"They're lucky to have you."

"I'm lucky to have them. They've always been there for me. Now it's my turn to be there for them."

She picked up her purse and he walked out with her. They'd left her car in the carport, but it was still covered with green pollen. He waited while she dug through her purse for her keys. When she found them, he opened the car door for her.

"Rachel, if you need a couple of days off to get other things done, I understand."

"I might. There's something…" She sighed. "Never mind. I'll see you tomorrow."

"Are you sure?"

She got in the car and he rested his arm on the vinyl top and looked in.

"I'm sure. I'll see you tomorrow. We have a lot to do before Molly's birthday Saturday."

"Okay, I'll talk to you later." He closed the door and backed away from her car. As she backed out of the carport, he waved and she smiled.

It seemed normal enough, but it didn't sit right. Whatever she had started to tell him mattered and he wanted to know what it was.

Chapter Fifteen

Boxes lined the walls of the living room and Rachel didn't want to empty the contents of the room into the brown cardboard. She sat down on the footstool and stared at the bookcases, the curio cabinet and the pictures on the walls. She loved this room with its pine-paneled walls. She loved the hardwood floors and the big windows.

She loved this house.

"The boxes won't pack themselves."

She turned and smiled at her mother. It was a good week. Maybe the excitement of the move had given Gloria Waters the extra energy. Or maybe her immune system was in check. Either way she had accomplished a lot in the two days since Rachel had been gone.

Twenty-nine years old, Rachel shouldn't be having this conversation, about moving, about starting over with her parents. She pulled a few books off the shelves and held them. Her mom walked into the room and sat in the rocking chair across from her.

"Rachel, don't go. Stay here."

"That's out of the question." Rachel stacked the books

in the bottom of a box. "I'm not going to stay here when the two of you are going to Tulsa."

"Are you afraid?"

Afraid? Rachel looked out the window. Across the road the neighbors were mulching their garden. Down the street a new neighbor had moved in. Her dad had already invited them to church. A church that would soon lose its pastor. She thought about that church, her teen girls, her Sunday school class and the nursery.

Rachel always became involved in her dad's ministry. The new church was larger, had quite a few paid staff, he'd told her. She didn't know what that meant for her. But the real reason she would go would be to help her parents. She cooked when her mother didn't feel up to it. She kept the house clean.

Afraid?

"Afraid to jump out there, find someone and fall in love. Are you afraid? I know that Tanner hurt you, but it was a long time ago."

Rachel didn't know how to process what her mother had just said. Tanner. She hadn't really thought about him in years. They had dated when she was twenty.

"It isn't about Tanner." About a man who had dated her for a year and then decided he couldn't handle her faith.

"I wonder sometimes. I know he hurt you."

Rachel smiled at that. "It hasn't hurt in a long time, Mom. I'm here because I want to be here, to help you and Dad. And I guess because I haven't found anyone to spend my life with."

"You will, honey."

"Will I?" She shrugged. "I don't know if I will. If I don't, it's okay."

"What about Wyatt Johnson?" Her mom smiled that secretive smile.

"Mom, I'm not fifteen and I haven't been doodling his name in my notebook. I love his girls and I'm glad I could help out, but that's as far as it goes."

Heat worked its way up her cheeks and she reached for another stack of books. Now if only her mom would walk away and let it alone. Instead, Gloria Waters laughed a little.

"I think it's far more than caring about his girls."

Rachel grabbed more books and stacked them in the box.

"Mom, Wyatt Johnson is a nice guy who still loves the wife he lost."

"He might always love her, Rachel. That doesn't mean he can't love someone else."

Rachel finished packing the shelf and her mom continued to rock in the rocking chair. When the bookcase was empty, Rachel turned to face her mother.

"Mom, he might love someone else someday. I'm not going to push myself into that position. It doesn't work that way."

She knew from experience.

"Does he know that we're moving?"

"No, I haven't told him. I started to, but I know that Dad is going to make an announcement this Sunday and I didn't want it to get out before Dad could tell people."

"Well, I think you ought to tell Wyatt. He's going to need someone to take your place, or a chance to talk you into staying. The more time you give him, the better."

Someone to take her place. The words ached in her heart. That meant someone else taking care of Molly and Kat, someone else coloring with them and helping them draw pictures of flowers and kittens. She had only been in their lives since last fall when Wyatt came back to town. The idea of leaving them shouldn't create an empty space in her heart.

But it did. All of the years of holding back and not getting attached and two little girls had changed everything. Two little girls and their dad, his smile, his eyes, his sweetness. She looked up, caught her mom watching her.

"You shouldn't let this go, honey."

"You're not giving up, are you?" Rachel smiled and folded down the flaps of the box.

"Not on your life."

At least someone had hope for her love life. Rachel had given up a long time ago. True, Wyatt made her want to have hope again, but common sense told her to go slow and not act impulsively.

What if she put her heart on the line, even stayed in Dawson, only to find out that he would never be ready to move on? Or when he was ready, what if it was with someone else?

Either could happen. Rachel smiled at her mom.

"I'm fine."

Her mom touched her shoulder and left the room.

Rachel opened another box and went for the curio cabinet. She packed porcelain dolls, a tiny vase and her heart. All the breakables went together in a box labeled "Fragile."

The horse lunged in a slow circle at the end of the rope Wyatt held. The doctor had told him to stay off horses for a couple of weeks. That was fine and dandy, but he couldn't stop working. A few years ago he would have ignored the doctor and went ahead with whatever he needed to do.

Now he had the girls to think about. He glanced behind him. They were on the swing, not going very high but jabbering nonstop. He started to turn back to the horse but caught a flash of red on the road. Rachel.

She'd taken yesterday off. The girls had missed her, moping around the house because he had fed them some kind of casserole he thought would be an easy fix. He'd been pretty wrong about that. His cooking skills, with or without Etta's cookbooks, were not improving.

The red car eased up his driveway. He hadn't expected her today either. There were a lot of things he hadn't expected but he didn't want to dwell on them. The girls jumped off the swings and started across the yard. He would have yelled for them to stop, but they paused a good distance from the driveway and the car that was pulling up.

He gave a quiet command and the horse stopped, waiting for him to walk up to it. He left the rope on the ground and the horse remained steady in the spot where he'd come to a halt. Ears forward, the animal turned its head toward him.

"Good job, boy. Real good." He unsnapped the lunge line and replaced it with a lead rope. "Let's get you out to pasture and see what's going on."

He led the horse to the gate and turned him loose. The animal went off at a fast trot, shaking his head. After a few minutes he burst into a full run, bucking his back end into the air. Wyatt turned and walked back toward the house and the girls. And Rachel.

"What are you doing here?" He opened the gate that led to the yard.

"Thought I'd stop and check on the girls and find out if you've heard anything about the twins."

"The twins will probably be home by the first of next week." He picked up Kat, wincing a little at the catch in his ribs. "Sis, you're getting heavy."

Kat shook her head no and rested her chin on his shoulder.

Rachel smiled at the girls and not at him.

"So, what's really up?" He put Kat on the ground. "You girls run and play."

Kat and Molly started to protest, but he shook his head. They ran for the swings, forgetting to be upset. He smiled as he watched Molly help Kat onto the lower swing.

Rachel stopped walking. She watched the girls, her eyes a little misty. "I came over to bake the cake for Molly's party tomorrow. But before the party and before church Sunday, I want you to know something. I want you to hear it from me."

"Okay." He pulled off his hat and waited.

"My dad is taking a church in Tulsa. My mom needs to be closer to the doctors there. They want to be closer because they're getting older and they feel like it will be better for them."

"I hate for the church to lose your dad." He waited, wanting to hear that she wouldn't leave. He glanced in the direction of the girls, wanting it to be about them. "Rachel, the girls love having you here."

"I know. I love them."

Unsettled shifted to anger. "You're trying to tell me that you're going, too, right?"

"I am." She continued to watch the girls play, but her

eyes filled with tears. He watched one slide down her cheek and then the next.

"I'd like for you to stay. We could work something out if you wanted to work for me full-time."

"I can't." She wiped the tears away, one finger across her cheek. "My brother and sister live so far away. I'm the only one here to help my parents."

"I see." He rubbed the back of his neck and couldn't think of a thing to say that didn't sound crazy.

He didn't want to hire another housekeeper. Joint cream and therapeutic socks were no longer appealing. He kind of liked butterflies, country music and the smell of wildflowers.

The thoughts were pretty dangerous and he didn't want to go there. He'd taken his ring off. Now he was contemplating how to keep Rachel Waters in his life. No, in his girls' lives.

That's why he needed Rachel. She made Kat and Molly smile again. She made them happy. And that made his life a lot easier.

"Would you think about it? Just consider it. If you don't want to leave, the job is yours."

"Thank you. And I will think about it." She smiled and the gesture trembled on wild cherry lips. He was about as confused as a man could get.

"Well, I guess you have to make this decision. I need to feed the girls lunch."

"I can help."

He brushed his hand through his hair and settled his hat back on his head. "If you have things to do, I can handle it."

"I came over because you need help. I'm going to fix lunch and then I'll get something in the oven for dinner."

"Right, that works." He leaned against her car and he couldn't look at her. "Man, this is rough."

"I'll be around for the next month. I can even help you find someone."

"No, I don't want to do this again." He managed a smile. "Maybe you can teach me to cook before you leave."

"I can do that. And for the next couple of days, we have a lot to do to get ready for Molly's party."

"Yeah, her birthday. She's counting on you for that. I can't braid hair and I sure can't decorate for a little girl's birthday."

"I'm not going to miss her birthday, Wyatt. I'll go ahead and bake the cake today. I'll decorate the cake and the house tomorrow before her guests arrive."

"Thanks, that'll be great."

She nodded, her smile still soft and trembling. "I'm sorry. I love the girls. I don't want them to be hurt."

"Yeah, but they will be. I know you have to go. I get that. But the girls are my priority."

"That's the way it should be."

"Well, I have to get back to work."

"I'll take the girls inside to help me with the cake."

He nodded and walked away.

This wasn't the way he'd expected his day to go. He'd almost prefer to get kicked by a horse. At least with a horse he knew what to expect.

Some things in life were honest and easy, always what you thought they'd be. And sometimes one choice changed everything. Jackson Cooper's words wormed their way into his mind. Rachel had definitely gotten under his skin.

But worse, she'd made Kat and Molly pretty happy.

For the first time in a long time they'd felt whole, the way a family should feel. Because of her.

And now they were back to square one.

The cake baked in the oven, making the kitchen smell like strawberry. Rachel had explained to Molly that pink cakes sometimes had flavors and since they were using a mix, pink happened to be strawberry. The little girl had stopped being offended after a small taste of batter confirmed that pink was not only a pretty color, it tasted good, too.

"What now?" Rachel leaned on the counter across from the two girls who sat on stools sharing a plate of cookies.

"We should draw pictures," Molly informed her, dipping a cookie in her cup of milk.

"Or play with frogs." Kat nodded her head, milk dripping down her chin and a circle of chocolate around her mouth.

The back door slammed shut. Rachel straightened and waited for Wyatt to join them. She heard him in the laundry room and then he was there, tall and lean, his jeans faded. He must have hung his hat in the laundry room because the crown of his hair was flattened from having worn it all day.

"How about the Mad Cow, girls?" His smile didn't include her. Rachel didn't blame him.

"Rachel is making omelets." Molly picked up her cup to drink her milk. "Because eggs are good and we have stuff to do."

"What stuff?" This time he did look her way, his brow arched in question.

"Party stuff. We're going to decorate for tomorrow."

Molly clasped her hands together and leaned toward her daddy. No way would he deny that little smile.

"I tell you what, you girls decorate. I'll order from the Mad Cow and bring it home for us." He shifted to face her. "If you write down what the three of you want and call in the order, I'll run upstairs for a quick shower and a change of clothes."

In a month, life would be ordinary again, missing them, missing Dawson. Rachel smiled because it didn't do her or the girls any good to let those thoughts take over.

He smiled back and then he left. She watched him leave, wondering how much pain he was in. He hid it well, his pain. The girls were tugging on her, asking questions about the cake and ice cream that she promised to make. Homemade, with strawberries, of course.

The oven timer went off. She grabbed an oven mitt and pulled out the cake. Strawberry pink. She put it on the top of the stove. The aroma filled the air, even stronger than when it had been baking. Both girls were off their stools and standing a short distance away.

Rachel wanted cake. She wanted chocolate. She really wanted to not be this new person she'd created, the one who jogged instead of eating cheesecake when she was depressed.

"It's going to be good." Molly grinned big.

"It is going to be good. And we'll put pink icing on it and pretty stuff."

"Flowers? And a ballerina?"

Rachel smiled. "Yes, flowers and ballerinas. We bought those in Tulsa, remember?"

"Bought what?"

Wyatt stood in the doorway dressed in khaki shorts

and a T-shirt. His feet were bare and his hair still damp from the shower. His tanned skin looked darker thanks to the white T-shirt.

"Decorations for the cake." Rachel ached inside because something had happened, something was gone and she knew she'd miss it for a long, long time after she left Dawson.

The thin thread of connection they'd shared had been broken. Because she was leaving and he didn't want his girls hurt. She didn't want them hurt either.

She was torn. Did anyone get that? She felt so responsible for her parents. She loved this town. She smiled at Kat and Molly. She loved them.

"Did you make the list of what we want to eat?"

She picked up a pen and grabbed a tablet from the basket on the counter. "Okay, what does everyone want?"

She didn't look at him and she hoped he wasn't looking at her. Kat jumped up and down and said, "I want fries."

"More than that, Kat." Wyatt smiled at his daughter.

Rachel wrote down the rest of the order. "I'll call Vera."

"Okay, let me know how long it'll be. I promised the girls they could ride their pony for a few minutes."

Both girls shouted and started to jump around the room. Wyatt smiled, watching them. And Rachel watched him. Molly and Kat ran into the laundry room to pull on boots and hats. And suddenly Rachel didn't know what to do, didn't know where she fit.

She knew she never wanted to leave here. The thought settled deep, like most bad thoughts. How many times had she moved as a kid? She'd lost track.

But she wasn't sixteen looking for a place to start over.

She was nearly thirty and some unseen clock was ticking an unfamiliar beat, one she hadn't expected.

Once again her gaze traveled to that cowboy. It was his fault, that much was obvious. It felt pretty good to blame him for making this difficult.

Kat and Molly returned wearing their boots and with cowboy hats on their heads. She smiled at little faces that were starting to tan. They had matching braids that stuck out from beneath their hats. Cowgirl hats, Molly had informed her, were important for cowgirls. They had bought one for Rachel, too.

She didn't look as cute in a cowgirl hat as they did.

She wouldn't need one in Tulsa. She turned away from the happy scene and started dishwater for the few mixing bowls and spoons she'd used to make the cake.

Footsteps behind her. She felt him close, felt the warmth of his exhaled breath, inhaled the spicy cologne he wore. His hand touched her arm.

"You okay?" His voice was close to her ear and she nodded, looking out the window at the barn, at fields with grazing livestock, at the dog sleeping under the shade of an oak tree.

"Yeah, I'm good."

"No, you're not."

She shook her head. She wasn't at all good. She was breaking inside, not just her heart but all of her. Because she loved them. She loved the girls and she loved him and for a few brief weeks she'd been a part of their lives, a part of their family. She didn't want to leave them, or Dawson.

She closed her eyes and waited for an answer, even a whisper. Nothing. Of course nothing, God knew. He had known this plan and He knew the rest of the untold story. He knew how much it hurt.

"I'm going to take the girls outside." His hand dropped from her arm. "You were good for us."

She closed her eyes and listened to him walking away from her. She wanted him to beg her to stay. Of course he wouldn't do that. He wanted her help finding a replacement because she really was just the housekeeper and the nanny. She wasn't a part of his family.

She wasn't… She opened her eyes and watched him with the girls, watched him hug them, watched him pick Kat up and set her on his shoulders, grimacing just a little as she settled.

She wasn't the woman he loved. How could she stay here working for him, feeling the way she felt? How could she stay here when she knew that her parents needed her?

In the end it was easier to walk outside and pretend she wasn't leaving. It was easier to watch the girls laugh as Wyatt led them on the pony and pretend she would always be in their lives.

Chapter Sixteen

The birthday party had been a pretty big success thanks to Prince the pony. Wyatt sat back in the lawn chair and watched some of the last visitors leave. He smiled at the sight of the poor pony with pink and purple ribbons in his mane and tail. That had been Rachel's idea. It had seemed pretty goofy to him, to do that to the poor pony. The kids had felt differently about it. Little girls loved ribbons. He'd have to remember that.

Little girls loved pink cakes and balloons. They loved pretty dresses and dolls, even when they were cowgirls with ponies and stock dogs. Rachel had taught him that about his daughters. She had taught him a few things about himself, too.

Someone sat down next to him. He turned and smiled at Robert Waters, Rachel's father. The older man smiled back and stretched long legs in front of him. He wore his customary slacks and button-up shirt.

Wyatt glanced down at his own khaki shorts and leather flip-flops. He smiled at Rachel's dad.

"Glad you were here." Not so glad to hear that you're

leaving. Since that wasn't common knowledge, Wyatt didn't mention it.

"Wyatt, Rachel told me that she shared with you that we're leaving. The elders know and a few others. I'll make the announcement tomorrow."

"I'm sorry to hear that you're going." Wyatt let out a sigh and shook his head. "The church hoped you'd stay a long time."

"You know as well as I do that we can never make plans for God." Robert crossed his left leg over his right knee, still relaxed, always relaxed. He was about the calmest man Wyatt had ever met.

"Yeah, things do happen without our permission."

"Have you given any more thought to the youth ministry? When I asked you to do that, I didn't know we were going to be leaving. I guess God did."

"I've thought about it. And yeah, I think I'm ready. I still have moments when I question God. He could have stopped her."

"No one blames you for that. I imagine we could all put together a list of things we question God over. Why someone we loved died in a car accident or why someone had to die young. And the only answer is that sin entered the world and we are allowed free will. We make choices that change lives."

Wyatt fought a real strong urge to say something about this move and if it was really what God wanted or was he giving Pastor Waters freedom to choose, right or wrong. But he knew that Robert Waters was a praying man. He didn't make hasty decisions. He followed what he felt God wanted for him.

He didn't want this man to leave. But maybe it really had been God's plan to have Pastor Waters in Dawson for this season to do the things he needed to do here before moving somewhere else where God had another plan.

"This isn't going to be an easy move for us." Pastor Waters sighed at the end of the sentence and shook his head. "Rachel loves Dawson. She loves taking care of your girls."

"They love her, too."

Pastor Waters glanced his way and smiled. "I guess you've asked her to consider staying?"

"I have, but she won't."

"No, I didn't figure she would."

Family issues, everyone had them. For Wyatt it was all about making his girls his first priority. His parents had never made that a rule. For his parents, life had been about parties and what made them happy. Their two boys were pictures they showed when they wanted to brag about something other than money or the land they owned.

He'd never be his parents. He ran the family business from a distance and his girls came first. Especially now.

Across the lawn Violet and Rachel were cleaning up the leftover party favors, the empty cups and paper plates that were blowing off the picnic table. They talked in quiet whispers like two old friends.

That scene made him a little itchy on the inside, so he turned to search for his girls. They were swinging, feet dangling and party crowns still on their heads. Molly had the biggest crown, the queen crown. And each girl had pink satin ballerina slippers.

He'd never seen so much pink in one place.

"I think I'll go check on my girls." He pushed himself out of the chair, wincing a little at the catch in his ribs and the pull across his lower back. He'd never been so glad to see a horse go as he had been to watch that buckskin loaded into the trailer yesterday afternoon.

He would have kept the animal around if Ryder had been able to take over training for a week or two. But they both had different priorities now.

"Molly, did you have a good birthday?" He stood behind his daughters, pushing one and then the other.

"The bestest one ever." Molly looked back at him, smiling big.

His gaze traveled the short distance to Rachel Waters. The bestest ever. He decided to feel a little angry with her and with God because she was going to leave them empty again.

Last night he'd had to tell the girls. They'd both cried and Molly had begged him to make Rachel stay. She wouldn't, he'd explained. She had responsibilities. Molly asked him what that word meant. He'd had to find a way to explain it to a four-year-old.

Things that matter. Responsibility is the things that we have to do because they matter, they come first. Family, the farm, a job. Those were responsibilities. Molly wanted to be Rachel's responsibility.

The things that come first.

Rachel laughed, the sound carrying. He tried to picture this yard, this house and their lives with her gone.

They'd be empty again.

He gave Kat an easy push. No, they wouldn't be empty. They would still have each other. And they'd have something else. They had the ability to move on and to laugh.

Two weeks after Molly's party, Rachel walked through a ranch house on the outskirts of Tulsa, just a few blocks from her dad's new church. The church was larger than any he'd ever pastored. The benefits were clearly the best. It was something wonderful for her parents. It meant having a real retirement and security.

It meant great medical care.

It meant Rachel moving into a small bedroom with purple carpet and green walls. Obviously a teenager had been here. Rachel felt a little dizzy, standing in the center of that room.

"It's a nice little house." Her mother stood at the window looking out at the tiny little yard. Rachel didn't want to look. She knew what she'd see outside that window. She'd had views like this before.

She would see other houses, back to back, side to side. She would see privacy fences and manicured shrubs. There would be a patio and eventually patio furniture. Her dog would go on a leash and they'd take walks around the neighborhood. They would talk to strangers who would possibly become friends.

They would adjust. They always did.

And she would live this life until? Until her parents no longer needed her. She smiled at her mom, who hadn't looked this happy in a long time. The idea of a big church with a large staff had taken a burden off her mother.

Gloria Waters wouldn't feel guilty, as if she was letting her husband or his congregation down because she couldn't take a more active role in the ministry. Rachel wanted to tell her mother that they had her, she took that burden. She carried that weight for them.

Cynthia, her sister, had called that morning as they drove into Tulsa. She had given Rachel a lecture about being a martyr because she didn't want to take chances in life. It was easy to stay with their parents, to not get involved in real life.

Rachel had ended the conversation with a blunt "Goodbye."

It was easy for Cynthia. Life had always been easy for the pretty blonde with the stick figure and the outgoing personality. Cynthia had married her college sweetheart. She'd never been rejected.

Her dad stuck his head around the corner. "Nice room."

Rachel smiled. "Love the colors."

"I thought you would." He stepped into the room. "You can paint if you want."

"I know." She smiled, pretending to love the idea of painting another room.

She would be thirty in a few months. Thirty and living with her parents. What did people think? Did they think she was somehow defective? Did they get that she wanted to be here to help?

"Let's take a walk around the neighborhood." Rachel's dad reached for her hand. "I think there's a pool down the block."

"Dad, I'm not fifteen."

He laughed a little. "Yeah, I know. But swimming is great exercise. You can jog one day and swim the next."

She remembered this from her teen years. Her parents always broke the news about moving by telling them how great the new place would be. Eventually Rachel stopped caring. She stopped seeing the moves as an adventure. It became about having to learn a new school, make new friends and reinvent herself each time.

She no longer reinvented.

But she did go for a walk with her dad. He held Wolf-gang's leash and they took their time, letting the dog sniff all of the new scents.

"Rachel, have you prayed about this move?"

"What do you mean?"

He stopped while the dog took particular interest in a sign post. "I mean, have you prayed for yourself? Is this move what you're supposed to do?"

"Dad, we're here. I'm here."

Her dad continued to walk and she stayed next to him, whistling to get the dog's attention when it appeared a little too interested in a neighbor's cat. That wouldn't be a good way to start this new life.

"Rachel, I want you to make a decision based on what *you* want."

"What I want is to be here helping you and Mom."

"I'm not sure about that. I kind of wonder if you aren't sacrificing your own happiness because of some sense of duty to your mother and me."

"You've been talking to Cynthia." Rachel took Wolfgang's leash because she needed to control something. Her life was obviously out of the question.

"I talked to Rob and Cynthia. They're both concerned that you're giving up what you want because you feel as if we need you."

"That's nice of them." The brother and sister who visited once a year suddenly knew what was best for her and for their parents.

The thought was unfair, but at the moment she didn't feel like being fair.

"Rachel, I'm about to do something I should have done a long time ago. I'm pushing you from the nest."

"Pushing me?"

She wasn't stupid, but seriously, where had this come from?

"Rachel, years ago God called me to this ministry. He

called me. He called your mother with me. We had children. Now our children are grown and it is time for you, my daughter, to find your own place. Your mother and I can take care of ourselves. We took care of you. We really are able to handle life."

"But when Mom is sick…"

He smiled and she felt ten again. "Rachel, I'm her husband. I can take care of her. Go and live your life, make your own choices. When I took this position I knew it was right for me, right for your mother. I think you have to pray about the right place for you."

"Here." She held tight to the leash and fought tears that burned her eyes.

"If that's what God's plan is, fine. With us, in Tulsa, or back in Dawson, it doesn't matter as long as you know it's the right place for you." He kissed her cheek. "Go do something for yourself, Rachel. Eat chocolate, find something you love. Or *someone* you love. Stop using us as an excuse to avoid your own life."

"Ouch."

He laughed a little. "Sorry, but the truth can hurt. You pray and if, after you pray, you honestly feel like it is God's will for you to move here, then I'll accept that."

"I'm starting to get a very big hint." The hint that her parents would like to be alone.

"I thought you might."

Right, so where did that leave her?

Wyatt backed the trailer up to the corral gate, watching the side mirrors as he eased back. He stopped when the open gate hit the back of the trailer. Perfect.

The dog that had followed next to his truck started to bark. Wyatt turned off the truck and watched Rachel's car easing up the drive. He let out a shallow breath, still not taking deep breaths because his ribs wouldn't give that much. He stepped out of the truck and waited for her to get out of her car.

He hadn't expected her today. For the last week she'd been packing, loading boxes and getting the church staff ready to take over her many jobs. They didn't have a new pastor, not yet. Wyatt and a few other men had prayed about the decision. For now they'd take turns preaching, just until they could find the right man.

The dog left his side and ran to hers, tail wagging. Rachel reached to pet the animal. It followed her back to him. He glanced toward the house. Violet was inside with the girls. She'd been interviewing housekeepers. So far he and the girls hadn't liked any of the candidates.

"I didn't expect to see you today."

She shrugged one shoulder and didn't look directly at him. Her brown hair blew around her face and her expression seemed a little lost to him.

"I hadn't expected to stop. I missed the girls and wanted to give them something I bought in Tulsa."

"They've missed you, too." He almost included himself, but he wasn't going there.

What did he miss? Her pancakes, coffee that didn't taste bitter, or music blasting as she cleaned?

"Do you mind if I go in and see them?"

"No, go ahead. I have to load some calves that we've sold." The reason he'd backed the trailer up to the corral. The bawling calves were huddled in the far corner of the corral.

"I could help you."

"I can get it." He tried not to move like someone who needed help. She laughed at his attempt.

"Let me help. I'll miss this." The faraway look returned. "We're moving into a neighborhood where our view is of the neighbor's back door."

"I've lived in those neighborhoods. It works for a lot of people. I guess it's a good thing we're all different."

"Yeah. So I can help?"

He pointed her to the gate. "I'll head them this way. You make sure they don't squeeze through there."

She nodded and headed for the spot he pointed to. She wasn't country at all, just wanted to be. That was okay with him. He enjoyed watching her standing there in her denim shorts, a T-shirt and sandals. Not exactly a picture of a cowgirl, but he didn't really know what a cowgirl was supposed to look like. He'd seen a few in his time that looked like anything but.

The calves moved away from him. His dog circled, keeping them together and moving toward the trailer. One angus steer tried to break from the group, the dog brought him back, nipping quick at the steer's hooves.

Ahead of him, Rachel stood next to the gate, her hand shading her eyes as the sun hit. He didn't smile, couldn't. He was picturing her in that house surrounded by neighbors.

The calves ran through the opening into the back of the trailer. He swung the trailer door, swinging the latch in place. The calves moved to the back of the trailer.

Wyatt slid through the gate. Rachel moved out of his way.

"You don't have to go."

Her eyes widened and she stared, waiting. He didn't know what to say other than what he'd said. He lifted a hand and rested it on the side of the trailer.

"I kind of do have to go. I don't have a home here. My parents are moving."

"Rachel, the girls don't want any other nanny. They already miss you and you're not gone."

"Of course, I know they'll miss me. I'll miss them, too. But I feel like I need to be close to my parents. If my mom gets sick, I need to be there."

"It isn't that far. What is it, just under two hours to their new church?"

"Something like that. But if she's sick, she needs daily help, not a visit."

"Right, you're right." He let it go because he did understand her loyalty to her parents. He got it.

"I'm going to go see the girls. I want them to know that I'll visit."

He smiled and tipped his hat. "Yeah, visits are good. I have to get these steers on down the road."

She turned and walked away. He watched her walk through the back door of his house and then he climbed in the truck and cranked the engine. He eased forward, watching in the rearview mirror as the corral gate swung shut. The trailer shifted as the cattle shifted.

In the house Rachel was telling his girls goodbye. Why did he have the sudden urge to hit something? It combined with a pretty nasty urge to turn the truck and stock trailer around.

And do what? Beg Rachel to stay? What would he tell her? He could tell her that his girls were happier with her in their lives. *He* was happier.

After that, what then? He would have her in their home as a housekeeper and nanny. She would cook for them, clean their house and hug the girls. He'd still have to deal with moving on.

Last night he'd pulled out photo albums. He'd glanced through pictures of Wendy in college. They were young and in love. Crazy in love.

He rode bulls and roped steers. She spent weekends working at a homeless shelter. They'd picked youth ministry together. After college they'd gotten married.

The pictures stayed happy for a few years, until after Molly's birth. That was when the story of their lives changed. He'd looked at those pictures and tried to figure out what he could have done.

But he couldn't change things. He couldn't undo them now. What he had was a future with his two little girls and memories of their mother. Someday he'd share the good memories.

None of that fixed the situation right now. Rachel was going to leave and Violet was hiring a new housekeeper. She'd talked about a lady named Thelda Matheson. He hoped she wore joint cream.

Chapter Seventeen

Rachel stood in the green-and-purple bedroom staring out a window without a view and knowing this was all wrong. She was in the wrong place, in the wrong life. It felt like wearing someone else's shoes.

Her parents were drinking coffee in the new kitchen, sitting in front of patio doors at a table they'd had for years. Same table, same parents, different kitchen. Same life. Their life.

She joined them at that table. They looked up, not asking questions. She got up to pour herself a cup of coffee and then she joined them again.

"You're right, this isn't my place anymore."

"What does that mean?" Her mom put her cup down and glanced at Rachel's dad. The two seemed to always know everything she was about to tell them.

When she had been sixteen and rebellious, nothing ever seemed to surprise them. They always seemed to know what trouble she'd gotten herself into.

"I left my ministry." Rachel wiped at tears that were rolling down her cheeks. "I left my home."

"Dawson?" Her dad smiled, as if he'd planned it himself.

"Yes, Dawson. The teen girls. My Sunday school class. Molly and Kat. I left it all because I thought you needed me here. But God called you to make this move, not me. It's just that I'm stubborn or afraid, I'm not sure which."

"And you thought I needed you." Gloria patted her hand. "Honey, I will always need you, but I'm really okay."

"I know you are. Maybe I wasn't. Maybe I've needed you."

"I think we just got into the bad habit of letting you take care of us." Her mom smiled. "What do you plan on doing?"

"I think I'm going to call Etta and see if I can still take her up on the offer to stay at her house. I'll call the church and ask if I can keep working with the kids."

"It feels good, doesn't it?" Her dad grinned big.

"Yeah, it kind of does feel good. This is right, Dad."

"I think I tried to tell you that the other day. Time to fly, Rachel. Go find your future."

She carried her still-full cup to the sink. "I think I'm going to start packing."

The one thing she wouldn't do was make this move about Wyatt. He'd hired a new housekeeper. The girls needed to get settled with the person he'd found. Rachel needed to make sure she was where God wanted her, not jump back into what felt comfortable and easy.

She needed to wait because she didn't want a broken heart her first day back in her new life.

Wyatt drove past the parsonage a few days after Rachel's last visit. It was empty. He let out a sigh and kept on going. She was gone and Mrs. Matheson had taken her place. He didn't like the lady. No reason, he just didn't like her. He didn't like her sensible shoes or the smell of eucalyptus that hovered over her as she moved through the house.

Kat and Molly weren't crazy about her either.

He pulled up the drive and parked inside the garage. Violet was still at the house. She assured him she would be leaving in the morning. They'd be fine without her.

Of course they would. He walked out of the garage and across the yard to the barn. The stallion he'd bought from the Fosters whinnied from the small corral at the side of the barn. Wyatt walked up to the fence and the big bay, his dark red coat gleaming, trotted up for a treat. Wyatt pulled an apple snack out of his pocket and the horse sucked it up, barely grazing his hands.

The back door banged shut. He turned. It was Violet. She walked toward him, her high heels sinking in the yard that was still soggy from last night's rain. He wondered if she would ever try to fit into these surroundings. He doubted it.

"Did you see Rachel before she left?" Violet stood next to him, holding her hand out to the horse but withdrawing it before the horse made contact.

"No, I didn't see her. I think they left last night."

"Right." Violet stepped back because the horse stuck his nose out to her.

"What is it you want to say, Violet?"

She smiled up at him. "Don't let her go."

"What does that mean? I offered her the job, she turned it down. How can I change that?" He really wanted to walk away from this conversation. "I've hired someone. Remember?"

"Don't be ridiculous, I'm not talking about hiring her as a housekeeper. I'm talking about what you seem to be ignoring or avoiding. You love her. It's obvious she loves you. Why in the world are you letting her go?"

The mother of his wife, pushing him to—what?

"Violet, this isn't the conversation I want to have with you."

"No, I'm sure it isn't. But I think I'm the best person to tell you that Wendy would want you to move on. She'd want it to be with someone like Rachel, someone who loves you and your girls. This kind of love doesn't happen often. For most people it happens once. You're blessed to have it happen twice. Don't let this get away."

"It's too soon." He pushed his hat down on his head, tipping the brim to shade his eyes.

"Who says?"

"I say." He backed away from the fence, from the horse, from Violet. "I say it's too soon."

"You can't control that. You're trying to hold on to her memory and the love you shared. I get that. But you can't say it's too soon. Not if the right person has entered your life and you're on the verge of losing her. If you haven't already lost her."

"I have to go for a drive."

"Fine, go for a drive. But if I was you, I'd spend time praying about this. I don't believe in chance, Wyatt Johnson. It was no accident that she was here, in your life and in the lives of your daughters."

"Violet, let it go."

She drew in her lips and shook her head. "Wyatt, you're stubborn."

He walked away, back to his truck, back to a few minutes alone. As he drove down the drive, he thought back to her words. He remembered telling Rachel that he wasn't ready.

He hadn't planned on ever being ready.

And Rachel had made a choice. He'd asked her to stay and she'd made the decision to go.

Because he hadn't asked her to stay for him. He called himself every kind of fool because he knew he'd asked the wrong question.

Fly, little bird, fly. Rachel smiled as the wind whipped through her hair. The radio blasted Sara Evans and she sang along to a song about suds being left in the bucket and clothes left hanging on the line.

Rachel Waters was finally leaving home. After the conversation with her parents a few days ago, she'd taken time to figure out exactly what she wanted. She knew it wasn't Tulsa. As much as she loved the city, she didn't want to live there.

And it had been pretty obvious her parents didn't need her. It had been more obvious that maybe they were a little relieved to hear that she planned on moving out.

She'd watched them together, watched her mom and dad taking care of each other, unpacking, planning. She'd watched herself on the outside of their circle, trying to be helpful, trying to take care of them. And all along they could take care of themselves.

She'd stopped taking risks. A long time ago she'd decided safe was good. Well, today was a new day. Today included giving in a little, maybe even giving in to temptation.

So on the way out of Tulsa she'd gone through a drive-through for a frozen coffee drink full of calories and a cookie laden down with chocolate chips. Take that, thighs.

Rachel Waters was done controlling her life. She planned on finding her path, her future, her today. With God in control.

Today. No more waiting for tomorrow. No more fear of taking risks.

She had called Etta who'd been overjoyed with the idea of Rachel staying with her for a while, helping on the farm and with her business. Vera had answered the next call and agreed to give her a few lunch shifts during the week.

Rachel cruised through Dawson, slow, taking it all in. Home. She smiled, loving that word. The one place she had loved more than any other and now it was her home. Her choice. She had a place to go and a nice savings account. It felt good. It felt better than good.

It felt pretty close to perfect until she drove past Wyatt's and saw the girls on the swing. It shouldn't hurt, that he'd offered her a job. But it did. He wanted her in their lives, but only as the person who cooked meals, gave hugs and went home at the end of every day.

She wanted more than that.

The old convictions were still strong, the belief that God would bring the right person into her life. As she got older she wondered if maybe that wasn't His plan. Not everyone had the same destiny. There was a point in time when a person just accepted what his or her life was and made peace with it.

Etta's house was a welcome sight. The big, yellow Victorian glowed in the setting sun. Rachel pulled up the drive and parked. When she walked around the corner of the house, Etta met her on the sidewalk.

"Well, aren't you a sight for sore eyes." Etta grabbed her in a tight hug.

"It's only been a few days."

"Longest days of my life, wondering if you'd get it right."

Rachel laughed and hugged Etta back. "I got it right."

Etta slid an arm around Rachel's waist and they walked up the steps to the porch. "At least partially right."

"How much more right do I need to be?"

Etta turned at the sound of a car coming down the road. No, it was a truck. Rachel's heart froze in place, refusing to pick up where it left off. She took a deep breath and her heart did the same.

"Hmm, someone else must be trying to get it right."

"No, Etta." Rachel refused to watch the truck drive on by.

"Oh, you kids. I tell you what, in the last year, I've had it up to my neck with silly young couples who take forever to get it right. It was simpler in my day. The man knew what he wanted and he went after it. The woman knew it was the right thing to do and she stopped running. Happy ever after."

Rachel wanted to laugh but she couldn't. The truck didn't go on down the road, it pulled into Etta's drive.

Etta chuckled a little. "Don't run, Rachel. I'm going inside and you let yourself get caught."

"I have a job. I'm going to work for you. He found someone else to watch the girls."

Etta had walked inside. The screen door closed behind her.

"Oh, honey, you are clueless."

Rachel stood on the porch waiting for Wyatt to get out of the truck and join her. He walked a little easier than he had the previous week. It hadn't been that long, she reminded herself. But honestly, the last week had felt like a lifetime.

"So this is where you went to." He walked up the steps. He took off his hat and held it in front of him, raising one hand and running it through dark hair flattened to his head.

She'd been right about him, he was heartache and she didn't need heartache, not even if it came in a package with lean, suntanned cheeks and a smile that nearly became a caress.

"I came back." She eased the words out.

"I know. I've been in Tulsa."

"What? Why?"

"To talk to your dad."

"Oh."

"And to see you." He stepped closer. His dark eyes held hers captive.

"Really?" Her heart took a hopeful leap forward but she pulled it back, reined it in. Maybe the new housekeeper hadn't worked out.

"Yeah, really." His smile was sweet, it melted in his eyes and melted her heart. Wasn't that the same heart she was trying to keep under control?

For some reason it wasn't working, that control thing.

"How are the girls?"

He reached for her hands. "The girls miss you."

"I miss them, too."

He tossed his hat on a nearby chair. "I miss you, too."

"I see."

"No, you don't. Rachel, I got up this morning and walked around a house that has never felt more empty. I realized what was missing. You." He teased her with another one of those smiles. "I realized I asked you the wrong question."

She didn't know what to say.

"You are the thing missing from our lives. From *my* life. I went to Tulsa because I wanted to see you. I wanted to tell you that I don't want you in our lives as a house-keeper or a nanny."

Her heart wouldn't let go of hope. It wouldn't stop its crazy beat inside her chest. She couldn't move, couldn't breathe.

"Rachel, I want you in our lives because we love you. I love you."

"You do?" She loved him, too, but she was afraid to say the words, afraid to believe this moment was happening.

He grinned and brushed a hand across her cheek. "I do. While I was in Tulsa, I asked your dad to do me a favor."

"What's that?" Was that her heart melting, pooling up inside her?

"I asked him if he would do the honor of officiating at a wedding."

"Oh."

"I told him I'd like to date his daughter for a few months." He pulled her close, touching his lips to hers, sweet, seductive and then gone. "And I asked him if he would walk you down the aisle and then step behind the pulpit and marry us."

"Wyatt." She whispered the word close to his ear and he turned, brushing his cheek against hers.

"So now I need to ask you, Rachel Waters, if you'll be the wife of one very hard-headed cowboy. This isn't about being ready to move on. This is about being ready to love you for the rest of my life."

Rachel closed her eyes, replaying his words, the words she'd been waiting for, wanting to hear. She'd dreamed of those words and how it would feel at this moment. And now she knew. She knew that shivers would tingle up her arms and down her spine. She knew that her heart would twirl inside her chest.

She now knew that he would lean and his hands would cup her cheeks as he dropped the sweetest kiss on her lips.

But in her dreams it had never been this wonderful.

"Rachel, will you marry me?" Wyatt whispered the proposal again after kissing her long and easy.

She nodded and tears pooled and slid down her cheeks. "Of course I'll marry you."

Wyatt held his breath as she said the words he'd been waiting to hear and then he released his hand from hers and fished the ring out of his shirt pocket.

"I was hoping you might say yes." He grinned, his face a little warm. "So I stopped at a jewelry store on the way home and told them I needed the most beautiful diamond for the most beautiful bride."

She stood in front of him, sweeter than cherry soda on a hot summer day and everything he wanted in life. He reached for her hand and slid the ring onto her finger. The diamond glinted, winking the promise of forever.

"I love you," he whispered.

He held her close, thankful to have her in his arms again. She felt good there, in his arms. She felt right. This felt right.

This was something only a fool would let go of. He

wasn't a fool. He might be a hard-headed cowboy, but he knew what he wanted and he knew when to hold on to it.

She moved her hands to his shoulders and then to the back of his neck as he captured her lips in a kiss that promised forever.

"I love you, too." She whispered close to his ear and he held her tight.

No way would he ever let her go.

Epilogue

Wyatt walked out of the barn and saw his wife and kids in the backyard. Ryder stood behind him. The two of them had been working cattle all day, giving immunizations and taking care of other details that had to be dealt with. Little bull calves were now steers. Ears were tagged.

The two of them were dirty and pretty close to disgusting.

Ryder slapped his back. "Brother, that's a nice little family you've got."

Wyatt smiled and he couldn't agree more. But he wasn't going to give Ryder room to gloat. He knew where Ryder was going with this conversation. Wyatt counted to three and waited for it.

On cue Ryder spoke, a big smile on his face. "Wasn't it just a couple of years ago that I said something about needing a boy in our family to protect all of these girls?"

Wyatt continued to ignore his little brother. Listen to Ryder, or watch his family playing together in the backyard. He picked ignoring the pest at his side. Even if he was right.

"Yep, that's one cute little baby boy you've got." Ryder,

loose limbed and way too sure of himself, took off across the yard. Andie had the twins in a big playpen, keeping the "little fillies," as Ryder called his girls, corralled.

Wyatt smiled when Rachel turned to find him. She was more beautiful today than she'd been on their wedding day. That day, dressed in a cream gown and walking down the aisle with her dad, that had been a day.

But today, with their little boy tucked safe in the pouch that hung around her neck, today she glowed. Today, just looking at her knocked him on his can.

He choked up a little, thinking about Rowdy's birth. He had feared losing Rachel. He'd been afraid she'd slip away.

Now those thoughts were pushed aside. He had a wife, two beautiful daughters and one handsome little guy.

"Are you going to come and push your daughters?" Rachel called out, bringing him back to earth.

"On my way." He hurried across the lawn. When he got there he kissed her first, holding her close for a minute, loose in his arms. And then he kissed the dark head of his little boy.

God had brought her to Dawson and then brought him home. Good planning, God. He smiled as he pushed Molly high and gave Kat a lighter push.

Good planning.

* * * * *

Read on for a sneak peek of
THE BOSS'S BRIDE by Brenda Minton,
available September 2013
from Love Inspired Books

Prologue

Gracie Wilson stood in the center of a Sunday school classroom at the Bygones Community Church. Her friend Janie Lawson adjusted her veil and again wiped at tears.

"You look beautiful."

"Do I?" Gracie glanced in the full-length mirror that hung on the door of the supply cabinet and suppressed a shudder. The dress was hideous and she hadn't picked it.

"Of course you do. You look like a fairy princess."

Gracie groaned. "Is this another height joke?"

Janie hugged her tight for one second. "Not at all. You look beautiful. And you look miserable. It's your wedding day, you should be smiling."

Gracie smiled but she knew it was a poor attempt at best. The frown on Janie's face confirmed it. She exhaled and looked again at her reflection in the mirror. Janie was right; a bride shouldn't look sad.

"Gracie, what's wrong?" Janie walked up behind her and peeked over her shoulder so that their reflections stared back at them.

"Nothing. I'm good." She leaned her cheek against Janie's hand on her shoulder. "Other than the fact that you've moved one hundred miles away and I never get to see you."

What else could she say? Everyone in Bygones, Kansas, and probably for miles around, thought she'd landed the catch of the century. Trent Morgan was handsome, charming and came from money. She should be thrilled to be marrying him. Six months ago she had been thrilled. Five months ago she'd still been happy.

But then she'd started to notice little signs. She should have put the wedding on hold the moment she noticed those signs. She should have slowed down and not worried so much about what everyone else would think. And when she knew for certain, she should have put a stop to the entire thing. But she hadn't. Because once the wedding wheels had been put in motion, she hadn't known how to stop it all from happening.

It made her feel weak. And she'd never been a weak person.

"You're not convincing me." Janie smiled tenderly, a best-friend smile reflected from the mirror. Gracie turned to face her friend, the skirt of the dress pushing them apart.

"I'm just tired, Janie. I mean, it's been a long three months of wedding planning, right?" Did she sound convincing?

"And Mrs. Morgan isn't a dream of a woman to deal with." Janie gave an exaggerated shudder to prove her point.

"Exactly." Gracie twirled in the lace creation that had a skirt that made her look like a dinner bell or a Southern belle, she wasn't sure which. "Do you care if I have a few minutes alone?"

"Of course not." Janie gave her another hug. "But not

too long. You dad is outside and when I came in to check on you, the seats were filling up out there."

"I won't be long. I just need a minute to catch my breath."

"Of course you do. And just think, after today you'll be going to Hawaii and you'll have a week on the beach to catch your breath. And then you'll move to Manhattan and your new home."

Gracie smiled and nodded her head, trying to pretend the idea excited her. A week in Hawaii. On the beach. With Trent.

Janie smiled back at her and then the door to the classroom closed. And for the first time in days, Gracie was alone. She looked around the room with the bright yellow walls and posters from the Sunday school curriculum. She stopped at the poster of David and Goliath. Her favorite. She'd love to have that kind of faith, the kind that knocked down giants.

She knew a few Davids. Ann Mars was a faith giant. And Miss Coraline Connolly. They both believed the town of Bygones could be saved. Not with stones and a slingshot, but with new businesses and new people.

And of course those new businesses made her think of her boss at The Fixer-Upper. Patrick Fogerty, one of the most genuinely nice people she'd ever met.

She closed her eyes and took a deep breath. Today was her wedding day. Instead of worrying she had to remember back to when she met Trent and how love had felt then. Not how it felt now, sadly lacking because he'd not only pulled away, he'd betrayed her trust. A knock on the door interrupted her thoughts.

"You almost ready, Gracie?" her dad called through the door.

"Almost."

She opened the window, just to let in fresh air. She leaned out, breathing the hint of autumn, enjoying the breeze on her face. She looked across the grassy lawn and saw...

Freedom.

She shook her head at the word. That was the wrong word. A bride shouldn't be thinking of freedom. She should be thinking of happy-ever-after with the man she loved. The word ached deep inside, mocking her. *Love.* It meant something, to love someone, to want to be with them forever. It meant loyalty.

She closed her eyes and thought back to that day one month ago when she'd meant to surprise Trent. She'd packed a lunch for them. She'd thought a picnic would be romantic. Instead she sat in her car watching him and then she'd eased out of the parking space, driving away as if she hadn't seen anything. That moment had confirmed her suspicions.

It all added up. He had been seeing someone else while she'd been busy at home, planning their wedding. He had texted the other woman while they'd been sampling cakes at the Sweet Dreams Bakery. He'd called her while he and Gracie had dinner with his parents.

Gracie hadn't known how to end a relationship just weeks short of the wedding.

But now she did.

Quiet as a mouse she slid herself and the hoopskirt through the window. Once she stood on the grass outside the window, her heart began to pound. She thought about how wrong this was. She thought about all the money Mrs. Morgan had spent.

She thought of how things would have been different

if her own mother had been alive and she'd had a woman to turn to, to talk to. If she didn't feel so responsible for everyone else.

It hadn't been her plan to sneak around the side of the church, to look out at the crowded parking lot. The limo was already decorated with cans, streamers and painted windows; two teenaged boys were finishing up with cans of shaving cream. She hadn't planned to slip away and then run as fast as she could down a side street.

But she did run.

And she felt freer than she had in months. She felt the breeze on her face, the coolness of the air, and knew she couldn't marry Trent Morgan. But she didn't know where to go or what to do now that she'd left her groom standing in the sanctuary of the church waiting for a bride who wouldn't be walking down the aisle. She only knew that she couldn't go through with this wedding.

Chapter One

The stockroom of The Fixer-Upper hardware store was dark, warm and strangely peaceful. Gracie sat on a stool, staring down at the white dress that hadn't made it down the aisle. She shifted the skirt, all lace and silk, that was the type of creation she never would have picked on her own. The only things of her own choosing were her white cowboy boots with sequins and the crystal ribbon on the flowers.

She studied the bouquet Trent's mother had picked, so different from the daisies Gracie had wanted. When Gracie had sneaked into The Fixer-Upper, she'd tossed the bouquet on a worktable. Even from several feet away she could smell the sweetness of the flowers, a reminder that this had never really been her wedding. Even the yellow roses, which would have been okay, had been enhanced with a few exotic blooms. Mrs. Morgan had a thing for over-the-top.

From the church to the decorations, Trent's mother had made all the decisions. Mrs. Morgan, wife of a prominent surgeon, had taken charge. After all, as Mrs. Morgan liked to point out, Gracie didn't have a mother of her own to take care of these things. And because Gracie's father's granary was struggling, like every other business in Bygones, Kansas, the Morgan family had been footing the bill for their only son to marry Gracie Wilson.

Gracie smiled as she leaned back against the wall and closed her eyes. She'd finally made a decision of her own. She'd made the decision to bail on the whole dreadful affair.

It seemed as if everyone was counting on this marriage. It had definitely been a big help to the Bygones economy, thanks to the Morgans. *Her dad.* Thinking of him, she felt guilty. He'd been happy, thinking she would never have to work hard again. She was marrying up, he'd said. She'd be set for life, her brother Evan had added.

She'd never agreed with her dad about marrying up. Her dad and her five brothers were the cream of the crop. Very few men could compete with those men of hers. Trent Morgan might have money but he was far from marrying "up." He'd proven more than once that he wasn't the man she wanted to share her dreams or her life with.

She drew in a deep breath and she didn't cry. As difficult as tomorrow would be for her, for her family, today she could breathe. She had made the right decision. She'd made the decision she'd been afraid to make weeks ago when she'd first caught him cheating. She'd made the decision she should have made months ago when first she realized something was wrong.

She'd started the relationship with Trent thinking it would be perfect. But they'd been two different people. She knew how to rely on her faith. He used his faith as a disguise.

She had tried to do the right thing for everyone. But she hadn't done the right thing for herself.

She only hoped she still had a job here at The Fixer-Upper hardware store. She hoped her boss, Patrick Fogerty, hadn't replaced her. She would definitely need the money, because she had a feeling Mrs. Morgan would want to be reimbursed for the wedding that hadn't happened.

Her dad couldn't afford the expense.

Somehow she'd make this right. She would get her life back. Tomorrow she'd admit to Miss Coraline Connolly, retired principal of the Bygones school system, that she'd been right. She and Ann Mars, owner of the This 'n' That, had both questioned her in the past few days, telling her she didn't look as happy as a bride-to-be ought to.

Outside The Fixer-Upper she could hear cars. People were probably looking for her. She guessed her dad would have gone home to search in all of her old hiding places. No one would think to check for her in the hardware store, a business that had been in town for only two months, with an owner few people really knew.

They'd like him once they got to know him, she thought, once they realized he wasn't just a city person looking for a fresh start. He was a decent man who really wanted to be a part of a community. She thought that about all the new business owners in Bygones. From the coffee shop to the bakery, they had made the town better. They were giving her hometown hope. The folks in Bygones needed hope.

She needed hope. She closed her eyes and prayed, something she should have been doing more of. She should have paid attention to her nagging doubts about this marriage. She should have listened to God. Instead she'd listened to everyone else, to all the people telling her how great it would be to marry a man like Trent.

Gracie swiped a hand across her eyes. A tear or two slipped down her cheeks, not for the marriage that wouldn't be, but for her dad, her family and her community. She thought about her mom and how things would have been different if Eva Wilson had lived.

The door chime dinged on the wall across from her. Someone had opened the front door of the hardware store. She scooted to the edge of the stool and glanced at the back door, her only way to escape. But running out the back door would set off an alarm and the overworked, understaffed local police didn't need more drama. They were probably busy looking for her.

She reached for a three-foot-length of rebar and held it tight in her hand, just in case the person coming in thought they could rip the place off since everyone in town was otherwise occupied. There had been some vandalism lately. As quiet as Bygones used to be, a break-in wouldn't be so surprising in this economy. The door to the storeroom opened. She held the rebar close, took a deep breath and waited.

Patrick Fogerty stepped into the room, all six feet four inches of him. He looked around and then spotted her. Gracie shrugged as she watched her boss take a few steps into the room, his ruggedly handsome face masked in shadows, his dark hair a little messy from the wind.

For the first time she really wanted to cry. It was a strange mixture of relief, sadness, guilt and anger that wrapped itself up inside of her like tangled string, none of it really making any sense. Tears sprang to her eyes and she blinked them away. Patrick offered her a sympathetic smile and that was when the tears really began to flow.

* * *

Gracie Wilson stared up at Patrick, her wide, dark eyes filling with tears. He watched her for a long minute, surprised to see her sitting in the stockroom of his store. When she hadn't walked down the aisle, everyone had been surprised. Everyone, that was, except Ann Mars. He'd been sitting next to her in the church, and, for whatever reason, she hadn't seemed all that shocked. She'd told him that it was because she was in her eighties and she knew a thing or two about life.

Miss Mars, instead of being worried, had seemed relieved. He'd thought he heard a few sighs of relief throughout the sanctuary of Bygones Community Church.

"Are you going to hit me with that rebar?" he asked, because he didn't know what else to say. Damsels in distress were not typically his cup of tea.

What else could he say to the woman he'd known for only a couple of months? She'd been recommended by Ann Mars, his worthy representative and guide to all things Bygones. Ann had promised him a worker who would be on time, work hard and know how to fix anything, as well as bring in customers. She'd picked the right person.

Gracie Wilson could handle tools, she could handle customers and she even seemed to know how to handle him. She'd kept him from giving up on this venture. After all, he was a city boy, born and raised. Moving to Bygones, starting a new business in a town that was struggling financially, that took faith. When his seemed to be in short supply, she loaned him hers the way neighbors loaned a cup of sugar in Bygones, Kansas.

He'd made a commitment. A business of his own in

trade for a commitment to stay for two years and make it work. There were several new businesses in Bygones. They had been painted and remodeled, and hopefully would be a cure for a town that didn't want to lose everything.

"I was prepared for a burglar," she whispered as tears trickled down her cheeks.

He stood there for a long minute, unsure of what to do next. Call the police? Call Ann Mars, his Save Our Streets sponsor?

She shifted on the stool. "Say something."

"Gracie—" he cleared his throat "—I guess I'm surprised to see you here."

She looked up, smiling a little as she brushed tears from her cheeks. She looked tinier than ever in the white creation of a dress, her dark hair pulled back with rhinestone clips and strings of pearls.

"I think there are probably a lot of people surprised," she said, brushing away her tears.

"Yes, surprised, and worried. They're searching for you." He focused on the rebar she still had a death grip on. "Other than the ones who decided to take advantage of the reception."

"It should be a good party."

"What happened?"

"I couldn't marry him." She laughed and then sobbed. "I'm going to be in big trouble."

"Seems to me the trouble would have been marrying him if you had doubts?"

She nodded but didn't speak. The tears were streaming down her cheeks again and he wondered if her doubts were real, or if she just had cold feet and needed a few minutes to get her thoughts together.

The Boss's Bride

"Can I help?"

She shook her head. "No. I mean, there's really nothing anyone can do. I just can't marry him."

"Are you sure?" He cleared his throat, not at all sure what else to say in a situation such as this. He'd never had little sisters. He'd dated but never been married.

He'd learned one thing about women: sometimes they walked when things looked difficult. At least that's what had happened to him.

He didn't think Gracie was the type to skip out on someone just because it got a little difficult.

Sitting on the stool she looked smaller than her barely five feet, especially in the billowy white dress that didn't seem to suit her style. Not that he was a guy who paid much attention to style. But even he could recognize when a woman needed someone, though.

He pushed aside misgivings and reached to hug her. First he took the rebar from her hand and set it on the worktable. She leaned into his shoulder and he wrapped his arms around her, keeping his face out of the protruding objects that decorated her hair. Avoiding the light scent of her fragrance took more effort. It matched the softness of her skin and the sweet way she leaned against him.

For a guy who didn't notice much, unless it had to do with home remodeling or electrical problems, he noticed a lot in those few minutes holding Gracie.

"I can't marry him," she finally whispered against his shoulder and then she backed out of his embrace. "But I'm going to have to face this."

"Yes, I guess you will." He reached for a roll of paper towels on the shelf and pulled off a few sheets for her to wipe her eyes. "I don't have a handkerchief."

She smiled through her tears and then laughed. "Wouldn't that be chivalrous if you did? Maybe a little too cliché?"

"I guess that's a good reason to never offer a woman a handkerchief. What guy wants to be cliché?"

"You could never be cliché." She smiled as she said it, dabbing her eyes with paper towels that were less than soft. "My dad is going to be embarrassed. Mrs. Morgan will be furious. I wonder if there's a bus out of this town tonight."

"I don't think a bus comes anywhere near Bygones. And if you caught a bus, who would work for me?"

"You haven't replaced me?"

"Of course not. And if you're up to it, I'll need you here Monday morning. Remember, you had that great idea to have the block party in a few weeks. I can't do that without you."

"You could."

"Yeah, but people trust you. They aren't always trusting of the city guy that has moved in and wants their business."

"They'll learn that you can be trusted."

"Thanks, Gracie." He reached for her hand and helped her down from the stool. "I like the boots."

"Thank you. I picked them out." She twirled in the dress that looked like white lace gone crazy. "I did not pick this. I think it makes me look like a bad version of Cinderella at the ball."

"It isn't that bad."

She wrinkled her nose at him. "It is that bad. You're just being nice."

"Okay, I'm being nice. I am a nice guy, haven't you heard?"

She smiled up at him. She was more than a foot shorter than him with a pixie face and dark eyes that could tease or flash with humor. Sometimes those eyes flashed fire if something got her riled up. She was twenty-four, ten years younger than his thirty-four years. She sometimes seemed younger, but more often seemed a decade older.

He knew she'd gone through a lot. She'd lost her mom fourteen years ago. Miss Coraline had given him tidbits and told him to take care of her girl, because Gracie acted strong but she needed to be able to let other people be strong for her. He'd gotten a lot of advice from Coraline Connolly since he'd moved to Bygones.

"You are a nice guy, Patrick." Gracie sighed and reached back for the veil that hung from a hook on the wall. "And my name is going to be mud. I'm glad I have one friend left."

"Want me to drive you home?"

She nodded. "Please. Unless, of course, you're willing to help me run away from Bygones. Far away."

"Sorry, I'm here for at least two years and I'd like for you to be here, too. If you stay, you know I'll have your back. I'll be here for you."

"Thank you. And I'm going to help you find a wife. You need a wife. A good country woman that can cook biscuits and gravy."

"The person who just ran from her own wedding wants to arrange one for me?"

"I guess you have a point. I don't think I'm the poster child for encouraging someone to take the walk down the aisle."

He grinned at that. "No, probably not."

"Can you get me out of here without everyone seeing me?"

"In that dress?"

She looked down. "I guess not."

"I have sweatpants and a T-shirt you could change into. They'll be a little big, but not as obvious."

"And then I can leave the dress here. Mrs. Morgan will want to return it if she can."

"Or maybe you'll change your mind?"

"About the dress or Trent? I don't think I'll be taking either of them down the aisle."

He didn't know what to say to that. He'd known her all of two months and he didn't think he should be the one standing here having this conversation. There were people in town who had known her all her life. The same people who had shared stories with him of a rough and rowdy little girl turned woman. A woman who seemed to know her mind and be able to handle almost any situation.

Sometimes when Patrick looked at her he saw seven shades of vulnerable in her dark eyes, and a whole lot of sadness. He thought maybe the only other person who saw that look was Miss Coraline. The retired principal seemed to see a lot in everyone. He guessed it probably had made her very good at her job.

He shook himself from those thoughts and gave Gracie an easy smile. "I'll get the clothes and you can change in the restroom."

"Thank you, Patrick." She had that soft look in her eyes, the one that said she might cry again if he said the wrong thing or got too close.

He backed away, made sorry excuses and headed for the exit.

He'd come to Bygones because his family business had closed down after a big-box store full of discount lumber and building supplies moved into their suburban Detroit neighborhood, the neighborhood that had supported them for years.

Bygones was his future, his dream. It seemed literally the answer to his prayers: a small-town hardware store, close neighbors, a place to start over.

He hadn't realized moving to a small town meant getting tangled up in the lives of the people who lived there. He hadn't realized they would pull him in and make him such a part of their families and community.

More than anything, he hadn't planned on someone like Gracie Wilson storming into his life.

Look for
THE BOSS'S BRIDE
by Brenda Minton
Available September 2013
from Love Inspired Books

Copyright © 2013 Brenda Minton

Love Inspired

Uplifting romances of faith, forgiveness and hope.

Use this coupon to
SAVE $2.00
on the purchase of
ANY
Love Inspired book!

Available wherever books are sold, including most bookstores, supermarkets, drugstores and discount stores. ✂

SAVE $2.00 ON THE PURCHASE OF **ANY** LOVE INSPIRED® BOOK!

Coupon expires October 31, 2013. Redeemable at participating retail outlets in the U.S. and Canada only. Limit one coupon per customer.

52611025

CANADIAN RETAILERS: Harlequin Enterprises Limited will pay the face value of this coupon plus 10.25¢ if submitted by customer for this product only. Any other use constitutes fraud. Coupon is nonassignable. Void if taxed, prohibited or restricted by law. Consumer must pay any government taxes. Void if copied. Nielsen Clearing House ("NCH") customers submit coupons and proof of sales to Harlequin Enterprises Limited, P.O. Box 3000, Saint John, NB E2L 4L3, Canada. Non-NCH retailer—for reimbursement submit coupons and proof of sales directly to Harlequin Enterprises Limited, Retail Marketing Department, 225 Duncan Mill Rd., Don Mills, ON M3B 3K9, Canada.

U.S. RETAILERS:
Harlequin Enterprises Limited will pay the face value of this coupon plus 8¢ if submitted by customer for this product only. Any other use constitutes fraud. Coupon is nonassignable. Void if taxed, prohibited or restricted by law. Consumer must pay any government taxes. Void if copied. For reimbursement submit coupons and proof of sales directly to Harlequin Enterprises Limited, P.O. Box 880478, El Paso, TX 88588-0478, U.S.A. Cash value 1/100 cents.

5 65373 00082 3 (8100)0 11871

LICOUPWBLBM

WIN *Vegas*
A **TRIP** TO

& **TICKETS**
TO CHAMPIONSHIP
RODEO EVENTS!

Who can resist a cowboy? We sure can't!

You and a friend can win a 3-night,
4-day trip to Vegas to see some real
cowboys in action.

Visit
www.Harlequin.com/VegasSweepstakes
to enter!

See reverse for details.

Sweepstakes closes October 18, 2013.

CONTESTWBL

NO PURCHASE NECESSARY TO ENTER. Purchase or acceptance of a product offer does not improve your chances of winning. Sweepstakes opens 7/22/2013 at 12:01 AM (ET) and closes 10/18/2013 at 11:59 PM (ET). Enter online at www.Harlequin.com/VegasSweepstakes. Open to legal residents of the U.S. (excl. Alaska, Hawaii, Overseas Military Installations and other U.S. Territories) and Canada (excl. Quebec, Yukon Territory, Northwest Territories and Nunavut Territory) who are twenty-one (21) years of age or older. Void where prohibited by law. One Grand Prize available to be won consisting of a 3-night/ 4-day trip for winner and guest to Las Vegas, Nevada (12/05/13 to 12/8/13); tickets for winner and guest for two single performances at championship rodeo events; and $700 USD spending money (Total ARV: approx. $3,990). Odds of winning depend on number of eligible entries received. Full details and Official Rules available online at www.Harlequin.com/VegasSweepstakes.
Sponsor: Harlequin Enterprises Limited.

LEGALWBL

Love Inspired

A FATHER'S PROMISE
by
CAROLYNE AARSEN

When the child she gave up for adoption shows up in
town with her adoptive father, Renee must overcome
her guilt to find true love.

Hearts OF
HARTLEY CREEK

*Available September 2013
wherever Love Inspired books are sold.*

www.LoveInspiredBooks.com

LI87836

Love Inspired

Allison True knows that in real life, romances end in heartache. She learned that the hard way in high school, when handsome Sam Franklin completely ignored her existence. Back in Bygones, Allison is older now, and wiser. Her only focus is keeping her new bookstore afloat, and her heart safe from Sam.

Before he was a single dad juggling rambunctious twins, Sam had a secret thing for Allison. Now a beautiful young woman has replaced the bookish girl in braids and glasses, and Sam must work twice as hard to keep his feelings in check. He swore off love after his ex shattered his heart and his faith. But Allison seems to know the secret to repairing both….

The Cowboy's Christmas Courtship

by Brenda Minton

Available October 2013
wherever Love Inspired books are sold.

Find us on Facebook at
www.Facebook.com/LoveInspiredBooks

LI87843

Love Inspired®

Uplifting romances of faith, forgiveness and hope.

Use this coupon to
SAVE $2.00
on the purchase of
ANY
Love Inspired book!

Available wherever books are sold, including most
bookstores, supermarkets, drugstores and discount stores. ✂

SAVE $2.00 ON THE PURCHASE OF **ANY**
LOVE INSPIRED® BOOK!

Coupon expires January 31, 2014. Redeemable at participating retail
outlets in the U.S. and Canada only. Limit one coupon per customer.

52611038

CANADIAN RETAILERS: Harlequin Enterprises Limited will pay the face
value of this coupon plus 10.25¢ if submitted by customer for this product
only. Any other use constitutes fraud. Coupon is nonassignable. Void if
taxed, prohibited or restricted by law. Consumer must pay any government taxes. Void if copied. Nielsen Clearing House ("NCH") customers
submit coupons and proof of sales to Harlequin Enterprises Limited,
P.O. Box 3000, Saint John, NB E2L 4L3, Canada. Non-NCH retailer—for
reimbursement submit coupons and proof of sales directly to Harlequin
Enterprises Limited, Retail Marketing Department, 225 Duncan Mill Rd.,
Don Mills, ON M3B 3K9, Canada.

5 65373 00082 3   (8100)0 11872

U.S. RETAILERS:
Harlequin Enterprises Limited will
pay the face value of this coupon
plus 8¢ if submitted by customer
for this product only. Any other
use constitutes fraud. Coupon is
nonassignable. Void if taxed,
prohibited or restricted by law.
Consumer must pay any govern-
ment taxes. Void if copied. For reimbursement submit coupons and proof
of sales directly to Harlequin Enterprises Limited, P.O. Box 880478, El Paso,
TX 88588-0478, U.S.A. Cash value 1/100 cents.

LICOUPWBLBM2